D1738885

Also by Tina Folsom

Samson's Lovely Mortal (Scanguards Vampires, Book 1)

Amaury's Hellion (Scanguards Vampires, Book 2)

Gabriel's Mate (Scanguards Vampires, Book 3)

Yvette's Haven (Scanguards Vampires, Book 4)

A Touch of Greek (Out of Olympus, Book 1)

A Scent of Greek (Out of Olympus, Book 2)

Lawful Escort

Venice Vampyr – The Beginning

ZANE'S REDEMPTION

(Scanguards Vampires, Book 5)

Tina Folsom

Zane's Redemption is a work of fiction. Names, characters, places, and incidents are the products of the author's imagination and are used fictitiously. Any resemblance to actual events, locales, or persons, living or dead, is entirely coincidental.

2011 Tina Folsom

Published in the United States

Cover design: Elaina Lee
Author photograph: Cheryl Grey, London

Printed in the United States of America

Dedication

This book is dedicated to the memory of my grandfather, Josef Veselak, prisoner #29658. He perished in the concentration camp at Dachau on July 26, 1942.

Chapter One

Zane heard a scream and blocked it out to prolong feeding from the succulent neck of the Latino kid he'd cornered in an alley in the Mission, the predominantly Mexican and South American neighborhood of San Francisco. It was a sketchy area; on one hand, trendy restaurants and nightclubs attracted the rich residents from the north side of town, on the other, poor immigrants toiled in dead-end jobs for minimum wage. Yet somehow, Zane had instantly felt at home when he'd first set foot in the neighborhood.

As his fangs lodged deeper to draw more blood, Zane listened to the thundering heartbeat of his victim, fully aware of the power he had over the teenager's life. If he took an ounce too much, the boy would bleed out, his heartbeat ceasing, his breath rushing from his lungs for the last time, leaving behind a lifeless shell.

It was how he liked to feed, not from a bottle of lifeless donated blood like his colleagues at Scanguards preferred, but from a human where he felt the life pulsing beneath his palms while the warm, rich blood coated his throat. There was no substitute for this feeling. It went beyond pure nourishment; it appealed to his need to feel superior, to be powerful, to be in control of the life in his arms.

Every night, the struggle to allow that life to continue renewed. Despite the fact that each night a different human was at his mercy, it changed nothing, and the battle inside him remained the same: to stop while the human was still alive or to give into the urge to destroy and assuage his need to avenge, for no matter whether he fed from a Latino kid, a black woman, or an Asian man, their faces were all the same once his memories of the past took possession of his mind. Their features morphed into those of a white man, his hair a dark blond, his eyes brown, and his cheekbones high: the face of one of his torturers, the only one he had failed to track down after chasing him for over sixty-five years. The only one he hadn't slain—yet.

Zane noticed the change in pressure of the blood rushing through the kid's veins, and drew his fangs from his neck. He quickly licked over the wound to close it and prevent any more blood loss as his fangs retracted back into their sockets, deep within his gums, satisfied for the moment. His own heart hammered furiously in his chest as he felt his victim slacken, but his ears picked up the faint heartbeat, assuring him that he hadn't gone too far. He'd won tonight's battle, but the restlessness he'd felt in the last few months was increasing and driving him to take more and more risks with his victims' lives.

He'd come to San Francisco nine months ago on an assignment for Scanguards, the vampire-run bodyguard company that had employed him for several decades. The assignment had turned into a permanent stay. At first, he'd thought that the change of venue from New York to this quiet West coast town that was frequently engulfed in fog would bring him peace, but the opposite was the case. The hunt for his torturer had stalled, then come to a dead end. With every day that passed after the trail had gone cold, this failure drove his anger and hatred higher. He needed to hurt somebody. Soon.

At a sound, Zane snapped his head to the side. He lowered the Latino kid to the ground, resting him against the wall of a building. He squeezed his eyes shut for a moment, concentrating on the distant voice he'd heard. Past the noise that indicated a vibrant nightlife, a low whimpering laced with fear and despair drifted to him. It was remote, but his sensitive vampire hearing identified it as a plea for help.

"Fuck!"

He shouldn't have ignored the scream he'd heard earlier. He should have known that something was wrong. Both his vampire instincts and his training as a bodyguard told him as much. Without casting another glance at his victim, Zane charged out of the alley and headed for the origin of the sound. He hoped he wasn't too late already.

A few drunks stumbled along the sidewalk, their incoherent mumbles temporarily blocking out the distressed sobs he was following. Had he lost the trail? Zane rocked to a halt at the next corner and forced his ears to concentrate. For a moment, everything was completely quiet, but then the sound returned and intensified his gut feeling that he was needed.

This time, the cry was accompanied by the low hissing voice of a man. "Shut up, bitch, or I'm gonna gut you."

Instinct took over as Zane raced around the corner and into the driveway where two shabby apartment buildings converged. His superior night vision assessed the situation instantly: a man was forcing a young woman face down against a dumpster, holding a knife to her throat. His pants bunched at his knees, and his bare ass moved frantically back and forth as he raped her.

"Shit!" Zane leapt at him just as the man's head turned, alerted by Zane's curse.

His fangs lengthened in mid-flight, and his fingers transformed into sharp claws capable of ripping an elephant to shreds. Zane pried the rapist off his victim with one swoop, his claws digging into the guy's shoulders, cleaving clear through his hoodie sweater.

The man's scream was first surprise, then pain as Zane's claws slashed deeper into his flesh. He relished the sound and dragged one hand, claws extended, through the entire width of his shoulder, tearing the flesh apart, rupturing muscle and nerve tissue. Blood spurted from the open wound, and the air became pregnant with its metallic scent. He flashed his fangs, making sure the asshole got a good look at them.

"Nooooo!"

The desperate protest of his victim did nothing to stop Zane's assault. Deliberately slowly, he allowed his other hand to tear through the muscles of the left shoulder, doing equal damage there. His arms dangling limp from his shoulders, the severed sinew and nerves not supporting their movement any longer, the rapist was defenseless.

At his mercy.

If Zane had had a heart, he would have ended it right there, but it was too late. One look at the frightened girl who gaped at him in horror, and his past took hold of him. Suddenly, the strawberry blond rape victim's features with the terrified blue eyes became a face he knew so well, a face he'd not seen in decades, yet never forgotten.

Her dark brown hair curled at its ends and caressed her pale shoulders as it framed her young face. Her chocolate brown eyes looked up at him, innocence lost, begging him to help her, to save her.

"Zacharias ..."

As her voice faded, he reached for her, but she shrunk back, petrified.

"Rachel," he whispered. "Don't be afraid."

Zane became aware of the man struggling against him and tore his gaze from her. He would kill the man who was hurting her, hurting his little Rachel.

Zane tossed the rapist against a wall a few yards away, hearing the cracking of his ribs with utter satisfaction. When he crossed the distance to his victim, his steps were deliberate. He allowed his body to harden and enjoyed the horrified look in the man's eyes.

But he didn't see the face of the rapist anymore. It had changed. He saw a dark blond man with brown eyes. And finally those eyes shone with fear and the knowledge that his time had finally run out. He was caught and would pay for his crimes tonight.

Without another thought, Zane slammed his claws into the man's chest and sliced it open with the infallible precision of a man who'd performed this task before. Ignoring the bloodcurdling screams, he plunged his hands inside and jerked the ribs apart. Blood spurted onto him, liberally gushing from the open chest. He inhaled the scent, the smell of life and death equally strong. Despite the fact that he'd only just fed, hunger surged, but it was a different kind of hunger this time, not for food, but for revenge. Sweeter than hunger, it begged to be satisfied by the only means possible.

Zane jammed his hand through the chest wall and reached for the beating heart. His palm clamped around it, the life-sustaining organ pulsing into his fist, its spasms still strong and fighting against the inevitable.

"You'll never hurt anybody again."

As he tore the heart from its body, the man's eyes went blank. Zane stared at the still-beating heart in his hand as the warm blood dripped from the torn veins and arteries and ran down his hand and wrist. A river of it tunneled under the sleeve of his black shirt, soaking it, pasting it against his skin. His heartbeat slowed to near normal.

It was done.

"Rachel, he's dead. You're safe now."

Zane pivoted, but Rachel was gone. In her stead, a strawberry blond, young woman cowered against the dumpster, whimpering and shaking like a leaf. Tears had dissolved her black mascara and left long dark streaks along her cheeks. Her lips quivered.

Zane blinked. Rachel wasn't safe. Rachel was gone, and he couldn't bring her back. But this girl here was alive, and her attacker was dead.

He took a step toward her to impart the good news, but she

scrambled back and away from him.

"Noooo!" she echoed breathlessly, her eyes frantically searching for an escape route as if she thought Zane was coming after her next.

"I won't hurt you." He stretched his bloody hands toward her, but his gesture only made her shriek in panic.

Zane knew what she saw. His jeans and shirt were soaked in blood. The sticky, warm liquid had even penetrated his boots. But that wasn't the worst. The girl he'd rescued saw his vampire side, the deadly claws, the sharp fangs that pushed past his lips, and the glowing red eyes that made him look like the devil. His bald head only accentuated the air of danger that always accompanied him even when he was in his human form. Even without his fangs extended, people feared him—as they should.

He'd massacred a man like a butcher slaughtered a pig and felt no remorse. He'd done what was necessary, even if most people would never understand it. Evil had to be eradicated instantly, before it had a chance to grow bigger and turn into a festering cancer that could destroy an entire people. As it had once done while the world had stood by and watched.

They'd stood by until it was too late, until the worst had been done.

"I'll make you forget," Zane promised the scared girl and allowed his mental powers to take hold of her mind, erasing everything that had happened tonight, including the rape. When she woke tomorrow, she wouldn't remember anything about the man who'd attacked her, nor the man who'd saved her from this monster.

Or was Zane the monster? Was he the one to be feared, the one who was evil for wanting to avenge what had been done to him and his family?

As he stalked through the night, the warm blood of his victim rapidly drying on his skin and clothes, once again the face of his torturer hovered before him, taunting him. He had to close this chapter of his life and find him, otherwise peace would elude him and happiness remain a foreign word.

Chapter Two

"What the fuck were you thinking?"

Samson, the founder of Scanguards, slammed a newspaper on the massive desk in his study and rose. He was over six feet tall and slightly broader than Zane who was leaner but not any less lethal than his fellow vampire. He'd rarely ever seen Samson angry, but tonight his boss was fuming.

Zane glanced at the headline: 'Monstrous killer cuts heart from innocent partygoer.' What a load of bull! He hadn't *cut* anything—those reporters should get their facts straight. And his victim had been far from innocent.

"He had it coming."

"Did I say you could talk?" Samson snapped, his fangs descending in the process and peeking past his lips. "You weren't thinking at all, were you? What was it, Zane, bloodlust? You couldn't stop this time? You couldn't confine yourself to just feeding from him?"

Zane's heartbeat accelerated as Samson hurled wrong accusation after wrong accusation at him. "I didn't feed off him."

Samson blinked in surprise. "You murdered him in cold blood?"

Zane swore he could still hear the guy's screams of pain and fear. The recollection caused his gums to itch, a sure sign that his fangs were eager to descend and come out to play.

"And I enjoyed every single second of it."

"My God, you have no heart." Samson took an instinctive step back, clearly taken aback by his admission.

"I wouldn't say that. For a while there, I had two."

Samson pounded his fist onto the desk, apparently not enjoying Zane's sense of humor. Zane didn't care; he wasn't Samson's court jester.

"Do you have any idea what risks you were taking? This could expose us!"

Zane lunged for the desk, bracing his hands on it. "What would you have done, huh? That fucking asshole was raping an innocent girl! At knifepoint!"

With satisfaction, he noticed the widening of Samson's eyes.

"Yes, that's right. But you always assume the worst of me, don't you?" Just as everybody else did.

"She was an innocent, and he raped her, just put a knife to her throat and violated her. What if that had been your wife, or your sister? What if somebody did that to your daughter? Would you then stand here, self-righteously talking about exposure? Or would you rip the jerk a new one?"

Zane thrust his chin up in challenge, and knew he'd won this round.

As a blood-bonded vampire, Samson was fiercely protective of his human wife, Delilah, and their two-month-old daughter Isabelle. He would gladly give his own life to protect theirs and wouldn't think twice about killing anyone who threatened them.

When Samson closed his eyes for a moment and raked his hand through his raven black hair, Zane relaxed his aggressive stance.

"You could have made it a clean kill. There was no need to butcher him."

"There was need." He'd needed it. He'd needed to see him suffer. A clean kill wouldn't have satisfied him. "Breaking his neck wouldn't have hurt him. I had to set an example."

"An example of what?"

"That evil will be eradicated; that rapists will pay for their crimes."

"You can't make an example of someone when nobody knows why you did it!"

Zane let out a sharp breath. "The fact that he had his pants down to his ankles didn't tell you enough? What do you guys want, a sign around his neck that says 'rapist'?"

"The article didn't mention anything about his pants being down."

"Then maybe you should check your facts with your contact at the police first before accusing me of being a cold-blooded murderer."

Because of Samson's friendship with the mayor, who was a hybrid—half-vampire, half-human—he had a direct line to the police department, a fact that came in handy on occasion. Maybe Samson should have used his contacts before he'd gone to town on him.

Zane straightened and turned toward the door.

"Oh, we're not done," Samson said calmly.

Zane raised an eyebrow as he spun around to face him.

"The fact remains that you slaughtered a man and left his body for anybody to find. It goes against everything Scanguards stands for."

As Samson paused, a nauseating feeling spread in Zane's gut. Was his boss planning on firing him? Scanguards was his life, his family, his only link to humanity. Without it, he would descend into darkness and give into his most evil desires. He would only live for revenge and nothing else, leading him onto a path that was sure to destroy him. He was smart enough to know that if Scanguards wasn't there to ground him in reality any longer, he'd lose the last bit of his soul and turn as evil as the men responsible for his transformation into a vampire.

"No ..." he choked out, feeling his throat constrict at the thought of losing everything that meant anything to him.

The faces of his colleagues and friends flashed before him: the scarred face of Gabriel, Scanguards' second in command and the man who'd first hired him; Thomas, the gay biker with the IT-Geek brain; Amaury, his linebacker-sized friend whose huge size detracted from the fact that he had the softest heart of any man Zane had ever met, particularly when it came to his blood-bonded mate Nina; and even Yvette, the prissy woman who'd been a pain in the butt until two months ago when she'd found her soul mate, the witch-turned-vampire Haven.

His thoughts wandered further, back to New York and his friend Quinn who was responsible for him still being alive. If Quinn hadn't pulled him out of the downward spiral he'd been in at the time and introduced him to Gabriel, he would probably be dust by now. He couldn't give all this up. Those were his friends, the only people he could rely on.

"Sit down," Samson ordered.

"I'd rather stand." If Samson was going to fire him, he would take it like a man.

"Suit yourself. I'll discuss this situation with Gabriel later, but I'm sure we'll be of the same mind."

Figured! When didn't those two agree on something, particularly when it came to the punishment of fellow vampires? Sticklers for rules, both of them! Fuck, he was a vampire, not some idiot human. He had his own rules.

"In the meantime," Samson went on, "I'm pulling you off your assignment and revoking your class A status."

Zane clenched his jaw shut. Having Scanguards' highest clearance revoked meant being ineligible for any dangerous or high-importance assignments. It meant being relegated to routine duties. Samson might as well have chopped his hands off.

"You can't …" He was no fucking rent-a-cop with a beer belly and a bad haircut sitting in the lobby of a deserted building all night, guarding empty offices.

Samson held up his hand. "Before you say anything you might regret later, I'd like you to listen."

Zane snorted. Regret wasn't part of his vocabulary. Neither was remorse.

"I can't risk having a loose cannon on my staff. Until we've figured out how to mitigate the risk you represent, you'll work in low-risk and low-stress areas. You'll have my final decision in two days."

Zane nodded stiffly. "Fine," he pressed out, barely parting his lips so he wouldn't bare the fangs that had descended the moment the rage had started to grip him.

Low-risk! Low-stress!

What the fuck was Samson insinuating? That he was having a nervous breakdown? Those were for fucking sissies, not for men like him! He'd shove a nervous breakdown up their asses if they gave him any more shit about this.

Zane left Samson's study and resisted the urge to slam the door. His long legs ate up the distance as he hurried along the dark, wood-paneled corridor that led to the foyer. He couldn't wait to get out of the Victorian home that suddenly felt oppressive. He needed to smash something.

"Low-stress!" he cursed under his breath.

"Evening, Zane!" Delilah's calm voice came from his left.

He whipped his head toward her and watched her walk down the broad mahogany staircase, her infant daughter cradled in her arms.

"Delilah." He was unable to be any more civil than that. After all, her mate had just insulted him.

She smiled at him when a beeping sound from the kitchen put a frown on her face. "Oh, no, the cookies, I almost forgot."

Before he realized what she wanted to do, she stretched out her arms and put the baby against his chest.

"Here, hold her for a moment. I've gotta take the cookies out or they'll burn."

Instinctively, his arms came up to hold the baby before Delilah rushed toward the kitchen. "But, I ..."

His protest was too late. Shit!

He looked down at the little bundle in his arms, not knowing what to do next when the baby opened its eyes. They were as green as her mother's and just as beautiful. The little girl looked straight at him. She was a hybrid, a half-human, half-vampire child, possessing the attributes of both species.

She could be out in daylight without burning, yet she would have the strength and speed of a vampire once she was fully grown. Even as a child, she was stronger and would grow faster than a purely human child. While she could eat human food, she could also sustain herself on blood. And once she had reached maturity, she would stop aging just like a full-blooded vampire.

The best of both worlds, she was a tiny wonder. Only vampire males were fertile, but they could only procreate with blood-bonded human females. Vampire females were infertile. However, this little girl had lucked out: her human genes assured she was fertile. She would make Samson a grandfather one day; and her children would be hybrids like her, no matter who the father was.

Fascinated, Zane stared at the miracle in his arms and stroked his knuckles over her rosy cheeks. He hadn't felt such softness and sweetness since his little sister had been a baby. Ten years her senior, he'd often taken care of her, fed her, and lulled her to sleep.

"You sweet little girl," he whispered and noticed how she opened her mouth to smile at him. Tiny little fangs peeked from her upper gums.

The baby's little hand reached for him, and he obliged her and allowed her to capture his index finger with her fist. Her grip was strong, pulling his finger toward her face with ease. Before he could register what was happening, she drew his finger to her mouth and wrapped her lips around it. Sharp fangs descended into his flesh.

"Ouch!"

He jerked his finger from her. Blood dripped from it. Zane looked back at the baby and saw her smack her lips together as if she wanted more. The little devil had bitten him!

He shook his head and looked up, his gaze colliding with Delilah's. Her mouth gaping open, she stared at his bleeding finger and then at her daughter's mouth.

"She bit you." Not a question, simply a statement. "She's never bitten anybody before. You do know what that means, don't you?"

Ah, shit, he knew only too well.

Chapter Three

Portia Lewis shut her laptop and slid it into her shoulder bag together with her course book, waiting for her best friend, Lauren, to do the same.

"Are you going to Michael's party tonight?"

Portia shook her head as she and Lauren fought their way through the throng of students exiting the lecture hall.

"I still have to prepare for tomorrow's criminal psychology test."

Lauren made a dismissive hand movement. "Piece of cake. Besides—" She bent closer and lowered her voice. "—you can always use your powers."

Portia jumped back and gave her a scolding look. "You know we're not allowed to do that!"

It had been drilled into her as far back as she could remember. Both her father, a full-blooded vampire, and her mother, a human, had instilled in her that she had to hide what she was at all times: a hybrid, half vampire, half human. The only reason she could even talk to Lauren about this was because her friend was just like her.

When Portia and her dad had moved to San Francisco after her mother's death in a car accident six months earlier, she had struck up a friendship with the mayor's daughter after realizing that Lauren was a hybrid too.

They were signed up for many of the same courses at the University of San Francisco, a private catholic school. Because the aura of hybrids was so different from humans, they had recognized each other instantly, both glad to have a best friend they had so much in common with.

When she'd told her father about her new friend, he'd seemed displeased, making Portia wonder whether he was somewhat envious that she had instantly found a friend while he still mourned the loss of his wife. She missed her mother terribly, but she knew she had to get on with her life.

Luckily, Portia had always been good at making friends quickly. It was a survival mechanism she'd developed early on, because her family rarely stayed anywhere for longer than a year. Her father always moved them to a new town just when she started to feel at home. She understood it to a certain degree. As a vampire, he had to be careful not to attract attention. Humans around him would eventually find it odd that he never ventured outside the home during the day, never extended or accepted dinner invitations, and didn't age. She had accepted it, but at the same time, she longed for a place to grow roots and stay.

"Eric will be there," Lauren baited her and brought her back to the present. "You know he likes you."

Portia felt her cheeks flame and wished that her vampire side prevented her from blushing, but unfortunately only full-blooded vampires didn't blush. As so often before, she covered her insecurity about guys with an offhanded remark.

"You know he's not all that hot. I've been with more exciting guys before."

What a big lie that was! She'd never had a boyfriend, but not even Lauren knew that. Despite the fact that they were friends, Portia still hadn't been able to confide in her that the prospect of getting naked with a guy not only made her nervous, but terrified her.

"Not hot? You're kidding me. Eric is pretty much the number one heartthrob on campus."

"Shh, not so loud," Portia cautioned. "I don't need everybody hearing us talking about him." She cast a nervous look over her shoulder, hoping none of Eric's friends were close.

Lauren put her hand on her arm, making Portia halt in midstride.

She turned to look at her friend, wondering why Lauren suddenly gave her this penetrating look. "What?"

Lauren's eyes bored into her. "Oh, my God, why didn't I see this earlier?"

"Hey, move along, or get out of my way," an impatient voice ordered from behind.

Portia stepped aside to get out of the person's way when Lauren dragged her into the closest doorway.

"What are you doing?" Portia protested.

"We've gotta talk," Lauren insisted as she darted cautious looks down the corridor as if about to reveal a big secret.

She opened the door to a small study room and, finding it empty, virtually pushed Portia inside, shutting the door behind her.

"Lauren, I've got another class in five minutes." Portia glanced impatiently at her wristwatch and hugged her bag to her chest.

"I've already told you that I can't go to the party because of that criminal psychology test. Honestly, I've been to plenty of parties in my life, and they're all the same. It really gets boring after a while. So don't be a nag."

Lauren blew out an impatient breath. "Forget the party. This is more important."

More important than a party when all Lauren lived for at present was entertainment? Listening to this was definitely worth being late for her next class.

"What changed your tune?"

"Tell me about your last boyfriend." Lauren's casual tone belied the intense look in her eyes, as if she were a tigress waiting to pounce on her prey.

Portia furrowed her forehead, wondering what her friend was suddenly so interested in. "There's really nothing much to tell. Why do you want to know about him?"

"Just answer the question."

"He was nice. We went out for a few months, we broke up, I moved. End of story."

"Oh, yeah? How was the sex?"

Instinctively, Portia's body tensed, and she pulled her bag closer to her chest. "It was fine."

"Fine, huh? Not hot, not exciting, not sweaty, not earth moving?"

Unease crept up Portia's spine at Lauren's insistent question. "What do you want, Lauren?"

"You've never *had* sex."

Portia took an instinctive step back, crashing into the desk behind her. She quickly steadied herself, forcing her face into an indifferent mask she used when she wasn't prepared to exposed her feelings.

"That's ... that's ludicrous. Of course, I've had sex." Admitting that she hadn't and that she was a total innocent, was just too humiliating.

"I can tell when you're lying. Your eyes do this thing ..." Lauren made a circular motion with her hand. "Anyway, I know you well enough by now to have figured that out."

Portia let out a sigh. Somebody had finally caught her in her deception. And there she'd thought she'd played this role well enough:

she'd pretended to be worldly and sophisticated, and whenever the subject of guys and sex came up in conversation, she'd talked as if she knew everything about it. She'd gone so far as to read everything about it, and even to chime in when other girls talked about their preferred brand of condoms.

What a huge lie all that had been. And she'd done it so that nobody would think her odd; so she'd fit in, when she knew she didn't.

Lauren waited patiently and flicked a strand of her long chestnut hair over her shoulder, drawing Portia's attention to her graceful neck and the pretty head that sat on top of it.

Raising her eyes to meet Lauren's, she collected all her courage. "I'm still a virgin."

"Not good," Lauren murmured, shaking her head.

"I'm just waiting for the right guy."

"I'm afraid you don't have that luxury." Lauren's voice became even more urgent.

Uncomfortable about the situation and disappointed about the fact that Lauren didn't seem to understand her, Portia spun toward the door.

"I've gotta get to my class."

In vampire speed, a blur to the human eye, Lauren blocked the exit. "You're skipping class today. There are more important things in life than school."

"Don't be so dramatic; just because boys and sex are important to you, doesn't mean everybody thinks the same. You and I, we're very different."

Portia squeezed her bag tighter as if it could protect her from the things she didn't want to face.

"I agree, boys aren't important. Sex is."

Portia rolled her eyes. "For you maybe."

Imagining herself in bed with any of the guys she'd kissed held no particular appeal. Lauren's standards, however, appeared to be somewhat lower.

"You're turning twenty-one in what, five weeks from today?"

Confused about the change in subject, she answered automatically, "In six weeks. Why?"

Lauren pressed her lips together and hummed to herself as if contemplating a massive problem such as the eradication of world hunger.

"Then we have six weeks for you to lose your virginity. Granted, that's not a lot of time, but there are enough horny guys out there we can take if we don't find anything better. I can count at least a dozen—"

"Hold it! What the hell are you going on about? I'm not just going out there to lose my virginity to some idiot. I'm going to have sex when it feels right. And besides, I'm not planning on dating until after college. I promised my father."

Her parents had always drilled into her that it was important to find the right person. And knowing how happy they had been together, she had to agree. The love between them had been palpable. Portia wanted the same for herself. She didn't want to throw her virginity away at some guy she didn't care about. So far, she hadn't met anybody who had even tempted her in the slightest to take this step.

"Weren't you listening? You don't have time to wait." Lauren made it sound like the world was going to end. "You have to lose your virginity by your twenty-first birthday or you'll be a virgin forever!"

"That's ludicrous! Even at twenty-one I'm still young enough to attract guys. Besides, once I'm twenty-one, I won't age anymore."

"Exactly!" Lauren waved her hands in a dramatic gesture. "And that's the point. At twenty-one your body will freeze into its final form. It'll be set in stone. Your physical form won't change after that. Which means, if you still have your hymen in place then, you'll always have it."

Portia's heartbeat stuttered to a halt. Her hymen would remain intact? "But—" It couldn't be.

"Every time you have sex after you turn twenty-one, you'll be in pain, because each time the guy you're having sex with will tear through your hymen. And every day it will grow back, because your body thinks you're injured and will repair itself. Sex will always be painful for you. Do you see now?"

Portia swallowed hard. Her knees buckled, and she sought support from the desk behind her.

"You can't be serious ... this can't be true."

Why was this the first time she'd heard about this? Her mother had never mentioned anything about that, and her father had only always cautioned her about boys. She raised her eyes to her friend, her head full of questions.

Lauren shook her gorgeous locks. "I'm telling you the truth. Go, ask my father. He made sure that I lost my virginity with plenty of time to spare. Hell, he screened the guys himself and helped me pick one."

Portia looked back at the few times she'd struck up friendships with boys.

"One time, my dad found me kissing a guy in the backseat of a car. We moved to another town a week later, but ..." Her voice faltered as she remembered the times she'd gotten close to boys, but it had never led to more than a few kisses and some touching. Before she could go any further with any of them, had she even wanted to, she'd found herself in a new town and a new school.

Lauren gasped. "Your father kept you away from boys? But he must know what he's doing to you. He can't *not* know."

Portia shook her head, not wanting to follow the implications of Lauren's words. "No! My father loves me. He would never do anything to hurt me."

She believed that. He was her rock. He'd always been there for her. Even more so after her mother's death. She only had him.

"You said you promised him not to date until after college. Did you come up with that or did he demand that?"

"Demand?"

She glared at her friend, yet at the same time she remembered how her father had explained that it would be better for her to wait. And she'd agreed with him, secretly relieved that she didn't have to deal with this issue until later.

"He didn't demand it. We discussed it."

Lauren tsked. "Do you always do everything your father wants you to do? Have you never rebelled?"

"I have no reason to rebel. Yes, my father is strict, but it's because he wants the best for me. And I only have him. Without Mom ... I have nobody else. No other family. You can't understand that. You've never been alone."

Lauren put her hand on Portia's arm. "I'm sorry. I didn't mean to upset you. But you have to face the facts: you have to lose your virginity. You have to get rid of your hymen."

"What if my father doesn't know about this? He never hangs out with other vampires. We weren't part of a coven or a clan. Maybe he doesn't know because we never integrated in vampire society. We moved around too much for that."

Lauren shook her head, her eyes full of pity. "He has to know. You don't raise a hybrid daughter without knowing this."

"I don't believe it."

And she would prove Lauren wrong.

"I'm going to talk to him tonight."

Chapter Four

The sun had already set over the Pacific, when Portia got home and found her father sitting on the couch poring over a file he instantly closed when he saw her.

"Evening, sweetheart, how were your classes?" Her father gave her a cheerful smile.

Portia dropped her bag at the bottom of the stairs and walked into the living room.

"Fine." She hesitated, not knowing how to start this difficult conversation. Shifting from one foot to the other, she avoided looking at him and instead stared at the wall behind him.

"Something wrong? You seem quiet."

"Uh ... well, there is something I wanted to talk to you about." She adjusted her gaze to look at him.

Her father sat up, his torso suddenly rigid. "Is somebody giving you trouble?"

She quickly shook her head. "No, it's not that. Everything's fine. It's just ... I found out something today that you're not aware of and ..." Portia broke off again, searching for the right words. This was harder than she'd thought.

"What is it? You know you can tell me anything."

Of course she knew that, but this was kind of awkward. In this moment, she wished her mother were still alive, and rather than broach this delicate subject with her father, she could confide her concerns in her mother.

"It's just that I found out today that once my body sets into its final form, I'll still ... I'll still have my hymen if I don't lose my virginity before that."

She swallowed. Now it was out and she and her father could discuss this matter like two adults.

"Who told you?" her father's voice thundered as he rose in the same instant. "Lauren!"

Taken aback by his harsh and seemingly angry reply, Portia nodded quickly. "You mean she wasn't telling me the truth?"

"It's none of her business to tell you anything. You know only what

I tell you, and that's it. I'm the one raising you!"

Raising her? She was grown up! "Father, I'm not a child anymore. I have a right to know."

"Silence! Lauren has no right to fill your mind with these things. Don't concern yourself with them!"

Confused, Portia opened her mouth again. "But was she right? Is that what's going to happen to me?"

Her father stared at her, his eyes glaring red in anger. "You are my daughter. And I say who you'll lose your virginity to and when."

In that instant, she saw the truth in his face. He understood the implications. He'd *always* known, but he'd chosen to keep her in the dark.

"Why? How can you do this to me?" How could he betray her like this? Didn't he love her? Tears welled up in her eyes.

"You'll understand eventually, and—" The beeping of his cell phone interrupted him. He glanced at it, then back at her.

"I have a meeting. Go to your room and study. I'll be back soon."

Then he turned and simply walked out like a man used to his orders being followed.

Portia just stood here. She had never felt so alone in her life.

Her father believed that it was his right to keep her ignorant, and what was even worse, he thought he could choose a man for her and decide when she would lose her virginity—whether that was within the next six weeks or not.

Tears streaked down her cheeks before she could stop them. Disappointment clamped around her heart like a tight fist, squeezing it until the pain was unbearable. Her father didn't love her, because if he did, he would never impose this fate on her. She'd looked up to him all her life. No longer.

She would be his obedient daughter no more.

This was her life, and *she* would decide how to live it.

***

The party was at a fraternity house not far from campus. The music was blaring from several speakers, the light dim at best, the place reeking of alcohol and smoke. Portia wrinkled her nose—it was not the legal kind of smoke.

It took her a good ten minutes to locate Lauren. Her friend looked fantastic in her low rider jeans and tight top that could have doubled as a wide belt.

"I thought you weren't coming." Lauren gave her a surprised stare.

"I wasn't, but I needed to talk to you and you didn't answer your cell."

Lauren motioned toward the crowd. "Too loud in here; couldn't hear it ring. What's up?"

"You were right." The admission cost her.

Instantly, Lauren grabbed her arm and pulled her from the room and down a corridor. A moment later, the two of them were locked in one of the bathrooms.

"What happened?" Lauren asked.

Portia sniffed. "I asked him. And he knew what he was doing to me. He knew I would remain a ..." Her voice broke.

Lauren drew her into her arms and stroked over Portia's hair. "I'm so sorry, honey."

Portia pushed back the threatening tears. She would not cry. She had to stay strong. Slowly, she stepped back, pulling from Lauren's embrace.

"I've thought about how to do it." She'd come up with the perfect idea of how to take care of her predicament, and now she needed Lauren's help.

"Good, Eric is here already. He was disappointed when I told him you weren't coming. I'll let him know—"

"No! That's not why I'm here. I need you to go with me to buy a dildo." She shuddered at the thought of walking into a sex toy shop on her own.

Lauren's eyes widened. "A dildo? What are you ... oh no, you don't mean to pierce your hymen with a dildo?"

"Yes, that's the easiest solution. I really don't want to have to sleep with anybody just to—"

"Not gonna work, Portia."

Stunned, she stared at her friend. "Why not? It's as big as a ... you know. I think it's a brilliant idea."

"Sure, if it worked, but it won't. It'll push through your hymen, but tomorrow it will have grown back. A man's semen is what will make it disappear for good."

Portia suppressed her urge to gag. "But then ... then ..." Her mind's wheels churned. "Then, why don't I get donated sperm. You have to help me." She took Lauren by her shoulders, almost shaking her. "Can't you get one of your 'friends' to donate some? I'm sure you can come up with some excuse for why."

Lauren tilted her head and gave a sad smile. "You know, your idea would really be great, but unfortunately, it won't work either. The sperm has to be ultra-fresh, and it has to be delivered with a flesh and blood dick. So whatever turkey baster method you're thinking of, it's off the table."

This revelation hit her just as hard as the disappointment earlier in the evening. She dropped her head. "Why? Why?"

"I wish I could tell you something different, but that's how it is."

Portia lifted her head. "What now?"

"I think we should look for Eric."

Portia felt her palms dampen at the thought. "Now? Why don't we wait a little while and see if we can figure out another solution. There must be something else."

Lauren shook her head. "There's no other solutions. Trust me, you're not the first hybrid. You'll survive. I hear Eric is good between the sheets."

Portia groaned.

***

A half hour later, Portia found out first hand that Eric was a passable kisser. Only, no matter the contortions he put his tongue through, she wasn't getting turned on. She remained strangely detached from the entire situation. In fact, none of the guys she'd kissed before had really made her feel like she wanted more. Sure, it had always been pleasant, just like sitting in the sun and eating ice cream was pleasant.

Was she frigid? Was that the reason why she hadn't pursued sex and why it hadn't bothered her that her father didn't want her to date yet?

This wasn't going to work, not with Eric. He was a nice guy and all, but for her first time she wanted to be wowed and not feel like it was a chore. She wanted to feel weak in her knees with her heart fluttering; she wanted a man who robbed her of her breath when he kissed her and whose touch made her skin sizzle. And Eric wasn't that kind of man.

She was about to extricate herself from his embrace when a sudden tingling on her skin arrested her heart. Another vampire had entered the bedroom she and Eric had found to have some privacy. Portia knew the signature of the vampire's aura only too well.

A split-second later, Eric was yanked from her and slammed against the wall. Her father's eyes glared at her when he pointed his finger in her face. "You, young lady, home. Now." His voice was a low growl, one she knew well enough.

He was angry. But so was she.

Portia lifted her chest and raised her head, adding another two inches to reach her full height of five nine. With her two inch heels she was almost eye level with him. "You can't tell me what to do!"

"I'm your father, and you'll listen to me!" His hand clamped around her wrist like a vice, and despite her own vampire strength, she was no match for her father. He was older and stronger than she.

"No! You have no right to order me around anymore!" He'd lost that right when he'd betrayed her.

"You're not of age!"

Portia froze. In vampire society, parents remained the legal guardians of their children until the child's body had reached its final form, which occurred on its twenty-first birthday. Only then was a hybrid considered mature. How could she have forgotten that her father had been the one who'd told her about this rule many years ago when she was a child? He had every right to issue orders. But she was done following them.

"I won't remain a virgin!"

"I'm not going to have you throw yourself at some dirty lowlife who doesn't deserve you! You'll only mate with someone your equal! Someone I'll choose for you."

She shook her head in quiet disbelief. No! She wouldn't bend to his will anymore. She was ready to rebel. Better late than never.

Her father yanked her toward the door. Portia glanced at Eric who still lay on the floor. He stirred, groans of pain coming from him. She extended her mind to him, directing her powers to erase his memories of the last half hour. She needed no witness to her humiliation.

Chapter Five

Samson motioned his friends Gabriel and Amaury to take a seat in his study as he continued pacing.

"He needs to be punished," Gabriel started.

Amaury shook his dark mane. "I disagree. Punish him and he'll derail completely."

"A crime like this can't be left unpunished." Gabriel shot a pleading look toward Samson, silently asking for support.

"I'm not saying that we won't do anything about it, but if we punish Zane outright, he'll go off the deep end. What he needs is rehabilitation," Amaury insisted.

A short knock on the door interrupted.

"Come," Samson answered, sensing who requested entry.

The door swung open and Thomas strolled in, his heavy biker boots scraping loudly against the wooden floor. He gave an apologetic smile as he pulled his second leather glove off and shoved both of them into his jacket pocket. Then he combed his fingers through his sandy blond hair, fluffing what his helmet had flattened. "Sorry I'm late; I had some problems with the bike."

Samson motioned to the couch, and Thomas let his leather-clad frame fall onto it, making the furniture groan. His leather outfit easily added fifteen pounds to his weight.

"I thought your Ducati was in top shape," Amaury wondered.

"I didn't take the Ducati. I was taking the R6 for a spin."

"That thing is a pile of junk," Gabriel commented, shaking his head.

"It's a World War Two antique," Thomas corrected. "I've been fixing it up for the last two months."

Samson smirked. Thomas' passion for bikes was legendary, and he spent every free minute tinkering with one of his many acquisitions. "As much as I'd like to discuss your talents as a mechanic, we have more urgent things to talk about."

Thomas nodded. "What are we gonna do about Zane?"

"Amaury was thinking rehabilitation rather than punishment." Then Samson addressed Amaury, "What did you have in mind?"

Amaury moved to the edge of his chair. "We expose him to the softer things in life."

"Excuse me?" Gabriel tossed his friend a confused look, the scar on his face, which reached from his ear to his chin, jumping at the same time.

Thomas scoffed. "Give him soft and he'll smash it to pieces."

"He'll spit in your face," Samson added.

Amaury's blue eyes sparkled. "He didn't spit in your daughter's face."

Samson didn't bother suppressing his scowl. Delilah had told him the minute Zane had left the house that Isabelle had bitten him. The first bite of a hybrid baby was a significant event. It meant that his daughter had chosen her mentor, her godfather. Only, Samson had hoped that she would pick somebody like Gabriel or Amaury, or better, Thomas who was a great mentor to Eddie, the young vampire under his wings, but not Zane. However, there was no way around this. Isabelle had tasted Zane's blood and would be instinctively drawn to him to seek his advice. While Samson and Delilah were Isabelle's primary caregivers, Zane would play an important role in her life.

"Which makes it even more important to deal with him now before this gets out of hand. I can't have a loose cannon around my daughter."

"Nobody wants that." Gabriel pulled the band around his ponytail tight and shifted in his seat.

"Suggestions then," Samson said and gave Amaury an expectant nod.

"First of all, no more high-risk assignments. You were right to pull him off his current one. He doesn't need to be in constant assault mode. We'll have to condition him to use non-violent responses to aggression."

"Interesting," Gabriel snorted. "Good luck with that."

Thomas shook his head. "Let's face it: take violence out of Zane's life and his shell will collapse. It's the only things that keeps him alive."

Samson raised his hand. "Maybe Amaury is onto something. What else have you got?"

"He needs to see Drake."

"You want him to agree to see a shrink?" Gabriel shook his head. "That'll go down well. Just make sure I'm not around when you tell him, 'cause I'd kinda like to keep my head attached to my neck."

"I didn't say it was gonna be easy to get him to go." Amaury shrugged. "We just have to make sure he knows what's at stake if he doesn't."

Samson stopped pacing. "You're right. The carrot and stick approach. Show him what he can have, then threaten to take it away. It could work."

"And what are we gonna take away?" Gabriel asked.

"His job."

"He won't be hurting for money," Gabriel countered.

His second-in-command was right of course. Any vampire who'd been around for a few decades had invariably accumulated wealth simply by investing money in low risk assets such as real estate and bonds. Knowing Zane, he'd probably taken a riskier approach and amassed an even greater fortune.

"Money isn't the reason he works for us," Samson explained. "We're his family. He needs us." Just like they needed him. Each and every member of Scanguards was essential, and the inner core, consisting of Amaury, Gabriel, Thomas, Zane, Yvette, Quinn, and himself was vital for the survival of the company. They were the driving force.

Slowly, Gabriel nodded. "True. Then I have a suggestion to make. Let's fly Quinn out from New York. He's the one closest to Zane. Quinn brought him in. If anybody can get to Zane, it's Quinn. He knows what makes him tick."

"Who will run New York headquarters in the meantime?" Samson asked.

"New York is such a well-oiled machine, it runs itself," Gabriel claimed confidently.

Thomas grinned. "I suppose that means we can put a monkey at its helm and it'll still run?"

"Almost." Gabriel nodded. "Unfortunately, I'm fresh out of monkeys. We'll have to use someone higher up the food chain."

"Who did you have in mind?" Samson asked.

"Quinn mentioned a promising vampire the other day. His name is Jake and he's been working with Quinn for six months now. He might be ready to take on more responsibility."

"Quinn vouches for him?" Samson contemplated Gabriel's words.

"He's diligent and ambitious."

"Fine, let's do it," Samson agreed. "Call Quinn and fill him in. Now, we need to keep Zane occupied. Do we have a desk job we can park him at?"

Gabriel shook his head. "Nothing open. I could shift people around though, unless—" He scratched his head before he continued, "We just got this babysitting job in."

"Babysitting?" Amaury echoed.

"I've gotta hear that," Thomas mumbled under his breath.

"Couple of vampires, moved here about six months ago. A father with his hybrid daughter. She's friends with G's daughter. Goes to USF. Her father is leaving for a business trip for two to three weeks and needs us to babysit her twenty-four-seven."

"She goes to college and needs a babysitter? Where's her mother?" Samson asked.

"Died in a car accident six months ago."

"But the girl is what, eighteen, nineteen?" Amaury asked, confusion pasted on his handsome features as he swept his shoulder length black hair back.

"Twenty, almost twenty-one," Gabriel reported. "But according to her father, she's a wild one: parties, guys, alcohol, the works. She's acting out since her mother's death. He fears she's on the verge of a nervous breakdown. He's very concerned about her and worried about leaving her alone. She's liable to hurt herself."

"So what does he want us to do?" Samson asked.

"Watch her and keep her away from any bad influence. No parties, no boys, etc. Piece of cake. I've put Oliver on the dayshift. It'll be an easy job for him to take on and get his feet wet."

Samson nodded. "I suppose I can't keep him as my personal assistant forever. He's got lots of potential." Oliver, a human, had worked as his daytime assistant for over three years, almost four.

"He'll do well. His assignment starts at daybreak."

"Aren't you guys overlooking something important?" Amaury interrupted.

Samson gave him a questioning look. "Oliver is well-trained. You've seen him in action. He's a great bodyguard. He's protected Delilah many times, and you know I would never provide my wife with sub-standard safety."

"Yes, but your wife is human. This charge is a hybrid. She's stronger than Oliver."

Samson nodded. "I'm fully aware of that. But we can't put a vampire on the dayshift. You know that as well as I do. And unfortunately, we don't have a hybrid on staff. They're still too rare. It'll have to be a human."

"And what if she outsmarts him and uses mind control to slip away?" Amaury challenged, not letting the subject rest.

Samson ran his hand through his hair, but was saved from answering when Thomas cleared his voice.

"Samson, do I have your permission to tell them?"

Samson met Thomas' gaze. Vampires themselves weren't subject to mind control, in fact, it would result in a mental fight to the death if two vampires unleashed mind control on each other. However, Thomas had recently figured something out. "Go ahead, Thomas."

"This is still in its early stages of experimentation, but Oliver and I have been working together over the last few weeks."

"What experimentation?" Gabriel asked tightly, clearly miffed that he had not been informed.

"I'm trying to teach him how to resist mind control."

Gabriel gasped. Amaury seemed unaffected by the revelation.

"But how?" Gabriel wanted to know.

"As you all know, mind control is my specialty. So, I've been trying to examine the underlying physical properties to figure out whether there's a way for a human to be able to recognize mind control at its onset, and then break the vampire's concentration."

"You can't be serious!" Gabriel jumped up. "If this works, then …"

"I know what you're thinking, Gabriel," Thomas said calmly, "but this will not become public knowledge. Only our most trusted humans, only the inner core, will know about it. I had the idea when Amaury told me that Nina was immune to his mind control even before they bonded."

Amaury nodded. "And what a pain in the butt that was."

Thomas grinned. "As if you would have it any other way."

"You knew about this?" Gabriel asked.

Amaury shrugged. "What Nina knows, I know."

Joking aside, I've had long conversations with Nina to figure out what she felt when Amaury was trying to use his powers on her. And I'm making progress with Oliver. He's very smart and strong willed. That helps."

"So, can he fend off mind control?" Gabriel asked impatiently.

"Not fully and consistently, but I've seen moments in him, where I could feel his mind pushing against my power. He's getting there."

"In any case," Samson interrupted, "we have no choice about putting a human on the dayshift. I'd rather have Oliver do this than any of the other human guards. I trust him. He won't disappoint us."

Gabriel nodded. "And Zane? Do you think this will work?"

Samson contemplated Gabriel's words. The assignment sounded low-risk and low-stress. "How difficult can guarding a twenty-year old girl be?" He caught Amaury's doubtful look. "What?"

"He's gonna flip a lid when he hears that." Then he grinned. "Can't wait to see it."

Thomas nudged him. "You're such a troublemaker, Amaury." Then he looked straight at Samson. "Let's just hope it won't backfire and blow up in our faces."

"We'll keep a tight leash on him," Samson said.

From the corridor, voices drifted to them, mingled with the yapping of a dog. A moment later, the door opened without a knock and Delilah stormed in, a yellow Labrador puppy in her arms.

"Sorry to interrupt, but I just had to show you, Samson." Her face glowed.

Behind her, Yvette and her mate Haven appeared. "Hi, guys."

Yvette looked stunning as ever, and the fact that she had traded her spiky short haircut for long dark locks, made her look softer and more feminine. Haven, the bounty hunter she'd saved from an evil witch, was responsible for Yvette allowing her feminine side to emerge. After Yvette had turned him into a vampire to save his life, Haven had blood-bonded with her. Yet, so far, he hadn't joined their ranks at Scanguards. Samson hoped that he would do so one day. An ex-bounty hunter would be a great asset.

"Hey Yvette, Haven," Samson and his friends responded. "What's going on?"

"Look what Yvette gave us for Isabelle! One of the puppies. She'll have her own puppy to play with." Delight shone in Delilah's face, and Samson's heart expanded. God, how he loved this woman. He'd never been happier in his entire life.

"Isabelle will love it." He stroked his hand over the puppy's soft head, and the dog licked him enthusiastically. Then he nodded toward Yvette and Haven. "Thank you, guys, that's so thoughtful of you."

Yvette smiled. "We have four more, so—" She looked into the round. "—if anybody wants one ..."

Amaury's face suddenly lit up. "Actually—" He winked at Samson who instantly caught on to his oldest friend's thinking. "—I think we have another taker. Don't you agree, Samson?"

Samson smirked. "I was just thinking the same thing."

***

Zane set the two fifty-pound dumbbells on the ground before dropping down next to them. One arm behind his back, he pushed off the floor with the other and started counting. Push-up after punishing push-up, he performed until sweat dripped from his naked torso. His gym shorts were soaked, but he kept pushing himself. Forty-nine, fifty. He changed arms and started counting anew.

His body was on auto-pilot, his muscles tearing and repairing themselves as he continued his grueling workout. Tonight, he couldn't stop. His usual two hours of extreme physical exertion weren't enough, because the rage that still ran through his veins like acid demanded that he hurt somebody. And tonight this somebody was Zane.

By the time he counted to fifty, a pool of sweat had collected on the mat beneath him. Zane rose and reached for the jump rope that hung on the wall.

When he moved to San Francisco, the first thing he did was to equip his private gym even before he'd had a bed delivered. Sleeping wasn't important to him. He rarely needed more than three to four hours a day, which left him with plenty of daylight hours during which he was confined inside.

And even during those three or four hours he slept, a part of him remained alert, always listening for danger, aware that just as he was hunting his enemy, the enemy could be hunting him. Because he was the only survivor left who could destroy the man who had escaped justice: Dr. Franz Müller. He'd memorized the name and face just as he'd committed the names and faces of Müller's colleagues to memory: Andreas Schmidt, dead; Volker Brandt, dead; Mathias Arenberg, dead; and Erich Wolpers, dead.

Zane's hands curled tightly around the handles of his jump rope as he remembered their last moments. Brandt had squealed like a pig when he'd found Zane standing over him with murder in his eyes. He'd made sure that his victim remembered who he was and why Zane had come after him before he'd killed him. Not that Brandt needed much of a reminder: Zane hadn't changed a bit since Brandt had seen him last, and it only took seconds for him to recognize his erstwhile prisoner. He remembered how he'd enjoyed the fear that had emanated from Brandt. He could smell it even now, and the scent filled him with satisfaction. But the four men he'd executed had played minor roles in his torture compared to what Müller had done. Their leader, Müller, was still on the run.

Maybe it would be smart if Samson simply fired him. At least then, Zane wouldn't be accountable to anybody and could devote every minute of the day and night to tracking down Müller. But as quickly as the thought came, Zane dismissed it.

Scanguards was his rock. He wasn't suicidal enough to let go of the support they provided him with. Just as he wasn't going to admit to any of them that he needed them to survive, the way he needed blood.

Zane hung the rope back in its place after counting one hundred jumps. He was about to lie down on the bench for more bench presses when a sound disturbed the silence in his basement.

He listened, remaining motionless and forcing himself to stop breathing. A few seconds passed before the sound repeated: footsteps sounded on the front stairs leading up to the entrance door.

Zane glanced at the clock on the wall. It was shortly past four in the morning and still dark outside. Snatching a towel from the rack on the wall, he hastily dried his upper body and headed for the stairs. His bare feet made no noise on the cold floor as he made his way to the main floor of his two-story house. He skipped the last step, knowing that it creaked, and planted his feet on the landing.

He peered through the darkness in the foyer. Not wanting to draw attention to the odd hours he was keeping, he was in the habit of never switching on lights unless he needed them. He was glad for it now since the darkness around him protected him.

The footsteps were gone. Had the person left, or was the unwelcome visitor still out there, planning to ambush him if he stepped outside to investigate?

Zane moved closer to the door and inhaled deeply, trying to pick up the scent of the person who'd walked up his stairs, but the door was too thick and too well insulated to allow his sensitive nose to pick up anything beyond the smell of his own sweat. Fuck, he needed a shower.

Not a sound came from the outside. Was he perhaps too much on the edge lately that he'd started hearing things? It wouldn't surprise him. Hell, half the time he was in a world where the edges between reality and fantasy were blurred. Maybe he'd finally lost his grip.

Cursing himself for his stupid thoughts, he reached for the doorknob and turned it. There was only one way to figure out what was going on out there: confront whatever fucking bastard was trespassing on his property.

Zane jerked the door open and barreled down the five steps that led to the sidewalk. At the bottom, he pivoted, facing the house. The entire action had taken less than a second. His eyes assessed the situation instantly. No attacker was waiting for him. The area was empty. Only the faint smell of a vampire lingered.

He drew in another breath and took the scent into his lungs: Yvette. What the fuck had she wanted, and why hadn't she rung the doorbell like any decent visitor? Annoyed that his workout routine had been interrupted, he stormed back up the stairs when another scent hit his nostrils.

His head veered to the left side of the door where a little niche housed a broom to sweep the stairs and driveway. Tonight, said broom wasn't alone. To its left stood a small cage. From it came the scent that had drifted his way. Zane hunched down and looked inside when the caged animal let out a whining yelp. A dog, more precisely a puppy, was now yapping away at him, his nose pressed against the metal grid.

"Shut up! You're gonna wake up the whole fucking neighborhood."

But the dog kept on barking, clearly unaware who he was dealing with.

"Ah, shit!" Zane grabbed the handle on top of the cage and carried it inside the house, shutting the door behind him. As he flipped the switch to illuminate the foyer, he noticed a note card stuck to the side of the cage that had faced the wall before. He pried it off and read it.

'My name is Zane, and I'm yours.'

He recognized the handwriting, too. That fucking bitch! She was offloading one of her puppies on him. She should have had her dog spayed if she didn't want to deal with a litter. And the gall she had to even name one of the useless creatures after him! He was ready to take Yvette's head off!

He would return this unwanted present as soon as he'd had a shower. She wouldn't get away with this crap. No wonder she hadn't rung the doorbell, because she knew that he would have tossed her down the stairs, cage in hand.

"That's right," he muttered.

The dog yelped, and his big brown eyes lifted and looked straight at him.

"What do you want?" he barked back.

The puppy's paw nudged against the grid.

"No, I'm not letting you out of the cage. You're gonna piss all over my house." He gave the dog a stern look, making him understand that he meant it. He wouldn't be manipulated like that.

Zane set the cage on the sideboard in the hallway and headed for the bathroom. The dog instantly yowled in the most miserable way he'd ever heard an animal cry.

"Ah, shit!" he cursed and turned back to the cage. He released the lock and opened the grid door. He reached for the dog and pulled him out, fully intent on setting him down on the floor so he could roam around. But when he felt the soft fur of the Labrador puppy beneath his fingers, Zane instinctively brought the animal to his chest and stroked his hand over its back. The dog turned his head and licked Zane's hairless chest.

Some of his anger dissipated. He couldn't really blame the dog for Yvette's actions. "And don't think I'm gonna keep you. It's just for the day." He glanced at the clock on the wall. "I won't have enough time to get you to Yvette's and back here before sunrise." He could if he rushed, but he wasn't in the mood right now.

The dog gave a soft woof as if he understood.

"And I'm not calling you Zane." He'd call him Z, but only for today. Tomorrow night he'd return the dog to Yvette and be done with it.

As he walked into the kitchen to get the dog a bowl of water, his phone rang. He grabbed the receiver next to the fridge and answered it. "Yes?"

"I believe you've found your gift by now," Samson said nonchalantly.

"I ain't keeping him. You can tell Yvette. She'll take that fucking dog back tomorrow or I'll dropkick him down her street."

The dog made puppy eyes at him, and Zane rubbed his thumb along his ear. Little Z probably had dirt for brains anyway and didn't understand a single word he said, so why did he get the sense that he'd just hurt the dog's feelings?

"He's part of the package, so treat him nicely, and that's an order."

Zane grunted.

"And a file with details of your next assignment is in his cage. You'll report tomorrow after sunset to relieve Oliver. Good luck."

A click in the line confirmed that Samson had disconnected the call, giving Zane no chance to comment. He slammed the receiver down.

"Asshole!"

The dog yelped. "Not you!" Zane stroked his hand over the dog's head and snout. Instantly, the dog rolled sideways in his arms, exposing his belly. Zane got the hint and rubbed his knuckles along the dog's fur.

A few moments later, he reluctantly set the dog on the floor and retrieved the file from the cage.

As he read through the detailed instructions, rage instantly boiled over.

"You fucking jerks," he cursed. "You want me to babysit?" They couldn't have simply relegated him to a desk job to punish him? No, they had to turn him into Nanny McPhee to a volatile, spoiled, and probably suicidal girl who was seeking attention.

"Oh, I'll show you, assholes!"

The dog tilted his head, giving him another dose of his puppy-eyed look. Zane crouched down to him and shelved his snout on his palm. "You're probably gonna get hungry, aren't you? So unless you like Mrs. Hernandez' home-canned plums, I suppose we have to go shopping for dog food tonight."

His neighbor, Mrs. Hernandez, had cornered him in the backyard a few times and palmed off some jars of plums from her garden on him. Instead of instantly tossing them in the trash, he'd stashed them in one of the many empty kitchen cabinets, not knowing what else to do with them. He wasn't used to people giving him things.

Chapter Six

Portia folded her arms across her chest as she leaned back in the passenger seat of the black limousine her bodyguard Oliver was driving. Bodyguard, her ass! More like a jailor! Did her father really think she was stupid enough to believe that he'd hired this guard to protect her while he was gone on another long business trip? His claim that there was some crazy murderer on the loose who only a few nights ago had killed a young man in the Mission, rang hollow. As a hybrid, she was as strong as any vampire and could easily defend herself against any assailant. Even though she'd never trained in hand-to-hand combat, her instincts told her that she knew what to do if the situation demanded it.

Hell, she could take down the guy they'd assigned her as a bodyguard. She gave him another sideway's glance. His tousled dark hair seemed to point into every possible direction, and any comb Oliver had tried had probably lost the battle against his unruly hair. His eyes were sharp and focused, and his body muscular. It was clear that he was in great shape and capable of fending off any attacker. Not even his fresh face could detract from that fact. If anything, his youthful looks—for he could be no older than twenty-five—most likely fooled any would-be assailant into thinking they'd have an easy target in him. At first, she'd been fooled too, but then she'd spoken to her friend Lauren.

According to Lauren's father, Scanguards bodyguards were the best-trained bodyguards in the nation, and apparently the most lethal. She'd gleaned from Oliver's ID, which he'd presented when he'd picked her up to take her to her classes, that he had a class A clearance. It had meant nothing to her until Lauren had explained that it was Scanguards' highest security ranking, and only the best of their guards, and those who knew about the existence of vampires would receive such honor.

Portia snorted. She could still take that kid and lift him right out of his fancy shoes. After all, Oliver was human. It appeared even Scanguards, which employed not only humans, but also a large number of vampires, didn't have a hybrid on staff to assign to her. And that put her in the stronger position. Whenever she was ready to make her move, she'd leave her human bodyguard in her wake while she went off to find herself a suitable candidate to take her virginity. Bodyguard or not, her father wouldn't win this fight.

"Do you want to get a takeout for dinner?" Oliver asked as he left the campus behind and navigated through rush hour traffic.

Portia wondered whether she should make him drive out of his way to get to some obscure greasy food place, but decided against it. She wasn't mad at the bodyguard but at her father, and she wouldn't let her anger out on an innocent. Oliver was just doing his job. Besides, he had behaved very discreetly all day while she'd had classes. Even though he'd followed her around, he'd blended in and not indicated to anybody that he was there to protect her. No, she corrected herself, watch her. At least, she'd been spared the embarrassment of everybody knowing she had a fucking nanny. Luckily, the others had just assumed he was a new student. At least for that she was grateful to Oliver.

"I'm not hungry. Besides, I can always snack on you later." God, she hadn't wanted to say that, but it was too late to take it back now. Maybe she should simply keep her mouth shut when clearly nothing civil was coming out of it at present.

He tossed her a get-real look before concentrating on traffic again. "Try it and you'll regret it."

Portia frowned. "You're bluffing." Not that she'd even for a moment contemplated making good on her threat. Truth was she'd never bitten anybody in her life. When she needed blood to supplement her human diet, she drank it from the bottles her father ordered from a vampire-owned medical supply company. She didn't particularly like the stuff, but luckily her hybrid body required blood just twice a week to maintain its superior strength. She'd realized during exam stress the year before that if she increased her intake of blood, she had more energy and could pull all-nighters if she needed to. It had come in handy once or twice.

"Just because I look unarmed doesn't mean I am."

"Whatever." Portia looked outside, not particularly in the mood for a chat. It was still January, and the sun was setting fast. In half an hour it would be dark. But even with her eyes closed, she would have known when sunset occurred. It was in her bones. For full-blooded vampires, this instinct was a survival mechanism, but for her as a hybrid it wasn't essential. She was lucky: she could be out in the sunlight whenever she wanted to. However, she preferred the dark. Even as a young child, she'd gotten up in the middle of the night to stare at the stars in the dark night sky.

"Why do you work for them?" She hadn't meant to ask, but her mother had taught her to make polite conversation, mostly to blend in. And she felt bad for having behaved so bitchy with Oliver so far.

Oliver shrugged lightly. "It's a good job. It pays well."

"Aren't you afraid of them? What if one of them bites you?"

Oliver suddenly chuckled. "You think I've never been bitten?"

Portia whirled her head to stare at him. "You just told me I'd regret if I bit you!"

"And that's still the case!"

"But you let others bite you? What's wrong with me then?" Was she some sort of outcast? Granted, she didn't know a lot about how vampire society functioned, but did that make her undesirable?

"Nothing's wrong with you. But I only let a vampire bite me when there's an emergency."

Her heartbeat accelerated by a notch. "What kind of emergency?"

"When one of the guys is wounded so severely that he instantly needs blood, I let him have mine."

"Wounded? Why the hell would they get wounded? They're just working as security guards, probably sitting in some office building all night." How dangerous could that be?

"You'd better not let them hear that. They'll take your head off. They're warriors, all of them. Their jobs are dangerous, and occasionally one of them gets injured. I've been on some missions with them. We were attacked many times. There were casualties."

Portia shook her head. Oliver was probably embellishing to make himself and Scanguards look more important. "You're trying to tell me that vampires are assigned as bodyguards to your human clients and will take a bullet for them?"

Oliver nodded, his expression serious. "We guard all our clients with our lives. And that goes even more so for the vampires. They will fight to the death."

She snorted. "Easily said when they're practically indestructible."

"Believe what you want to believe, but I warn you not to underestimate any of us."

"No need to be rude! I guess protecting a client and being polite at the same time is too much to ask." Not that she could really blame Oliver. He was probably just paying her back for her own rudeness earlier.

Oliver bent toward her, never taking his eyes off the traffic in front of him. "Your father is our client. You, my dear Portia, are what we call a charge. We'll take care of the charge, but we only take orders from the client."

At the mention of her father, Portia expelled an angry huff. Like she wanted to be reminded of him right now! She spun her head to the passenger window, making it clear that she was done talking to him. Well, maybe just one more word. "You're just a human, I could take you anytime I wanted to."

Oliver didn't oblige her with a comeback, so she kept quiet until they reached the little house in Noe Valley her father was renting for them. It was a two story home with a garage underneath and a flat yard out the back. Upstairs were three bedrooms and two bathrooms, and downstairs was a large open-plan living and dining area with an adjacent kitchen with a small laundry room and a half bath. Portia had liked the house the moment she'd set foot in it for the first time, but at the same time she tried not to get too attached to the place. For all she knew, her father would be moving them again in a few months. He always did. And she would have to—hell no! She was going to be twenty-one, and soon her father would have no power over her anymore. Next time he wanted to move somewhere else, she could simply refuse and stay where she wanted to stay.

Portia jumped out of the car as soon as it came to a halt in the driveway. Her sudden epiphany lightened her steps as she sauntered to the entrance door and turned her key in the lock. Now all she needed to do was trick Oliver into thinking she was going to sleep early and then sneak out the back when he wasn't looking.

With Lauren's help, she'd made a date with Michael, the guy who'd thrown the party the other night. She didn't want to give Eric another try. He'd suffered enough, even though she'd made sure to wipe his memory so he didn't actually remember any of it. But she was sure he was still in pain from the injuries her father had inflicted by tossing him against the wall, and was probably scratching his head about how he'd obtained them.

Portia tossed her bag on the floor in the foyer. There would be no studying tonight. She marched into the kitchen and opened the fridge.

Oliver followed her and leaned against the kitchen island. "I thought you said you weren't hungry."

Without turning, she continued perusing the contents of her nearly empty fridge and chuckled, making sure Oliver understood that her next comment wasn't malicious. "I also said I could always snack on you."

A strange tingling at her nape signaled danger, but before she had a chance to turn, she received a reply to her remark, a remark that was merely meant to needle Oliver.

"I don't think that would be wise." The deep voice of a stranger sliced through her body as she spun around to face the intruder.

Before she even laid eyes on him, she knew he was a vampire, and she felt waves of power rolling off him.

When she lifted her eyes, the stranger standing calmly next to Oliver took her breath away. She'd never seen a vampire like him. His head was bald. Not a single hair graced his nicely shaped skull except for the thin eyebrows and the dark lashes that framed his eyes. Brown eyes; not ordinary brown though. There seemed to be a rim of gold around the irises and flecks of the same gold sprinkled all over.

His lips looked hard and unyielding, and there were no laugh lines around his mouth. His nose was long and straight. He was over six feet tall and lean, extremely lean. The stranger was dressed in black jeans and a long-sleeve black shirt, and he made the simple outfit look like a million bucks. The top two buttons of his shirt were open, revealing a glimpse of his chest. Apparently hairless too, just like his head.

Portia allowed her eyes to travel lower to his narrow hips and strong thighs. Her stomach flipped, and her knees suddenly felt weak. Looking at a man had never before made her feel like this, so … so feminine. She suddenly regretted that she hadn't taken better care of herself this morning, not bothering to apply makeup. Why hadn't she at least moistened her lips with lip gloss before she'd left campus?

"You done?" the vampire asked, catapulting her head first into a wave of embarrassment at being caught checking him out. And unlike a full-blooded vampire who couldn't blush, the cheeks of her hybrid body burned, and she knew she was flushing the shade of a bottle of blood.

"Who are you?" she fired back. "And what the hell are you doing in my house?"

The vampire gave Oliver a sideways glance. "I take it she's the brat I'm supposed to guard?"

Portia's heart sank. Figured! The first man she felt the slightest bit of excitement for had to be the enemy. Right now she was ready to throttle her father. "Oh, this sucks," she muttered.

***

Zane forced himself to remain calm when inside he was anything but. Years of practicing his stony expression helped him keep his cool. Samson was messing with him. Why the fuck had he assigned him to guard this … this vixen? How else could he describe her?

Her green-brown almond shaped eyes had traveled over his body while she'd licked her red lips, making them appear even plumper. He'd noticed her heartbeat accelerate and her breaths turn irregular, drawing his attention to her shapely breasts. She wore a bra under her casual tight sweater, something he shouldn't even notice. But he did, just like he noticed her slim waist and those long, toned legs that were hidden in her jeans. She was tall for a woman, but that fact didn't detract from her femininity.

Zane had expected to find a teenager; instead, he was faced with a grown woman. While that in itself shouldn't bother him, his reaction to her did.

He was tempted to step closer to allow her tantalizing scent to wrap around him. He wanted to bury his face in her long black hair while his hands explored her body, peeling her out of her clothes. The thought of what he would do next made his pants feel tighter instantly. The teeth of his zipper dug into his aroused flesh, threatening imminent release. He'd heard of spontaneous orgasms, but he'd never imagined being so close to having one. Shit, he had more control than letting a beautiful face and an enticing scent screw him over like that!

"Zane!" Oliver was trying to get his attention.

He jerked his gaze away from Portia. "Yeah?"

"I'll be back a half hour before sunrise. Will that give you enough time to get home or shall I get you a blackout van?"

It gave him way too much time in the presence of this walking sin called Portia for starters. Zane cleared his throat. "That's plenty of time."

He barely noticed Oliver leaving as his eyes moved back to his charge who still gripped the fridge door as if her life depended on it, her knuckles white as if she were riding a rollercoaster.

"I thought Oliver was my bodyguard."

Zane shrugged, shaking off the feeling her melodic voice conjured up as it sank deep into his chest. "Even a bodyguard has to sleep, and your father doesn't pay us for sleeping." Had she really thought that they would make it easy for her to go against her father's wishes?

"Nothing is going to happen to me while I'm at home. You might as well save yourself the trouble and take off." She slammed the fridge door shut, signaling her contempt for him.

"Nice try, baby girl, but I'm staying." Hell, what had he just called her? Baby girl? Was he losing it? He wasn't one to toss out endearments like beads during Mardi Gras in New Orleans.

Her eyes flared, a red glint appearing in them as she planted her hands on the kitchen island. "My name is Portia. Use it if you must, but call me anything else and I'll have you fired." Then she turned and marched to the door, the clicking of her heels in synch with his rapid heartbeat. "And now I'm going upstairs to be alone."

"Suit yourself," he grumbled under his breath, his eyes glued to that backside she moved as if wanting to enthrall him.

Great, it had taken him under thirty seconds to get her to hate him. That had to be a record, even for him. Unfortunately, while he normally couldn't care less who hated his guts and why, in this instance he had a sliver of regret. This time, his subconscious had done all the work for him, pushing her away with the ridiculous endearment he'd used, making sure she'd never look at him the way she'd done during the first ten seconds of their meeting. There'd been desire in her eyes, and that was the last thing he needed if he wanted to survive this assignment.

It was bad enough that he was alone in the house with her, charged to protect her from herself. Who would protect her from him? The only thing standing between him and running after her now, throwing her onto the nearest flat surface and burying himself in her was his loyalty to Scanguards and the veiled threat Samson had issued. If he screwed this assignment up, he'd be out. Once more, he'd be without a family.

As he stalked into the living room and slunk into the soft couch, he tried to find more reasons why he shouldn't go up to Portia's room and make a play for her. He came up with plenty: the girl was unstable. According to her father, she was on the verge of a nervous breakdown and was acting out. Grief for her mother had made her emotionally unbalanced. No wonder she had first looked at him as if she wanted to devour him, and in the next instant hurled insults at him. Perhaps his endearment had triggered something. For all he knew, her mother had called her baby girl.

There was no way he would get involved with a volatile woman who would probably stake him if she was in one of her moods. He didn't need shit like that. He was here to do a job: watch her and make sure she didn't harm herself. Her father couldn't come home fast enough to suit Zane. The sooner this assignment was over the better. And hopefully once he'd proven to Samson and Gabriel that he could be trusted and wouldn't derail, they'd reinstate his class A status and assign him to a real job.

Zane snatched a magazine from the coffee table and paged through it while his senses remained on full alert. He heard Portia rummage in her closet upstairs. In the bathroom next to her, a faucet dripped. The occasional car drove by the house, and a neighbor walked his dog. That reminded him of the puppy.

He'd left Z at home and set out bowls with water and dog food on the kitchen floor. He couldn't drop off the dog at Yvette's—yet. Samson had made it clear that the puppy was part of the deal, like it or not. For now, he was stuck with the animal, but as soon as this was over, the dog would end up right where he belonged—with Yvette and Haven. No way was Zane gonna keep him.

Chapter Seven

Portia applied the finishing touches to her makeup and glanced at her watch. She didn't have much time left to make it to her date on time. Sneaking down the stairs and past Zane would be a wasted effort since the vampire had installed himself on the couch in such a way that he could see anything happening on the first floor. Her only chance was getting out through the window on the second floor.

While she wasn't one for climbing, she could jump. From the window in her room down to the back yard, the vertical distance was less than fifteen feet. No big deal for a hybrid. Portia pushed the sash window up as far as it went and peered outside into the dark. Beneath it, the grass came up to the wall, allowing for a soundless landing. She wouldn't have to worry about Zane seeing her jump either since her room was over the garage and the laundry: there was no window where she was about to land.

Portia lifted one leg out the window and caught a glimpse of her shoes. Jumping with high heels was definitely not advisable. She swiftly took off her pumps and dropped them into the grass below. They made a soft thumping sound. Portia's heart stopped. Had Zane heard it? She kept herself motionless and stopped breathing, listening for any sound in the house, but it remained quiet.

Relieved, she swung her legs out backwards and twisted her body under the window. She cursed the sash window, because unlike a regular window, it only opened halfway, forcing her to lower herself out of it facing the wall. Her hands still on the window sill, she pushed herself away from the wall and let go. She dropped into the cold and damp grass, her knees going soft to absorb the impact. Portia smiled to herself. In a gymnastics competition she would have received a perfect ten for her landing.

She brushed her hands on her skirt and turned to gather her shoes.

Shock wasn't the only thing that catapulted her against the wall at her back.

"Going out?" Zane asked as his hands captured her shoulders and pressed her against the siding.

With her heart stopping and no oxygen reaching her brain, Portia's ability to respond was severely impacted. Or was it the fact that Zane's body was only inches from hers that turned her speechless? She felt his heat as if tiny flames jumped from his body to hers, igniting her cells like kindling in a fireplace. If she didn't stop this from happening, her entire body would go up in flames. Already now, heat traveled to all her extremities, and even her naked feet felt warm as if she were wearing bunny slippers.

But the heat wasn't the comforting heat she knew from a cashmere sweater or a woolen blanket. The heat she felt now was consuming, engulfing, destroying. Instinct told her to stay away from this fire or get burned, but everything feminine in her rebelled against the thought of pushing him away.

Oh, Zane was mean, she knew that. He'd proven that with the few words they'd exchanged in the kitchen. She also realized that he saw her as a necessary evil to perform his job, and the last thing he saw in her was a woman. To him she was a child; when he'd addressed her as baby girl, he'd made that abundantly clear. But despite the overwhelming evidence to the contrary, the way he looked at her now said otherwise.

His gaze was heated, and she liked to imagine that it was desire rather than fury that blazed in his eyes. Zane's fingernails dug into her flesh, and while she barely felt the pain, she noticed their sharpness, wondering how close his vampire side was to emerging. The cords in his neck bulged, and she saw the pulsing vein that ran along its side.

She could fairly smell his blood, and for the first time she wondered what it would be like to bite somebody, to sink her fangs deep into his flesh and taste him. Furious at herself for the direction her mind was taking, she clenched her jaw, sending a clear signal to her fangs that they were not allowed to descend under any circumstances.

"Look at you, all dolled up." Zane roamed his eyes over her face before his lids dropped as he perused her low-cut top. Her cleavage was clearly visible, and from his vantage point he could most likely see all the way down to her navel.

"Enjoying the peep show?" she hissed, suppressing the shudder that went through her at the thrill of Zane admiring her boobs.

One side of his mouth tilted up, but he wasn't going for a smile. She doubted he knew what a smile was. "You've got nothing I haven't seen already."

If he wanted to deliberately hurt her, he'd succeeded. "Jerk!"

"Unlike you, I don't care what people call me." He made a deliberate pause. "Baby girl."

Her fists clenched, and before she could even finish her thought, she'd raised them and aimed at his face. Zane was faster. Her fists landed in his palms, which he instantly wrapped around them, preventing her from doing any damage to his arrogant visage.

"Violent, too?" He shook his head and tsked. "They left that out of your file."

File? They had a file on her? "What are you saying?"

"I'm saying that I know what you're all about, so don't think you can get anything past me or—" The ring of a cell phone interrupted his little speech. He released one of her hands and dug into his pocket. "Another attempt at hitting me and I'll have you hogtied in ten seconds flat."

She didn't doubt his words for even a fraction of a second.

"Yes?" His tone was more bellow that greeting.

"Hey, Zane, what's going on?" Portia heard the male voice on the other end clearly.

"Quinn, good to hear from you." Despite his words, Zane didn't crack even the beginning of a smile. That confirmed it: he was incapable of smiling.

"Listen, I need a vacation. Do you mind if I come to visit?"

"No problem. When are you flying in?"

"I was thinking tomorrow night."

"Who's picking you up from the airport?"

"I'll ask Oliver."

"I'll give him a key to the house for you. See you."

"Hey, man, are you all right?"

"Never been better." Zane disconnected the call and shoved the cell back into his pants.

If it was true that he was feeling better than ever, then Portia wondered what he was like when he was in a pissy mood. She wasn't gonna stick around to find out.

"Now," he said slowly and focused his gaze back onto her. "Where were you heading?"

"None of your fucking business." She twisted her hand from his grip and pivoted, trying to get away from him.

***

Zane wasn't ready to let go of her and snatched her arms, preventing her from brushing past him. Not that he minded a little brushing here and there. He enjoyed the contact with her body far too much, despite the fact that she held herself rigid.

If it wasn't for the old sash window he'd heard grinding against its wooden frame when Portia had opened it, she would have escaped him. Luckily, he had been prepared for her to pull a fast one on him and had refrained from making any noise downstairs so he could hear what she was doing. When he'd heard the doors of her closet close, he'd figured that she was getting changed. It could only mean one thing.

And he'd been right. The flimsy top she wore screamed 'fuck me' as if she'd had it tattooed on her forehead. Her short skirt wasn't any better. It hid nothing of her amazing figure and her lush curves. Considering her age and her height, she should be skinny as a rail, but instead, her hips were nicely cushioned, and her breasts …

Zane tore his gaze away and swallowed. It wasn't good to go down that road. Only a fool would allow himself to be swayed by her enticing package, and he was no fool. She was a job just like any other, and he'd be damned if he'd do anything that could jeopardize his decidedly shaky position at Scanguards. If Samson and Gabriel thought they could throw a wrench into the works by dangling this temptation in front of him to test him, then he'd do his damnedest to pass that test, even if it meant passing up some hot piece of ass.

"Fine. I don't care what your plans were, because guess what, they've changed." He released her arms, his palms burning from the touch, the need to press her against him too savage to acknowledge. "Back inside."

When she turned to round the side of the building, he grabbed her top and pulled her back.

Portia whirled around, her hair flying, her face furious. The sight nearly undid him, undermining his resolve to treat her with indifference. "I was going inside," she bit out.

Zane shook his head once before motioning to the window above him. Her eyes followed his look. When her jaw dropped, he knew she'd caught onto his thinking.

"You've got to be kidding me!" she protested.

"Do you see me laughing?" He doubted that he even remembered how to laugh or smile. It had been so darn long since he'd made his facial muscles perform that particular action.

"And how am I supposed to get up there?" She gestured to the window.

"You managed to get down on your own. I'm sure you can figure out a way to get back up there."

He crossed his arms over his chest and leaned against the wall, waiting and indeed curious to see what she'd come up with. In particular, he wanted to see how she managed to get up that wall and through the window without him getting an eyeful of her hot legs and whatever else she had hidden under that short skirt of hers.

While he couldn't touch, nobody could slap him on the wrist for looking. And he was gonna do some looking, a whole bunch of it. Not that it would aid in tamping down the beast inside him that demanded its due.

Portia stepped further back into the garden and looked up at the window. Her forehead furrowed as she assessed the situation. He could almost see the little wheels in her mind turn as she narrowed her eyes. She briefly glanced at him and lifted her chin in a clear show of defiance. Suited him fine. He wasn't here to make friends with her.

When she suddenly took off toward the back of the garden, he was taken by surprise. It took him half a second to recover and launch into a sprint to follow her. She was about to vault herself over the garden fence when he reached her and pulled her down. Without ceremony, Zane slung her over his right shoulder, her head dangling over his back, his hands imprisoning her legs.

"Let me go!" she yelled and pounded her fists into his lower back.

He didn't care. She was touching him, and at present it was all he could think of. The faster he got her into the house, the more of a chance he had to keep his hands off her, because even the rough treatment she doled out right now was turning him on. Add to that the way he was carrying her, her shapely rump level with his face as if he needed an invitation more obvious, and he'd already lost. He kept her bare legs restrained by his arms, but couldn't prevent his thumb from straying and swiping over her soft skin in a hushed caress.

Frustration howled through him, and it had nothing to do with his charge's failed attempt at escape and everything to do with the thrill he'd felt at the short chase. As if he were hunting prey.

He deliberately turned his head away from Portia's sweet backside when he lengthened his stride and moved toward the house, but not even that prevented her female scent from infiltrating his sensitive nostrils and clinging to the tiny hairs inside his nose. The ten second sprint was pure torture.

And he was a sucker for torture.

Zane kicked the front door shut with his boot and plopped Portia onto the couch. But if she thought he'd let her off this easily, she was sorely mistaken. Before she could make a move, he was on her, pinning her down with his body hovering over her, daring her to make another attempt at escaping.

It wasn't fear that lashed at him from her fiery eyes but annoyance. He ignored it and lowered his head so only an inch of air separated them. One inch away from a kiss if he were so inclined.

"Maybe I forgot to mention something very important," he started. "Let me make it clear to you now: don't underestimate me. What I say goes."

Her breath hit him as she parted her lips, and he drew in the scent. All it served was to make him even harder. If she could feel him, she gave no hint, riling him up even more.

"I'll have you fired," she spat, her breasts rising and brushing against his chest.

Zane suppressed the urge to groan at the contact. "I'd say join the club, but I'm afraid the membership roster is overly full."

"I hate you!"

He narrowed the gap between them, then slowly turned his mouth to her ear, their cheeks almost touching. He took in a long, deep breath, unable to get enough of her scent. But it wasn't all he enjoyed: her breasts now connected fully with his chest, her nipples pressing against him. "It seems you keep choosing the wrong clubs to join. Alas this one has a long waiting list as well. You see, I really don't care who hates me."

"Don't you?" she challenged.

Zane raised his head to look at her. Her long, curved lashes fluttered for a brief moment before sweeping upwards as her eyes opened fully, her gaze suddenly pinning him with more intensity than before.

Did Portia suspect that he didn't want her to hate him, that the emotion he most wished from her was as far away from hate as humanly possible, yet at the same time was only separated from it by a sliver as thin as the thread of control he had left?

"Hate is the only reliable emotion left." Love couldn't survive the challenges in this world.

"Hate is the most destructive and useless of all feelings."

Zane cocked an eyebrow. "That's because you've never experienced true hate. You have no idea of its power."

It was a power that drove him, that contributed to his survival. Without it, he wouldn't have survived the first few weeks as a vampire. Only hate had kept him alive then. It had become a trusted companion, one he could rely upon not to desert him.

"There's a greater power than hate."

"If you're getting religious on me, you might as well—"

"I'm talking about love," Portia interrupted him.

Instinctively, he pulled back and noticed the responding satisfactory glint in her eyes.

Her lips quirked. "So that's what you're afraid of. Love."

Her words catapulted him upright in a millisecond. Zane rose as fast as if she was pointing a stake at his chest. In one fluid movement he turned his back to her. "I think you should go to your room now. It's past your bedtime." *And safer for you*, he wanted to add.

He heard the sound of the couch cushions as she shifted and stood. "Well, I guess I hit that one out of the park." Portia marched past him, and from what he could tell, she deliberately brushed her body against his side, the brief touch searing him like a branding iron marred the flesh of a calf.

"You think your Psych 101 makes you an expert in analyzing people?"

"I'm a Psych major, so, yes, I do."

Pride dictated that he not let her win this argument. "You know nothing about me, and you never will."

She didn't turn as she set her foot on the first stair. Her words were low as she murmured as if talking to herself, but he heard them all the same. "Watch your back, tough guy."

Watch yours, or you'll find yourself on it soon, he wanted to respond but didn't.

Chapter Eight

The door snapped in behind Zane as he entered his foyer, the rising sun on his heels. He'd preyed on an unsuspecting pedestrian on his way home, feeling so agitated by his argument with Portia that he had taken longer than normal to feed. And even after the two full pints of blood he'd taken, his body felt unsatisfied. He knew only too well what he needed to gain the satisfaction his body demanded, but that knowledge didn't bring him any closer to obtaining what he so desperately sought: a taste of Portia, not simply a kiss or a quick fuck, but more, a taste of her blood, her arousal, her heart.

Her words and the look on her face when she'd spoken them had whirled his insides up like a tornado ripping through a Midwestern town, leaving only destruction and devastation behind. Suddenly, he hadn't been the one in charge. She'd taken over the reins and whipped him by exposing his greatest fear.

To love again.

He'd loved his parents and his sister. He'd loved the words he'd used to craft beautiful masterpieces. He'd loved the sound of birds singing in the back yard.

He'd loved life.

Then they had robbed him of everything: his parents, his sister, and his passion. And finally, his life.

They'd taken everything away from him because of who he was and replaced it with nothing but a heart full of hatred and a drive for revenge. To love again would only serve as a painful reminder of his loss. The fraction of his soul that was still intact would shatter from the impact of another loss, one that surely would occur if he allowed his heart to soften.

He'd made a promise long ago that justice would be done. Only if he remained stalwart could he achieve his goal and make good on his promise. Love had no place in his life.

Zane shrugged off his leather coat and tossed it over the chair in the hallway. His next step landed him in something soft. The accompanying smell he only now registered because he'd been too preoccupied when he'd entered his house, confirmed that he had a mess on his hands.

"Z!" he yelled. "Where the fuck are you?"

He knew it had been a bad move to leave the dog alone at home. He should have locked him outside in the yard. Flipping the light switch, Zane lifted his boot and inspected the damage. Great! The grooves of his soles were caked with dog shit.

"I'm going to kill you, Z!"

The dog clearly knew his lesson on self-preservation because he didn't show his snout anywhere. Not that it would save him from punishment. Hiding would only delay the inevitable.

Fuming, Zane charged into the kitchen and yanked a towel from the rack. As he cleaned up the dog's mess, he cursed Yvette once more. She could have at least housetrained the pup before palming him off on an unsuspecting new owner. Owner? Not if he could help it. Tonight the dog would be history.

He tossed the dirty towel on the floor to be disposed of later. His boots landed in the kitchen sink before he stalked barefoot into the living room. It was empty. Well, almost: there was an oversized leather couch facing a monstrous high-definition TV. Apart from those two items, the living room was bare; no rug, no coffee table, no paintings on the white walls. He'd still not gotten around to decorating the place beyond the bare necessities, despite the fact that he'd bought the house over five months ago.

"Zee-eee, daddy's home," he cooed, but the damn animal didn't respond.

Zane inhaled and, ignoring the stench from the dog's shit, he concentrated on the underlying scent of the dog's fur. He lifted his head. "Gotcha."

Making no sound, he walked up the stairs to the second floor and headed for his bedroom. The upstairs floor had originally had three bedrooms, and he'd chosen the largest one, which faced the garden and was leading out to a small deck, as his master bedroom. He'd converted the second bedroom into a large bathroom and dressing room, leaving the second bathroom on this floor as a guest bath. Considering he never had guests, it was an unnecessary luxury. He halted for a moment, remembering that Quinn was due to arrive the next day. He wasn't sure yet whether to look forward to his visit or dread it. Right now, he had too much stuff on his mind to make a decision about that.

When he entered his bedroom through the open door, he heard the dog's shallow breaths. He closed the door behind him, making sure the little pup had no chance to escape. Not seeing the animal in the room, it wasn't hard to figure out where he was hiding. After all, there was only one item of furniture suitable as a hiding place.

Zane switched on the light, allowing the forty watt bulb hidden underneath a hideous looking shade he'd inherited from the previous owner to illuminate the room. It reminded him once more that he desperately needed to put his own touch on the rest of the place just as he'd done with the bathroom. But first things first.

He dropped to the floor and peered under the bed. As expected, Z was crouching underneath it, right in the middle of the king-sized piece of furniture, safe for now. His round eyes were wide as they stared at him. Did that dog know what he'd done, or was he simply reacting to Zane's fury? Zane took a breather. Hell, he didn't know the first thing about dogs. He should be the last person to own one.

"Come on, little Z, be a good dog and come out." Zane felt like a fool as he coaxed the stupid animal with a voice only reserved for babies and, well, dogs. If anybody saw him like this, he'd have to silence that person forever.

Z set one paw in front of the other, and, tilting his head, he crawled forward a few inches. Zane reached his hand underneath the bed, but the dog shrunk back from him. He clenched his jaw. Stupid animal!

"Come now, Z, you must be hungry," he tempted the pup, dropping his voice to a sweet cooing sound.

The animal took another few tentative movements toward him. Zane dropped his hand on the floor, laying it flat, palm up. "Come to daddy." Ah, shit, he was turning into a complete idiot.

A moment later, Z licked over his palm and came within striking distance. Zane acted, snatching the dog around his neck and pulling him from his hiding place as Z made a futile attempt to dig his hindquarters into the wooden floor, making a scratching sound with his claws.

"Gotcha!"

Zane rose with the pup in his arms. When the animal curled into him and made puppy eyes at him, all steam went out of Zane. He couldn't punish the animal. Yet, somebody needed a talking to.

Holding onto Z, he dug into his pants pocket and pulled out his cell, pressing the speed dial button with his thumb. When the call connected a few moments later, he pressed the phone to his ear.

"The fucking dog isn't housebroken!"

Haven's calm voice responded, "Ah, Zane, figured you'd call sooner or later."

"I wanna talk to your wife!"

Haven's voice turned quieter. "Baby, Zane's a tad pissed off. Do you wanna talk to him or shall I handle him for you?"

"I'M NOT PISSED OFF!" He was livid.

Z gave a frightened whine. Instinctively, Zane stroked his thumb over the animal's neck, calming it.

"Morning, Zane."

Hearing Yvette's voice, he repeated his accusation. "The dog isn't housebroken!"

"Of course he's housebroken."

"Then why is he shitting all over the house?"

"What do you expect him to do?" Yvette protested. "Open the door and let himself out when he needs to go?"

Zane opened his mouth and shut it again instantly. Shit, he hadn't thought of that. "Oh."

"So, either you lock him out in the garden when you're gone, or you'll have to build in a doggie door."

"I'm not keeping him!" At the words, Zane dropped his gaze to the dog who contently rubbed his snout against his shirt.

"He's perfect for you. Besides, you can't just return a gift. It's not polite."

"You call that a gift? And since when do I care about being polite?"

"He'll grow on you," she assured him.

"He'll piss on me, that's what's gonna happen." But he couldn't refute Yvette's claim entirely. The little creature had its undeniable charm. That alone was annoying as hell. He wouldn't be felled by an animal he could easily squash with one hand if he chose to do so.

"Not if you get that doggie door. Listen, I'll call the guy who built mine in. He does a great job and he's fast. I'll send him right over. See ya!"

"Hell, no—" But Yvette had already disconnected the call, not giving him a chance to protest any further.

"Guess I'm stuck with you," he said to the dog and rubbed his neck.

Z turned his head and licked over Zane's arm as if wanting to thank him. Clearly the dog didn't know yet that Zane wasn't exactly the most jovial of masters—or he had an extremely forgiving nature. He would soon wish he was back with Yvette in her cozy cottage, surrounded by all that love. In the meantime, before the dog deserted him, Zane shrugged off the odd sense that a wave of change was sweeping into his life. The jury was still out regarding who would ultimately benefit from this change.

When the doorbell rang twenty minutes later, he had to hand it to Yvette. At least she kept to her word, and she'd clearly not praised the worker too much: he was fast.

Zane pressed one of the many buzzers he'd installed throughout the house so he could open the front door during the day without leaving the security of his darkened rooms. He listened for the door to open while he refilled the dog's water bowl from the kitchen faucet.

His dirty boots were still stinking up the place. That and the excited yapping of the dog at his feet distracted him from his visitor until it was too late.

"Zacharias Eisenberg."

Zane whirled around. It took him a millisecond to recognize several things: the intruder was a hybrid vampire of average height and build, he wasn't here to install a doggie-door, and he knew of Zane's past. Addressing him by his real name confirmed that, which also made one thing clear: the intruder was here to kill him.

The water bowl dropped from his hands, its contents spilling on the tile floor as Zane lunged for his would-be assassin. His claws extended and his fangs descended from their sockets, ready for the kill.

An iron fist blocked him and jerked him to the side as his shoulder took the impact of the strike. Instantly, Zane refocused, ignoring the temporary pain, and swiped his claws against his opponent's chest, but only sliced through the outer layers of clothing and skin.

Z yapped and snarled from the sidelines.

The hybrid's face barely registered the pain. Instead, he kicked his legs high against Zane's thighs and hips, slamming him back against the sink. Zane pushed off the counter, using the momentum to barrel his full weight against the fractionally lighter assassin. They crashed against the glass hutch, breaking every pane of it.

His jaw clenching in concert with the tension in his body, Zane pounded his claws into the man, but he got as good as he gave. The attacker's claws were sharp and relentless, and only now Zane noticed that the intruder's hands were covered in cutoff gloves, protecting his palms while allowing his claws to emerge.

"Shit!" Zane cursed.

A nasty grin flashed on the hybrid's face and disappeared just as quickly as he continued to use his claws against Zane. Despite his average size, he matched Zane in strength and ferocity, dealing blow after blow without showing any outward signs of exhaustion.

Zane drew his arm back to prepare for a strike when a kick into his kneecap temporarily halted his movements while he tried to absorb the pain. In the next instant, he felt a searing sensation on the front of his neck, followed by the smell of burnt flesh and body hair rising into his nose. Silver! Zane recoiled from the pain and toppled backwards. The action sent him careening to the floor.

His attacker landed on him. With his glove-clad hands, he pressed a silver chain against Zane's neck. Zane fought for air, his hands instinctively coming up to his neck, trying to pry the silver away from his skin.

"Finally got you," the assassin bit out.

Zane recognized an accent, most likely South American in origin, even as he fought against the silver's effect. As it was the only metal that could injure or kill a vampire, he feared silver as much as the next vampire, but even though the pain was excruciating and incapacitating, Zane knew he couldn't give up. He wasn't ready to die.

His fingers singed when he touched the chain, but he continued nevertheless, ignoring the taunting grin on the stranger's face. "Murderer! You'll pay today!"

Not if he could help it. Zane kicked his legs against the asshole that held him down, but with his energy quickly draining from his body as the effect of the silver intensified, his kicks had no more effect than the frantic yapping of his dog.

His eyes darted toward the animal, but there was no help to be expected from it. Maybe if he'd had a fully grown dog who was trained to fight, but Z was more likely to lick the guy to death than bite him.

"Wait until Müller finds out I found you. Now I'll get my reward," the assassin announced and lifted his torso, reaching into his jacket with one hand as he pressed the silver chain against Zane's neck with the other.

Zane wasn't surprised that the intruder had been sent by Müller. Sooner or later, it had to be expected. But he couldn't allow the bastard to win.

Zane removed his hands from the burning metal, unable to stand the pain any longer and reached above his head for anything he could use as a weapon. His fingers encountered a cold, wet cloth, and he gripped it. Just as the attacker's hand emerged with a stake, Zane flung the cloth into his face: it was the same he'd used to clean up the dog's shit.

As the poop-covered towel hit the hybrid's face, the hand on the chain loosened for a short moment. It was enough for Zane to jerk it from his neck, freeing himself.

The assassin yanked the towel from his face, just as Zane swiped his claws across it, ripping open his left cheek. The half-vampire howled, and Zane tossed him off, slamming him against the stove.

Zane scrambled to his feet and jumped, kicking both his feet into the stranger's chest. As several ribs cracked, his opponent picked himself up and, murderous intent in his eyes and dog shit on his cheeks, blindly barreled toward Zane.

Zane snarled and sidestepped him. Now he had the upper hand: his enemy was pissed, and it made him an emotional fighter who didn't think.

"Your time to die," Zane whispered behind the intruder's back and jumped onto him, locking his head in a vice grip. The stake still in his right hand, the attacker tried to twist, but Zane tightened his grip like a noose at the same time that he kicked into the back of his knees, making him collapse.

"Fucking bastard!" the guy pressed out, his hands flailing.

Zane's eyes swept over the kitchen to find where the silver chain had landed. Keeping his opponent's head lodged in his arm hold, Zane pushed him ahead of him. He snatched a towel from the counter and wrapped it around his damaged palm, covering as much of the surface as possible. Then he forced his prisoner to his knees and picked up the chain with his towel-covered hand.

As he kicked the assassin facedown, Zane released his arm hold and wrapped the chain around his neck, twisting it into a knot at the nape. "See, that's how it's done right."

The hybrid screamed in agony as his flesh burned. His attempts to remove the chain were futile. Zane now used both his hands with the towel as a barrier against the silver to hold the chain tightly around his neck. The stake dropped from the assassin's hand.

"See, you made a mistake. You started your obligatory villain speech before you had me subdued. Big mistake," Zane announced. He wrenched him up and dragged him toward the oven. Before the asshole had any time to react, Zane attached the chain to the stove top, hooking it around one of the iron burners.

As he stepped back and retrieved the stake his prisoner had dropped, he briefly glanced at Z who watched him with interest but had finally stopped barking.

Zane looked down at the hybrid, perusing him. While he was sure he didn't know him, there was something about him that was familiar— and it wasn't the dog shit that still clung to his face. The odd crook in his nose and the blue of his eyes reminded him of someone.

"Who are you?" he demanded.

The man spat, but his defiance was instantly punished by the chain around his neck that made his flesh sizzle even more with each unnecessary movement.

Zane went for the intruder's pockets in search for an ID, but neither his jacket pocket nor his pants pocket held any wallet or identification.

"Talk and I'll loosen the chain." Not. His own neck still burned, and the damaged skin and flesh would need an entire day of sleep to regenerate. His hand tightened around the stake as he took another step toward the assailant.

"Now, before I grow impatient," he commanded and bit back the pain. He needed blood, but a look toward the closed blinds over the sink told him that the sun had long since risen, and he couldn't venture outside.

His victim's blood assaulted his nostrils. He inhaled deeply, picking up the distinct undertone of human blood in the hybrid. A thought intruded. Since the assassin's blood was a mix between human and vampire, it would nourish and strengthen Zane just like pure human blood would.

His gaze zeroed in on the guy's wrist. "Not talking? Guess you'll only be good for dinner then."

Zane snatched the hybrid's wrist and pulled it to his mouth. His fangs dug into the flesh and quickly pulled on the vein as the stranger struggled and hit him with his other arm, kicking his legs to boot. But Zane held him off. With every ounce of blood that replenished his body, he felt his strength return. As soon as he had enough to heal, he released the guy with disgust.

His eyes were shut, his face contorted in pain. But the sight conjured up no feelings of pity in Zane. This man had come to kill him. "Who are you?"

His eyes flew open, their intense blue colliding with Zane's dark gaze. "I'm Volker Brandt's son."

Shit! He'd killed Brandt the year before down in Brazil and thought he had closed this chapter. "Then you'll die like your father. You're poison, you're evil just like him. Nothing coming from any of them can be good. Their seed produces only evil."

Brandt's son tried to thrust his head forward, but the chain made mincemeat out of his efforts to underscore his defiance physically. "I'm not alone. You kill me, the others come after you. They find you, just like I found you."

Zane shrugged off the guy's false bravado. "Only a few minutes ago you said Müller would be happy to hear that you found me. Guess that means he has no idea where I am."

"He knows," he spat.

"If he knew, he'd be here himself and finish me off."

The hybrid squeezed his eyes shut to avoid Zane's stare, but Zane interpreted the action as confirmation of his guess. Big fucking deal!

Defiance shot from Brandt's eyes when he reopened them. "He'll find you."

"Not if I find him first. Which hole is he hiding in?"

"I don't know."

Zane punched his face, whipping it sideways, skin sizzling in response. "Where is he?"

"Nobody's seen him."

"You're lying. Where is Franz Müller?"

"If I knew, do you think I would have come alone?"

Zane digested the words. Either the asshole really didn't know, or he was too loyal to tell. Either way, it made no difference. He'd find Müller himself. One day. "Then you're no use to me."

With one powerful thrust of his right arm, he slammed the stake into Brandt's heart.

"No use at all," he whispered as the hybrid dissolved into dust.

The silver chain fell slack, and several metal items dropped clinking to the floor: a small key, a few loose coins, and a pin. Zane bent to pick up the items. He stared at the symbol embossed on the pin.

He'd never seen anything like it, but he'd bet his last clean shirt that it would somehow lead him to Müller. The dead hybrid was Volker Brandt's son, and the older Brandt had been Müller's right hand. They had to have been in contact somehow. And he wouldn't leave any stone unturned until he figured out where Müller was hiding.

Chapter Nine

Portia looked back in the mirror and examined her face. Was it obvious that she'd put on a little more makeup than usual? Hell, who was she kidding? She rarely ever wore more than the occasional eyeliner, and today she sported not only that, but also mascara, lip gloss, some rouge, and a little eye shadow. Another critical look in the bathroom mirror confirmed it. She had lost all her good senses and painted her face for the one person who would ignore her anyway: Zane.

Portia tossed the washcloth in the sink, annoyed at herself. There was no reason why she should be attracted to this jerk whose only mission was to keep her away from her male fellow students or any other men who could become a danger to her virginity. And who was keeping her away from Zane? Was this her father's ultimate punishment, to dangle the hottest stuff since the invention of the Chippendales in front of her when she knew Zane saw her as only a pesky annoyance?

Well, she'd show him that he could shove his indifference up his ass and prove to everybody that there was somebody out there who'd be more than happy to liberate her from her virginity.

Portia heard the front door open and Oliver exchange a few words with Zane. At the sound of his voice, her knees wobbled, and butterflies fluttered in her stomach. She braced herself on the sink for support. This was not good. If she couldn't bring her body's reactions under control, she couldn't face him.

His vampire hearing would pick up on her rapid heartbeat as well as on the fact that she was emitting pheromones. She'd learned enough in biology to realize that much, and her own acute senses told her that her body was doing exactly that. This wouldn't work. Portia grabbed her cell phone and typed a text message to Lauren: *wr lots of Chanel & bring it w/ u. C u in 15.*

With a deep breath, she opened the bathroom door and went downstairs. As she'd expected, Zane had installed himself on the couch at an angle that allowed him to see both the stairs and the front door.

She didn't miss the instant flaring of Zane's nostrils the moment she reached the foot of the stairs. The accompanying spark in his eyes could have been an optical illusion, had he not instantly clenched his hands into fists as if trying to fight something or someone off. There was no doubt in her mind that he could smell her arousal. A thought shot through her mind. Maybe that was actually a good thing and would make her plan for tonight easier to execute than she'd thought.

"Evening, Zane," she said politely and approached the couch. Oh, yeah, it was best if he got a really good whiff of her tonight.

His eyes narrowed in suspicion even as he answered her greeting. "Portia." Then he swept a long look over her before his eyes lingered on her face. "Up to something tonight?"

The mocking tone in his voice almost made her lash out at him, but she reigned herself in. "I'm wearing jeans and a t-shirt, hardly an outfit for going out."

He didn't buy it. "What's with the makeup?"

"What are you suddenly, my father? I can wear makeup whenever I please."

Zane jumped up, and a second later stood only a foot from her. "You wouldn't be wearing that makeup for me, would you?"

Anger churned inside her, but she used all her restraint not to let this arrogant jerk see it. It wouldn't serve her, not tonight. "Please! You're my bodyguard, nothing more." Her heart beat high into her throat, making it difficult to keep her voice even and indifferent. "I wear makeup all the time."

Zane moved closer, his sinful body now only inches from touching hers. "Is that so?" His eyes lowered to her lips, and she instinctively licked them.

The rumble coming from Zane's chest could only be a suppressed groan. Maybe he was feeling not quite as indifferent toward her as he pretended.

Portia closed her eyes for a second, allowing her other senses to guide her. The first thing she noticed was his masculine scent. It was stronger now than when she'd first entered the living room. As she took it deep into her lungs, she couldn't stop her body from reacting to it. A shiver slithered down her back.

Heat suddenly seared her body, making her open her eyes to find the source. Zane stood flush against her. Had he crossed the remaining inches of space between them or had she? She wanted to pull back and sever the contact when he pressed his palm into her lower back and yanked her against him. In an instant, all her previous thoughts fled to be replaced by a single realization: Zane was turned on by her. The hard outline of his erection pressing against her soft flesh left no doubt about it.

His heartbeat echoed hers, and his eyes glowed now. There were only two instances when a vampire's eyes glowed: when in fighting mode, or when aroused.

With each breath she took, her breasts brushed against his chest. Her nipples tightened in response. The clenching of his jaw was sign enough that he noticed her body's responses to him. Responses which, in truth, she was unaccustomed to. Not even when kissing a guy had she ever felt so turned on, so boneless as she felt now. And Zane hadn't even made any attempt to kiss her. Instead, his hand on her lower back moved slowly, his thumb drawing lazy circles on her waist before dropping further down and repeating the same motion on her backside.

She should push him away and not allow him such liberties when she knew he couldn't stand her, but her body simply melted into him and didn't obey. The sensation was so new and exciting, she couldn't bring herself to stop what they were doing. Not that Zane was really doing anything. He only stood there, his body a pillar of stone, hard and unyielding, with only his hand and his fingers moving, caressing her ever so softly. Everything else remained motionless, except maybe his erection, which seemed to grow.

Portia shifted, aligning her core with his hard length, and felt a whimper escape her lips.

"Fuck!" he ground out.

Panicked, she lifted her lids and crashed into his heated gaze. His head moved closer. Her pulse stuttered: Zane was going to kiss her.

When his lips brushed lightly against hers, her lips parted on a sigh and her eyes fell shut.

Ding Dong! Ding Dong!

***

"Fuck!" Zane cursed and pushed himself away from Portia, turning in the same instant so she wouldn't be able to see how she affected him. As if that would make it any better. He'd pressed his swollen cock against her so hard and for so long, there was no doubt in his mind that she knew exactly what she was doing to him.

"The door," she said, her voice no more agitated than as though she were ordering pizza, and not being interrupted at the most inconvenient of moments.

Maybe he should be grateful to whoever had rung the doorbell for saving him from the biggest mistake of his career, if not his life: kissing a woman he was charged to protect. And for all he knew, the kiss would have led to much more. Within minutes, he would have had her flat on her back on the couch with his cock pounding into her and his lips devouring every inch of her skin.

"I'll get the door." Portia's voice penetrated his haze.

He swiveled. "I'll get it." After all, he was her bodyguard and had to make sure no harm came to her. Yeah, that was working out really well.

He stalked to the door and spied through the hole.

"I'm expecting my friend Lauren," Portia said from behind him.

Zane opened the door and scrutinized the young woman who wore sunglasses even though it was night. She was about Portia's age and from what he'd read in Portia's file, she was the mayor's daughter and a hybrid. He sniffed. Her scent was masked by perfume so strong, it was almost imperceptible. Only her aura identified her as a hybrid.

"Hey, Lauren, come in."

The girl pushed past him. She opened her grey Parka and lowered her hoodie, revealing the same long hair as Portia. Her high heels echoed on the wooden floor as she hugged her friend as if the two hadn't seen each other in weeks.

"Let's do some work," Lauren said.

"We'll be upstairs. No interruptions please. We're studying for a test," Portia requested with barely a look at him. The little bitch had seduced him, and now she was giving him the cold shoulder.

Zane seethed as he slammed the front door shut and walked back to the sofa.

"What was that all about?" Lauren whispered.

Despite the fact that she'd reached the top of the stairs, Zane could still hear her, as he could Portia's response. "Don't mind him. He's just a bodyguard."

Zane's fangs lengthened. Just a bodyguard? Oh, he'd show her what he thought of that statement, right when Lauren was gone. If Portia thought she could get away with dressing him down like that after she'd come onto him, she'd have it coming. How dare she press her body against him like that, the scent of her arousal wrapping around her as though she were in heat, and minutes later toss him aside as if he were chopped liver?

He growled low and dark. Oh, he'd give her a piece of his mind.

For the next two hours, he alternated between watching TV on mute, pacing the length of the living room, and staring holes into the wall, all the while trying not to listen in on the conversation between Portia and Lauren. Not that there was much to overhear: they rarely talked, and when they did, they did so quietly. The fragments he picked up centered around a psychology test that presumably was scheduled for the next morning. All in all, the wait got on his nerves, and the time stretched longer than he thought was bearable.

Zane rubbed his neck, noticing the flawless skin that had grown over his injuries. He would do better asking Samson for a few nights off so he could investigate Brandt's son and find out where he'd been before he'd arrived at his house. With a bit of luck, it would lead him straight to Müller. He was clearly wasting his time here.

When he suddenly heard a door open on the upstairs floor, he sat up straight.

"Thanks so much for helping me out!" Portia drawled.

"Anytime. What are friends for?" came Lauren's predictable reply.

Blah, blah, get out! Zane cursed inside.

"Can we go through the questions once more right before class?" Portia asked.

"Sure. Shall we say a half hour before? We'll meet at the cafeteria?"

"Perfect."

Footsteps sounded on the stairs. Zane quickly slunk back into the sofa cushions and grabbed a news magazine from the coffee table, pretending to read.

Lauren's god-awful perfume spread in the living room as she came down the stairs. From the corner of his eyes, he noticed that she'd already pulled the hoodie of her grey Parka up as she wandered to the door. He gave a quick nod acknowledging her presence, but didn't look at her. That was all he needed: Lauren telling Portia that he gave a shit.

When the door closed behind her, he tossed the unread magazine back on the coffee table and impatiently tapped his foot, trying to stop himself from jumping up immediately to storm into Portia's room. At least he could keep up the pretense of control and not make it obvious that his need to take her to task about her earlier seduction was outweighing his common sense and his restraint.

He managed about ten minutes of holding himself back, before he shot up from the couch. "Fuck it!"

Lauren's perfume still hung heavy in the house as he reached the upstairs landing and became even more intense as he neared Portia's room. How Portia would be able to sleep at all tonight with that stink filling her room was beyond his comprehension. He for one was positively choking on the stuff.

Zane halted in front of the closed door, hesitating for an instant. Should he knock? The thought instantly pissed him off. Of course he wouldn't knock. This wasn't a social call where he begged to be admitted. He was here to dole out punishment for her earlier behavior. There would be no friendly knock to announce his arrival. Maybe she had already sensed him approach, even though, as always, his footsteps had been soundless, and with the fucking perfume stinking up the house, she would have a hard time smelling him, as he would her.

His heart suddenly rocked to a halt. He couldn't smell her. He yanked at the knob and swung the door open, charging into the room, already knowing what he would find.

"That little bitch!" She'd outsmarted him.

On Portia's bed, Lauren lay stretched out, lazily flicking through the channels on the TV. When she saw him, the remote fell from her hand, and she sat up in a start.

"Ah, shit!" Lauren had the good grace to look somewhat guilty at being caught at the deception the two had concocted.

"Your fucking perfume!" he growled. The two women had purposefully screwed with his sense of smell so he wouldn't notice Portia sneaking past him. The thick grey Parka with the hood and the wide, dark sunglasses had topped off the disguise. "I should have known it was a trick!"

"Shoulda," Lauren replied with a shrug.

Zane snarled, not bothering to hide his fangs. "Where is she?"

"I don't know."

Zane recognized a lie when he heard one. He was in no mood to play a little cat and mouse game with a juvenile hybrid. Without warning, he pounced, snatched Lauren's arms and pinned her against the wall at the head of the bed. The girl stared at him, stunned. She clearly hadn't expected him to get physical.

"Now I'll repeat my question: where is Portia?"

"My dad is going to have your ass for this." She thrust her chin up in defiance.

"Your father is going to ground you for what you did and he'll pat me on the shoulder."

Lauren pressed her lips together. "He won't."

"Talk, or I'll haul your ass to your father and we'll find out, shall we?"

The standoff took thirty seconds, and Zane didn't blink a single time. He was good at this, and Lauren was a mere amateur and obviously not as sure about her father's sentiments as she pretended.

"Fine. She went to a party."

"Where?"

"At one of the fraternities."

The moment Zane had the address, he punched it into his cell phone's GPS and charged out the door.

Chapter Ten

The fraternity house was hopping. Music blared from oversized speakers and filled the entire three story Victorian mansion. The place was packed with students holding beer bottles or plastic cups with hard liquor. In the front room, people danced, but on the fringes of it, others tried to talk over the din of the music.

"Oh, come on, Michael, don't be mad at me." Portia batted her eyelashes at her fellow student. "I told you my father had an emergency last night and I had to rush to get to him. I would have called earlier if I could."

Michael pulled her into the hallway where it was only marginally quieter. "All right, but just so you know, I'm not someone to be pushed around. You're hot, Portia, but I'm not letting you dance on my nose."

She put her hand on his arm. "I know, Michael. Why don't we find a place that's a little quieter?" She motioned her head to the stairs that led to the upper floors.

As Michael took her hand to lead her upstairs, she waited for the spark of excitement to flare, but nothing happened. She glanced at him sideways. He was an inch or so taller than she, quite handsome for a twenty-two-year-old, and well built. She could do worse than Michael. But even though he held her hand firmly in his, and the touch wasn't unpleasant, there were no bolts of electricity, no flames of fire licking her skin, as when Zane had touched her.

Maybe once they started kissing, she would get in the mood. She had to. Surely, it couldn't be all that difficult to get in the mood for sex. Hell, one touch by Zane, and she'd been ready to explode like Mount St. Helens. If an unfriendly guy like Zane could do that to her, it shouldn't be beyond the capabilities of a nice guy like Michael. All they needed was a little privacy, and well, the right mood for it: a dark room, some candles, a fire in a fireplace, some pillows on the floor.

Ah shit! She shouldn't be dreaming up something romantic. This wasn't about romance. All she wanted was to lose her virginity. She had no interest in a romantic relationship with Michael. Did he know that?

As they reached the landing, she tugged on his hand. He turned toward her.

"It's only for tonight," she stammered, a little at a loss as to how to make it clear to him that she wasn't interested in a relationship.

"Don't worry, Lauren explained."

Shocked, Portia's mouth fell open. "What did she say?" She hoped Lauren hadn't blabbed more than was absolutely necessary. This was embarrassing enough as it was.

He grinned, showing his cute dimples. "Don't look so horrified. She said you're a little shy when it comes to guys, and that you just want to do it once to get over your shyness. Could have fooled me, but hey, I don't mind."

Portia cringed, but swallowed her anxiety. Lauren was right, she just had to get through this once, and then she could go on with her life and wait for the right guy. And even better that Michael understood. That way, there would be no awkwardness afterwards, and they could remain friends.

Portia looked at the few people who littered the upstairs corridor, wondering if they knew what she and Michael were planning, but they seemed too preoccupied with their own lives to even notice them. She was grateful for that.

"Okay then." She forced a smile and took a step toward one of the bedrooms. A strong hand on her shoulder jerked her back and spun her around. "What the—" The words got stuck in her throat.

Zane towered over her, his face a mask of anger. "You thought I wouldn't find you?"

Not really; but she hadn't thought he'd find her before she'd taken care of, well, business.

"Hey, who are you?" Michael interfered. "Leave her alone. She's with me."

Zane glared at Michael, and Portia instantly felt sorry for him. He wouldn't fare any better than Eric had at her father's hands. And she really didn't want that on her conscience.

"She's not *with* you. So, shove off." Zane grabbed her arm and pulled her toward one of the doors.

"Let her go!" Michael insisted.

Portia tossed him a pleading look. He would only get hurt if he tried to fight Zane. And while she wanted to fight Zane herself, she knew she had to pacify Michael first. "It's all right, Michael. He works for my father."

Michael tilted his head. "Are you sure? I can call the police."

Portia shook her head. "No, please, don't. My father will only get angry."

Finally Michael nodded. He graced Zane with another weary look before he turned away.

Zane swung the nearest door open. A couple making out on a bed shrieked.

"Are you blind? This room is taken!" the guy yelled.

"Out, both of you," Zane ordered with a voice that brooked no refusal. "I'm not gonna say it twice." His hard face only underscored the fact that he wasn't bluffing.

The two students scrambled from the room. Zane slammed the door shut behind them and turned the lock. Click. She was alone with him. And he wasn't happy. Oh no, he was pissed, and by the looks of it, he'd unleash his foul mood on her any second now.

***

Zane couldn't keep his anger leashed any longer and allowed his fangs to descend. Portia had been about to disappear into one of the bedrooms with that guy to—Christ, he didn't even want to complete the thought, because imagining that guy's hands on her, brought his blood to boiling point. And once there, he'd have no means to cool it down.

"What the fuck do you think you were doing?" he accused her, unable to hold his fury in check.

Portia raised her head in defiance and leveled an angry glare at him. "None of your business!" The *fucking* was implied in her tone.

Zane growled. Her words had just blasted the top off his piss-o-meter. He grabbed her and hauled her against the door, then pinned her there with his body. "You are my business, like it or not."

Her breath hitched, and he ground his hips into her, his hard cock eager for a connection with her softness.

"You jerk! I can do what I want!"

"Not on my watch! I was warned about you: parties, boys, drinking, drugs." What nobody had warned him about was how he would be drawn to her. How much he lusted after her.

Her eyes widened, her mouth dropping open in disbelief. "Who said that?"

"Who do you think? Your father. He hired us to protect you from yourself. And that's exactly what I'm doing." Well, not exactly, because protecting her from herself didn't require grinding his erection against her. His horny body was doing that all by itself.

"He lied to you! That's not why he hired you!" Her voice was furious, and her eyes gleamed with anger.

"He said you'd say that." As if he was going to believe one word this woman said to him. All she wanted was to manipulate him. She'd done so from the moment he'd laid eyes on her.

"That's a lie! Do you really want to know why he hired you? Do you?"

Portia didn't wait for his answer, not that he was ready to give one. Did he want to hear any more of her lies?

"He wants to keep me away from guys so I won't have a chance to lose my virginity."

Zane's response was automatic. "Bullshit. You're no more a virgin than I'm a lamb."

Portia struggled against him, but all that did was turn him on even more.

"And you know how I know that?" he asked and lowered his head so his lips hovered above hers. "You don't smell like a virgin. Even now, your body is readying itself for sex." And the scent drove him nuts. "Seductress!"

He hastily retracted his fangs, getting ready for his next move.

"You—"

But her next words were drowned out by his lips on hers as he captured her mouth and took the kiss that had been denied him earlier in the night.

Zane wasn't prepared for the effect she had on him. At first, she tried to resist and held herself stiff in his arms, even hit him with her fists a couple of times. But as he pressed his lips against hers with more urging and licked his tongue over their seam, she slowly parted them and allowed him to enter.

When her flavor hit his tongue, his heart clenched, stopping for a second only to restart at triple the pace. Her lips yielded to him, and she angled her head to give him better access. As he slanted his lips and explored her warm and inviting mouth, he felt her hands come around his neck, pulling him closer.

He growled his approval and drove his thigh between hers, parting them to rub against her sex. Even through the denim, he felt the warmth and wetness there, evidence that she was as aroused as he.

Zane licked, sucked, and stroked, diving deep into her delicious mouth, until she finally stroked her tongue against his. The contact sent a thrill through him he'd never felt before. He couldn't stop his fangs from descending. Unable to hold back, he deepened his kiss and purposefully licked along her teeth, tempting her to unleash her vampire side.

Her pulse quickened, her heartbeat reverberating against his chest. His hands traveled up her torso, caressing along her sides until one met with her breast. He slid his hand over it, teasing the nipple that sat on top. No bra impeded his touch; only the fabric of her t-shirt provided a barrier between her skin and his hand.

Zane stroked over her nipple, turning it hard. Portia gasped into his mouth, and in the same moment, he felt the sharp tips of her fangs.

"Yes!" he groaned and stroked his tongue over one fang, licking it carefully and thoroughly.

Portia ripped her mouth from his. "Oh, God!" Her eyes were wide with shock.

Had nobody ever licked her fangs?

"Let me lick them," he growled and lowered his mouth back to hers.

Fangs were a vampire's primary erogenous zone, and to lick another vampire's fangs gave the most erotic sensations short of full-blown sex. Did Portia not know that? He severed his mouth from hers.

"Has nobody ever licked your fangs?"

Portia shook her head and lowered her lashes, seeming embarrassed. "I've never kissed another vampire."

He understood. With a human she wouldn't be able to let herself go and allow her fangs to emerge. But with him …

Zane took her lips once more, and this time, he very slowly and very deliberately swiped his tongue over her fangs, caressing and stroking. She moaned, and it was the purest sound he'd ever heard. So beautiful, so innocent. And he wanted to hear it again, so he continued his sensual assault.

Meanwhile, Portia's fingers caressed the back of his neck before one hand trailed upwards to stroke over his bald head. He shivered at her touch. The women he slept with rarely caressed him, and if they did they steered clear of this bald head and concentrated on areas lower down. But for some reason, being touched there by Portia felt intimate.

When she lowered her hand to his shoulder, he reached for it and led it back to his head. She obliged him and brushed her soft fingers over his scalp once more. He moaned out his pleasure, interrupting his kiss.

"Make love to me," she whispered. "Please. I want you to take my virginity."

Her words catapulted him backwards. He regarded her with suspicion. "You don't kiss like a virgin, so why don't you drop the act."

"It's not an act!" she yelled, fury darkening her lust-drenched eyes. "I'm a virgin."

Her rapid heartbeat echoed in his ears, and he could fairly smell the blood that rushed through her veins to color her cheeks in a delightful blush—an almost virginal blush. Zane watched as her eyes darted past him as if she were ashamed of something. He let his training as a bodyguard guide him, looking for physical tells that would expose the lie, but found none.

Slowly he shook his head. She couldn't possibly be telling the truth. Everything about her screamed passion, desire, and lust. Could a virgin really conjure up those feelings?

"... and I have to lose my virginity before I'm twenty-one or ..." She blinked her eyes shut as her breath stuttered and forced back a sob. When she opened her eyes and raised her head, her gaze was one of ... resignation.

That's when it hit him. He'd sensed her innocence, her purity, and her hesitation in responding to his kiss. Could it really be true that she was a virgin? Could he have been so wrong simply because all he saw was the woman who tempted him beyond all comprehension? Was that why he couldn't see her as a virgin? But what if she was right, what if her claim was true? She was only a short while away from her body setting into its final form. So, if she spoke the truth and was really a virgin ...

"You'll always be a virgin," he finished her sentence.

Her solemn nod was too serious to dismiss.

Shit! Portia was telling the truth. He saw it in the stubborn curve of her brow and the hard outline of the lips she now pressed together as if she were trying not to cry.

Shit! Shit! Shit! He wasn't in the business of deflowering virgins, and he wouldn't start now.

"So, please. We only need to do it once, I promise," she begged.

Who was she kidding? If he buried his aching cock in her once, he'd want to do it again, and again, and again. Didn't she realize that? He shook his head. "No."

Her body jolted at his harsh rejection. Quickly her arms wrapped around her waist. "You owe me. You just destroyed my chances with Michael."

Fury burst from his lungs. "You were going to sleep with that kid? You can do better than him!" His cock agreed wholeheartedly, but he wasn't going to listen to that lecherous appendage.

"Then why don't *you* do it? You sure didn't mind kissing me!" she accused and lowered her gaze to his groin.

Great! Of course she'd know he was turned on, and now she was using it against him.

"Trust me, you don't want me to be your first. No woman in her right mind would want that." He wasn't gentle, he wasn't kind. He wasn't the right man to initiate a virgin.

"My twenty-first birthday is in five weeks. I'm running out of time," she pleaded, tears now rimming her eyes.

Zane tore his gaze away, not allowing himself to be swayed by her plight. This wasn't part of his job. On the contrary: his job was clearly to keep her away from parties, booze, and men.

"I can't help you."

"I hate you."

He nodded. Good. As long as she hated him, at least she wouldn't repeat her request to take her to bed. Not that it made much of a difference anyway. Now that he'd tasted her and felt his body's reaction to her, he would have one hell of a time keeping his hands to himself.

"I'll take you home."

"No!" Suddenly, the fight was back in her voice.

He glared at her. "You're not staying here."

She glowered back. "I'm not facing my twenty-first birthday as a virgin, so if you're not doing it, I'll find somebody else."

"Over my dead body!" he snarled.

"You don't have a say in this!"

"I'm your bodyguard, so I do!"

"You sound more like my father, and he doesn't get a say in this either. Do you have any idea what he's condemning me to? A life full of pain! I won't have it!"

Zane sighed. Maybe there'd simply been a misunderstanding between Portia and her father. "Perhaps he's not aware of the implications."

"He admitted it! And you're not any better than he, otherwise you'd help me!"

"Help you?" He tilted his head. "I don't think you understand, baby girl. I'm not a gentle man; I'm not the right man to touch a virgin. When it comes to sex …" He raked his hand over his bald head. "I'm rough. I fuck hard. I only think of myself; I wouldn't care if you liked it or not."

Zane averted his eyes so Portia wouldn't detect his lie. Yes, he was rough, but with her, he could care; with her, he would see that she enjoyed it. For her, he could do that. But he didn't want her to know, because this was never going to happen. If he took Portia, he'd consume her, devour her, and then, when she wanted to leave him, he'd force her to stay with him, because he wouldn't be able to let her go. One taste of her, and he knew that much with certainty. There was no need to tempt fate and take this any further.

"It doesn't matter if I like it."

He shook his head. "Don't say that. You have no idea what you'd be missing out on."

"Then show me," she challenged.

Zane clenched his hands into fists. "I told you I can't."

Not only would he hurt her, he'd betray his boss' and colleagues' trust. And if he lost Scanguards, he'd lose his family. He'd be alone again, because no matter what, Portia wouldn't stay with him. She was young, she had her whole life ahead of her; she had choices. All he was was a means to an end. Once he'd done the deed, she'd toss him aside and find somebody who was more suited for her.

When he noticed one solitary tear slide down her cheek, a dull ache spread in his gut. Before it had a chance to travel north, he grabbed her arm and dragged her from the room and out of the fraternity house. On the way back, she didn't say a word. Only her eyes spoke to him. And he didn't like what he heard.

He'd disappointed her.

But if he gave into her wishes, the disappointments would be much greater. For both of them. And the pain would last longer. Maybe an eternity.

Chapter Eleven

Zane slammed his front door shut and instantly heard the excited yapping of his dog. Z came running from the living room and crashed right into his feet. He bent down and picked up the hyper animal. Z immediately licked his neck.

"Hey, I wasn't gone that long," he whispered to the pup and rubbed his fingers over the soft fur.

"You didn't mention you had a dog."

Zane looked to the door of the living room where Quinn leaned casually against the doorjamb. Even though Quinn was about a century older than Zane, he didn't look it: his features were frozen into those of a twenty-something kid. His blond hair and hazel eyes added a boyish quality, and if he'd wanted to, he could have passed for a college freshman, given the right clothes.

Zane set the dog to the floor and straightened. "I'm not keeping him. He's just a loaner."

Quinn grinned. "That's funny, cause I thought I saw a doggie door going out to the backyard. Looked pretty permanent to me."

Zane shrugged. "Dog's gotta go when I'm at work." Then he walked toward his friend and clasped his arm. "Good to see you."

"Same. Nice digs." Quinn motioned his head to encompass the entire house. "Sketchy neighborhood."

"Amaury assures me it's a great investment. Besides, the nightlife is plentiful."

Quinn's face split into a huge smile. "And by nightlife I guess you mean juicy necks at your disposal?"

"If you were honest with yourself, my old friend, you'd admit that the bottled stuff just doesn't cut it."

Yeah, his friends and colleagues at Scanguards might drink blood that a shell company posing as a medical facility acquired, then bottled and shipped to vampires nationwide. But Zane didn't touch the stuff.

"There's nothing better than warm blood straight from a vein. But you go right ahead and keep lying to yourself." Zane stepped into the living room and let himself fall onto the couch.

"What's gotten your dander up?" Quinn followed and plopped down next to him.

Trying to deflect from what really bothered him, Zane decided to steer the conversation onto a more tangible subject. One that was much more clear cut, yet just as dangerous. "Someone tried to kill me yesterday."

"Shit!" Quinn turned sideways. "Who was it?"

Z waddled into the room and tilted his head, looking at both of them.

Zane twisted his mouth. "An assassin."

He made an inviting hand movement toward Z, and the dog jumped and settled in his lap.

"I killed his father last year. He wanted to avenge him by killing me."

Quinn nodded. "Did he get away?"

Zane scoffed. "Do I look like I'd let an assassin get away?"

"Hey, I'm not trying to insult you."

Zane grunted. He almost regretted having told Quinn about his past—or at least part of it—in a weak moment over five decades earlier. It was the only reason Quinn didn't judge him for the murders he'd committed. Because those murders had been executions. And it allowed him to speak to at least one person about the things he'd done. On occasion, it had been a relief.

Zane pulled out the pin and the key from his jeans pocket and tossed both at Quinn who caught them effortlessly. "I found these on him."

Quinn perused the items. "The key looks like it belongs to a locker."

Zane nodded. "I came up with the same. How about the pin? Have you ever seen this symbol before?"

Quinn shook his head and twisted the item in his hand. "Hmm. Odd, those two parts," he commented. "That wave in the middle could be a river, but it could also indicate that something is broken in half."

He held the pin closer to his eyes. "The one symbol on the top of it looks like a 'u' without the down stroke but with a handle to the right instead. And the symbol below is its mirror image." He looked up. "Could it signify some mathematical equation?"

Zane reached for the pin, taking it from Quinn's hands to give it another look. He'd stared at it for hours after he'd killed Brandt's son, but couldn't make heads or tails of it.

"I've never seen a mathematical symbol like this."

"Maybe the broken line in between means the two pieces belong together," Quinn suggested.

Zane refocused his eyes and imagined the line gone. As the two pieces moved closer to each other, they formed a symbol he was only too familiar with.

"It's a broken Swastika."

"You sound surprised. Given who the man was you killed last year, you shouldn't be."

Zane shook his head. "I never found anything like this on Brandt or the others. So why on his son? And why break the Swastika in half? Why not admit to what they are?"

"Maybe the broken line means something else."

Unease skidded over Zane's back and crept up to his neck. "It's too obvious. I don't like it. Almost as if the old guard is still there, but now their children have taken over and put their own stamp on things."

"To do what? The Nazis will never rise again. No government on this planet will allow it."

"What if they don't look like Nazis? What if nobody realizes that they're one and the same, just dressed up differently?"

Quinn took a deep breath. "I think you're reading too much into this. The guy wanted to avenge the death of his father, that's all. Anybody would have done the same. It doesn't mean there's a grand conspiracy behind all this."

"What are you saying? Spit it out!"

"Have you ever thought that you might be getting a little paranoid, believing that they're still after you?"

Zane jumped up, the dog in his lap sliding off him, whining in the process. "Paranoid? You think I'm paranoid? Brandt said he couldn't wait to tell Müller that he'd found me. He's still out there somewhere."

Zane pointed his hand toward the window, his gaze instinctively following its direction. Somewhere, that bastard was still hiding and living a life he didn't deserve.

"Maybe it's time to quit," Quinn suggested.

Zane snarled, allowing his fangs to descend to underscore his disapproval. "I will quit when Müller is dead and not a minute earlier." He raised his hand, clenching it the way he would wrap it around

Müller's neck right before he strung him up by silver chains and hung him out to wait for the rising sun. A stake was too good for Müller. Too humane.

"It's eating you up."

"What are you, my psychiatrist? I thought we were friends, but if that's too much to ask for, you know where the door is. Use it." He needed no friend who didn't have his back, or would try to lead him away from his mission.

Quinn sighed. "What do you need me to do?"

Relieved, Zane gave a nod of approval. He would never admit it, but if Quinn had decided to leave, it would have been hard to take.

"Send out a drawing of this symbol to your contacts and she if anything shakes. Somebody has to have seen it before. It must mean something."

"Do you know anything else about the assassin?"

Zane shrugged. "He had a South American accent. To be expected from Brandt's son, but his English was good. It tells me he's been in the country for a while. He had nothing on him but the key, the pin, and a few coins. Even if he lives in this country, he would have had to stash his ID and some money somewhere. I suspect there's a locker somewhere. He also mentioned that Müller would reward him."

"So, he sent him."

"Possibly. But Müller doesn't seem to know where I am. More like the guy was on a little freelance mission."

"I'll check it out. We should be able to find something on the symbol, and the key should be routine. I'll start at the airport and see whether he used a locker there. It would be the most logical place if he flew in from out of town." Quinn paused, then smiled. "And now that the nasty business is out of our way, tell me what's really going on."

Zane slumped down on the sofa. Instantly, the dog made puppy eyes at him. He slapped his hand on his thigh once, and the animal jumped into his lap.

"Nothing new, same old, same old."

And that answer would be the extent to which Quinn would hear of that subject. No way would Zane talk about his current assignment and more specifically about Portia, the woman who'd scrambled his brain as if she'd tossed it in a blender and flipped the switch.

Portia looked away and pretended to be interested in the food on her plate. The cafeteria was virtually empty. Oliver hung around the door, watching yet giving her privacy. She and Lauren had skipped a class to have time to talk. Now she wished she'd never said a word about what was bothering her.

"That nasty dude? You're kidding, right? Please tell me you're kidding," Lauren urged and placed her hand over Portia's forearm.

Portia shook her head. "When he kissed me ..." Her world had turned upside down with that one kiss. She'd suddenly realized what she'd missed out on all these years.

"You can do better than him," Lauren claimed.

"Funny, he said the same thing." But she didn't buy it. Why would any man who was attracted to her—and he clearly was—turn down her offer of no-strings-attached sex? "He's out of his mind."

Lauren raised her eyebrows. "You both are! You can't do this, not with somebody like him. I mean, can you imagine his bald head hovering over you while he's ... eww!"

"I find his head attractive, and actually, I think he's quite sensitive there." It hadn't escaped her that he'd shuddered when she'd caressed his scalp. And how he'd wanted her to do it again.

"Eww!" Lauren waved her hands before her face. "Erase, erase, erase! You can't sleep with him."

"Don't go all Mother Teresa on me. Besides, he turned me down. I mean, can you believe it? As if I were some ugly duckling." It had hurt having put herself out there only to be coldly rejected.

"He what?"

"You heard right."

"What an asshole! He has no business rejecting you. He should be grateful that you even considered him. Who does he think he is?"

The hottest guy she'd ever laid eyes on, Portia wanted to scream but refrained from the urge, not wanting to give Lauren more ammunition to use against her.

"Exactly," she tossed out instead.

"He can't get away with that! How dare he treat you like you're a wallflower? Jerk!" Lauren pounded her fist on the table, making the trays on it rattle. A student sitting close by glanced at them, before dropping his head back into his book.

"You can have any man you want, Portia." Lauren let her eyes glide over Portia's body. "You're pretty, you have a great body, nice boobs. Any guy would be happy to do you."

Portia cringed at the crude words.

"Sorry," Lauren said sheepishly. "I'm just calling it the way it is."

"Right." But Portia didn't want any guy; she wanted Zane.

He was the first man who'd ever made her feel anything. Her body had hummed under his touch, his kiss so searing hot she'd thought she'd go up in flames. With him, she wasn't afraid that her first time would be some tepid, clinical affair. If Zane touched her and made her a woman, she knew she would enjoy it despite what he'd warned her about.

She didn't believe that he would be cruel to her. His kiss hadn't been cruel. On the contrary, he'd coaxed her. Yes, he'd been demanding, but he'd waited until she'd allowed him to go further. And when he'd licked her fangs, she'd practically exploded. She'd had no idea how arousing it was to have another vampire caress her fangs like this. With so much gentleness, yet so much passion.

"What will I do now?" Portia lifted her head and stared at her friend.

Lauren gave a resigned smile. "Are you sure I can't talk you out of this?"

Portia nodded. "I want him."

"What exactly did he say when he rejected you? And be specific; don't leave anything out. Every word is important."

Trusting in her friend's experience with men, Portia nudged forward on her chair and lowered her voice. There was no need for anybody to overhear what she had to say.

Chapter Twelve

When Portia heard the front door opening without having heard a car drive up, she knew it was Zane. She wondered why he didn't drive but walked instead. It could only mean that he didn't live far. She made a mental note to put Lauren on the task of finding out where he lived. She was sure that Lauren, as the mayor's daughter, had a way of finding out Zane's address. There was a chance it could come in handy one day. She wasn't going to leave anything up to chance.

Portia glanced in the mirror. Her low-rider jeans showed off her flat stomach, and the t-shirt was at least a size too small and short enough to leave her midriff bare while it stretched tightly over her boobs. She had to admit that Lauren was right: she had decent boobs, full and round, and actually a little more shapely than most of her fellow students.

As a hybrid, she had developed faster during her teens, and her body was more mature than that of a nearly twenty-one-year-old human. Just as well: it would be dreadful to be stuck with a gangly teenage body for the rest of her life. But the body she had now, she could work with.

One way or another, Zane would give in to her. Even if she had to throw herself at him. She had five weeks left, and during those five weeks she would chisel away his resistance. No man could be that stoic and say no to something that was dangled in front of his nose every single night, not even Zane. He would crack sooner or later. Did that make her just a tad desperate?

Portia blew out a big breath and planted her legs wider apart, placed her hands on her hips and tried a seductive look in the mirror. She cringed. Maybe she needed a little more practice with that look. It didn't appear quite right yet, unless Zane was turned on by a cheesy grin accompanied by some waggling eyebrows. Maybe some more lipstick, she mused, and twisted the cap off her latest acquisition. As she dabbed her lips with more of the blood-red color, she knew she couldn't stall any longer. The night wouldn't last forever, and eventually Zane would be gone to be replaced by Oliver again.

Her hands clammy, she turned the door handle and left her room. Her heart beat so loudly, she was sure Zane could hear it downstairs in the living room. Slowly, she walked down the stairs, her bare feet making barely any sound. Only the creaking of several steps echoed through the old house. When she reached the landing, she could tell from Zane's stiff posture sitting in an armchair that he'd already heard her.

"Hi."

He looked up briefly, muttering an indistinguishable greeting, and lowered his head again to read the magazine he was holding. Or pretend to read. His eyes didn't appear to move from left to right, but seemed to stare at some random spot on the page.

Zane wore what he always wore: tight-fitting jeans, a black long-sleeved shirt, and boots that looked like he could kick the shit out of someone with them. His leather coat hung over a chair near the entrance. And damn it if that simple outfit didn't make him look like sex-on-a-stick. Why Lauren insisted his bald head was unattractive, Portia didn't understand. She had, in fact, never seen anybody who carried the loss of hair off the way Zane did, with his 'take it or leave it' kind of attitude, as if he didn't give a shit what anybody thought of him. Maybe that's what she liked most about him.

Liked? That was too strong a word. She didn't really 'like' him—more like she had the hots for him—and that was a totally different cup of tea. 'Like' had nothing to do with it.

"Are you done looking?" Zane grunted.

Shit! She hated it when he called her on it like that. She could only hope that she hadn't been drooling.

"Not much to see; you're wearing too many clothes."

His head shot up, his narrowed eyes glaring at her. "That kind of talk is dangerous."

She took a few steps in his direction, easing closer. "Afraid of me?" Surprised at her own boldness, her pulse beat faster and more erratic than before.

He scoffed. "Don't you have homework to do, baby girl?"

Annoyance kicked in, lending her courage. "If you think by calling me 'baby girl' you can fool yourself into thinking I'm not a grown woman, go ahead."

Zane's knuckles gripping the magazine turned white. She was clearly getting to him, just as she'd anticipated. Unfortunately, however, instead of turning him on, she was pissing him off. Perhaps she wasn't that good on the flirting front. And why would she be? She'd never felt the need to flirt with anyone before, so she'd never bothered.

"I don't care if you're a grown woman. How often do I have to repeat myself? I'm NOT INTERESTED in you!"

Shocked by his violent outburst, she swiveled on her heels and headed for the kitchen. "Liar," she mumbled to herself before she tore the door open and went for the fridge.

Well, that was going brilliantly! Lauren had warned her that a man like Zane wouldn't be swayed easily. After this disaster she had to check in with her friend to see how she should proceed now. Lauren had a lot more experience with men. She would come up with something to salvage the situation.

Portia grabbed a coke, needing the sugar and caffeine rush, and closed the fridge door.

A split-second later, she found herself pressed against the cool stainless steel surface. Zane's face was inches from hers. The coke can dropped from her grip and landed on the floor, making a loud noise on the tiles.

His teeth clenched, Zane issued his warning, "Never call me a liar!"

Her chest heaved from the sudden effort of breathing, her boobs pressing against his lean body with each breath, her nipples chafing and reacting instantly. When she tilted her hips forward, one realization infused her with courage to speak: he was sporting an erection.

"I'd call you lover, but you give me no choice."

Zane closed his eyes, his nostrils flaring at the same moment. "I'll never be your lover," he countered, all anger drained from his toneless voice. "Go play with somebody else before you start something you can't handle."

He thought she couldn't handle him? He was wrong! She would prove it to him.

Abruptly, Zane released his hold on her, but before he could step back, she framed his face with her hands and pressed her lips to his.

"Don't," he whispered but didn't pull back.

Portia licked her tongue over the seam of his lips, urging him to surrender. A thrill charged through her body when Zane moved. His lips parted, and the next moment she felt herself sandwiched between the fridge door and his hard body.

Her hands dropped from his face to wrap around his neck, making sure he wouldn't change his mind.

"You'll regret this," he murmured against her lips.

"I won't."

"I know *I* will." But despite his contradicting comment, he stroked his tongue against her lips before he delved into her, capturing her mouth in a move indicating ultimate possession. He held her so tightly, not even with her hybrid strength would she have been able to escape him had she wanted to.

Zane kissed her as if he wanted to punish her, his tongue the whip that lashed her until she was raw, his lips the ties that bound her to him as his hands traveled over her torso in a frantic race to touch every inch before either of them had a change of mind.

Tasting the raw hunger in his kiss, the obvious desperation to possess and devour, Portia's heart recognized her own need: to give herself to this man, this vampire, and to surrender to her desires, desires she'd never felt before. Everything was new and unknown. How had she lived until now without knowing what a touch and a kiss could do, how it could consume a person like a wildfire consumed a forest, leaving nothing behind but a charred surface?

That's how she felt, her skin seared as if hot lava touched her instead of the sensual long fingers of the most enticing man—human or vampire—she'd ever met. And those fingers did things to her, incredible things, exciting things: their touch was poison and soothing medicine all at once, first stirring up her insides, then calming them.

Their rhythm matched her breath, the tremors inside her reaching earthquake levels. Wherever Zane's body connected with hers, she burned—and burned for more. Like an addict, she pulled him closer, moaning her approval and her surrender in one breath. Yet he didn't seem to understand, continuing to unleash his devastating sexual prowess onto her when he could have stripped her of her clothes already and be driving into her without preamble.

Portia ripped her lips from his. "Take me now."

Zane didn't listen. His response was a growl, a sound only an animal could make. His eyes were glowing a deep orange, and his breath rushed from his lungs. Without a response, he took her mouth again, continuing where he'd left off as is she'd never interrupted.

Trying to ease the ache between her thighs, Portia drew up one leg and wrapped it around his thigh, making him press closer. She felt the hard outline of his erection against her soft core and rubbed herself against him, trying to find relief.

A groan rumbled from his chest and reverberated against her ribcage. One of his hands went to her backside, hauling her fully against him, increasing the friction between their bodies.

She went on tip toes to feel his erection pressing lower where her clit throbbed in concert with her heartbeat. Her hands went to his ass, her nails digging into the jeans she wished he wasn't wearing.

All of a sudden, Zane lifted her, forcing her legs farther apart, compelling her to wrap them around his hips as he thrust against her.

The fridge behind her rattled, containers inside tumbling from the shelves. She didn't care. Every time he thrust, his cock hit that little bundle of nerves that was swollen and aching for release. All she could think of was for him not to stop, for this never to end.

"I need …" she whimpered against his lips, unable to control her body's reactions any longer.

A moment later, she felt his fangs grazing her lip, nipping slightly. Her nose detected blood, but her tongue would never taste it, because Zane licked her blood off her lips and swallowed it.

"Fuck!" he cursed and closed his eyes.

She didn't know what he meant, nor did she care. "More!" As her hips ground against him, his cock dragging over her clit with every movement, she pulled his head back to her.

Ding Dong! Ding Dong!

No, not now! She would ignore it. Portia pressed her lips onto Zane's, hoping he hadn't heard the sound in his lust-drugged state, but he pulled back. In the next instant, she stood on her own two feet again, feet that were shaking uncontrollably, her entire body trembling with need.

"No!" she protested. She reached for him, but he turned his back to her.

"Fuck!" she heard him curse under his breath as he stalked out of the kitchen without another word or a look.

***

He'd lost it.

Portia had called him a liar, and she'd been right. But he hadn't wanted to see the truth. So he'd punished her for finding him out, and punished himself even more. Because knowing what it would be like with her, yet having to make sure it never happened was going to kill him. It was as certain as a stake through his heart.

A second longer of feeling her legs around him, of smelling her arousal and tasting her hot lips, and he would have torn her clothes to shreds with his claws and fucked her against the cold steel of the refrigerator, not caring that she was a virgin who needed gentle, not rough.

Using his shirt sleeve, Zane wiped the sweat off his forehead. Shit! What the fuck was he going to do now? He couldn't continue this assignment. Every second in Portia's company would be torture. And what if she provoked him again? Would he simply take what he craved? And once she realized how savage he was, would she change her mind? By then, it would be too late. He'd take it anyway—take what he considered his.

He should never have bitten her lip and tasted her blood. That one drop had been enough to make his vampire side yearn for something he didn't dare claim: a woman of his own. It wasn't right. How could he expect to love and be loved when he lived only for hate and revenge?

He wasn't done with revenge yet. Justice still required one more kill, one more name to be added to the list of those who were responsible for so much misery, so much death, and for robbing him of the life he never got to live. He couldn't give up now; he was too close.

If he took Portia and gave into her, she would see deep into him, and she would hate him, because he'd feared for a while now that he'd become as bad as the men he'd been chasing. If she saw it, it would be confirmation. He couldn't allow it. Nobody should see what lurked inside him, because he couldn't face it himself.

Ding Dong! Ding Dong! Ding Dong!

The door bell rang more urgently, reminding Zane why he'd rushed out of the kitchen. He straightened and cleared his throat. Shit, he still had her taste on his tongue, and his cock pressed hard and heavy against his zipper, still expecting release. In vain.

Through the spy hole in the door, he identified Thomas and Eddie.

What the fuck did they want from him now? He wasn't in the right frame of mind to deal with his colleagues now, particularly not with the ever cheerful young Eddie who was Amaury's brother-in-law. Neither did he have the stomach for Thomas, the ever perceptive mentor who'd never done a wrong thing in his life—well, maybe just once when he'd hooked up with Milo, his lover who'd later betrayed him.

"Listen, Zane," Thomas suddenly said from behind her door, "we know you're standing right there, so open the damn door."

There were times when Zane hated the enhanced senses every vampire possessed. Tonight was one of those times.

He opened the door and moved aside, hoping that the smell of the old house would distract his colleagues from the scent of Portia that was all over his body and his clothes. But the moment Thomas walked in, wearing, as always, his biker duds, consisting of leather and more leather, the flaring of his nostrils and narrowing of his eyes were indication enough that he had noticed something. Figured.

As Eddie followed Thomas and closed the door behind them, Zane glared at Thomas, silently daring him to make a nasty comment. Thomas' age and experience won out over the impulse that sat clearly on his lips. Now all that had to happen was for Portia to stay out of the way and remain in the kitchen, so Thomas would know only that Zane wore the smell of a woman, not that it was the scent of the charge he was guarding.

"What's up?" Zane kept his jaw tight.

"Hey, Zane," Eddie greeted him and looked around.

Thomas merely nodded. "I'm here to relieve you."

Relieve him? Shit! How could they already know what he'd done, how he'd violated Scanguards' code of ethics?

Thomas inclined his head toward Eddie. "Eddie will take you to Drake for your appointment."

Appointment? Zane's gaze snapped to Eddie, then back to Thomas. His heartbeat kicked up. "I'd know if I had an appointment with that quack!" That about summed up what he thought of the shrink who appeared to be a favorite among Scanguards staff.

"Samson figured that would be your reaction, so he decided not—"

"He decided? Samson doesn't get to decide my life!"

"You wanna keep working for Scanguards, you follow his rules."

Zane's gums itched for a bite. "So that's how it's gonna be? And you two, you're playing his messenger boys because he doesn't have the guts to tell me himself?" He thrust his chin up in challenge, daring Thomas to give him a reason to launch his fists into his colleague's too-pretty face.

Thomas moved in vampire speed to go face to face with Zane. "Be very careful, my friend, what you say about Samson. He's been my friend for a very long time, far longer than either of us has known you. If I decide to repeat our little chat to him, you're not one of us anymore. Does that get through your thick skull?"

"What's going on here? Who are these people, Zane?" Portia's voice came from behind him.

Shit, his luck had just turned.

Zane moved his head, seeing her approach with caution. "Colleagues," he pressed out.

"Oh, well then …" She gave Thomas and Eddie a warm smile.

Had she ever smiled at him like that? He couldn't recall. The realization hit him like somebody was driving a stake through his chest: Portia didn't like him at all, otherwise why wouldn't she smile at him the way she smiled at Thomas and Eddie now?

When Eddie walked over to her and shook her hand, Zane clenched his fists. He was touching her! The tips of his fangs descended as he fought the urge to separate their hands.

"I'm Eddie. You must be Portia."

From the corner of his eye, Zane noticed Thomas shake his head in stunned disbelief.

"Yes, hi Eddie."

Zane snapped his head back to Thomas who still hadn't moved and stood only inches from him.

"You little shit," Thomas hissed so low, only Zane could hear it. "What the fuck do you think you're playing at?"

Zane blinked and dropped his voice to the same level. Thomas had connected the scent on him with that of Portia. "Why don't you go fuck Eddie and leave me the hell alone!"

Thomas' face dropped, shock rolling off his features. Zane knew the blow was low, but somebody had to finally say it. Maybe if Thomas wasn't frustrated with his own situation, he wouldn't stick his head into things that didn't concern him.

"You fucking asshole. You're going to see Dr. Drake now, no protests, or I'll report this to Samson and your gig is up."

The sternness in Thomas' voice and face was undeniable. It left Zane no choice but to give into blackmail. Without a word to Thomas, he turned fully and motioned to Eddie. "Eddie, we're leaving. Now."

"Where are you going?" Portia's tone had accusation written all over it. Her smile had disappeared.

Before he could find the right words, Thomas spoke up. "Zane has a prior engagement. I'll be his relief for the next couple of hours." He went to Portia and extended his hand. "I'm Thomas. Pleasure meeting you."

Zane stalked to the door, Eddie on his heels.

"You can take my bike," Thomas called after him, but Zane didn't bother replying.

"Asshole," he muttered under his breath.

Chapter Thirteen

Cool night air greeted him as he walked into the driveway. Zane halted for a moment for Eddie to catch up with him. Still seething about Thomas' blackmail, he glanced around and noticed Eddie's motorcycle parked near the gate. He craned his neck.

"Where is Thomas' Ducati?"

"He didn't take his Ducati today. He brought the BMW," Eddie replied and sauntered past him.

Zane followed. "I didn't know he had a BMW."

"That's because he just only finished restoring it. It's an antique."

Zane reached Eddie's bike and rounded it. Behind Eddie's Kawasaki was a smaller motorcycle. Zane jerked to a halt, his heart stopping in the same instant.

"It's an R6, a 1937 model," Zane echoed with the remaining breath in his lungs before his vocal cords ceased working.

"Yeah, you're right. Thomas is quite proud of it. Paid a high price for it. But he did a great job, don't you think so?"

Eddie's words faded in the background while Zane's eyes took in the features of the bike he remembered well. It was all black and chrome, just like the one he'd had back then; the R6 that had belonged to him when he'd still been Zacharias, when he still had hair and a promising future ahead of him.

Even now, he could feel the wind ruffling his hair as he rode through the streets of Munich.

The cobblestones sent tiny shocks through his body as he throttled up and passed a car. Behind him, his sister Rachel sat on the miniscule luggage rack, which wasn't really meant for passengers, and held onto him for dear life, her legs stretched out toward the curb.

"Not so fast, Zacharias!" she cried out but giggled at the same time. She was having as much fun as he was.

"Are you scared?" he teased and laughed. There was no better feeling than being on his bike and feeling the air rush past his ears.

"No, but Papa will be mad if we fall and hurt ourselves."

"Don't worry about Papa."

His father wouldn't have given him this birthday present—a 3-year-

old BMW R6 motorcycle that looked like new—if he didn't want him to use it and enjoy it. Rachel was still too much of a child. At only fourteen, she obeyed her father and mother one hundred percent, whereas he had rebelled from time to time. At one point, he'd been close to moving out from home, but his mother had thought it a ridiculous idea. Besides, as an aspiring poet, he still relied on his parents' money for survival.

"We should go home. Mama is waiting with supper," Rachel urged.

"Just one more time around the block," he cajoled and twisted the grip to increase the speed.

One more time became three, and by the time they reached their parents' townhouse, it was dark already. Rachel hopped off, and Zacharias rolled the bike toward the garage, when he noticed the armed uniformed man at the entrance door to his home.

Instantly, panic surged through him. Had something happened to his parents while he and Rachel had been out having fun? He parked the bike hastily and rushed toward the door Rachel had already reached.

"Mama? Papa?" His sister's voice echoed against the walls in the narrow street.

"Has something happened to our parents? What's going on?" Words spilled from Zacharias' lips like water rushing down a waterfall.

The officer with the tell-tale SS emblem on his uniform responded with a stoic look. "Zacharias and Rachel Eisenberg?"

Zacharias nodded automatically. "That's us." He reached for his sister's hand and squeezed it. A thought invaded his mind: he'd heard of SS personnel showing up at other families' homes, rumors of decent citizens being taken away.

The SS officer motioned his head to the hallway behind him and unblocked the way to let them through. Continuing to hold Rachel's hand, Zacharias ran toward the back of the house where he heard voices. Every room he passed was lit brightly.

Anxiety made his heart beat like a locomotive by the time he finally reached the living room. His mother sat on the couch, her head in her hands, and his father stood next to her, his body visibly coiled in tension. He darted nervous looks at the men in the room: three more SS members, the black uniforms and shiny boots gleaming in the artificial light.

"Are those your children?" the tall, blond officer asked.

Zacharias' father nodded and cast a regretful glance at Zacharias and Rachel.

"Father?" He tried to swallow past the lump in his throat, but to no avail. The presence of these officers in his home could only mean one thing. The rumors were true; he knew it when he looked at his parents' faces.

His mother's face was tearstained. Zacharias rushed to her and took her hands as he crouched down.

"They're taking us away. All of us." She sobbed, and behind him he heard Rachel's shocked gasp. "They are arresting us."

Zane snapped his head to the intruders. Even though he knew the answer, he nevertheless asked the question: "Why?"

As a nasty grin spread on the blonde's face, Zacharias felt as if an icy hand wrapped around his neck and squeezed the life out of him. A sense of foreboding slammed into him.

"Why?" The officer exchanged a look with his colleagues. "Because you're Jews, that's why. Dirty Jews."

Dirty Jews. The words still echoed in his head when the SS guards led him and his family outside and into a waiting van. He turned his head to look back, glimpsing one last time at the bike he'd come home with only minutes earlier. He'd owned it for only a day—one single day in 1940. He was twenty-four years old, and his life as he knew it had just changed forever. How drastically, nobody could have guessed.

Zane tore his gaze from the bike and looked back at Eddie. "I can't ride that bike."

"Of course you can. It works no different than—"

"I said, I can't ride that bike," Zane bit out from behind clenched teeth and glared at Eddie.

His colleague did well not to ask any stupid questions. "Fine, hop on with me."

***

Zane felt numb when he walked into Drake's practice. He scowled at the Barbie doll receptionist and ignored her protest that she needed to announce him first. Instead, he simply barged into the doctor's office and slammed the door behind him.

Drake sat behind his desk. He looked up only briefly, seemingly undeterred by Zane's dramatic entry.

"I'm here," Zane bellowed when the shrink looked back down at his paperwork. He hated being ignored.

"I'm not blind," Drake announced calmly.

"And if you don't start this session now, I'll make sure you'll fit into an ashtray," Zane muttered under his breath.

"Nor deaf," Drake added and closed the file he was reading and put it aside. "I hadn't expected you to be so eager to start."

Zane rolled his shoulders. "If your skills as a doctor are as sharp as your ability to interpret a person's intentions, I suggest you find another profession." As if he was here to get through some stupid psycho-analysis and let this quack probe around in his head! Like he had wacko tattooed on his forehead. The guy wouldn't get a single word out of him, Zane swore.

"I'd offer you a seat but I get the impression that you'd rather stand, so I won't."

"Wrong again," Zane answered and let himself fall onto the ghastly coffin-couch, propping his feet up on one of the wooden panels that served as an armrest. Sure, he would have preferred to stand, but he wasn't going to give that asshole one inch. In five minutes, he would be done proving that Drake was incompetent. And to top it off, he'd have Drake agree with him.

"Nice furniture," he lied. He'd throw the doctor so far off his track by feeding him wrong answers, he'd be heading for China next.

A raised eyebrow indicated that Drake was onto his deceptive tactics. "Your boss warned me that you had peculiar tastes."

Zane kept his face impassive even though a storm was raging inside him. "I doubt he sent me here so you could discuss my peculiar tastes with me. What do you want, Drake?" He crossed his ankles, affecting a relaxed pose.

"That's entirely up to you."

"Don't give me this line. We both know it's not true. You were given specific instructions by Samson as to what he wanted me to talk about." Remaining as calm as he could, he continued, "So let's just cut to it: I killed that asshole. Did I enjoy it? Immensely. Do I have any regrets? No. Remorse? No. Second thoughts? Hell no."

Zane dropped his feet to the floor. "And now that that's out of the way, go ahead and charge Samson the full hour and take the rest of the time off." He rose.

The doctor clapped, slowly and deliberately.

Zane shot him an icy look.

"Fabulous, excellent! I love a good performance as much as the next vampire. Have you ever thought of becoming an actor?"

"Piss off!"

"No, honestly." Drake rose and rounded his desk. "I see a lot of talent there."

Zane narrowed his eyes at the doctor's obvious sarcastic remark. "We're done here."

"Not so hasty. As you're probably aware I am to report to Samson if you miss any of your sessions or if you leave early." He gave his wristwatch a deliberate glance. "You've been here just five minutes. That's indeed a record." Then he looked back at Zane. "This is not speed dating."

Zane clenched his fists and took a deep breath. Fine, the doctor required him to stay the full hour? He could do that. "As you wish," he pressed out.

He lay down on the coffin-couch, stuffed one of the pillows under his head and closed his eyes. "Wake me in fifty-five minutes."

There was silence in the room. Zane started counting. One minute passed and another one. Then the laughter of the psychiatrist echoed through the room. Zane's eyes shot open, pinning the man with a furious glare.

"And there your colleagues keep telling me you don't have a sense of humor," Drake claimed.

"You're annoying as hell." Almost as annoying as Portia could be.

Fuck, he wasn't going to think about her and what had happened less than an hour earlier. Nor wonder about what could have happened had they not been interrupted. Damn it, he wasn't going to fuck a virgin. Hell, she shouldn't still be a virgin. It was all wrong.

"What do you know about hybrids?" The question was out before Zane even knew he was going to ask it.

"I suppose you're not talking about cars."

Zane shot him a get-real look.

"You're not the only one with a sense of humor," Drake chuckled.

Zane rolled his eyes. God damn it, why did Drake have to be the only psychiatrist in the city? Well, the only vampire-psychiatrist anyway.

"Hybrids are the product of a male vampire and his blood-bonded human mate, or, in other cases, the children of hybrids."

With an impatient jerk, Zane sat up. "Even I know that much."

"Then maybe you'd like to rephrase your question and be a bit more specific about what you want to know." The doctor sat down in the armchair opposite the coffin-couch.

Zane shifted on his seat. Heck, maybe he should forget the whole thing. It wasn't his business. It would be smarter to stay out of it. But his damn mouth had its own motor. "Is there a reason why a parent wouldn't want a hybrid female to lose her virginity before her body attained its final form?"

"What?"

"I thought you weren't deaf!"

"Oh, I heard you loud and clear. I'm simply stunned by your question."

"Well?"

Drake steepled his fingers. "I'm assuming you refer to the fact that her hymen will still be in place at her final turning?" He acknowledged Zane's nod before he continued, "Frankly, it makes no sense. Only a masochist would do that to somebody. How old is the hybrid in question?"

Zane stiffened. "It was a hypothetical question, doc."

Drake frowned. "How old is your hypothetical hybrid?"

"A few weeks short of her twenty-first birthday."

"I suggest that you take her mother aside and inform her of the implications."

"Her mother is dead."

"Her father then."

"He keeps her practically imprisoned so she won't meet any men."

"So you think this is deliberate?"

"What else can it be?" The instructions Scanguards had received from Portia's father had been crystal clear: keep her away from boys.

Drake contemplated the question. "Why is it that you're so interested in this hybrid?"

Zane jumped to his feet. "I'm not interested." Ah, hell, not even he believed that crock of shit.

"Hmm. Could have fooled me."

Zane ignored Drake's comment as another thought crossed his mind. "Can't a hymen be removed by other means than sex?"

"No"

Zane blinked. Was he really sitting in the psychiatrist's office discussing sex organs with him? He must have gone off the deep end without noticing.

"But ... I've heard that even in humans a hymen can easily be broken by vigorous physical activity. So couldn't she have already torn her hymen herself?" He'd seen her jump out of the window and run like she was being chased by a pack of wolves. Wasn't that considered vigorous physical activity?

Drake raised an eyebrow.

"So I watch the Discovery Channel. Sue me!" Zane scoffed.

Drake cleared his throat. "To get back to your question, sadly, the answer is 'no'. A hybrid's hymen isn't susceptible to such permanent injury. Yes, it can be torn, but it will repair itself during her restorative sleep. Not even finger-fucking her, excuse the crude words, would rip it permanently. Only full intercourse assures that the hymen is destroyed and won't repair itself."

Drake moved forward on his chair. "It takes a flesh and blood penis and live semen to dissolve the hymen in its entirety. There is no other way. I guess, somehow our creator wanted to make sure we continued procreating." He shrugged. "What do I know?"

Zane swallowed. "So that leaves sex."

Sweaty, passionate, heart-stopping sex with Portia.

Chapter Fourteen

After leaving Drake's office, Zane rode back to Portia's house on the back of Eddie's motorcycle, still contemplating the doctor's words and not at all in the mood to talk. Luckily, when he reached the house, Thomas informed him that Portia had gone to bed. At least he wouldn't have to face her right now when he was too conflicted about what to do next.

He was glad when Oliver showed up shortly before sunrise to relieve him.

"Can you come an hour and a half before sunrise tomorrow?" Zane asked the human.

"What for?"

"I have to see Samson about something."

"Sure. Not a problem."

"Thanks, buddy." He slapped Oliver on the shoulder and stalked out into the dark.

On the way home, Zane fed off a street person he found sleeping in a doorway and almost gagged on the man's blood. After having tasted that tiny drop of Portia's blood, everything else now tasted like battery acid. Shit, he'd really screwed himself, hadn't he? While he'd never much cared where his next meal came from as long as it was dripping from a pulsing vein, his taste had just become more refined.

He'd been a McDonalds kind of guy; now he'd suddenly acquired a taste for 3-star Michelin food. Perfect!

When he got home, Quinn took his mind off the disturbing thought.

"You're not going to believe this."

Zane raised a tired eyebrow and slumped down on the couch. Z jumped onto his lap and curled up. "Has he eaten?"

Quinn nodded. "I fed him after our walk."

Zane looked down at the dog. "Thanks. So, what am I not going to believe?"

"The pin you found on the assassin: I've found the symbol."

A bolt of excitement charged through him. Finally, something he could concentrate his energy on. "What does it mean?"

"Get this: it's a group of vampires and hybrids who have banded together to create a superior race."

Zane's ears rang from the news. "A new race?"

"Not new, superior. They are selecting vampires and hybrids for a breeding program to give birth to stronger, *superior* hybrids."

Zane shuddered. It sounded too much like something he knew. "As the Nazis did in their attempts to create their Arian super race: select tall, blond men and women with above average intelligence, physical strength and beauty and have them produce babies."

Quinn nodded. "Only this time, it's not blond and blue eyed individuals they want, it's mostly hybrids. They'll take vampires too, but only extraordinary ones: stronger than others, more lethal, more intelligent, more skilled. They want to breed these traits into the next generation of hybrids."

"How did you find out?"

Quinn shrugged. "A disgruntled vampire who was rejected by their program responded to one of my contacts."

"Disgruntled? Not exactly the most reliable source of information. People like that are known to exaggerate."

"He seemed genuine."

Zane frowned despite the fact that Quinn had an uncanny ability to figure people out. "Doesn't sound right to me. If I were to try something like that, I wouldn't exactly broadcast to every possible recruit what this is all about. Only once somebody is accepted into the program, would I give the recruits more information, and even then only what they needed to know."

Quinn looked as if contemplating his words. "My informant strikes me as the kind of guy who does his own digging around if you know what I mean."

A vampire who stuck his nose into things that didn't concern him? Well, at least Zane could find out what he knew. Didn't mean he had to believe it.

"Does he know who runs the program?"

"He didn't know. Only those who are accepted get to eventually meet the top brass."

At least that sounded right. "What else did he know?"

"The location of their headquarters is secret. Only the few at the top know. Everything is kept secret: the number of recruits, the number of new hybrid babies produced."

"Does he know anything at all? What is the goal of this group? There has to be a reason why they're doing this."

"I think we can guess from the symbol they have chosen: it's indeed a Swastika, a broken one, as indicated by the line running between the two pieces. One thing the rejected vampire was able to find out was that the symbol changes over time. Every few years, a new pin is issued, and each time the line grows fainter and the two pieces of the Swastika move closer together."

Zane cursed. A symbol like that could only mean one thing. "They're trying to resurrect the Third Reich."

"Maybe not exactly, but they're taking ideas from it to create stronger, more indestructible hybrids. And because they aren't full blooded vampires, they can be out in daylight. They can blend in with the human population and propagate in their midst, unchecked, unhindered. Imagine how powerful that will make them. And the rest of us, the full-blooded vampires, are hamstrung by being able to counteract them only at night. If this superior breed has any designs on world domination ..." Quinn didn't have to finish his sentence.

"The ultimate master race with the skills and advantages of both the human and the vampire species, but without any of their weaknesses," Zane breathed. And there was no doubt in his mind that his biggest enemy was behind it. "Franz Müller, he's their leader."

"You don't know that."

Zane gave a bitter laugh. "The scheme is evil." He tossed his friend a glare, and continued, "If anybody is capable of pulling something like this off, it's Müller. His background fits; he's got the medical knowledge to understand what traits would work well in a breeding program, and he's got all the connections. He and his colleagues could have started this right after the end of the war. Once they figured out that they could breed with humans and create hybrid children, they had all the tools they needed."

"You make him out to be some sort of Über-villain. He's nothing of the sort. Aren't you taking this personal vendetta a little too far? He's only a vampire who's eluded you so far."

Zane shook his head. "Don't underestimate Müller. You underestimate him, you die. He's evil to the bone. And his ambition only fuels the evil in him. If he's got something in his mind, he'll do it. It was his research and cunning that led the program at Buchenwald. He was the one who figured out how to create vampires after one of the guards stumbled on a vampire feeding on the prisoners. He was the one who saw an opportunity there. And he took it."

Quinn put his hand on Zane's forearm. "But a master race? Don't you think that even for Müller that's too much to chew on?"

"He has a God complex. He is a psychopath."

Quinn sighed. "What are you gonna do?"

"There's only one thing I can do: find him and take him down. Knowing how he operates, he trusts no one. He'll be the only one with all the information about how the program is set up and how it works. If he falls, the program will dissolve into nothing."

"That is if he's the head."

"He has to be." Müller had always hated authority, and even back in Buchenwald, resented his superiors. As a civilian, there was no chance in hell that he would take orders; Müller would be nobody's underling. He would be the leader.

"How are we going to find him?"

"Let's continue with Brandt's son. He'll lead us to him. Anything on the key?"

Quinn shook his head. "Guess what, there are no lockers at the airport. Homeland Security crap I suppose. I'll check out the Greyhound and train stations tonight."

"Do that. He couldn't have gotten here without anything on him. He has to have stashed his stuff somewhere."

And hopefully Brandt would lead them right to the organization. Even though Brandt had claimed not to know where Müller was, it didn't mean much. If only the top brass in the organization knew where headquarters was located, and therefore where Müller could be found, then it could only mean that Brandt wasn't part of the top brass. Simple as that.

Zane slammed his fist into this palm. He was itching to find Müller, now more than ever. If he was really head of this neo-Nazi breeding program—and Zane was convinced he was—then he needed to be taken out as quickly as possible. Vampires and hybrids were already superior to humans in strength and speed. Allowing Müller to create a race, which was even more superior—combined with his motivation to dominate as many people as possible— would put all of humanity at risk.

Zane couldn't allow that to happen. This evil had to be annihilated.

***

"You can't just show up at his house," Lauren whispered as she turned off the faucet in the ladies restroom at the University. "He won't let you in."

Portia combed her fingers through her hair. "I'm not going to just show up and wait for him to open the door. I'm going to break in."

Lauren shook her head. "You do know that everybody is going to blame your behavior on my bad influence, don't you?"

"Nothing will happen to you. By the time anybody finds out, the deed will be done."

"Are you sure about that?"

Portia nodded. "You weren't there, but I'm telling you, Zane was all over me. If his colleagues hadn't shown up, we would have had sex last night. Unfortunately, by the time he came back, I was asleep, even though I tried to stay up and wait for him."

Lauren applied lipstick to her lips. "Why not wait until tonight?"

She couldn't wait. Throughout her morning classes, she hadn't been able to concentrate, and had relived Zane's kiss and touch a hundred times. She was burning up. If she had to wait another hour, all the fire trucks in this city wouldn't be able to douse the flames.

"I can't." The need to have him, to feel his body joined with hers was growing too fast and too strong.

"How are you planning on getting rid of Oliver?" Lauren motioned her head to the door, on the other side of which Oliver was waiting for them.

"Don't worry. He's only a human. I'll be gone so fast, he won't know what hit him."

"Careful. Nobody else can get a hint of your vampire speed, or we're both in deep shit."

"You worry too much." Portia smiled to herself.

Ever since she'd met Zane, she'd become more confident in herself. She was willing to take risks for what she wanted, because what she wanted was worth it. Zane's hands on her were worth it. And once they'd had sex, maybe he would want more. Because she wanted more. She wanted to get to know him, to explore what was under his mask of indifference and violence. To see what he was hiding from the world; to discover what he was protecting so fiercely.

Yes, she admitted it, if not to Lauren or anybody else, to herself: she should probably run as far as she could from Zane, but she knew she couldn't. The force that drew her to him was too strong, like a current she couldn't swim against any longer. It was better to give up the struggle and allow herself to drift to him and land in his arms.

"Are you ready?" Lauren's eyes pursued her in the mirror.

"Yep. You have the address?"

Lauren pulled a piece of paper from her purse and handed it to her. "It's in the Mission."

Portia looked at the address Lauren had scribbled down. "I'll find it."

A shiver of anticipation skidded down her back as she opened the restroom door and walked into the hallway.

"I was about to check on you," Oliver remarked.

"You really don't have to treat me like a baby. I'm perfectly fine being in the restroom by myself." Portia darted looks up and down the hallway. There were too many students around for her to simply launch into vampire speed and run. She would have to do something a little more devious.

Chapter Fifteen

Zane dropped the weights and exhaled. He was bathed in sweat from his vigorous workout. He'd tried to sleep after his conversation with Quinn, but his mind wouldn't shut off, making it impossible for him to rest. Quinn was sleeping soundly now.

As he walked upstairs, he didn't bother being quiet. This was his house, and if anybody didn't like it, they could leave. Besides, Quinn was used to him being up half the day. They'd shared a place in New York for a while, and Quinn had learned to ignore Zane roaming around the apartment most of the day.

Fuck, he was in a pissy mood. The suspicion that Müller was leading a group that was breeding a new master race gnawed on him. He blamed himself. If he hadn't failed at finding the bastard and killing him, this wouldn't even have happened. He'd had more than sixty years to chase Müller down, only to be evaded at every turn.

Zane headed for his shower and stripped. When the warm water ran down his naked skin, he closed his eyes and leaned his forehead against the tiles. It was time to admit that the reason he was really pissed was Portia. He desired her against all reason. But to take what she offered would violate so many rules, Samson would throw the book at him.

And even if he wasn't violating Scanguards' code of ethics by touching her, he had his own scruples to deal with.

Zane looked down at himself. Figured that his cock was hard and ready the moment his thoughts had turned to Portia. But he wouldn't let this get any further. With a painful flick of his fingernail against the tip of his erection, he deflated the horny appendage. After soaping his body and rinsing it, he turned off the water and stepped onto the soft mat in front of the shower.

The dog's bark made him listen up for a moment. The animal roamed around the house and the garden all day long, barking at anything from a passing truck to a bee sitting on a flower.

He shook his head and continued drying off. At least somebody in this house was having some fun. He dressed in his robe and pulled the sash tight when he heard one of the stairs creak. Was Quinn up?

Barefoot, Zane stole out of the bathroom and into his bedroom, snatching a stake from his dresser drawer on the way. If another assassin was trying to get him, he'd be prepared this time. His fingers reached the light switch, and he flipped it, cloaking the room in darkness. Let the assassin think he was asleep.

No more sounds came from the hallway. Had he imagined the sound? Maybe the old house was simply making noises by itself? Zane strained his ears as he waited, his body pressed against the wall next to the door, poised to strike.

He held his breath, not wanting to give his position away, when the doorknob turned slowly. The hinges moaned as the door eased open. The shadow moved, and Zane pounced, slinging his arm over the intruder's head and around his neck, yanking him against his chest, his other hand holding the stake.

Finally taking a deep breath, he inhaled a fragrance he was all too familiar with. He hadn't smelled it earlier because he'd held his breath.

Zane reached for the light switch and flipped it, bathing the room in light.

"Shit! Portia," he breathed, releasing her from his neck hold.

She turned, her eyes instantly running over his barely clothed body. Instinctively, he tested the sash, making sure it hadn't loosened.

"Hi."

He slapped his hand over her mouth, horrified that her greeting might have woken Quinn.

Zane dipped his head to her ear. "What the fuck are you doing here?"

She mumbled against his hand, but he didn't release her.

"I'm not alone in the house. So, unless you want me to be fired as your bodyguard, keep your voice down," he whispered through clenched teeth.

She nodded, and he dropped his hand. Portia instantly moved her head to his face. Shit, she smelled so good, he didn't know how long he could refrain from touching her.

"I wanted to see you." Her voice was low and seductive.

Had she always sounded like that, or was he just getting more desperate the longer he denied himself the thrill of taking her and making her his?

"You broke into my house."

She shrugged. Then her hand connected with his chest, and her fingers played with the lapels of his robe. Before she could slip her hand onto his naked skin, he grasped it and imprisoned it in his palm.

"Stop that."

No, do it, he wanted to howl.

Her other hand came up too fast for him to react and pushed the robe apart so her fingers connected with his hairless chest. Her touch burned like the fires of hell, so tempting, so tantalizing, yet so forbidden. Maybe only for a second he could allow himself to soak in her essence, to allow her enthralling scent to permeate his body.

"I want you," she murmured and pressed her lips against his skin.

Her lips moved, sliding along his heated body, moving upwards to his neck. He tilted his head, unable to resist the pleasure she was offering. Excitement coursed through him when she pulled his skin between her lips and suckled.

His hands grabbed her backside and hauled her against his thick erection.

"Bite me," he demanded, his voice hoarse.

Portia's head jerked up, her eyes looking at him, stunned.

"Yes," he said, louder now, "that's what it would be like. We'd be like animals, wild, no holds barred. That's what being with me would be like." He released her and stepped back. "Admit it: you're not ready for that. All you want is some nice tame lovemaking. I can't give you that."

"That's not true. I want … more."

He shook his head. "Go home, baby girl." Then something hit him. "Where's Oliver?"

"I escaped him."

"How?"

"Mind control."

"You devious little …" Yet he couldn't really blame her. Like her, he'd do anything if he wanted something bad enough.

"I didn't hurt him."

"He has to pick you up and take you home." He turned to reach for his cell phone on the dresser, but Portia's hand clamped over his wrist.

"No!"

"You don't get to choose."

"You're a big bully!"

Zane shrugged. What else was new?

"Zane?" Quinn's voice was accompanied by a knock on his door.

Shit! He shot Portia a scolding look.

"Is everything all right?"

Zane motioned to Portia and then the bed. She understood and hopped in, putting the covers over her up to the neck, turning her head away from the door.

"Everything's fine," he said calmly, as he opened the door halfway so Quinn could see Portia's long, dark hair but not her face. If he hadn't opened the door, Quinn would have only become suspicious.

Quinn glanced inside the room. "Hey, I was just worried because of the assassin the other day." Then he grinned. "Anybody special?"

Zane shook his head. "Just a one-nighter."

"You can send her over to my room when you're done with her," Quinn suggested with a lascivious grin.

In his dreams! "By the time I'm done with her she won't be able to stand."

Quinn chuckled. "Lucky bastard."

Zane slapped him on the shoulder and shut the door. When he turned back to the bed, he saw Portia pushing down the cover and taking off her shoes.

"Stop it right there," he warned, not wanting her to take any more clothes off. The temptation was big enough when she was fully dressed. If she were naked, he'd have a snowball's chance in hell of keeping his hands off her.

"What are you gonna do? Scream for help?" she teased.

Zane jumped onto the bed and snatched her arms, holding her down. "You, baby girl, listen to me now. You have a choice: either you behave and I might let you stay until tonight, or I'll call Oliver right now to pick you up."

Hell, what was he saying? Letting her stay? To do what? To torture himself for the next few hours by having her close, without being able to touch her? Was he going completely insane?

Portia pursed her lips. "Can you clarify what you mean by 'behave'?"

"Don't play your games with me, Portia, I'm warning you."

"Or you'll do what?"

Kiss you. Fuck you. Bite you. Those were the words he wanted to say to her, but couldn't. All he could do was stare at her and lose himself in the green depths of her eyes, wondering what could have been if they'd met under other circumstances, in another time. If he were a different man, one not consumed by hate and revenge, maybe he could even make her happy. But he was who he was.

"You have to leave." He released her wrists and rolled to the side.

"But you just said if I behaved, you'd let me stay."

He shook his head. "It's better for both of us if you leave now."

She turned to her side, angled her elbow and rested her head on her hand. "Because you think I don't want what you want?"

"You have no idea what I want."

"Then why don't you tell me?"

"I don't want to talk."

She lifted her hand and stroked it along his cheek. Zane closed his eyes, warring between pushing her away and pulling her onto his body. He did neither, her touch felling him like a bullet would a deer. He felt just as vulnerable in Portia's hands.

"I want to touch you," she whispered.

"You're already touching me." If she did anything more intimate to him, the last thread of his control would snap.

"I want to touch the rest of your body."

Zane groaned. "Please don't." *Please do.*

"You might like it."

"That's what I'm afraid of," he muttered under his breath.

Shit, he'd never felt so weak in his entire life, not even when he was human, but as much as he knew he should stop her and make her leave, his body didn't obey any signals from his brain and simply lay there, coiled tightly in anticipation of her caress.

When her hand slipped beneath the fabric and stroked along his chest, his pulse quickened and his breath stuttered. Her fingers were softer than he'd expected, and wherever they touched him, his skin burned like he was being lathered in hot tar. Pain and pleasure joined with every lingering stroke and every sensual caress.

"Didn't you say you were a virgin?" he breathed, unable to comprehend how the touch of a woman as inexperienced as Portia could have such devastating effects on him.

"I'm following my instincts."

And her instincts told her at this moment to loosen his belt and pull his robe aside.

He'd never been shy about his body, and he'd always been comfortable with nudity with women as well as around his friends and colleagues, but this time it was different. He felt bare before her, exposed and vulnerable in his desire for her. There was no way he could hide from her now, hide how much he wanted and needed her.

He watched as Portia's mouth dropped open when her gaze lowered to his cock. His fully erect cock. He couldn't remember ever having been this hard.

"You are ..." She licked her lips. "... big."

But despite the apprehension he sensed in her, her hand traveled farther south, traversing his stomach with seeming determination and a clear idea of where it was going. If he didn't stop her soon, she would touch his hard shaft, and within seconds he'd spill in her hand, unable to hold back any longer.

"Portia, please ..."

Her hand reached the nest of dark curls that surrounded his cock.

"... stop. Don't ..." Air rushed out of his lungs as her fingers reached the base of his erection and touched the sensitive flesh.

He jerked and gripped her hand in the next instance. "No."

"Zane, I want to—"

The ringing of his cell phone saved him. Glad to have an excuse, he jumped from the bed, wrapping the robe tightly around him, and answered the phone.

"Yes?"

"Zane, sorry to wake you. It's Oliver. I need your help." Oliver sounded agitated, and Zane had a pretty good idea what had him in such a tizzy.

"What's up?"

"Shit, man, I lost Portia. She tricked me and ran off. I don't know what to do. Samson and Gabriel are so gonna fire me. You need to help me."

"Calm down, Oliver. I'm already on it." Was he ever! "Portia came to see me. She's here." But was she safe?

"Oh, thank God! I'll come right over and get her. I'm so grateful."

Then suddenly Oliver's tone changed as if he'd just caught on. "Hey, why would she go to your place?"

Ah, fuck, that kid was smarter than he'd given him credit for. "Listen, I won't tell Samson about your fuck-up if you don't tell him about this."

"What's she doing at your place?"

"What do you think she's doing?" *Seducing him,* that's what she was doing to him.

"You tell me."

"You need to pick her up. Right now." He ignored Portia's protest behind him. "But be careful. Quinn is staying here. I don't want him to hear you. Is that clear?"

"Yes. I'll be there in ten."

There was a click in the line.

Zane turned to face Portia, make that a furious Portia.

Her hands at her hips, she stood next to the bed, glaring at him. "I told you I wasn't leaving."

"You are, baby girl. Voluntarily."

"Hah!" she huffed. "You can't make me. Oliver can't restrain me. I'll escape him again."

"No, you won't."

"Watch me!" she threatened.

With a calm he didn't feel, Zane took one of her hands and led it to his face. He nuzzled his face in her palm and pressed a kiss into it, seeing Portia melt in front of his eyes.

"You won't do anything of the sort. If you do, I'll ask my boss to take me off this assignment, and you'll never see me again." His threat was a bluff, but he was good at bluffing, his face remaining a stony mask of indifference, a mask he'd worn for decades. It had gotten easier with the years, but tonight, it was the hardest thing he'd had to do.

"You wouldn't!" Her eyes searched his, but he held steady and didn't flinch.

When she finally lowered her lids, he saw the disappointment that swept over her face. "You've won, but only for today. This is not over."

He didn't stop her when she walked down the stairs, but he followed her to the top of the stairs and watched her as she waited for Oliver to arrive. When his car pulled up in the driveway, she opened the door and left without looking back at him even though she had to know he was standing there.

Knowing he couldn't sleep now even if he tried, he walked into his living room, where Z slumbered peacefully.

"You're some watch dog! You bark at everything and you couldn't warn me about her?"

The dog only blinked briefly before continuing his siesta.

Chapter Sixteen

Quinn knocked on the door to Samson's private office and took another deep breath. He felt like a rat. It wasn't right that he'd been ordered to keep an eye on Zane. After all, he was Zane's oldest friend and should be supporting him. But there was also his loyalty to Scanguards and his own worry that his friend might be heading for a cliff.

He'd always seen it in Zane, the desperation that would sometimes grip him when he felt he'd failed in his mission to bring those monsters to justice—monsters like Müller and Brandt. Yet he'd never breathed a word about Zane's past to anybody in the organization. Nobody knew what Zane had been through. Even Quinn knew only the sketchiest of outlines. The rest he'd puzzled together by himself—and wished he hadn't. There was such a thing as too much information, and this particular information could turn anyone's stomach.

"Come," Samson's voice sounded from the study.

Quinn turned the antique doorknob and let himself in.

Samson wasn't alone. As expected, Gabriel was in attendance, like Samson waiting for his report on Zane's state of mind. After an obligatory shaking of hands, Quinn sat down on the comfortable armchair and looked straight at Samson.

"Glad you could join us. How was your flight?"

"As always, I was in the lap of luxury."

Samson grinned. "Yeah, we just upgraded the jet. With Delilah and the baby I wanted to make sure there's a little place for her to lie down."

"Little?" Quinn chuckled. "That bedroom suite is larger than my entire home in New York."

Gabriel rolled his eyes. "If you're angling for a pay raise, try again."

Quinn made a face. "Lucky me that I like to slum it."

Samson laughed. "Is that what they call it these days on Park Avenue?"

Quinn shrugged. "It's only a condo."

"A five thousand square foot full floor condo if I remember correctly," Gabriel added.

"In need of upgrades."

"Pleasantries aside, does Zane suspect the reason for your visit?" Samson asked.

"I don't think so. He was his usual abrasive self." Before entering the room Quinn had already made up his mind not to divulge anything about the assassin Zane had met with. It would require explaining the why and how, and he couldn't betray Zane's trust by giving away the secrets of his past.

"Good. Let's keep it that way."

Gabriel nodded in agreement and shifted his foot. "Have you noticed that he's more aggressive than usual?"

"Actually, no. In fact, he seems calmer than normal. Maybe that dog is doing him some good. Nice little beast." The puppy was a rambunctious little rascal and the perfect companion for Zane. "The dog even listens to Zane. Whenever he sits down, the pup jumps onto his lap. And Zane doesn't seem to mind."

Samson exchanged a grin with Gabriel. "Looks like my idea wasn't that bad after all."

"We'll see," Gabriel replied. "He's only had the dog for what, three days, four days? I'd like to see what long term effect he has on him."

"Is he sleeping?" Samson asked, looking back at Quinn.

"The dog? All day long."

"Not the dog, Zane."

Quinn couldn't suppress a grin. "He sure wasn't sleeping much during the last day."

Samson frowned, but Quinn waved him off quickly. "It's not what you think. He wasn't brooding. He had a woman over."

"I thought he never took women to his place," Samson mused.

Quinn shrugged. "Surprised the hell out of me too, but hey, there she was in his bed. And he wasn't even willing to share her. Must have been quite a catch. Hey, not that I'm pissed or anything. I can get my own women. But hey, it was quite a departure from his usual modus operandi." Which generally meant a quick fuck in the backroom of a club or bar, or even in an alley.

"Do you know whether he hurt her?" Gabriel asked.

Knowing that Zane wasn't one to shy away from mixing a little pain with his pleasure, Quinn wasn't at all surprised at Gabriel's question. However, he had no answer for it. "I was up for only a half hour or so. I didn't hear any screams if that's what you're asking. And this evening I found Zane sleeping on the couch with the dog curled up by his side. Must have been quite a day for him to be so exhausted. I had to wake him to make sure he got to his assignment on time."

Samson quietly contemplated Quinn's words before he spoke. "Well, at least it appears he's calm and under control. I spoke to Drake earlier. Of course, his ethics don't allow him to disclose what Zane spoke about in his session, but Drake knows when to warn me about erratic behavior. And there seemed to be none."

"Do you think he's trying to fool us by pretending to be calm and collected when he's not?" Gabriel asked, staring at Samson.

"He's doing a good job if that's the case," Quinn chimed in, not wanting them to suspect how agitated Zane really was.

The encounter with the assassin and the discovery that Müller was most likely behind a master race breeding program had shaken Zane up; Quinn could see that. Having a woman over for a little playtime had probably helped calm his nerves a little, but Quinn knew all too well that this wouldn't keep Zane calm forever. Only one thing would: finding the headquarters of the breeding program and eradicating its leader and top ranks.

Once the last of the monsters of his friend's past were destroyed, perhaps he could finally find peace.

"Keep an eye on him. If anything changes, alert us immediately. We don't want another killing."

Quinn nodded in agreement and rose. "I've got a few things to take care of. I'll check in with you periodically."

"Thanks, Quinn, you're a great help." Samson offered his hand in thanks, and Quinn shook it.

When he stalked out of Samson's Victorian home in Nob Hill and walked down the hill, he felt a heavy stone lifted from his shoulders. He hadn't said anything negative about Zane; he'd given nothing away that would even border on betrayal. Of course, Zane wouldn't see it that way. He'd still call him a snitch and toss him out on his ass. But if he were honest, even Zane would have to admit that Quinn was only helping him. As long as he could keep Samson and Gabriel pacified and make sure they found Zane to be no longer a danger to anyone, he was helping his friend rather than betraying him.

Having already checked out the Greyhound station on his way to Samson's, Quinn headed for the train station, hoping to have better luck finding the locker that could be opened by the key Zane had given him.

The rush hour crowd had long left the station, and only those individuals who worked late were now waiting for trains to take them home. Quinn surveyed the platforms. Two trains were in the station, a couple of dozen passengers loitered along the gates waiting for their train to show, and a station agent wandered near the ticket windows, consulting his watch on and off.

Everything looked normal. Yet Quinn had worked in security long enough not to be fooled by the appearance of normality. He was never lulled into complacency, or any sense that this would be an easy task. At any time, another attacker could strike. If Brandt's son had taken the precaution of not having identification on him so he couldn't be traced anywhere, it was clearly information others were guarding, and Quinn knew to exercise caution in trying to unearth such information.

Instead of heading straight for the lockers that he spotted at the entrance to platform one, he perused the departure board. Only five more trains were scheduled for the remainder of the night. He looked over the passengers waiting on the platforms. His suspicious nature was appeased when he confirmed that only those platforms where trains were due in the next half hour were occupied by people. Good. At least on the surface, it appeared as if only genuine travelers were at the station.

Quinn turned and wandered toward platform one. He'd memorized the number on the key and now scanned the rows and columns of lockers, looking for it. There weren't many, and he was lucky; his number was among them. He glanced over his shoulder and noticed the station agent pacing.

Turning his attention back to the lockers, Quinn reached into his pocket and pulled out the key. He inserted it into the lock and was encouraged momentarily when it turned, but there was only a click. He pulled, but the door didn't open.

Steps from behind him made him spin on his heels, ready to attack.

"If it doesn't open," the station agent drawled, "then you gotta put more money in it." He pointed toward a red flag over the lock that screamed EXPIRED.

"Oh, thanks." Quinn pulled a few coins from his jeans pocket and dropped them in. After the third coin, the flag switched to green. He twisted the handle and heard another click.

The little hairs on his nape stood in alert. Quickly, he sucked in a deep breath. Shit! A familiar scent reached his sensitive nostrils.

"Still not opening?" The station agent's hand came up and reached for the handle. "Sometimes you've gotta yank it." And he did.

"NOOOOOO!" Quinn screamed to stop the man from pulling on the door and jerking it open, but it was too late.

The explosion rocked him back and, acting purely on instinct, Quinn jumped, grabbed the man and hauled them both several feet down the platform. As he covered the station agent with his own body, searing heat passed over him and debris scattered. Luckily, his heavy leather coat provided some protection from the heat as well as the metal items that flew through the air.

"Shit!" he cursed again. He'd smelled the residue of the explosive the moment the station agent had gripped the door and yanked it open.

Excited voices and screams came from the waiting passengers, and from the corner of his eye he saw several people running. Quinn turned his head, surveying the crowd, but his eyes strayed into the distance to the far platform where one man stood, not having moved.

Their gazes met for an instant, and even from a distance of three hundred yards, Quinn recognized the aura of a vampire. He could have sworn the guy hadn't been there earlier.

Fuck!

He lifted himself off the station agent, who, although shaken, appeared uninjured. Helpful hands reached for him, but the good Samaritans were only getting in his way. When he looked back at the vampire, he was already gone.

Now all he could do was damage control. He counted: two dozen people had witnessed the explosion. He needed help. Pronto.

Chapter Seventeen

"Zane, I need you at the train station on 4th and King, now," Quinn's frantic voice sounded through his cell. In the background, Zane heard a commotion. "There was an explosion."

"Fuck! I'll be there in ten minutes."

"Make that five. We need damage control."

Zane flipped the phone shut and looked toward the stairs that led up to Portia's room.

"Portia! Come down now!" he yelled.

To his surprise, she rushed down the stairs a few second later, a stunned look on her face. "What's wrong?"

A hell of a lot of things, but he didn't have the time to explain.

"I have to take care of something right now. You'll have to come with me."

He snatched her arm and dragged her to the door.

"Hey, I'm coming, I'm coming. There's no need to be brutal."

Instantly, he released her arm. In his haste, he hadn't realized how roughly he'd grabbed her. "We have no time."

He shot out the door, Portia following on his heels. Luckily, he'd come with his Hummer today since he'd planned on seeing Samson toward the end of his shift. Since Samson lived clear across town, he'd decided not to waste time by walking. He was glad now that the car was parked right in the driveway.

He jumped in. A moment later, Portia entered through the passenger door, and he gunned the engine, shooting out of the driveway and down the hill seconds later.

The Hummer was built like a tank in more ways than one. Zane had only just recently had the windows coated with specially designed UV protection Thomas had invented. They, in effect, turned the car into a blackout van that a vampire could drive during daylight. No harmful rays of the sun could penetrate the windows. From the outside, the windows looked no different than the tinted windows of any SUV.

But not even the specially coated windows eliminated all risks a vampire took when driving a car. Getting into a traffic accident would be life threatening if it happened during the day, and any traffic stop was always a risk. At least, using mind control on some unsuspecting traffic cop would take care of being pulled over and forced to open the window, but if the windows broke during an accident, he'd be toast. Which was why the Hummer was also equipped with shatterproof and bulletproof glass. All precautions had been taken.

"Where are we going?"

Zane turned a tight corner and barreled down the narrow street trying to avoid the mirrors of the parked cars on either side of the street. "Train station."

He concentrated on the traffic, his superior senses alerting him to other cars, giving him a chance to avoid any collisions despite the fact that he was reaching speeds of fifty miles an hour.

Avoiding busy Sixteenth Street, he took a side street and pressed down the gas pedal further. Three minutes had passed since Quinn's call, and he was closing in on his destination. Depending on how many witnesses had seen the explosion, and how many people were injured, it would require both him and Quinn to make sure that the scene was contained, and that nobody would have any memory of Quinn.

"What happened?" Portia's voice pushed through his thoughts.

"An explosion."

Her mouth dropped open. "Oh my god. Is anybody injured?"

"I don't know." If they were, at least he and Quinn could heal them with vampire blood, but if somebody had died, they'd be too late.

The train station came up on the right, and he pulled the SUV to a stop, the tires screeching. He killed the engine.

"You stay here."

"But, I can h—"

He glared at her. "You stay here. Don't leave the car!"

Zane jumped out and slammed the door. It would have been better if he'd been able to come on his own, but he couldn't risk leaving Portia alone in the house. She might use the occasion to run out on him and go to whatever fucking party was happening tonight. Those students for sure had a party each night.

At least with her only a few yards away, he'd be able to catch her if she pulled a runner.

He charged into the station and scanned his surroundings, spotting Quinn instantly. A group of people stood around, talking excitedly.

Some were on their cell phones, most likely alerting the authorities or their friends.

Zane rushed to Quinn's side.

"Help me wipe their memories of me," Quinn requested. "There are too many for me to stop them from calling the police. All we can do is make sure they've never seen me."

Zane nodded. "Are you all right?"

"Yes."

"Anybody injured?"

"No. Help me." Quinn pointed to a few people now sitting on benches. "I already took care of those."

Zane concentrated and let his powers flow to the group that was standing near the lockers, gawking at the damaged structure. Warm energy flowed through him as he sent his thoughts out to them, infiltrated their minds and planted his own suggestions in them, erasing any memory of how the explosion had happened and who they had seen.

Minutes passed in tense silence as he and Quinn worked side by side.

"I think we got them all," Quinn whispered.

Zane looked at him. "Now tell me what happened."

"Is anybody injured?" Portia's voice came from behind him.

Zane whirled around and glared at her. "I told you to stay in the car."

She planted her hands on her hips. "I wanted to see if I could help."

Portia craned her neck to look past him, but he simply grabbed her elbow and led her outside. He could sense Quinn behind him and cringed, hoping that his friends wouldn't be able to connect Portia to the smell of his visitor from the day before.

"Hey, Zane, don't you wanna introduce us?" Quinn planted himself next to Zane and smiled at Portia.

"Portia, that's Quinn," he grunted reluctantly.

When Quinn shook her hand and inhaled, Zane noticed his nostril flaring. A sideways glance confirmed that Quinn indeed recognized her scent as that of the woman in his bed the day before. Well, maybe all could still be saved. Quinn never needed to know who she was.

"Nice to meet you, Quinn. Are you a bodyguard like Zane?"

He nodded. "One of the best. And you?"

Portia opened her mouth to respond.

"Quinn, can we talk about the explosion?" Zane tried to steer the conversation into another direction.

"Oh, I'm Zane's assignment," Portia talked over him.

Shit, he shouldn't have risked taking her along.

"Assignment?" Quinn's head turned slowly and his gaze crashed into Zane's glare. He lowered his voice. "This is your *charge*?"

The warning was clear in the tone of Quinn's voice. After what he'd seen last night, he would assume the worst. "It's not what it looks like."

"Where have I heard that before?"

"Can we talk about the explosion now?" Zane gritted between his teeth.

Quinn narrowed his eyes. "Fine. But this discussion isn't over."

Police sirens blared in the distance.

"Let's get out of here before the police arrive," Quinn suggested.

Zane couldn't agree more and pointed toward his Hummer. "Get in."

As soon as they'd all climbed in the car, Zane started the engine and drove down the Embarcadero. At a quiet spot, he parked the car and turned in his seat, looking at Quinn who occupied the back seat.

"Now give me the lowdown. What happened?"

"The locker was rigged with an explosive device. I smelled it, but that stupid station agent pulled the handle before I could stop him and the whole thing blew apart. We were lucky nobody got injured. I think your assassin planned for every eventuality."

"Assassin?" Portia echoed. "Somebody is trying to kill you?"

Zane turned his attention to her. He shouldn't have brought her. There was no reason for her to know all this. Yet, at the same time he wanted her to know what his life was like, the dangers he faced daily, the dangers she would face if she were with him. Was it so she would run the other way, or was he trying to gather sympathy from her? What the fuck was he trying to do?

He shrugged. "There's always somebody out there who wants to kill me. What else is new?"

"But, that's terrible." Her hand clamped over his forearm. Shit, she was offering sympathy. He should have known that this kind of news wouldn't make her shy away from him.

"It's not all," Quinn added, undeterred. "Somebody was watching. I saw him just after the explosion."

"Human or vampire?" Zane asked.

"Vampire, possibly Hybrid. I couldn't tell from that distance. But he saw me, and he knew I was trying to get at the contents of the locker."

Zane clenched his jaw. "Do you think they sent him after Brandt didn't come back?"

"Very possible. They probably knew what he was planning and had instructions to come look for him if he didn't come back."

Zane was afraid that Quinn was right. "Then they know now that we're onto them. They're warned."

"Who are they?" Portia interrupted.

She already knew too much. He wasn't going to tell her anything else. "You don't need to know." Then he looked back at Quinn. "Anything salvageable from the locker?"

"I lifted a cell phone. It's all mangled and melted."

Zane twisted his lips. "If he left his cell phone in the locker, I'm guessing he rigged the locker himself."

"Could have been the vampire I saw after the explosion."

"We both know how these things work: you go on a mission, but you don't want to be traced in case things don't work out. So you stash away any items that could identify you or where you came from, and you protect them."

"With a little bomb," Quinn interjected.

"Right. If everything goes well, you disable the bomb and get your stuff back. If it doesn't, you make sure your enemies get blown to bits if they find the locker." Zane made a movement with his hands, indicating an explosion.

"I would tend to agree with you. Unfortunately, there's no way to know now if the bomb he planted could be easily disabled by Brandt. Therefore, we can't rule out the possibility that the vampire I saw planted the cell phone and the bomb so we'd get a false lead."

"In either case, we need to follow this lead."

Quinn nodded in agreement. "I'll give the cell to Thomas. Maybe he can get some info from the chip, if he can pry if out of that mess."

"It's worth a try. Can you have him look at it without telling him what it's for?" All he needed right now was Scanguards finding out what shit he was in right now. Besides, this was private. It had nothing to do with Scanguards.

"He owes me a favor. He won't ask any questions."

"Then do it." Zane started the engine.

***

Even after Zane had dropped Quinn off, Portia's head was still spinning. She realized how much of a sheltered life she'd really lived so far, because while she was certain that her father, like any vampire, probably had enemies, or had to hide from people, she'd never felt the kind of danger that Quinn had just escaped. And that Zane might still be facing.

"Somebody is trying to kill you?"

Zane gave her a sideways glance before training his eyes back on the street, driving much slower than before. "Wouldn't be a first."

"But why? What did you do?"

"Why does it have to be something *I* did?"

Portia let the words sink in. "Oh. Then what do they want from you?"

"You don't want to know."

"I do."

"Let me rephrase that: it's none of your business." Despite the reprimand, his voice was even.

"What happened to the assassin Quinn mentioned?"

"I shouldn't have brought you with me."

"That's not an answer. So, what happened to him? Did he get away?" She wouldn't rest until she found out what was going on.

"What do you think?" he challenged.

A shiver ran down her arms, creating goose bumps under the sleeves of her sweater. Instinct answered the question for her. "You killed him."

"Does that shock you?"

She swallowed and contemplated her next words. Was she shocked? Disgusted? Afraid? "No."

Zane turned his gaze toward her, clearly stunned. "I killed him without a second thought. And I would do it again."

"If you're trying to scare me, it's not working." Hell, why wasn't it? Why was she not afraid that if Zane could so easily kill somebody, he wouldn't hurt her? Hadn't she pissed him off often enough to warrant his wrath? Wasn't that reason enough why she should be careful around him now?

When he simply grunted to himself and concentrated on traffic, she slid her palm onto his thigh. Instantly, his muscles shifted under her touch.

"Shit, Portia, stop that."

She couldn't. Her body was on fire, the knowledge that he was in danger making her quest to have him even more urgent. "Are you gonna hurt me if I don't?"

She noticed how tightly he clenched his jaw together as if to ward off some invisible pain.

"You could pull over somewhere and lock the doors. Nobody will see us. The windows are tinted. Nobody would ever know what we did."

Zane slammed on the breaks and yanked the car to the curb. His eyes glaring red, he grasped her hand and pulled it off his thigh. "You're playing with fire, Portia. Can't you get that into your head? I'm a killer, I'm brutal, and I can't be controlled. You don't want me."

"I do," she whispered, ignoring her thundering heart and her galloping pulse. More than ever, she wanted to scream, but the last remaining shred of pride she had wouldn't let her.

"You shouldn't, baby girl. I'm no good."

The sad look he gave her tore her heart in two. And whenever he called her 'baby girl', something inside her just melted, even if he didn't mean it as an endearment but derogatorily, as a way to put her in her place.

Instinctively, she raised her palm and reached for his face, wanting to stroke his cheek and show him that he too deserved love. But he was too quick; he pulled back and slipped the Hummer in gear.

She was crazy, but now that she knew he was in danger, she felt this inexplicable urge to protect him. It was stupid, of course. After all, he was a bodyguard and there to protect her, not the other way around. Besides, he didn't want her help. His abrasive behavior was clear indication that he wanted to keep his distance from her.

"Can we go for a drive?"

"Why?" he retorted.

"I don't want to go home yet. I feel cooped up there."

"I understand."

Surprised at his response she looked at his profile. Maybe they weren't that different after all. They were both essentially alone. And while she didn't have an assassin gunning for her, she had a deadline looming over her head that felt just as urgent. Five weeks to her birthday and the day her body would set into its final form, never to change again. She had choices to make: how long she wanted to keep her hair, whether she should lose a pound or two before, things that seemed trivial all of a sudden.

"What's it like to be turned?" She'd been born into it, but for a vampire like Zane, who'd been human once, it had to have been a different experience.

The knuckles of Zane's hands grew white as he gripped the steering wheel tighter. "It's hell."

Her heart clenched instinctively. "I'm sorry."

"Why?"

"Ever heard of compassion?" Could he not even accept that she was sorry for the pain he'd gone through? That she wished so much to be able to soothe it?

Zane ignored her remark. "I survived. But they've paid for it."

"Paid?" She held her breath, not sure whether she wanted to know or not.

He graced her with a sideways glance. "The men who turned me."

"There was more than one?" She didn't quite understand.

"There was a group of them. They're dead now, all but one of them." Then he sought her eyes, locked his gaze with hers, and continued, "I killed them, one by one, slowly and painfully."

Portia gasped, her heart stuttering to a complete halt. She wanted to say something, but no words came over her lips. He'd killed the men who'd turned him. Men? "I don't understand. Did several vampires turn you?"

He shook his head and looked back at traffic. They were driving through a golf course now, but Portia didn't look out the window to enjoy the view.

"There were five of them. And they were human."

"But—"

Zane cut her off. "I don't want to talk about it. So, either you stop asking about it or I'll drive you home now."

Portia clamped her mouth shut and nodded.

A few moments later, Zane stopped the car and turned off the engine.

"There's a great view of the Golden Gate Bridge from here."

He opened the door and climbed out. Portia followed him and crossed the street. Beyond it was another hole of the golf course, and past that she saw the San Francisco Bay and the Golden Gate Bridge which stretched over its entrance. Illuminated by lights, it shone in red and orange colors.

"It's beautiful," she admitted, and stopped next to Zane.

"Beauty has its price. Eleven men died during construction."

Portia sighed. "Do you always have to see the negative in everything?"

"I try not to forget that where there is beauty, misery isn't far behind."

"Have you always been a pessimist?"

"Only youth is optimistic because they don't know any better," he countered.

"And you do?"

He nodded. "I've seen more in my life than I ever cared to see."

"But not everything can have been as bad as you make it out to be. You must have experienced good things: friendship, love."

If only he would allow her closer, perhaps she could be the one who he would share those emotions with. The cool night air made her shiver, or maybe it was the tension between them that suddenly made the air between them seem to tingle.

"It's getting late. I should get you home. You've got classes tomorrow."

The moment was gone. Zane wouldn't let her get any closer tonight, she understood that much about him. She might as well pack up and save her energy for tomorrow night.

Chapter Eighteen

It was still dark outside when Oliver showed up to relieve him. He looked tired, and Zane felt compelled to ease his mind.

"She won't give you any trouble today."

Oliver raised a doubting eyebrow. "Right." Shrugging off his jacket, he stepped farther into the living room. "I swear that girl is more difficult to guard than a hardened criminal."

Zane almost wanted to smile—almost, but of course, he didn't. He never smiled. "I know what you mean." Did he ever! "I talked to her about the stunt she pulled yesterday. Trust me, she won't do it again."

"And how do you know that? The moment you turn around, she's gonna use mind control on me again and escape."

"She won't. She knows what the consequences are."

"What did you threaten her with? Torture?"

"Something like that." Unfortunately, if he really made good on quitting this assignment if she gave him any more trouble, it would be more torture for himself than for her.

"I tell you, it sucks that she's part vampire, and I'm not. Puts me at a huge disadvantage."

This wasn't the first time Oliver had praised the advantages a vampire had over a human. Zane always wondered if the kid would one day ask Samson for permission to be turned. But did Oliver really know what he was asking for?

"Being a vampire isn't all that it's cracked up to be."

"In what way?" Oliver shot back.

"For starters, no more days on the beach," Zane responded lightheartedly. For a moment, he wondered whether he really missed the sun. He'd been living in the dark for so long that he could barely remember what it would be like to enjoy the rays of the sun on his skin. Besides, the darkness suited his mood. Particularly right now.

"Like there's ever any beach weather in San Francisco. The entire summer is fogged in, and when we do get our obligatory three days of hot beach weather, it happens on a Wednesday afternoon when everybody has to work."

There was some truth to Oliver's statement. "Yep, the weather is a little temperamental here. Of course, you could always call in sick."

Oliver frowned. Nope, the kid wouldn't neglect his duties. His loss.

"So, if that's the only thing I'm giving up by becoming a vampire, it's not a hard choice to make."

Zane shook his head. "The turning is painful."

"I'm no wuss."

"Nobody's saying you are."

"For gaining immortality and all those awesome powers I don't mind going through some pain."

"With all those powers comes vulnerability. Besides, a long life can be very lonely." Like Zane's. Lonely and consumed with hatred.

"I wouldn't worry about that." He flashed his charming grin. "Imagine, I can have all the girls I want."

"Right." As if that had anything to do with being a vampire.

Zane consulted his watch. "I'd better go."

"See you tonight."

Zane headed for his Hummer and drove to Samson's house in Nob Hill. Since it was well before sunrise, the streets were nearly deserted. He preferred it that way.

He pulled in front of Samson's garage and parked the car. Lights were ablaze in the Victorian mansion. He knew that even Delilah had adjusted her habits to be awake during the night and asleep during the day so she and Samson could live a near-normal life. Well, as normal as living with a vampire could ever be.

Samson opened the door himself and ushered him inside.

"You wanted to see me?"

Zane nodded.

"Let's go to my office."

Zane followed on Samson's heels and practiced in his head how to start the conversation. Unfortunately, he wasn't one for diplomacy, and there was really no easy way to talk about what he needed to say.

When he shut the door behind him, Samson turned to face him, resting his butt on the massive mahogany desk.

"So, what's going on?"

Zane shifted his feet and tried to adopt a casual stance but failed. "It's about my assignment."

Samson raised a hand. "Hold it right there. We've gone through this.

We decided that you'd have a low stress, low risk job for a while until things have blown over and we can be sure—"

"That's not what it's about. We shouldn't have accepted the job."

Samson gave him a stunned look. "What? Listen, Zane, just because you're not keen on this assignment doesn't—"

Zane interrupted once more. "We shouldn't have taken it, because what we're doing to this girl isn't right."

Samson narrowed his eyes. "Are you questioning Gabriel's and my decision?"

Zane widened his stance. "Yes, I am."

"Explain yourself."

"Do you have any idea what her father is asking us to do?"

Samson clenched his jaw. "If you need clarification beyond what's in your briefing file, I'm more than happy to explain it to you again: she's a volatile young woman who's grieving for her mother and acting out. We're there to make sure she doesn't hurt herself."

"Bullshit!" Zane spat. "That's what her father is trying to make us believe. It's a lie."

Samson pushed himself off the desk and squared his stance. "You'd better have something to back up that accusation."

"Portia's father is trying to keep her away from any men so she won't have a chance of losing her virginity before her twenty-first birthday."

"Get real."

Zane could virtually see what was going through Samson's mind. As a father of a hybrid daughter himself, he knew what this meant. And by the frown on his face, Zane understood that Samson would never impose this fate on his own daughter. He would make sure she would lose her virginity well before her body set into its final form, even if he had to line up potential lovers himself.

"Nobody would do that to his own daughter." Samson's voice was firm as he ran his hand through his full, raven-black hair.

"He's doing it."

"And how would you know that?" Impatience crept into Samson's hazel eyes.

"She told me." The circumstances under which he'd found out, however, were none of Samson's business. Hell, they were nobody's business but Portia's and his own.

"Just like that?"

"I caught her trying to escape, so she told me." Well, that was close enough to the truth. That they'd kissed for the first time that night didn't matter. The truth was still the truth.

"Interesting," Samson mused. "And the fact that she's trying to manipulate you with this sob story hasn't crossed your mind?"

Of course Portia was manipulating him, but not the way Samson suspected. She was trying to get him to sleep with her. And fuck, he wanted that. "She's not manipulating me."

"I think you're being played."

Zane cursed. "Nobody is playing me! Don't you see what he's trying to do to her? She'll be twenty-one in five weeks, and she'll still be a virgin. Do you really want that on your conscience?"

"I've figured you for a lot of stuff, Zane, but gullible wasn't one of them. You have a lot to learn about young women. She's practically a teenager. She'll do anything to get around her father's rules. She'll lie, she'll make up stories to elicit your sympathy. Heck, that's why we chose you for this job: because you don't soften when somebody tells you a sob story."

"It's not a sob story. Her father is condemning her to a life as a virgin. Do you have any idea what that means for her?"

"Don't lecture me on this issue. I know what it means. And I know that no father in his right mind would want that on his daughter. He loves her. All he's trying to do is protect her from herself."

"That's a lie!"

Samson huffed. "Fine. You wanna know how I know she's lying to you?" He rounded his desk and opened a drawer. A moment later, a manila file landed on top of the desk.

"Open it, look on page three."

Hesitating, Zane took a step and reached for the folder. He slowly opened it and turned to page three. He scanned the notes. Halfway down, his eyes stopped.

One of her favorite lies is to claim she's a virgin and her father is trying to prevent her from losing her virginity, it read.

"No …" Zane shook his head. Had she lied to him? Had she made it all up so she could gain his sympathy and goad him into sleeping with her? Was she some sort of nymphomaniac who couldn't keep her hands off the men around her?

No, he couldn't believe it. At the beginning, her kiss had been so innocent. Her reactions to him were honest.

"Do you believe me now?" Samson asked.

Just because it was written in black and white, didn't mean it had to be true. But he didn't contradict Samson any further. Samson was wrong; they were all wrong about Portia. He knew her better. He'd seen her tears when she'd told him about her fate. He'd looked deep into her and understood that there was no pretense, no lie to her words.

"She wouldn't lie to me."

Then he turned and left Samson's office, ignoring his boss' voice calling after him.

***

Samson tossed and glanced at the clock on his bedside table. It was still mid-afternoon.

"I know it's bothering you," Delilah said softly and sat up.

It was one of the drawbacks of being blood-bonded: your mate always knew when something was wrong, and when he couldn't sleep, Delilah couldn't either.

"I'm sorry, sweetness," he said and turned toward her, pulling her into his arms. "But something doesn't feel right."

"Do you think that Zane's claim has any merit at all?"

"No. You know as well as I do that no father would do that to his daughter. You know I wouldn't."

She smiled at him, and he felt the love between them radiate. "I suspect you'll run background checks on any man who comes near Isabelle?"

Samson grinned. "You bet. But as soon as she's eighteen, she'll be entertaining offers. And he'd better be gentle with her, or I'm gonna take his head off."

Delilah pressed her lips to his cheek. "What's really bothering you about what Zane said if you don't believe he's right?"

"It's not what he said, but how he said it. As if he knew something that nobody else did. Delilah, he believed her. Zane isn't someone to trust or be easily fooled. Something happened there. He wasn't as cold and indifferent as he normally is. He was passionate about this issue."

"You don't think there could be something going on?" She shook her head instantly. "Zane is more loyal to Scanguards than anybody else. He would never do anything that goes against your rules."

"I'm not so sure about that anymore. When he was here earlier, I sensed him wanting to rebel. He questioned my judgment without being able to back it up with facts. That's not like him. He's acting on emotion."

"Isn't that a good thing? Wasn't that always your worry about Zane, that he's too cold, too emotionless? Maybe Drake's getting through to him."

"After one session? I doubt that very much. No, something else must have happened."

"With the girl?"

Samson hoped he was wrong, but somehow his gut told him to check it out. He would never forgive himself if something happened because he hadn't done his due diligence.

"What are you gonna do?"

He sat up and reached for the phone. "Check in with Oliver. See whether she told him the same story."

Delilah already knew what he was thinking, their telepathic bond sensing his next thoughts. "If she did, then she's playing everybody, but if she didn't, then it's got to do with Zane."

Oliver's cell rang only once before he picked it up and answered it quietly. "Samson?" In the background, there was chatter. Samson figured that he was still at the university.

"Can you talk?"

"Sure. Portia is just saying good-bye to her friends. We're heading back home in a moment."

"Listen, this might sound like an odd question, but has Portia fed you any sob story about what her father is trying to do to her so you'd let her out of your sight?" Samson deliberately didn't say anything about her claim that she needed to lose her virginity. He didn't want to ask a leading question.

There was a short hesitation on Oliver's part before he answered. "No, she's been fine. Hangs out with Lauren mostly. She goes to all her classes like a model student and is pretty agreeable."

"So she hasn't tried to escape you or tried to gain your sympathy?"

"No. Definitely not."

Odd. Samson exchanged a look with Delilah who shrugged.

"Thanks, Oliver, good job."

He disconnected and dialed another number. He wasn't satisfied with Oliver's answers. Model student? That didn't sound like the girl her father had been describing to Gabriel.

"Hey, Samson," Thomas answered his phone, his voice a little groggy. "Please tell me there's a good reason you're interrupting my sleep."

"Sorry, Thomas, but I'm worried about Zane."

"What has he done now?"

"Nothing, it's more like what he *said*—or didn't say. I need your opinion."

"Sure."

"You covered for him when he went to Drake's. What kind of impression did you get of Portia?"

"I'm not sure what you mean. She seemed nice, polite even."

"Did she try to gain your sympathy by giving you some bull story about why her father has us protect her?"

"No. What was she supposed to tell me?"

"Zane came to see me tonight. He claimed that she told him that her father is trying to keep her imprisoned so she won't have a chance at losing her virginity before her twenty-first birthday in five weeks."

There was a pause. Then, "Oh, shit."

Thomas' curse made Samson's body coil in tension.

"Does that mean she told you too?"

"No. But—Samson, this is not good." Thomas cleared his throat.

Instantly alert, Samson pressed the phone closer to his ear. "What do you know? Tell me now."

"Listen, Samson, I'm not one to rat of my friends, but … when I went to Portia's house the other night … I could smell her on him. As if they'd been kissing."

"Fuck!"

"I can't be sure," Thomas hastened to add.

"Fuck, Thomas, you should have told me!"

"Damn it, Samson, I couldn't. I warned Zane. He knew he was on notice. But this, I mean, knowing that she wants to lose her virginity, that changes things."

"It's all a lie, Thomas. There's no way she's still a virgin. No father would allow that to happen to his hybrid daughter. She's using the story to manipulate him so she gets what she wants. And Zane is stupid enough to fall for it."

"You have to pull him off the assignment."

"I should have never put him on it in the first place. It was a huge mistake. He can't be allowed to ever touch her again."

"I hope it's not too late," Thomas mused.

Samson shook his head. He hadn't smelled anything suspicious on Zane and was pretty sure he hadn't touched Portia last night. But he couldn't risk having Zane near her any longer. It would violate the trust their client had placed in Scanguards: to keep his daughter safe. Exposing her to a vampire who would go against her father's strict instructions would break that trust and jeopardize Scanguards' integrity.

"I need you to take over from Oliver at sunset." At least with Thomas he knew there would be no problems: he was not susceptible to a woman's charms, no matter how enticing she might be. It was one advantage of having a gay vampire on staff.

"I'm on it."

"Thanks." He pressed the disconnect button.

"And now?" Delilah asked.

"Zane is in for a dressing down." A major dressing down.

Chapter Nineteen

Zane reared up from his bed, for a brief moment wondering what had awakened him, when he heard the sound once more: his cell phone was vibrating. He snatched it from the bedside table and looked at caller ID.

Shit, it was never good to get a call from one's boss at this time of day.

"Samson, what—?"

"I'm taking you off your assignment. As of immediately!" Samson's voice sounded decidedly pissed off.

An instant curse escaped him before he could clamp his mouth shut. "Fuck!"

"Yeah, you fucked up big time. I want to see you in my office a half hour after sunset!"

"What the fuck did I do?"

"Oh, you know very well what you did. You touch that girl once more, and I'll have your head for it. Are we clear?"

Shit, fuck, crap!

Quinn!

That bastard had told Samson that Portia had been at his place, in his bed even. And Zane had pretended that night that he'd had a woman there for sex. Quinn, that fucking traitor, had promptly run to Samson and ratted on him.

"In my office a half hour after sunset!" Samson repeated and disconnected the call.

Zane slammed his fist into the mattress, his mood as dark as it had ever been. He bolted from the bed, ready to beat his friend to a pulp. Friend? He had no friend!

How could Quinn go behind his back like that? Without even a warning!

Black hate chased disappointment as he considered Quinn's action and what it meant. Two things came to mind instantly: Portia would remain a virgin her entire life, and Zane would never see her again.

Both options hurt equally. Hurt him, the man who thought he could feel no more pain because he'd felt it all before. But it was as strong as ever: white hot pain as if somebody were driving a hot iron through his beating heart. Yes, it was beating, harder than before, but not because he needed his heart to pump blood through his veins, but because he felt compassion for another person: Portia.

Despite the things that were written in her file, in his heart he knew that she had told him the truth. She might have tried to manipulate him in other ways, but he couldn't deny what was in her eyes.

And he'd be damned if he'd desert her now and leave her in the care of people who didn't believe her.

He rocked to a halt in front of Quinn's bedroom and retreated. It wouldn't do him any good to satisfy his need for revenge right now. Quinn would get the beating he deserved soon enough. For now, Zane needed to take care of more important things.

As quietly as his anger allowed him to move, he went into his bedroom suite and got dressed. A quick look at his watch confirmed that it was still at least two hours to sunset. It didn't matter. He had to act now and get a head start before anybody caught onto what he was planning.

Zane snuck down the stairs, carefully avoiding those that creaked. In the hallway, he turned toward the door that led into the garage.

A soft whine made him spin around. Z looked at him, eyes big, his tail wagging excitedly.

"Go back to sleep," he whispered.

Apparently the animal didn't understand and jumped up his leg, hugging his calf.

Zane crouched down. "No, you can't come."

Big round eyes begged him to reconsider.

Ah, shit!

"Fine," he growled low and dark. "But don't complain if you're freezing."

He grabbed the dog and hooked him under his arm, then slid through the door into the garage. He didn't bother switching on any lights, and instantly opened the door to his Hummer, plopping onto the driver's seat quickly.

He set Z onto the back seat and eased the door of the vehicle shut.

When he started the engine, he cringed inwardly, hoping that the noise wouldn't wake Quinn. His bedroom was in the back of the house, away from the garage, and since his guest hadn't gotten used to the particular noises of this neighborhood, he could only hope that Quinn thought the sound of a car starting or the garage door opening belonged to the adjacent house.

Zane pressed the automatic garage door opener and backed out of the garage as soon as it had lifted sufficiently enough. It closed behind him as he backed onto the street and drove off.

Traffic in the late afternoon in the Mission was murder. It was always a risk to be out during daytime, even in a specially equipped car or one of the blackout vans Scanguards possessed to transport vampires during daylight hours. One accident was enough to put a vampire at risk for death. It was one of the reasons he'd bought a Hummer. Very little could damage the car that was practically built like a personal tank.

He was as safe in this car as he'd ever be outside during daytime. Still, it was a risk, but one he couldn't avoid today.

As he navigated through traffic, he dialed Portia's cell number.

It took two rings before she picked up. Before she could say a single word, he issued his order. "Say 'hi, Lauren'."

"Hi, Lauren." Portia's voice shook for a second, but she caught herself immediately. "What' going on?"

Relief flooded him at her quick comprehension. "Listen carefully. Do you still want to lose your virginity?"

"Yes, of course."

"Are you sure you want me to do it?"

"Yes."

"Don't just give one word answers, it sound suspicious if Oliver is listening."

"Oh, that would be lovely, Lauren. When do you think we could do that?"

"That's more like it."

"What made you think of that?" she asked.

"My boss is pulling me off the assignment."

"Oh, no!"

"Knowing Samson, he'll assign somebody to you who won't give you a chance to get away."

"That's so unfair." She paused. "Lauren, that sucks."

"Go up to your room now. Pack a few things, warm stuff mostly, sturdy shoes, a thick jacket. Things you need for a few nights."

"A few?"

"Unless you don't want to."

"No, I'd really like that, Lauren."

"Good. I'll give you ten minutes. As soon as you hear Oliver's phone ring, climb out your window like you did the other night. I'll keep him on the phone and distract him. Run through the back garden and climb over your neighbor's fence. I'll be in a black Hummer on the street behind you. You know how to get there?"

"Sure. That's a great idea."

"When you get in the car, make it quick. I'm not in the mood for a sunburn."

"Thanks. I appreciate it."

Zane disconnected the call and steered the car clear of a truck, which was double parked. His car sped through the next light before he finally left the Mission behind him and entered Noe Valley.

Traffic was lighter once he crossed busy Twenty-fourth Street and reached the predominantly residential area. One block from Portia's house, he turned off her street and went around the block to turn into the street parallel to hers. He counted the homes and parked right in front of the home that was directly behind Portia's.

Zane put the car in park and turned off the engine. He couldn't risk Oliver hearing the engine running over the phone when he called him.

After sending a text message to a contact, he consulted his watch. He waited two more minutes, hoping he'd given Portia enough time to throw a few things into a bag. Then he picked up his phone again and dialed Oliver's number.

The kid picked up on the second ring. "Hey, Zane. You're up early."

Zane forced himself to sound casual. "Damn dog keeps waking me up in the middle of the day. I swear I'm gonna give him back to Yvette."

"Yeah, that's why I don't have pets. Too much responsibility."

"Yep. Listen, Oliver, about what we talked earlier, about you thinking it would be cool to be a vampire."

"Yes?" Oliver's voice lifted in interest.

Perfect, he'd found the right subject to keep Oliver busy for a few minutes. He wouldn't hear Portia open her window and jump out in the garden.

***

Portia felt giddy with excitement. It was really happening. Zane had decided to help her. Tonight, she would lose her virginity, and it would be at Zane's hands. Whatever had made him suddenly make this decision, she didn't want to investigate right now. His claim that his boss was taking him off his assignment of protecting her probably had something to do with it. But there had been no time to ask him about it, particularly not with Oliver within earshot.

At least she'd fooled him into thinking she was talking to Lauren, even though she'd said goodbye to Lauren only a short while earlier.

She rummaged through her closet and pulled out a few pieces, not really knowing what she should take. Darn, if he'd only given her a little more warning, she could have figured out what to wear and maybe even gone to Victoria's Secret to get some suitable underwear. Now all she could find in a hurry were boring panties and a plain bra without frills. Great! That didn't sound very romantic!

When she heard Oliver's cell phone suddenly ring from downstairs, she suppressed a curse and threw the garment in her hand into her backpack and zipped it up. She snatched her boots from the bottom of her closet and rushed to the window.

As quietly as possible, Portia shoved the window open and threw out the backpack, followed by her boots. She quickly lowered herself out of the window and let go of the sill. Her landing made no sound. She was getting good at this.

She darted cautious looks to her left and right and listened for any sound from inside the house, but it was quiet. Picking up her backpack in one hand and her boots in the other, she ran toward the fence and vaulted herself over it with ease despite the height. Vampire strength and speed were handy at times.

The neighbor's garden was empty, and she hoped nobody would see her and alert Oliver to her escape. She ran along the low bushes and hit the tiled garden path. Her socks soaked up the dirt from the ground, but she didn't want to take the time to put on her boots until she was at a safe distance.

Running past the trashcans, she reached for the gate and flung it open. The street beckoned.

"Hey!" a male voice called after her, but she didn't care what her neighbor thought.

Portia didn't turn and continued running into the street, her eyes searching for the black Hummer. It sat double-parked in front of the house to her right. The headlights flashed at her.

Zane!

For a fraction of a second, she wondered whether she was making a mistake by trusting a man she barely knew and allowing him to practically kidnap her. But the thought fled just as quickly as it had come. Her heart beat faster, not from the brisk run, but from the knowledge that she would be with Zane, the man who excited her beyond all others.

She could still turn around now, but then she would be no further than before. No, Zane would keep her safe.

As she reached the Hummer, she remembered his words to be quick about entering the car. She jerked the door open, threw her backpack and shoes to the floor of the passenger seat and jumped in, slamming the door shut with the same movement.

The engine howled, and she was jolted forward, bracing herself on the dashboard.

"Hold on tight."

Zane's voice was on edge, driving home the fact that what they were doing was against not only her father's wishes but also Scanguards' rules. She knew that he would get in trouble for this. But there was no turning back now.

"Where are we going?" she asked as she tugged on the seatbelt and clicked it.

"Somewhere where nobody will find us. Make sure your cell is turned off."

She pulled her phone from her pocket. "Why?"

"Scanguards has your number. They'll be able to triangulate your location with the help of signals between the cell towers."

She shivered at the thought that they were running away.

"Are you afraid?"

Portia quickly shook her head. "No." She wasn't afraid; she was terrified. Terrified of what was going to happen. What if she didn't like it? What if this was a mistake? But she couldn't chicken out now. She had to do this. Zane was most likely risking his job for her; she couldn't bow out now.

"We can still turn back if you've changed your mind."

She looked at him, and he turned his face to her, his eyes gleaming with understanding. But beneath it, she saw the disappointment that loomed there, disappointment that would surface if she pulled back now.

A bark from the backseat bought her time to answer. She leaned sideways and found a Labrador puppy staring at her.

"You have a dog?"

She already reached for the little pup and pulled him onto her lap.

"You're going to spoil him. He's not trained, and by the looks of it, he never will be."

Portia petted the animal's soft fur. "What's his name?"

"Z."

"Z? Just one letter?"

"That's all he gets. He's a pest." Despite the words, Zane's voice was warm, attesting to his affection for the dog.

Zane hadn't just left him behind. He'd brought the puppy with him. Didn't that mean that he cared, that he was responsible, and definitely not as indifferent as he tried to make himself out to be? A man who had a dog, especially such a cute one, was a man who had a heart and feelings.

It sealed it for her. She could trust him. He would take care of her just like he took care of the dog. "Let's get wherever you want us to go."

There was something in his face that could almost be called a smile, or at least the beginning of one: his lips twitched and curved upwards by a tiny fraction of an inch.

"How far is it?"

"We'll be there in four hours."

"I can't wait." She lifted her hand from the pup and slid it onto Zane's thigh, suddenly feeling courageous. His muscles bunched just as they had the last time she'd done that. No reprimand followed her bold action.

"Maybe I can make that three and a half hours," he conceded and placed his hand over hers, not to remove it, but to capture it where it was.

"I'd like that." Portia had never heard her own voice sound that husky before.

When their gazes collided for a fleeting moment, awareness made her body burn with unquenchable lust, a lust she saw reflected in Zane's eyes.

Yes, this was the right decision. The only decision. Zane would be hers. Soon.

Chapter Twenty

Quinn slammed the door to the empty garage shut and pressed his cell back to his ear.

"Shit, he's taken the Hummer. And the dog is gone too."

On the other line, Oliver let out a low curse. "Damn it! I was hoping she'd run to him. Have you checked his bedroom?"

"He's gone, Oliver. And by the looks of it, he's taken Portia with him." Why hadn't he seen that coming? That was exactly the kind of thing Samson had asked him to come and watch Zane for—and to prevent.

"Shit, what am I gonna do now? Samson will have my hide for this." There was fear in Oliver's voice.

Quinn felt for him. This was his first big assignment, and he was screwing it up royally. No, actually, Zane was screwing him over big time.

"Pick me up at Zane's house. Let's go to Samson's together."

"Thanks, Quinn."

Ten minutes later, a glum-looking Oliver picked him up with one of the limousines. In another twenty minutes they were in Nob Hill and parked in front of Samson's house.

Oliver switched off the engine and took a deep breath. "This is so fucked up. I should have said something before."

"About what?"

"That Portia used mind control on me and left me in the dust the other day. When I called Zane for help, he told me she was with him. Fuck, why would she do that? Why would she trick one bodyguard just to run to the other?"

Quinn slapped him on the shoulder. "I guess you haven't noticed how those two look at each other."

Oliver gave him a stunned look. "You've seen them together?"

"Last night. Long story. But I'm telling you something: when two people look at each other like that, there's nothing you can do. Best to stay out of it."

"Zane has the hots for Portia? No way!"

"Not only that, I think she has the hots for him. And I'm not even sure it's just that. I know Zane too well. He doesn't turn all territorial over just any woman. So here's my advice: keep your mouth shut about what happened the other day. Nobody needs to know about that. It'll only get you in hot water with Samson."

Oliver ran his hands through his impossibly messy hairdo. "Are you sure? What if somebody knows about it?"

"I'm the only other person who knows, and I won't blab. So, take my advice. As for what happened tonight, they both tricked you. It's not your fault. He's duped me too, and I know him better; I should have seen the warning signs."

Besides, he should have heard the garage door opening and closing, but with the constant noise in the neighborhood and the hustle and bustle that went on there during the day, he'd tried to block out any sound so he could sleep, and had used earplugs.

"Okay then," Oliver finally agreed.

"Just let me talk. And don't volunteer any information that's not asked for."

Oliver trotted next to him up the five steps to Samson's house. Quinn rang the door bell and was surprised when the door was opened almost instantly.

Samson had his cell glued to his ear. When he noticed Oliver, he pointed at him.

"Hold on, Thomas, it's Oliver." Then he almost glared at the young human bodyguard. "Where's your charge?"

Oliver flinched. "She tricked me and got away."

Quinn shoved his colleague into the foyer and shut the door behind him.

"Fuck!" Samson cursed. "Thomas, I'm putting you on loudspeaker." He pressed a button and held his phone out on his palm.

"When Thomas got to the house at the end of your shift, the house was empty. What happened?" Samson demanded from Oliver.

"Why would Thomas take over from Oliver? It was Zane's shift," Quinn interrupted.

Samson glared at Quinn. "Zane fucked up. I suspended him and assigned Thomas instead."

"Ah, shit, no wonder he's gone," Quinn responded.

"What?" Samson shifted his gaze between Quinn and Oliver.

"Zane is gone. He took the Hummer and the dog," Quinn replied.

Oliver nodded. "And most likely Portia."

"He took Portia?" Samson yelled.

"Zane called me an hour or so before sunset. He kept me on the phone so Portia could get out the back."

"How do you know that?"

"Her window was open, and I found footprints in the back yard. He must have been waiting for her."

"Shit!" Samson cursed.

"I'll see if I can get a lock on the GPS in his cell or his Hummer," Thomas' voice came through the phone.

"Do it now," Samson instructed.

"Call you back in a few."

Samson looked up from the phone and stared at Quinn. "Did you not realize he was leaving the house during the day? I thought you were keeping an eye on him."

Quinn shifted his weight from one foot to the other. "You know yourself how stealthily he moves. Didn't hear a thing. Not even that damn dog barked. When did you suspend him?"

"Around four this afternoon."

"That's probably what ticked him off."

"Ticked him off? You don't get it, Quinn. He was getting involved with his charge! That's not only against Scanguards' rules, it's against her father's—our client's—orders. She's a minor!"

"She's twenty," Oliver chimed in.

Samson lashed a glare as his once trusted assistant. "In our world that makes her a minor. God knows what he told her so she'd go with him."

Quinn raised his hand. "Samson, it takes two to tango. From what I hear about this girl, she's rather headstrong. I don't see her being manipulated by Zane. I think she knows very well what she's doing."

"Zane is dangerous. He killed a man in cold blood only a few days ago. Have you already forgotten?"

Make that two, Quinn thought to himself and was instantly glad, that Samson had no idea about the assassin. He would keep it that way. "He had a reason. The guy was a rapist."

"Zane should have let the authorities deal with him. Fuck, Quinn."

Samson raised his arm and pointed at the door. "Zane is out there with the girl. Do you have any idea what he's going to do with her?"

Fuck her senseless, if he'd read Zane right when he'd seen the two together. Yet, Quinn kept his mouth shut. There were times when it was better not to answer a question, particularly when it was clearly rhetorical.

Samson's cell rang. He answered it instantly, pressing the speaker button. "Yes?"

"The GPS on his Hummer is disabled, and I can't get a location from his cell either. We're blind."

"Shit! Call Gabriel and have him reach out to all our vampire contacts in Northern California. Get them a picture of Zane as well as the Hummer's license plate. Nobody is to approach him. Just get me his location."

"I'm on it." Thomas clicked off.

"Oliver, you're going over to Lauren's house. I'll notify the mayor to expect you. Interrogate her and check her cell phone to see if she's had any contact with Portia in the last few hours: calls, text messages, voicemails. Check her email account too."

Oliver nodded dutifully. "I know she spoke to Lauren only a few minutes before ..." Suddenly he scratched his head. "Ah, shit, that was probably Zane calling her. I thought the conversation sounded a little stilted, but ..."

Quinn cupped Oliver's elbow, reminding him silently not to volunteer any information like they'd discussed. He'd only get himself in trouble if he did. Samson was mad enough, and with good reason. If they didn't find Portia soon, they'd have to decide what to tell her father. It was a conversation nobody looked forward to.

"Talk to Lauren now. We need to know what she knows."

"Yes, Samson." Oliver turned to the door and left.

"Quinn, this wasn't supposed to happen."

Quinn nodded and took a deep breath. "He won't hurt her."

Samson shook his head. "You don't know the whole story. He came to speak to me last night. Claimed that Portia's father is deliberately keeping her a virgin even though her twenty-first birthday is in five weeks. Apparently she told him all that."

"Is it true?"

"I don't believe so. Her father warned us ahead of time that it's one of the stories she uses to gain sympathy. She's lying to him."

"Did you tell him that?"

"Of course I did. I showed him the file. But I don't think he was convinced."

"How could he?" Quinn murmured under his breath.

"What?" Suspicion flared in Samson's eyes.

"I'm saying knowing Zane, he won't believe it just because it's written in a file. You know him: he'll investigate himself to find the truth."

His mind went back to the night before when he'd seen them together. Their interactions had indicated that while there was clearly something between them, they hadn't been intimate yet—despite the fact that Portia had been in Zane's bed.

"That's exactly what I can't have him do. In either case it would be wrong: if she's not a virgin, he'll be furious about being duped by her, and who knows what he'll do then."

Quinn raised an eyebrow. "And if she *is* a virgin?"

Samson blinked. "If her father is really intent on keeping her a virgin until her final turning, he'll kill Zane for robbing her of her virginity."

"If he finds him," Quinn added.

"We have to find him first and stop him before he does something that can't be reversed."

Quinn gave his boss a long look, wondering whether to ask his next question or keep his mouth shut. This time though his sense of justice won out. "What about the girl?"

"What about her?"

"If she's really a virgin, we can't allow her father to prevent her from losing her virginity before she turns twenty-one." His own conscience wouldn't allow him to stand idly by and do nothing, when somebody was clearly doing the girl wrong.

"I know that, and it's bothered me all day. I just hope for all our sakes that she lied to Zane. Because fighting her father on this issue is not a fight I look forward to."

Chapter Twenty-One

Zane pulled into the garage underneath his mountain cabin and brought the car to a complete stop, the chains he'd put on the wheels before reaching the mountains clacking loudly against the concrete floor. The moment he killed the engine, Portia stirred and opened her eyes. She'd nodded off only a half hour earlier with Z curled into a ball at her feet. The picture was so utterly unfamiliar, yet it warmed his heart.

"Are we there?" Her eyes darted around the garage then back to him.

"I'll get the bags. Why don't you and Z go in already?"

Portia opened the door, and Z jumped out, excitedly sniffing his surroundings.

"I can't believe you have a cabin in Tahoe!"

Zane rounded the Hummer, Portia's backpack in hand, and opened the trunk. For emergencies, he always kept a bag in his car that was stocked with everything he needed for a few nights.

"It's not big, but it's all I need. I always come here alone." He stopped himself.

This was his sanctuary. He'd never brought a woman here. Not even his friends and colleagues at Scanguards knew about this place. He'd even made sure not to ask for Amaury's real estate expertise when he'd purchased the house, wanting this to be his own little getaway that nobody knew about.

Zane grabbed his bag and shut the trunk. Portia was still waiting next to the passenger door for him. Their eyes met.

"I don't need much space," she whispered and licked her lower lip. "We only need one bed. As long as you have that ..."

Her cheeks colored a pretty pink. Zane dropped the bags and crossed the distance between them with two large strides, stopping only inches from her. "Go inside now, Portia, and do me a favor: don't mention words like 'bed' until we're inside the house or your first time will happen right here in this garage with your back against the car."

He kept all menace out of his voice, but he couldn't suppress the lust that coursed through him. It made him sound hoarse. During the entire drive he'd fought with himself, fought against the need to stop the car and pull her onto the back seat to take her right there and then. Because now that he'd made up his mind to make love to Portia, he couldn't wait a minute longer.

Her lashes crashed against her eyelids as she raised them in one smooth move. "Don't make me wait." Then she turned and ushered the dog through the door to the interior.

Wait? That word had just been expelled from his vocabulary and been replaced by the only possible replacement: now. Zane's heart beat a violent staccato against his ribcage, and his cock, which had been semi-hard during the entire ride, surged to a full erection.

Picking up the bags once more, he charged after her. Inside, he dropped the luggage onto the floor and straightened. As always, a sense of tranquility poured over him when he entered the great room of his cabin. The vaulted ceiling and its wooden beams added an air of space to the small house, belying its size of less than a thousand square feet. The décor was rustic and not something he'd first thought he'd like, but it had grown on him.

"There's a fire in the fireplace," Portia noted, her voice tinged with a sliver of alarm. "Is somebody living here?"

Zane shook his head. "I texted my caretaker before I picked you up to prepare the place for us. Check the fridge. It should be stocked with human food for you." He would have to go out hunting for blood later, unless … He quickly pushed away the thought before it could form in his mind. One thing at a time: first sex, then maybe later he could—

"The fridge is chock-full with food. Who does your caretaker think I am? A three hundred pound gorilla?" She laughed and turned to him, her hair falling in her face.

"I didn't know what you liked, so I had him get a bit of everything."

It was so much easier with blood. There were only eight varietals, four positive and four negative. And he liked them all.

"That's sweet of you."

Sweet? Nobody had ever said that anything he'd ever done was sweet. Slowly, but with purpose Zane walked toward her and noticed how she stood completely motionless with only her eyes moving as he approached. He stopped a foot away from her and reached for the strand of hair that had caught on her cheek, brushing it away from her face.

"Don't make the mistake of seeing me for something that I'm not. I don't have a sweet or gentle bone in my body, and if that's what you're looking for, I should take you back now."

As soon as the words were out, he knew that if she wanted to leave, he couldn't allow it. She was in his secret lair, and the only way she would leave this place was as a real woman, her virginity a memory.

Portia raised her hand and slid it to the back of his neck, shaking her head as if to reprimand him. "Don't even think about it."

He liked that about her: she never backed down from a challenge.

"You could have chosen anybody you wanted. Why me, baby girl?"

Did she not know how desirable she was, that any man with eyes in his head would see the passionate woman that was ready to burst to the surface?

She leaned closer, her mouth hovering opposite his. "Because when you kiss me, I feel something."

With her free hand, she took his and led it to her chest where her heart beat in a rapid rhythm.

"Here." She pressed his hand against her heart, then pushed it lower past the waistband of her jeans before he could enjoy the softness of her flesh. But she rewarded him by guiding his hand to cup her sex.

Raising her lids, Portia gazed into his eyes. "And here."

Warmth radiated into his palm as he pressed against her pussy, any closer contact impeded by the thick fabric of her pants. Nevertheless, his cock rejoiced.

He groaned, unable to hold back the lust that barreled through him. "Since we're honest here," he husked and drank in the green of her eyes, "I think you should know where I feel something when you kiss me."

Zane took her hand and guided it to his cock, letting her glide it over his entire length and feel the hardness that dug into his zipper. "Here."

She squeezed his shaft, making him clench his jaw to fight off his imminent release.

"Woof, woof!"

Z's barking made him shift his attention away from Portia and her tempting hands.

"That's really bad timing, Z."

Portia dropped her hands from him and turned toward the dog. "I think he needs to go outside."

Zane frowned, but knowing what kind of mess his dog could make, he realized there was no way around this. "I'll take him. Why don't you make yourself comfortable in the meantime? I'll be back in ten minutes."

Or maybe in five: for sure the little pup had never experienced snow. The mountain was covered with a fresh snow pack, and the temperature, now that it was dark, was below freezing. He bet that Z would be freezing his ass off in three minutes tops and wanting to return to the warmth in front of the fireplace.

***

Portia's eyes followed Zane as he escorted the dog out into the snowy wilderness. Darn, that man filled out a pair of jeans just the right way despite his lean body. His muscles shifted with every step, and she wondered what it would feel like when they were finally both naked, his skin sliding against hers.

When he drew the door shut behind him, she stopped holding her breath. She'd better use the time he was gone. There had been no time to change into fresh clothes, even less to take a shower. Considering what they were planning tonight, she felt the need to groom herself, not just to be ready for him, but also to boost her self-confidence. She'd never touched a man as intimately as she'd already touched Zane today, and she hoped that instinct would guide her so she wouldn't turn out to be a klutz in bed.

In the bedroom, Portia quickly shimmied out of her jeans and sweater, then tossed her socks, panties and bra on a chair. Realizing how uninspiring her underwear looked, she picked it up again and chucked it under the bed. No need for him to see what cringe-worthy panties she wore. It would only serve to turn him off, not on.

A look at the king-sized bed with its decidedly masculine dark striped cover made her shiver despite the welcoming warmth in the small house. In a short while, they would lie in each other's arms there, naked, wrapped only in their own passion and desire.

Not wasting any more time, Portia hurried into the en-suite bathroom and stepped into the large shower. Soft pebbles caressed the soles of her feet, the same smooth stones that also graced the shower walls. The warm spray of the water ran down her body as soon as she turned the faucet.

She reached for the soap and lathered her skin. When she inhaled, she realized that the soap was unscented. It surprised her, particularly because the scent that Zane gave off was so intensely masculine that she'd thought it came from a scented soap he used. But it appeared that the scent she felt so drawn to was all him. She should have guessed as much. A vampire like Zane, whose raw power and energy constantly bubbled to the surface, would carry such a potent smell.

Portia didn't bother washing her hair. It would take too long to dry, and considering that Zane was entirely bald, she bet he didn't have a hairdryer. She quickly rinsed her body clean of the soap and stepped onto the soft rug in front of the shower, reaching for the towel that hung on a wall rack.

"When I said 'make yourself comfortable', I didn't realize I'd be missing something important."

Her head snapped toward the door, where Zane filled the frame.

Reflexively, she pressed the towel to her front, covering her nakedness, at the same time as a gasp escaped her.

His eyes darkened and honed in on the towel. "You won't need that."

Hesitantly, she lowered her hands, pushing the towel down past her nipples, which were suddenly hard and erect, and exposed to his hungry gaze.

Zane's nostril's flared, and his body moved. With two steps, he reached her and clasped his hand over hers. She relinquished the towel to his control. It dropped to the floor a second later.

Zane's shirt brushed against her breasts as he drew her against his body. "I could have watched you shower if that damn dog wasn't so inexplicably fond of snow."

She raised her lashes and lost herself in the golden flecks of his eyes. "Or you could have helped me."

With a groan, he sank his lips onto her mouth and captured her. Her lips parted on his demand, welcoming his forceful invasion. Pure and unadulterated lust careened through her veins instead of the blood that normally ran there. Her pulse quickened to a pace faster than any human dance when Zane's tongue stroked against hers in a relentless assault, asking for her surrender.

Instinct guided her responses. Portia greeted his masculine taste with a feral growl of her own, sending him an unmistakable signal that if he wanted surrender, she demanded the same from him.

Without giving her reprieve from his searching tongue and pressing lips, his hands slid around her back and down to her behind where he filled his palms with her flesh. In the next instant he hauled her toward him, his cock as hard as before with only his cold jeans as a barrier between them. A barrier she wanted gone.

She tugged on his shirt, pulling it out of his pants, and fumbled with the buttons. But she was shaking so much with the need that he'd awakened in her that her fingers didn't find purchase.

Zane moaned, and the rumble sank deep into her core, heading straight for her womb, where it crashed against the waves that her body created. When he ripped his mouth from hers, she wanted to scream, to protest, but before she could, his lips connected with the sensitive skin of her neck, as she obligingly offered it to him.

A wave of white hot heat skated over where his firm lips suckled her damp skin, evaporating the remaining pearls of water from her shower.

"Zane," she murmured, not knowing really what she was asking for, but certain that whatever it was, she wanted it. Wanted him.

"Easy, baby girl," his husky voice breathed against her neck as his lips nibbled toward her earlobe and sucked the soft piece of flesh between them.

A painless bite stole her breath, making her breasts heave and brush against the cotton of his shirt, reminding her once more that he was still fully clothed. But she needed to touch him. Without thinking, hands curled into fists gripping the lapels of his shirt. One forceful rip, and all buttons went flying.

Finally, there was skin she could touch: warm, smooth skin. Hairless, just like his skull. Her fingers glided over his chest, where sinew and lean muscle flexed, and where his heart beat violently.

"Oh, God, Portia," he groaned and threw his head back, his hands on her stilling for a moment. When she looked up at his face, she watched his fangs lengthen and the glow in his eyes intensify.

A thrill of excitement shot through her at the knowledge that she could reduce this man to a creature who only lived for this moment of passion and desire.

"I want you," she whispered and felt her own fangs itch beneath her gums.

His eyes flashed with lust, and his nostrils flared before he dropped his head back to her. But instead of kissing her lips or her neck, he moved lower and captured her breasts, a word bouncing against them that she wasn't sure she'd heard correctly.

Yet, it still echoed in her head: *mine.*

Chapter Twenty-Two

Mine.

Zane would never give voice to it, yet the thought bounced around his head, forbidden and unattainable as it was. But just because he couldn't act on it, it didn't stop the wish from repeating again and again. *Mine, mine, mine.* Like a song on a loop it came around as regularly as seconds ticked away on a clock. With no means to tell his mind that he had no right to make her his, to claim her for himself, he did the only thing he could: he lavished her body with the passion that had been locked up inside him for so long.

His lips locking around one taut nipple, he swiped his tongue over it and relished the breathless moan Portia released. She was more responsive than he'd expected a virgin to be. At the same time, her responses to him were pure and unaffected as only those of an inexperienced woman could be. He found that it appealed to him more than the artificial moans and grunts the prostitutes and sluts he frequented played for him.

Every moan and sigh from Portia's lips felt like a gift. And selfish as he was, he coaxed more of them out of her by sucking harder and working her other breast with his hand, squeezing and molding it in his palm. So firm, yet so soft, her body was a contradiction in terms.

Unable to get enough of her, he sank down to the tile floor and pulled her with him, laying her down on the soft bathmat. His hands roamed her body, exploring unchartered territory.

When he trailed kisses down her stomach, her head reared up. "Zane? What are you doing?"

It wasn't an admonishment, but a question colored in surprise and disbelief. He raised his lids and collided with her intense gaze, her green eyes glowing with lust. She had to know what was coming. Even as a virgin, she couldn't be that ignorant.

"I need to taste your pussy."

Her breath hitched, and his nostrils flared as the scent of her arousal intensified.

"You don't have to do that," she whispered a weak protest, but her eyes said otherwise. She wanted his lips on her, his tongue inside her.

"I have to."

Not a horde of vampire hunters chasing him with stakes could stop him now. Lowering his head, he moved his hands to her thighs and pushed them apart, opening her for his own pleasure.

A triangle of dark curls greeted his approach, and the tantalizing smell of youth and purity beckoned him to move farther south. He sank his face between her spread thighs and inhaled, allowing her scent to engulf him. Everything else faded into the background. The cold tile floor was suddenly forgotten. And even the soft woofing of his dog in the next room subsided. The only things his senses were able to process were her scent and the feel of her silken flesh under his hands. Her soft, almost inaudible moans provided the background music to this enticing tableau of ripe and willing woman.

Zane stroked his fingers up her thighs, allowing them to converge at the moist folds of her sex. As he brushed against the warm cleft, Portia jolted.

"I'll be gentle," he heard himself reassure her. Gentle? Could he really be that? Could he be tender and careful with a woman as precious as her? Or would his desire for her unleash the beast in him?

He wanted to pull back, to try to get himself under control so he wouldn't hurt her, when her hands suddenly stroked over his skull, her fingernails softly grazing his skin. He lost his ability to move. A shudder went through him and right through his cock, making pre-cum ooze from the slit.

Zane licked his tongue over her flesh, lapping up the juices that coated it. His entire body went rigid with his first taste of her innocence.

Holy hell!

He'd never tasted anything as delicious, and he'd eaten a lot of pussy in his life. This was nothing like he'd ever had. Her tangy flavor was rich and ripe, the texture of her flesh so soft and smooth, teasing his lips and tongue by making them tingle. His pulse raced, his heart pounding through his chest as if it wanted to jump out of his body and into hers.

Portia was better than the best blood he'd ever drunk.

Need to possess her charged through every single cell of his body.

Mine, his mind screamed again, deafening him. Warring emotions battled in his heart, the need to have her on one side, and to protect her from himself on the other. In between those two forces, a third reared its head: the will to protect himself from falling for her, from giving his heart away only to have it crushed when she ran from him.

Zane pushed away the thoughts, forcing himself only to live in the moment and take what she was willing to give him: her body, nothing else. He would have to content himself with it, even though he wanted more now. He would do his darnedest to tempt her to give him more. He'd already violated Scanguards' ethics, and one-by-one was breaking every single rule he'd ever put in place for himself: never to get involved, never to care, and never to hope for love.

It was all shot to hell now.

All because of Portia and the way he reacted to her. Just like she reacted to him. Her body twisted beneath his mouth, her pelvis rocking against him, and her hands kept caressing his sensitive skull.

For the first time in his vampire life he was grateful for the fact that he was bald. It had made his skin more sensitive to touch, and now acted as one of the most erogenous zones of his body besides the one now struggling to escape his pants.

With his tongue, he explored her beautiful pussy, nipped, sucked and licked this way, then that. When he stroked upwards and connected with her clit, she let out a breathless cry.

"So sensitive," he mumbled against the fully engorged bundle of nerves.

But Zane gave her no reprieve. He wanted to taste her passion, her lust, and her desire. He needed to feel her come apart in his mouth, to know that he could give her something that she would remember, a feeling she would never forget and always associate with him.

While sex had always been a power play for him, never to be confused with affection or love, as Portia writhed beneath him in obvious ecstasy, he felt his heart soften, the wall around it crack. Not wanting to examine the implications of this, he doubled his efforts and pulled her clit between his lips, pressing them together.

Her moan was followed by a shudder. Wave after wave crashed against his lips as her orgasm broke.

His own release was only prevented by the tightness of his jeans and the zipper that dug painfully into his aroused flesh. Had he been naked, he would have spilled his seed onto the tile floor.

Zane groaned and kept licking over her clit, igniting her once more. Then he lifted his head and looked at her face. Her eyes were closed, her lips parted, showing the tips of her fangs, and her chest heaved. He'd never seen a more beautiful sight in his long life.

"Next time you come, I'll be inside you."

Her eyes flew open, and she pinned him. "Now."

Her breathless word did something unfamiliar to his facial muscles. They twisted, his lips pulling up into a curve, parting as they did so. He brought a hand to his face to see what was happening to him and realized to his surprise that he was smiling.

He hadn't smiled in over six decades.

***

Languid pleasure made her body feel boneless. Portia had masturbated a few times before, and while it had made her feel good, it couldn't compare to what Zane's hands and mouth had done to her. She felt weightless.

When she opened her eyes, she looked at Zane's smiling face. He looked so different now, younger and so much happier than she'd ever seen him.

Zane rose from between her thighs, thighs she'd so willingly spread for him only thinking of her own pleasure. With fluid grace, he pulled her into his arms, cradling her against his naked chest, still wearing his shirt and pants, and carried her into the bedroom.

She pressed her head into the crook of his neck and slid her lips against his skin, kissing him. She sensed him tilt his head to allow her closer access. Sighing her approval, she brushed her fangs against his neck, sensing the pulsing vein beneath that screamed for her to tear his skin so she could drink.

Zane growled. "Careful, Portia, if you bite me, you might be getting deeper into this than you want to."

She met his eyes and noticed a strange glint there. Was he rejecting her, regretting what he'd just done? She averted her eyes. "I'm sorry."

When he lowered her onto the bed, she scooted away from him, his rejection stinging. She cursed her inexperience. If she'd been with a vampire before, maybe she would know more about the etiquette around biting. As it was, all she had to go by was her instinct, and it told her that she wanted his blood just as much as she wanted his cock inside her.

Zane's hand tipped her chin up, making her face his scrutinizing look. "Don't get me wrong. I'd be honored if you drank my blood."

Her heart jumped. "But then why—"

"Taking another vampire's blood creates a connection …"

She knew all about blood bonds, her mother had explained it to her. "But if you don't bite me at the same time, it won't create a blood bond."

"That's not what I was talking about. Even without that, there'll be a closer connection than if we were simply sexual partners."

She frowned. Sexual partners, how clinical that sounded. "I see." All he wanted was what she'd asked him in the first place: to help her lose her virginity. Nothing more, nothing less.

"You don't."

Zane shrugged his shirt off and dropped it to the floor. Then he stretched out his right arm, revealing the inside of his forearm. With the finger of his other hand, he pointed to the tattoo that marred his skin.

Portia's eyes followed the direction, and her pulse skidded to a full stop. There, on his skin, six numbers were imprinted. It took her less than a second to realize what they were. She knew their significance from somewhere—from reading, or some class she'd taken, or maybe one of the many TV documentaries she'd perused. In any case, she knew that Zane had survived a Nazi concentration camp.

"This is what I am, Portia. I did unspeakable things to survive. You don't want my blood, believe me. I'm an animal."

Stunned at his self-hate, she stopped breathing.

"I'm a dirty Jew, Portia. Is that really what you want?"

He hated himself for being a Jew? She shook her head, unable to comprehend how he could have these feelings about himself. When he pulled away and lowered his lids, she realized he'd misunderstood her movement as an answer to his question.

"No!" she cried out and reached for his hand, pulling his arm closer to her. "Whoever said that of you is wrong." How long had they repeated those words to him that he now believed them himself? What had they done to him to make him think he was dirty because of his heritage?

But Zane had already shut down again, his smile wiped off his face, his mask of indifference firmly in place.

"I want you."

He shook his head. "I don't want your pity or your political correctness."

"It's neither." Damn it, why was he so stubborn?

Unconcerned with her nudity, she nudged to the edge of the bed and turned her head to his forearm once more. She brought it to her mouth and pressed a kiss onto the first number.

"Portia, stop …"

His protest died when she kissed the second number, then the third. By the fourth Zane was moaning softly, and when she kissed the fifth and then the last one, his other arm had come around her and his fingers combed through her hair.

"To me you're beautiful, honorable, and strong. You're the first person I've ever wanted to bite. But if you don't want me to …"

Portia let her words hang there, giving him a chance to make a decision.

"You've never bitten anybody?"

"I was raised on bottled blood."

The news appeared to surprise him. She watched how his eyes changed, how he seemingly fought an invisible enemy. A few tense moments passed, before Zane suddenly pulled her into his embrace and buried his face in her hair.

"When we make love, when I push through your hymen, I want you to sink your fangs into me and take as much blood as you want."

"What if I can't stop?" The way his blood smelled, she wasn't sure she could withdraw in time.

"It would be a very sweet death."

She pulled back and glared at him, only to realize that he was smiling. "How can you make a joke like that?"

"Who said it was a joke?"

"You have a very dark sense of humor, do you know that?" Because this had to be a joke.

"There are a lot of things about me that are dark, baby girl. And for your sake, I hope you'll never see them."

Before she could answer, his mouth was back on hers, drowning out any protest on that subject.

Chapter Twenty-Three

Zane deepened his kiss at the same time as he worked himself out of his jeans. Thanks to Portia's enthusiastic help, he was naked a few moments later. Finally, he pressed her back into the mattress and covered her body with his.

Even though history had taught the world about the atrocities the Nazi's had committed, and that the Jews weren't the only ones who'd been marked for elimination, he'd never been able to shake the words they'd used to break him: dirty Jew. A deep-rooted belief that he deserved to be the vermin they'd turned him into at Buchenwald remained, as did the conviction that he'd never be able to cleanse himself of the acts of brutality he'd committed in the years after it.

He could have easily hidden his tattoo from her for a while longer, but something had urged him to point it out to her, eager to see her reaction. He hadn't expected her to be so kind. However, when Portia had kissed the numbers that had once identified him as a prisoner, he'd felt the chains around his heart loosen. If an innocent like Portia could see past the mark that daily reminded him of his past, then maybe there was hope after all. Hope that one day he'd be free from pain and the need for revenge.

Free to love.

He banned the thought from his mind, and instead brought his attention back to Portia's enticing body. He was one lucky son of a bitch that she'd gotten it into her head to have him be her first. Knowing that something like this would never happen to him again, he didn't want to rush the moment. And the fact that she would take his blood while he was deep inside her, made the whole prospect so much sweeter.

Her lips tasted of surrender, and her hands that now roamed freely over his naked torso, spoke their own language, one of desire and passion, of eagerness and curiosity.

He severed his lips from hers and gazed into her face. Her cheeks flamed, and her breath came in shallow pants.

"We'll take it slowly," he assured her.

To his surprise, Portia shook her head. "I don't want slow. I don't want you to hold back."

"But you're a—"

She pressed her finger to his lips, silencing him. "I'm a hybrid. You can't break me. Please."

Zane stroked his knuckles over her cheek. "What do you want from me, baby girl?"

"Treat me like a woman you're passionate about. Pretend you can't control your desire. It doesn't matter that it's not real. Just make me feel it."

Zane searched her eyes. "Pretend?" He leaned his forehead against hers. "I can't pretend."

There was a disappointed sigh, and it almost made him smile.

"I don't have to pretend." He brushed his lips over her eyes and kissed them. "You see, Portia ..."

He took her wrists and pinned them on each side of her head. Her heartbeat instantly kicked up but she didn't give him any resistance.

"... what I want is you panting when I thrust into you, and screaming for more, begging me to fuck you harder. Can you pretend for me?"

Portia's eyes lit up, sending a bolt of heat through him. "What if I don't need to pretend?"

Zane let a low growl of approval emerge from his chest. "Even if I hurt you?"

"You can't hurt me."

He closed his eyes for a second. There were so many ways he could hurt her, despite her being a near indestructible hybrid. "So you want real. You want sex without restraints, without holding back?"

"Yes."

Without another word, he nudged his thigh between hers, spreading her. The scent of her arousal intensified, filling his bedroom. His cock brushed against her inner thigh, relishing the heat from her body.

Releasing her wrists, he cradled her closer and centered himself above her core. When he drew his hips back, his cock slid into the space between her thighs, stroking against her damp center. The brief contact almost undid him.

Slowly, he probed at her entrance, the tip of his swollen cock pressing between her outer lips, feeling the membrane guarding her virginity.

"God, you're tight," he whispered at her ear.

"Do it," she urged and caressed his neck with her lips.

Zane tilted his head, anticipating what would happen next.

Portia's pelvis pushed against him. Without a thought, he plunged forward, pushing through the hymen that represented the final barrier to her treasure, seating himself.

In the same instant, Portia's fangs sank into his neck, piercing his skin. When she drew on his vein, intense pleasure speared through him, equaling the pleasure he felt being lodged deep inside her exquisitely tight pussy.

Fuck!

Her muscles squeezed him, making him clench his jaw shut to avoid a premature release. He allowed the moans that built in his chest to emerge freely, unconcerned about exposing himself and the depth of pleasure she gave him. Portia's hand on the back of his head held him to her hungry mouth, but even if she hadn't held him so tightly, he wouldn't have pulled back. Her fangs in his neck were the most intimate sensation he'd ever experienced.

There was only one way to top it. Zane withdrew from her sheath only to plunge back inside, driving his cock harder and deeper into her than before. She was slick with her arousal, and every glide into her was pure silk on silk.

His triumphant growl joined her soft moans when the realization of their actions finally sank in. Portia had given him not one gift, but two: she'd accepted his blood and given him her virginity. In return, he would do what she'd asked for; unleash his passion on her and make her feel desired. Because she was.

The sounds of flesh slapping against flesh filled the room. Comingled with soft moans and sighs from Portia and the much more pronounced groans from him, a concert of lust and passion played out in the small house that had, until now, known only a quiet existence. No longer. The sounds of lovemaking bounced against the rafters and fell back onto them like waves crashing onto a beach.

Their bodies moved in perfect rhythm as if they'd done this a thousand times. At the same time, everything was new. And while Zane knew that Portia had never been with a man, he felt the memories of other women vanish from him as if somebody had wiped his slate clean.

He felt as much like a virgin as the pliable woman in his arms. Never had he felt anything as sensual and as beautiful as the union of their two bodies. He had no memory of ever having touched other women. Only Portia counted, only her pleasure was important. Because if he could pleasure her, it would only serve to double his own satisfaction.

He worked his cock in and out of her, slamming his pelvis into her hard and fast, just the way she'd demanded earlier. He realized now that there was no way he could have gone slowly. Too much pent up lust drove him to pound his cock into her, to claim her pussy for himself, to make her want only him, no other man.

The desire to brand her flitted through his mind, but he knew she was really branding him. Not only with her bite but with the imprint of her fingers on his skin, fingers that had turned into claws and dug into his flesh.

Zane suddenly felt her withdraw her fangs from his neck and lick over the incisions, closing the skin with her saliva.

"Don't stop," he urged her and lifted his head.

She gazed back at him, her lips smeared with his blood, her eyes shining. She was even more beautiful now.

"I love your taste."

Her admission made him want to howl at the moon like a wild animal. She carried his blood now, and she loved it. He couldn't ask for more. It was already more than he'd ever expected. And now that his blood was running in her veins, he knew she was stronger. His blood would have a potent effect on her, one he was more than willing to exploit.

Zane withdrew from her and lifted his body, only to flip Portia onto her stomach.

"Oh!" was all that escaped her lips.

"You did say not to hold back," he reminded her and captured her hips in his hands, pulling them up.

Her heart-shaped ass drew back, and her thighs spread.

"Good girl," he praised.

She moaned when he slipped his hand between her cheeks and along her cleft before he thrust a finger into her warm slit.

"I'm gonna fuck you from behind. You wanna know why?"

"Why?" The word was more moan than voice.

He positioned himself at her center, pulling out his finger and guiding his hard shaft to her glistening folds. Her skin was red and swollen, but he wouldn't give her reprieve. She could take him.

"When you're on your hands and knees, I have complete control over you. I can fuck you as hard as I want to. You'll be at my mercy."

"Yes … oh, God, yes …"

Zane drove into her, ramming his rod into her to the hilt so hard, her entire body lifted and moved a couple of inches toward the headboard. He gripped her hips harder and pulled her back, impaling her so his entire length was buried in her.

"Again," she spurred him on.

She didn't need to tell him twice. Zane repeated his action and found a rhythm that was driving him quickly toward the abyss. But he couldn't allow himself release before he'd made her come. Releasing her right hip, he slid his hand over her stomach and down to her nest of curls, finding her clit.

Fully engorged, it peaked from beneath its hood. Drawing juices from her pussy, he moistened his finger and rubbed it over her sensitive organ, eliciting a pronounced moan from Portia.

"Oh, God!" she gasped.

Zane rubbed his thumb over it again, back and forth, then in a circle, steadily increasing the pressure. He watched for her reactions and honed his caress to her preference, all the while thrusting deep and hard into her from behind.

When suddenly her interior muscles clenched around him, it hit him out of nowhere. His cock convulsed inside her, spewing his seed into her womb as she continued to milk him. He only slightly eased the pressure on her clit, allowing her to ride the waves that wracked her body. When they slowly subsided, he caressed the responsive bundle of nerves again, taking her over the edge once more until she finally collapsed beneath him.

Refusing to leave her body, he rolled to the side, taking her with him. He pressed her cute ass into his groin, keeping himself lodged deep inside her. Her back molded to his chest as she sighed contently.

Zane pulled the blanket over them and wrapped his arms around her.

"Zane," she murmured languidly.

"Yes, baby girl?" He smoothed her hair back behind her ear.

When she didn't answer, he craned his neck to look at her face. Her eyes were closed, and her even breath confirmed that she was asleep.

Asleep in his arms, trusting him to keep her safe. A virgin no more.

Chapter Twenty-Four

Quinn paid the cabbie and jumped out of the taxi, waiting until it disappeared down the hill before he walked back two blocks and turned into the next street, blending into the shadows of the large trees that lined it. Paranoia was hard to shake, and his years as a vampire had taught him never to let his guard down, even if he had no reason to believe that he was being followed. The last thing he wanted to do was to put one of his fellow vampires in jeopardy, particularly when he was here to ask for a favor.

Just because Zane had disappeared with the girl didn't mean that his other problems had just vanished with him. Finding out where the assassin had come from was still paramount, and once Quinn had a lead on that, he could use it to force Zane to come back. He knew his friend well enough to realize that once he had crucial information about Müller's whereabouts, nothing could keep Zane from pursuing his ultimate goal: revenge. Not even a piece of ass as enticing at Portia—he hoped.

With a sigh, he stopped in front of the modern home that sat high on Twin Peaks. Its floor-to-ceiling windows wrapped around two sides of the house, the back reaching into the mountain behind it. While impressive, it felt by no means out of place in this neighborhood. Just like a vampire's home was meant to be: possessing all the amenities necessary for a comfortable life, yet fitting in and not attracting any unwanted attention.

Quinn walked up to the entrance door and rang the bell. It took only a moment before it opened, yet it wasn't Thomas who greeted him, but Nina, Amaury's hot-headed mate. Her blond curls were tousled, and she looked slightly out of breath. Her sweat smelled sweet and ever so tempting. He could only imagine how her blood must taste, but he would never know for sure how rich and delicious it was. Only Amaury did. And he would kill anybody who touched her.

"Oh, hey, Quinn."

"I won!" Eddie's enthusiastic shout came from behind her.

"Hey, Nina. Is Thomas in?"

She opened the door all the way and motioned him to enter. "He and

Amaury are downstairs in the garage."

Quinn entered the large open plan living area with the set of computers nestled in one corner and a large flat-screen TV mounted on one wall. Eddie, Nina's brother stood in front of it, a white plastic object in his hands.

"What are you guys doing?" Quinn asked, pointing at the screen, which showed some sort of green field.

"Wii Tennis," Eddie answered and grinned. "And I'm kicking my big sister's butt!"

Quinn smirked. Well, who wouldn't want to kick that cute butt, or rather, slap it? Another thing he'd never get to do if he didn't want to find himself at the end of a stake.

"It's only the second set; we said three out of five," Nina reminded her brother and snatched the Wii controller from him.

Starting a new set, she moved into position and swung her right arm as if she were holding a tennis racket. Pinging sounds came from the TV. Her boobs bounced as her arm came full circle, and Quinn had to tear his eyes away from the lovely sight. He definitely had a thing for hot women, particularly those who belonged to other men. At least that way, he knew for sure that none of them would snare him in her net and force him to settle down. Getting married was furthest from his mind—who'd ever heard of a married playboy? And that's what he was, a playboy. Hefner was an inexperienced schoolboy compared to him.

Quinn grinned to himself and headed down the stairs that led into the garage. As he approached, he could already hear Thomas' and Amaury's voices.

Knocking briefly at the door at the bottom of the stairs, he entered.

"Hey, guys."

Thomas and Amaury both looked at him and greeted him with enthusiasm.

"About time we get to see you," Amaury said and clasped Quinn's hand.

"Hey, Quinn." Thomas waved a hand in greeting then wiped it on his grease smeared pants.

Quinn cast a quick glance at the motorcycle next to him, noticing that half the engine seemed to be missing. "Working on another bike?"

"Just a few minor repairs."

Quinn raised a doubting eyebrow. "If you say so." If taking an engine apart and putting it back together was minor, then how hard could it be for this technical genius to pry a computer chip from that mangled cell phone Quinn still had in his pocket?

"So, about Zane," Amaury started and gave him a long look.

"Yeah, not a good situation," Quinn felt compelled to say.

Thomas took a step closer. "Kind of strange that you didn't notice what was going on inside him, particularly since you've known him the longest."

Quinn shrugged, not willing to give away his secrets. "You know how unreadable he is. Hey, what's done is done. Any sightings of his Hummer?"

Amaury shook his head. "Nothing so far. He's vanished."

Thomas interrupted. "I have an automated software program running right now to get into Zane's personal accounts. I tell you, that guy's paranoid. Everything is encrypted to the hilt. But I'll get in sooner or later."

"What do you hope to find?" Quinn asked.

"He must have had an idea where to take Portia. He wouldn't just go to a hotel; that's too dangerous once it's daytime. I'm guessing he has a place somewhere."

"Not that Zane ever mentioned any of that to us," Amaury added and gave Quinn a penetrating look. "Maybe he's said something to you. Has he contacted you?"

"Listen, Amaury, and you too, Thomas, just because I'm his oldest and closest friend doesn't mean he tells me shit. I'm the first one to admit that Zane is on the edge, but I don't like it when you guys insinuate that I should have known, or that I know something I'm not telling. I'm as loyal to Scanguards as the two of you." Offense was better than defense; he hoped this would take the heat off him.

Amaury raised his hands in capitulation. "Hey, no offense. We're just all a little agitated."

Thomas nodded in agreement. "I blame myself. I should have said something earlier, but I figured a warning would be sufficient."

"Said what earlier?" Quinn wanted to know, his hackles rising.

"That I noticed something going on between him and his charge. But by the time I told Samson, it was already too late."

Shit! So Thomas was the one who'd ratted on Zane. Quinn gritted his teeth.

Thomas held up his hand. "I know what you're thinking, but it wasn't like that. Samson already had a suspicion. I only confirmed it. And I would do it again. What I regret is that we didn't tell Zane to his face. If we'd done that maybe we would have realized what he was planning."

Quinn kept his anger in check. It would do no good to pick a fight with Thomas, particularly since he still hadn't come to what he was there to ask for.

"I doubt even that would have made a difference. Zane hides his emotions better than anybody," Amaury added and gave Thomas a friendly slap on the shoulder.

"Hey, Thomas, given your sentiment about how things went down with Zane, maybe you wanna help me try to coax him back," Quinn baited his colleague.

Thomas' eyebrows went up. "Coax Zane? How?"

Quinn pulled the mangled cell phone from his pocket, drawing both Amaury's and Thomas' gaze onto it.

"There's some information he's after, and I'm pretty sure that if I can get it for him, he'll come running back."

Even though he'd promised Zane not to let Thomas know that this had anything to do with him, this was a promise he couldn't keep. Thomas would work on this problem with much more speed and energy if he knew it could bring Zane back.

"Information in that piece of shit?" Amaury asked full of doubt.

"What kind of information?" Thomas added.

"Phone numbers, contact info, anything you can pry out of it."

Quinn tossed the phone to Thomas who caught it in one hand. He turned it between his fingers and looked at it from all sides.

Then he raised his eyes. "Explosion?"

Quinn shrugged. "Can you salvage the chip?"

"Maybe."

"I thought you were a genius," Quinn needled him.

"And I thought you were loyal to Scanguards."

"It's nothing to do with Scanguards," Quinn protested. "And that's all I can tell you."

"For now," Thomas said calmly, "I'm going with it, but if something turns out to be fishy, I'll demand the whole story."

"Fair enough."

Chapter Twenty-Five

Portia traced her fingers over Zane's arm, feeling an intimacy and connection that she'd thought impossible before. Being in Zane's arms had exceeded all her wildest dreams. The pain of losing her virginity had been fleeting and had been instantly replaced by intense pleasure that had built and built until she'd thought she could take no more.

She purred like a content cat and snuggled closer to Zane's lean body.

"My sentiments exactly," he husked at her ear, and pulled her lobe between his lips, humming softly.

Her smile intensified as if wanting to permanently imprint itself on her face. "I liked it."

"Just 'liked'?" he growled while his hand on her stomach pressed her firmer into the curve of his body—his still very hard body. "You practically passed out."

Her cheeks flamed. "I nodded off. Sorry."

He lifted her chin with the tip of his fingers and turned her face to him. "Don't be. I like holding you."

"Just 'like'?" she teased back.

His eyes sparkled in response. "What do you think?"

Portia turned in his arms and stroked her hand over the spot on his neck where she'd bitten him. The skin had instantly mended, repairing itself, but she could still visualize the tiny wound.

Zane's eyes darkened, and a moan issued from his chest. "I can still feel your fangs there." He pulled her closer.

She licked her lips, remembering his rich taste, suddenly hungry for more. "Can we do it again?"

"Just the biting?"

"No. Both."

"Biting and making love?"

Portia felt warmth spread in her belly. "I want both."

"Anytime, baby girl. You just tell me when you're ready for me."

Encouraged by his tender voice and the warmth she felt from him, she brushed her fingers over his forearm again, lingering over the tattoo on its inside. She dropped her gaze to it and felt him shift.

"You don't have to tell me if you don't want to …"

"Portia …"

His muscles tensed.

"You must have gone through a horrible time." She'd sensed earlier that whatever things he'd experienced in the death camps, had shaped his beliefs about himself. And now that she'd experienced the passion that was inside of Zane, she wanted more. She wanted to understand him, to find out what else was inside him. If he let her in.

"It's best to forget it."

"But you haven't forgotten." Beneath her fingers, the tattoo seemed to burn.

Zane squeezed his eyes shut. "No. I can never forget."

Her hand went to his cheek, cupping it. He jerked for a split-second, then placed his own palm over her hand.

"Why do you want to know about it?" He opened his eyes and gazed at her.

"Because I want to know who you are." She collected all her courage to speak the next words. "Because I'm falling in love with you."

A flash of despair lit in his eyes. "Oh, God, Portia. Please don't … You're young. This is your first experience. You don't know what you're feeling."

Portia shook her head. Her feelings toward him were intense and honest, and most of all, very clear: it wasn't simply desire that held her captured in his arms, it was something deeper and more potent than anything else she'd ever experienced. "I know what I feel."

"You don't know me."

"Then help me get to know you."

He stared at her, his jaw tight, his chest heaving as if he had trouble breathing.

"Please," she whispered. "Tell me who you are."

Zane closed his eyes in a motion of surrender. "Promise me something."

"Anything."

"Don't judge me for what I've done."

She leaned to kiss his lips in agreement. There was a sense of desperation when he kissed her back, and a reluctance to let go of her.

She reacted by shifting closer.

"I was human when I entered Buchenwald. I escaped it a vampire. Between those two events lie five years of misery, pain, and death. The first two years in the camp was hard labor, working in an armament factory, supporting a cause I didn't believe in. We lived in miserable conditions, and I thought I was in hell. But then they selected me and my sister for another program."

"What program?" Portia echoed.

"They called it medical research, but it was much more than that. It was evil."

***

"The barracks looked no different from the others where the general inmate population was kept, yet inside the wooden structure, hell had been recreated. Rooms, or rather cells, lined the entire length of the building. On the other side, laboratories with ominous looking glass containers with mysterious contents gleamed in their sterility, belying the otherwise squalid condition of the camp."

"It must have been horrible," Portia interrupted.

Zane nodded. "Unimaginable. Are you sure you want to know about this?"

"Yes. Go on. What happened in those barracks?"

"Here, the prisoners were fed well. Their bodies were clean, and the doctors in attendance monitored their health on a constant basis. On its surface, it looked like a state-of-the-art hospital with every type of medical equipment available in the early 1940s. Any casual visitor would have seen nothing more frightening than two dozen inmates dressed in hospital whites, rather than the striped prison uniform worn by their fellow prisoners in the other barracks.

"But these men and women didn't count themselves lucky; each and every one wished they'd never been picked from the vermin-infested barracks where the rest of the Jews, Gypsies, homosexuals, and political prisoners were kept. Had they known what would be their fate, they would have gladly returned to the hard labor that the other, more fortunate ones, were performing daily."

Zane felt Portia holding her breath in anticipation.

"But they'd had no choice. They selected my sister Rachel and me in 1942, two years after we entered the camp. The day they brought us to the research barracks was the day I saw my parents for the last time. I don't know what happened to them after that."

Portia's hand stroked over his arm, comforting him.

"My hair was no longer than half an inch by that time, but they shaved what remained so they could attach the electrodes they used for some of the experiments.

"The medical chief of the facility was Dr. Franz Müller. There were four other doctors working under him. They did everything he demanded. Nobody questioned his methods. Even the commandant of the camp, Standartenführer Hermann Pister, didn't interfere. Müller was given free reign. His official orders were to conduct experiments that would help the German military in the recovery of their wounded soldiers. And mostly, it was what all these doctors did, not only at Buchenwald but also at other camps like Auschwitz and Mauthausen. Müller was as cruel as Mengele, and as mad as the Führer himself. But worst of all was his obsession with two things: immortality and a master race."

"Oh my God, I always thought some of those stories were just rumors."

Zane shook his head. "The inmates were his guinea pigs to experiment on as he wished. Cruelty was part of the program. At the beginning, he tested the threshold of pain a man could endure, applying injuries upon injuries, cuts, burns, and whippings to determine what the human body was capable of enduring. The experiments were more cruel and brutal than anybody could have imagined: bone, muscle and nerve transplants from one prisoner to the next—without the use of anesthetics; freezing experiments to figure out when hypothermia set in, and at what body temperature it was irreversible."

He felt Portia shiver next to him as if she physically felt the cold he was talking about.

"The head injury experiments were among the most savage: prisoners were strapped to a chair, and sustained repeated hammer blows to their heads. The screams were bloodcurdling, and the results inevitable: irreversible brain damage and eventual death.

"Müller went through hundreds of prisoners. They were disposable. When he breached a threshold, killing a test subject, he called for the guards to bring him more from the other barracks. There was limitless supply. Each day, more came in trains, herded in like cattle. Buchenwald wasn't an extermination camp, but the prisoners outside the research barracks died just as quickly as those inside from the experiments, and those working in the armament factories from sheer exhaustion and malnutrition.

"Eventually, Müller had enough data to take the tests further. He knew the limits of how far a human body could be taken before it would give in to death. But he needed more. He injected the prisoners with different compounds, testing what would allow them to endure more pain, live longer, or make them stronger. All so he could advance the Reich's racial ideology: to create a master race, humans who were superior to others, so they could rule the world. As many died from the injections as from the beatings and other injuries."

Portia let out a sigh. "How could those poor people even survive for as long as they did?"

Zane glanced at her for a moment. "I wished so many times to die then. But I wasn't that lucky." Neither was his sister.

"They did the same to the women. Even now, I can't get the screams out of my head. Rachel's screams. She was sixteen then, and her life was over before it began. Knowing what she went through, hurt me more than what they did to me. And I was powerless to stop it, powerless to help my baby sister."

He took a steadying breath, trying to lend his voice the strength it always lost when he thought about his sister.

"The experiments, of course, led nowhere. The entire program was a failure, but Müller wouldn't give up. With every month that passed, his desperation to reach his goal manifested itself in more and more brutality and cruelty... Müller's face had turned into a mask of madness, his eyes often wild with obsession, his hair in a constant mess because he couldn't stop raking his fingers through it as he contemplated his next move and thought up new ways of advancing his so-called research. Then one day in the winter of 1944, the solution fell into his lap.

"Just as Hitler was obsessed with the occult, Müller too believed in the supernatural, as did the men who worked for him. There was a strange occurrence in the camp one night, and guards investigated. They found a man feeding off some prisoners. Drinking blood. Later I found out from a local prisoner who was in the barracks with me that there had been rumors about vampires in that region, but those had been dismissed as stories to scare unruly kids.

"They managed to trap and capture the vampire. When they brought him to the medical barracks, chains as thick as my wrist wrapped around him, Müller couldn't have been more ecstatic."

"How? A vampire would have been much stronger than those humans."

Zane nodded in agreement. "The vampire killed several of the guards before the others could overpower him. It turned out that he was near starvation himself and too weak to fight them any longer."

"What happened then?"

He put his hand over hers and squeezed it. "Terrible things happened, baby girl. Things nobody should have to experience."

Chapter Twenty-Six

"A vampire," Müller echoed, his eyes wide with surprise.

From the treatment chair he was chained to, Zacharias witnessed what would become the turning point in Müller's research.

Immortality suddenly within his grasp, the evil doctor approached the creature. He looked human, except for the large fangs that protruded from his mouth, and the hands that looked more like the claws of an animal than human fingers. His body gaunt, his cheeks hollow he appeared starved, almost as starved as the prisoners in the other barracks. The snarls the man-beast released as he fought against the heavy chains the guard had wrapped around him, reverberated against the walls of the barracks and woke the test subjects in the nearby cells.

Zacharias closed his eyes. It was the only way he could hold onto his sanity, by thinking of the others not as humans, but as test subjects. Only when it came to his sister, when he saw her in her cell when passing on his way back to his, or when he heard her cry and whimper, did he remember that they were all human. During those moments, he wished for a way to end his life. But there was none.

"I will kill you all!" the vampire snarled in Czech, his voice hoarse and weak.

Zacharias had picked up a few Czech words from fellow prisoners, enough to understand what the vampire was saying.

"It speaks!" Müller marveled, then looked at the guards. "Do we have anybody who speaks Czech?"

Both of them shook their heads.

"Quickly," Müller instructed curtly, "find somebody and get him here."

When the captured vampire clawed at the guards and snapped his teeth in a futile attempt to attack them, Zacharias gazed at the poor creature. His heart filled with pity. Maybe he was an animal, a dangerous demon, but subdued by the vicious Nazi guards, the vampire would become just as much a test subject as the others in their midst. A quiet sob escaped him. None of the guards seemed to hear it. Yet, the vampire's gaze clashed with his. For a moment, he only saw the man inside the creature.

Zacharias mouthed one of the few words he knew in Czech. "I'm sorry."

He didn't know it then, but that brief connection from one soul to another was what would eventually save his life.

Müller rubbed his hands. "Chain him to the gurney. Wake Brandt and Arenberg, and get them in here now. We have work to do."

By the time the two subordinates arrived a few minutes later, nobody seemed to remember that Zacharias was still chained to a treatment chair in the other corner of the room. Everybody's eyes were on the vampire.

Müller's instructions were simple. "I want to analyze his blood."

Brandt proceeded to draw blood from the chained vampire, while Arenberg assisted. Müller watched from a safe distance.

Coward, Zacharias thought. With the weak human inmates, Müller had no problem doling out injuries and pain himself, but with a vampire who was stronger and who had already killed several guards during his capture, the doctor wanted to play it safe.

Nobody knew how strong the vampire was, and whether the chains would hold. Already now, as Zacharias watched in fascination, allowing his eyes to examine the strange man, it appeared as if the chains were stretching, the iron groaning, as the vampire's body fought against the restraints.

Without eye contact to the vampire who now lay face up on a gurney, Zacharias wasn't able to communicate with him without giving away that he understood some Czech. His instinct told him that it was a secret he needed to keep.

When the sound of snapping metal suddenly filled the room, and one of the vampire's hands broke free from its restraints, Müller's colleagues started screaming.

"He's breaking the chains!"

Instead of helping his colleagues, Müller retreated to safety, his eyes wide with fascination. "So strong," he whispered to himself.

Right then, Zacharias could fairly read Müller's thoughts. He would try anything to tap into the vampire's strength, harness it, and use it for himself.

"Scheiße!" Brandt screamed before the vampire's hand wrapped

around his neck.

As they struggled and Arenberg tried to subdue the vampire by plunging a syringe with unknown contents into his neck, the silver chains Arenberg liked to wear around his neck, made contact with the vampire's exposed skin.

A sizzling sound was followed by the stench of burnt hair and skin, and mingled with the vampire's scream, at the same time as he released Brandt's neck. Brandt coughed and jumped back.

"The silver!" Müller yelled. "It burns him."

He rushed toward Arenberg and ripped the two chains off his neck, then quickly wrapped them around the vampire's.

The prisoner howled in pain, his skin burning as if they'd poured acid over him. His movements weakened.

"Get me more silver!" Müller ordered.

From that night on, they chained the vampire with silver. It weakened him, making it impossible to escape. The next weeks were agony, not only for the vampire, but also for the other prisoners. It took many botched attempts before Müller and his colleagues figured out how they could turn other prisoners into vampires. Simply injecting them the blood of the captured vampire wasn't enough. While it healed the prisoners' injuries, it didn't in turn make them stronger or turn them into vampires.

Only when they figured out that the person they wanted to turn had to be on the verge of death and ingest vampire blood at that point, did they meet with success. After they turned the first prisoner into a vampire by using the Czech vampire's blood, they made sure to keep him weak and deprived him of human blood so he would be easily subdued.

Zacharias was in the cell next to the Czech vampire, and during the times when Müller and his colleagues weren't in the hospital barracks, and only a few guards were in attendance, they often whispered to each other. During those hushed conversations, Zacharias learned what he could from the vampire.

"Our kind is capable of mind control," he said one night.

"Mind control?" Zacharias wasn't sure he'd translated correctly.

"Yes, I can send my thoughts to others to make them do what I want."

"But then why don't you tell them to release you?"

A tired smile crossed the vampire's lips. "I was too starved and weak when they captured me, and even now, they're keeping me too weak to have enough strength for the task. I need more human blood."

Zacharias immediately reacted by moving away from the bars that separated them. "No," he whispered to himself. It was a ploy. If he allowed the vampire to feed off him, he'd grow too weak and die himself. And then who would save Rachel?

"Give me your blood and I'll help you escape."

Zacharias shook his head, too scared to believe the man. "You'll kill us all."

In retrospect, it was a mistake to deny the vampire. He could have saved them all, had Zacharias not doubted his words.

In March of 1945, a month before the camp was liberated by Patton's approaching army, Müller turned both Zacharias and Rachel into vampires to study the effects on both male and female of the species. Rachel endured the most horrible experiments: they amputated fingers and toes only to watch them re-grow during her restorative sleep. While the pain would eventually subside, Zacharias recognized that his sister's mind was going; the mutilations and the on-and-off deprivation of blood took their toll on her mind and drove her mad. Her eyes had an emptiness to them that made Zacharias despair.

His own turning had been painful, but what was worse was the constant hunger for blood he experienced right after the turning. He'd thought the hunger he'd lived through in the first two years at the camp had been excruciating, but there were no words to describe the horrendous cravings his body went through, or the shame that came with it. He was an animal now, no longer the sophisticated son of a lawyer who wrote poetry and loved music. No longer the man whose name was once Zacharias Abraham Noah Eisenberg, but only a shell of it, a shell that no longer deserved that name. All that was left of his humanity was a fraction of what he'd once been: Z.A.N.E.

But if he'd thought he'd been through the worst, he was wrong.

One night, he overheard the guards saying that the camp was being partially evacuated and that the hospital and all its inmates were to be destroyed so the approaching allies would find no evidence of the research Müller was conducting. Desperate to save both himself and his sister, he asked the Czech vampire for help.

"Now you come to me," the other vampire said weakly. "Too late now. We're too weak. We both need blood."

"Tell me what to do." His survival instinct was still strong, and Rachel was suffering.

He stared into the hollow eyes of his cellmate.

"They drained me and bottled my blood. I think they'll use it later to create more vampires. You want to escape? The silver will prevent it. And mind control is a skill that takes lots of energy."

Z.A.N.E. shook his head. He couldn't give up. Rachel depended on him. "Teach me. Tell me everything you know."

"Remember the day they captured me?"

He nodded.

"You told me then you're sorry. Your words gave me strength, and had one of them not worn a silver necklace, I would have escaped that night. I owe you for that." He closed his eyes briefly, before continuing, his voice getting weaker by the minute. "Now listen, my friend, I don't have much time left, but you can perhaps make it. A vampire's blood is potent. They may be depriving you of human blood to keep you weak and easily controlled, but if you drain the last of mine, there is a chance you can garner sufficient strength to use mind control on the weakest of the guards to make him untie you. Once he loosens your silver chains you'll have to drain him. Do it quickly. It'll heal your body and strengthen you."

Z.A.N.E. swallowed. The thought of stilling his hunger overwhelmed his scruples of killing. "And the mind control. How does it work?"

"You have to concentrate on what you want most. You'll feel a warmth starting in your belly. It'll engulf your entire body. When you feel the heat, focus your mind on the person you want to influence. Tell him what you want him to do, and he'll do it. Never lose your concentration. Forget the pain the silver is inflicting. Only think of your goal."

The breathing of the other vampire slowed.

"I'm sorry."

As the vampire's eyes flew open, a faint glint sparkled there. "It is time to die. Good-bye my friend, and promise me, you'll kill them all, you'll kill the men who did this to us."

Z.A.N.E. nodded and lowered his head to the man's neck. When his fangs sank into his flesh, he pulled on the vein and sucked the vessel until it was dry, until the heartbeat inside the shell disappeared. He felt his own body fill with the life giving liquid, his muscles strengthening, his mind thinking clearer now.

He was a killer now; nothing would ever change that.

The Czech vampire had been right. With his blood, he was feeling stronger, and his tenth attempt at mind control finally produced the expected result: he was able to control one of the guards and mentally forced him to free him of his silver chains while the second guard had nodded off.

He drained the guard who'd freed him and dropped his lifeless body to the ground. He felt a surge of strength and power in his new body, but before he could reach the second guard, he'd awakened and sounded the alarm. From everywhere, more guards came running.

In an effort to create confusion, Z.A.N.E. managed to open several cells so some of the inmates could escape. He used the uproar to search for his sister. Shots were fired, and a battle broke out between the released prisoners and the guards. Desperation, and the hope of a rumored rescue by the Allies, lent the human guinea pigs more strength than the guards expected, and more than they would have had before the rumors.

But there was no time for Z.A.N.E. to rejoice. He found Rachel in one of the treatment rooms, strapped onto a gurney. Her head thrashed wildly. Her body was broken: they had carved her womb open while she was still alive. He could only assume so they could examine if she had working reproductive organs.

His heart clenched. "Rachel."

She opened her eyes then. At first, they didn't focus, and she stared blankly, but then a flash of recognition lit in them. "Zacharias."

"I'm here now. They can't hurt you anymore."

She shook her head, her eyes filling with tears. "Let me go."

"Yes, we're going. I'll help you heal. Human blood," he murmured. He would get one of the remaining humans and have her drink from him, so she could heal.

"No. Let me go. I can't live like this. Let me go," she begged, and he finally understood.

"NOOOO!" he wailed.

She stretched her hands toward him, her eyes repeating her wish. Then her eyes darted toward a table with instruments. He followed her gaze and saw the wooden stake the doctors had fashioned. Whenever they were done with one of the vampires they had created, or when they feared the creature would become too strong, they used it to be sure it would not.

His feet moved before he knew his brain had made the decision. When his palm wrapped around the smooth wooden surface, he felt as if somebody was ripping his still beating heart from his body.

But when he looked back at Rachel and saw her give him a faint smile, he knew it was the only solution.

"I love you, Zacharias."

Then he did what he had to do. It was the last time tears streamed down his face.

Heavy sobs brought him back to the present. The tears weren't Zane's but Portia's.

"Baby girl, why are you crying?"

"They hurt you so much."

The chains around his heart loosened further. "Don't cry for me. I'm a killer."

She shook her head, her long hair caressing his chest in the process. "They're responsible. It's not your fault. They're the monsters."

"Most of them are dead now."

He tipped her head up with his thumb and forefinger and wiped her tears.

"The assassin Quinn spoke of the other night. Is he one of them?" she asked.

"He was Brandt's hybrid son."

Shock widened her eyes. "But Brandt was human."

"They used the blood they drained from the vampires they created and fled with it the same night I escaped. They knew how to turn a human into a vampire, so they performed the transformation on each other. It was what Müller always wanted: immortality and a master race. He had what he wanted."

"How do you know that's what they did?"

"I had my suspicions when they fled and all of the vampire blood was gone. And it was confirmed later when I found one of them. He was a vampire then. And I killed him. First Wolpers, then Arenberg, then Schmidt, then Brandt."

"And Müller?"

"He's still out there. He's the one who sent Brandt's son after me, I'm sure. He wants me dead. He knows I'm hunting him. And he knows I won't stop."

Portia's hand came up to caress his cheek. "I hope he dies a horrible death."

Zane put his finger to her lips to stop her from speaking. "Shh. I don't want you to be infected by my hatred. This is my business."

"You've been through so much. I want to support you."

He sighed. "Oh, baby girl, you shouldn't get entangled in this."

"Too late," she whispered and brushed her lips against his.

Her tempting scent washed away the memories of his past and reminded him why they'd come to his cabin. "God, you feel good," he mumbled as he drew her closer.

"Can we make love again?"

"As often as you want to." And even that wouldn't be often enough. But at least for a few hours or maybe even a few days, he could forget that he had a past, and how uncertain his future was, and live only in the moment.

Chapter Twenty-Seven

Daylight came and went, their time in bed only interrupted by short trips to let the dog out and feed him.

Portia rolled to her side and noticed that she was alone in bed. Zane's scent still lingered. She must have fallen asleep sometime around sunset. Her eyes fell onto the clock on the bedside table. It was just past nine o'clock.

Stretching her pleasantly aching muscles, she slid out of bed and snatched one of Zane's t-shirts from his closet. Dressed in only the shirt that reached almost to mid-thigh, she wandered into the living room.

Zane sat at a small desk with his back to her, dressed in a t-shirt and boxer shorts. On tip toes, she snuck up, but her silent approach was announced by the happy barking of the dog.

"Z!" she admonished. "You're spoiling everything."

Zane turned to her, revealing the computer screen that had been hidden by his body. "What were you trying to do? Wrestle me to the ground to have your way with me?"

Portia bent to pet the puppy as it excitedly moved around her legs. "Would I have to fight you for it?"

She stepped within Zane's reach, and his arms instantly came around her waist, drawing her closer.

"I'd wrestle with you any day." He buried his face in her stomach, audibly inhaling her scent.

Portia's gaze fell onto the monitor where an email program was open. "What are you doing up?"

"I was checking messages." He motioned his head toward the computer. "Can't switch on my cell phone; otherwise my colleagues can trace me, and there's no landline in the cabin. But I have a program that logs into my cell messages and transcribes them."

"It sends them to your email?" she asked. "That's useful. But can't your colleagues trace from where you accessed your messages?"

"Chances are very low. Everything is encrypted and routed over several servers." He pulled her onto his lap, his lips seeking her neck and nuzzling there. "But I needed to know what's going on back in San Francisco."

"Anything to worry about?"

He shook his head. "My colleagues are livid. Nothing new otherwise."

Portia's eyes honed in on a sentence of the message currently displayed on the screen and read it. "Quinn has a lead on the assassin? And you're telling me there's no news?"

Zane didn't even move his head and continued nibbling on her skin. "Quinn is lying. He's got nothing. It's a trap."

"How can you be so sure?" She read more of the message where Quinn talked about a cell phone chip and several phone numbers that were programmed into it.

"He's trying to trick me into coming back, and he's using the one thing I want most to do it."

"But what if he's telling the truth?"

Zane lifted his head and looked at her. "Quinn was the one who ratted me out to my boss. He's the one who told them about us. That's why they pulled me off the assignment. Trust me, he's trying to play me right now."

"Oh, but he seemed such a nice guy."

"Nice? That's what everybody thinks because he has the angelic face of a college kid. Don't let that fool you. He's a dangerous man. And he's no longer a friend." There was a harsh undertone in Zane's voice.

Portia pressed a soft kiss onto his lips. "I'm sorry."

"It's not your fault."

She shook her long locks. "It is. If I hadn't pestered you to do this, you wouldn't have lost your friend."

"Pestered me?" He smiled softly. "I guess that's a way of looking at it." He slanted his mouth over hers.

"Then come back to bed," she whispered, feeling his hunger physically. Her body instantly responded to him, her nipples tightening into hard points, hot lava shooting through her veins instead of blood.

"I can't." Zane pulled back.

His refusal jolted her. Had he already had enough of her? Disappointment stood at the gate, ready to enter.

"I have to go feed." He lifted her from his lap and stood. "Let me get dressed. I promise you, I'll be back within an hour."

Dumbfounded, she stood there for a second as he walked toward the bedroom. Then her lips parted and words tumbled from them. "Why don't you want my blood?"

Zane rocked to a dead stop.

Her eyes bored into his back, and she noticed his shoulders tense.

"Portia," he started before his voice faltered.

"Why?"

In slow motion, he turned. His eyes were glowing red and his sharp fangs protruded from his lips. As her gaze swept lower, she noticed his boxer shorts tenting. Her mouth watered in response, and she realized that the thought of drinking her blood turned him on.

She took two determined steps in his direction, yet he still didn't move.

"You do want my blood, don't you," she husked.

Her hand came up to stroke over the pulse on her neck, drawing his attention to it.

"Then why not take it? Why not sink your fangs into me and drink from me?"

She licked her lower lip, the image her words painted making her knees weak and her pulse pound against her skin.

Zane's feet finally moved, his hesitant steps bringing him closer until he stood only a few inches from her.

"Yes," she breathed. "I want your bite."

Her hand dropped to his boxers, brushing against the hard shaft beneath. It jerked as she pulled the waistband down and freed it.

"And I want your cock inside me."

She wrapped her hand around it, feeling the heat beneath her fingers. "Deep."

She stroked down its entire length. "Hard."

His ragged breath bounced against her. "Fuck, Portia."

His hand clamped down over hers, stopping her from repeating her movement. "If I take your blood, I won't be able to stop."

"When," she corrected him. "When you take my blood, we'll both make sure you won't hurt me."

***

Zane closed his eyes, the sensations coursing through his body too intense to bear. "Portia, are you sure you want this?"

Had she really offered him her blood or was he hallucinating because he needed blood so badly? After everything she knew about him now, did she still believe him worthy to take this gift, to allow him this ultimate intimacy of feeding from her?

The last twenty-four hours had depleted him. He could barely remember when he'd last fed, but he knew it had been too long ago. Making love to her all night and day had robbed him of his reserves, and now he was wiped. If he didn't get blood in the next six hours, his hunger would grow to frightening proportions, and his control would snap. Hell, he'd probably even attack the dog to feed, even though animal blood would provide him with little nourishment.

Knowing how close he was to giving into the bloodlust that hovered just below the surface, how could he accept her offer? What if he couldn't stop?

His dark side reared its head. She would taste delicious, better than anything he'd ever tasted. To fuck her at the same time would make it all the better.

"You want it," her voice repeated.

"But do you?"

"I want what you want. When I drank from you, it was the best thing I've ever tasted."

Zane's eyes dropped to her throat where her pulse jumped against her skin.

"The best thing I ever felt," she continued, her voice a mere breath. "I want you to feel the same."

It wouldn't be the same. It would be much more. Her blood was so much more potent than any pure vampire's blood. Hers was laced with the sweetness of human blood. Not only would it nourish him and strengthen him, it would make the connection that already existed between them more pronounced.

He'd felt it instantly the moment Portia had taken his blood, and then again later when they'd made love again and again. There was something between them that couldn't be denied, even if he wanted to. He wanted to claim her as his, damn the consequences, and she would agree, he read that much in her expressive face. But it wouldn't be right. She was young and he was her first experience. He had no right to bind her to him when this was only a temporary infatuation on her part.

"Portia, don't tempt me any longer."

She brought one hand to his lips and brushed her index finger over his fang. A flame of desire shot through him.

"So you *are* tempted."

Despite the hand he'd clamped over hers that clasped his cock, she managed to move it to stroke his shaft.

"Fuck!" he hissed.

"Bite me. Take my blood."

Ah, fuck it! Even he didn't have enough strength to resist. In one fluid motion, he lifted her off her feet and carried her to the sofa, letting himself fall onto it as he positioned her in his lap. Her legs spread, and the t-shirt that she wore rode up, revealing her lack of panties. He let out an appreciative grunt.

The scent of her arousal instantly wrapped around him, only intensifying his hunger.

"This won't be gentle," he warned before he rammed his shaft into her soft core. Liquid silk engulfed him, the warmth and wetness of it intoxicating.

Her head fell back, exposing her neck to him in all its vulnerability. The ivory skin beckoned him, the pulse that beat against it acting as a countdown to his approach. Tap-tap-tap, it called, but his eyes drifted lower.

He'd had his teeth in so many necks in the last decades, that he wanted something that would set this time apart from all the other times. His hands came up to grip the collar of her t-shirt. He ripped it, tearing it into two right down the middle.

Portia gasped, her eyes widening as understanding bloomed. "What—?"

"Too late, Portia." Too late to protest now.

His action couldn't be stopped, not by her, and certainly not by him. With one hand, he cradled her full breast, enjoying its weight in his palm. Underneath the pale skin, his keen eyes noticed the blood vessels that sat close to the surface, close enough for him to smell their sweetness.

His throat constricted and his cock jerked inside her.

"Ride me," he ordered gruffly.

She lifted herself onto her knees, making him withdraw, then came back down, impaling herself again.

"Harder!"

His body tensed, welcoming her movements. He'd hoped to savor this moment, but his control what shot to bits. Without another coherent thought, he sank his lips onto her breast, pulling the nipple into his mouth. As he licked over it, his fangs drove into her flesh to either side of it, drawing the blood from her tit.

Portia jerked under his hold only for an instant, before her breathless moan drifted to his ears. Her rich blood ran over his tongue and down the back of it, trickling down his throat, different flavors bursting on his taste buds. Spicy and sweet at the same time, it was everything he'd ever dreamed of and more.

He groaned, his hips thrusting in synch with Portia's movements as she continued to ride him, her tight muscles clenching around him on each down stroke and releasing on each withdrawal.

When her hand cupped the back of his head to hold him closer to her breast, Zane's heart jumped with joy. He felt accepted and wanted by a woman who could have anybody. Yet, she'd chosen him to show her what pleasure and passion meant. Would she want more from him? Could he hope that despite her youth and inexperience, her heart could feel the same as his did?

He shook the thought of it off, not wanting to taint this experience with the inevitable disappointment that would follow. All he could ask for was this moment, the moment of total possession, of acceptance, of surrender.

Portia was in his arms, moaning out her pleasure, riding him hard and fast, urging him to take more of her blood. Only the present counted. There was no past, no future. Only the here and now.

With her blood filling him, reaching every cell in his body, he felt like the richest man on earth, a man who had everything, who lacked nothing. And at the same time, he had nothing to give her, only his body, only the love that was inside him, bottled up and hidden. He could admit it to himself now, but he could never tell her. It was the one secret he had to keep from her. Because if she knew his feelings, she would feel obligated to offer him more. She was too sweet to leave him. She would confuse her own feelings with love, when the things that she felt were merely desire and lust for something she'd only just discovered:

sex.

To burden her with his own feelings was wrong. Yet it didn't stop him from hauling her closer to him, from digging his fangs deeper and drinking more of her sweet essence. And it didn't stop him from thrusting harder into her, filling her tight channel with his hard length that was ready to burst.

And it didn't stop him from wishing to leave something of him behind, of wanting his seed to take root in her. To create another life. At the same time he knew it was impossible: only blood-bonded couples could conceive, and he would never force this bond on her. If he did so now in the heat of passion, she would never forgive him for binding her to him for eternity.

"More," she whispered and lowered her head to his ear.

But he knew he couldn't take any more. Already, her movements had slowed and her voice sounded lethargic. He dropped his hand between their bodies and rubbed his thumb against her clit, stroking first gently, then harder.

Zane removed his fangs from her breast, licking over the incisions his teeth had left. His saliva closed them instantly and mended the skin.

"Oh, God!"

He felt her orgasm rock through her body and let go of his control. His release went through his cells like an atom bomb, obliterating everything in its path.

Portia collapsed against him. He discarded the torn t-shirt and cradled her against his chest.

"Baby girl," he murmured into her hair. There was so much more he wanted to say but couldn't.

Her breath hummed against his neck. "Promise me to always feed from me."

Zane's muscles tensed. He could make no such promise as much as he desired what she was offering. "I can't."

She pulled herself away from him, and her face told him everything he needed to know. She was so easy to read, and in this moment, he wished it were different. But he saw what was written there: hurt that he was rejecting her. And like a stake, that same kind of hurt drove into his heart.

Portia shifted to get out of his lap, but he captured her arms and stopped her, moving his hips at the same time to drive himself back into her.

"You don't understand, Portia."

She lashed an angry glare at him. "Oh, I understand. You've had enough of me already."

Zane bared his teeth. "You're wrong!"

She struggled against his hold. Angry at her defiance, he flipped her onto her back, and braced himself over her. There was no escape now, even though she pushed against him.

"It's not I who doesn't want you." Why was he even telling her that? He owed her no explanation. However, his stupid mouth didn't get the message and kept on moving. "It'll never work between us. You have your entire life ahead of you. Why would you want to chain yourself to somebody like me?"

She shook her head, her body suddenly going soft beneath his, molding itself to him. "But I want you."

"You say that now. You say that because we have great sex. That's all this is. You're confusing love with lust."

Her eyes focused on him, and something lit in them, a flicker of understanding. Maybe he'd finally gotten through to her.

"And you, are you confusing lust with love? Or do you know the difference?"

Her challenge was clear, and hell, he should be wiser than to accept it, but whatever it was—the aftermath of his orgasm or her blood pulsing in his veins—he couldn't resist answering.

"Of course I know the difference!" he bit out between clenched teeth.

"Then tell me, smart ass! Tell me that it's lust for you and I'll leave you alone. In fact, I'll pack up right now and go home. And you'll never have to set eyes on me again."

Never see her again? His heart clenched painfully at the vile thought. He searched her face to discover if she was bluffing, but nothing gave away what she was thinking. Was she giving him a way out, a way to make a clean break without losing face?

"Tell me you don't love me." At the last two words, her voice trembled.

He closed his eyes, trying to fight against the feelings that her demand conjured up. He should lie to her, lie and be done with it. But that final tremble in her voice had driven too deep into him, demanding he'd be honest with her.

Without opening his eyes, he admitted what he should have kept to himself. "I love you."

As he made a motion to lift himself off her, she hooked one leg around his, holding him back. His eyes flew open, and he pinned her.

There was a warm smile on Portia's face. "I think I should explain the rules to you again," she said softly.

"What rules?"

"As long as you love me, you don't get to leave."

He raised an eyebrow, surprised at her easy tone. "Does that rule go both ways?"

Her finger swiped over his lips in a slow and lazy stroke. "Why don't you ask what you really want to know?"

He suddenly felt lighthearted, her playful attitude helping him relax. Maybe he could give this a try. "Tell me you don't love me and I'll let you go now."

"When I'm near you, I can feel you in here." She pressed her hand against her heart. "And when you're gone, there's an emptiness there. And it hurts. And the pain only goes away when you're close again. Tell me, Zane, tell me what that is."

Her eyes were round like saucers and as beautiful as he'd ever seen her. Laced in those eyes was the knowledge that she knew the answer to her question, but that she wanted him to acknowledge it. She wanted him to accept it.

"Does it feel like your heart will tear into pieces at the thought that we'd never see each other again?" Because it was what he felt. And the pain was unbearable.

Portia nodded.

"Baby girl," he murmured and brushed his lips against hers. "Are you sure?"

Instead of another nod, she pressed her lips against his for a slow kiss. Her breath bounced against him when she parted her lips to speak.

"Have you figured it out yet?" she mumbled against his mouth.

Zane drew back a few inches so he could look into her eyes. "You love me."

How, he didn't know, but in her eyes shone the love he hadn't wanted to see at first.

"I love you, Zane."

Would he ever be worthy of it? He tried not to think of it, not to worry that she would change her mind and walk away from him one day. He wouldn't survive it, because losing her would rob him of the last piece of his heart and turn him into the monster that lurked in the shadows.

Chapter Twenty-Eight

Gabriel had expected the call, but not so quickly. But when he heard Lewis' voice asking about his daughter Portia, there was no doubt that the shit would soon hit the fan.

As discussed with Samson earlier, he quickly patched him into the call. This situation needed to be handled with care.

"It's Robert Lewis, Portia's father."

"Damn!" Samson cursed. "Have you told him anything yet?"

"No. But we won't be able to stall him."

"I know. Get him on the line."

Gabriel pressed a button and heard the other man's breathing on the other end. "Mr. Lewis, you're on the line with Samson Woodford, the owner of Scanguards."

"Where is my daughter? She's not answering her cell, and nobody's picking up the phone at home." There was a good deal of impatience in his voice.

Samson cleared his voice. "Let me assure you, Mr. Lewis, that your daughter is well."

Well? Gabriel felt the urge the scratch his head at Samson's conversation starter. How could Portia be well with Zane? His fellow vampire and second in command was a raving lunatic! He'd kidnapped his charge. Didn't that sum things up nicely?

"What are you saying? What happened to her?" The impatience in Lewis' voice was instantly replaced with panic.

Gabriel immediately realized that he cared for his daughter. After the things Samson had relayed to him about Zane's bizarre claim that her father wanted to keep her a virgin for some perverted reason, Gabriel hadn't expected him to show the kind of concern that was now evident in his voice. It only cemented his own belief that Zane had to be wrong.

"She's still in our care."

"What does that mean?" Lewis yelled into the phone, prompting Gabriel to move the handset away from his ear.

"What Mr. Woodford means is that no harm has come to her," Gabriel interjected.

"Get her on the phone! NOW!"

"Uh, Mr. Lewis, there's something I need to discuss with you before you can speak to your daughter."

A snarl ripped through the line. This wasn't going well, and why should it? The man had a right to speak to his daughter, and he knew it. No amount of stalling was going to get them out of this quagmire.

"Your daughter has made certain claims, and I'm afraid that we're compelled to investigate these alleg—"

"What lies has she been telling you?"

"We're not sure at this point whether they are lies. Your daughter has convinced at least one of our employees to take her allegations seriously, and considering the seriousness of her claim and the potential implications on your daughter's future, we have decided to look into this."

Look into this? Samson was twisting the truth just a little more than usual. The one who was looking into this, or more likely *thrusting into this* was Zane, Gabriel thought with a bitter laugh.

"You have no right to deny me access to my daughter! She's a minor, and by law, she—"

"There is more than one law that governs vampires and hybrids," Samson interrupted, a dangerous edge to his voice now. "And while I understand very well that the right of a father is a primary one, it does not override the laws of our society."

"I don't give a fuck about your laws. My daughter is mine! All I asked you to do was protect her. And what do you do? Listen to her stupid blabbering."

Gabriel's jaw clenched. So much for the care for his daughter. It wasn't concern for her wellbeing that had shown through early in the conversation, it was something else entirely. He pushed the thought away, not wanting to follow it to its conclusion.

"Mr. Lewis," Samson continued undeterred. "We can discuss this—"

"Oh, we'll discuss this!" Lewis yelled. "As soon as the sun sets, I'm on the next plane to San Francisco, and my daughter had better be waiting for me, or some heads will roll!"

With his threat, the call disconnected.

Samson exhaled on the other line. "You still there, Gabriel?"

"Yep. This didn't go well."

"I didn't expect it to go well. But at least we have a few more hours before we have to face him. Anything new on Zane's location?"

Gabriel shook his head. "Our contacts have come up empty. Lauren hasn't heard from Portia either, even though those two are thick as thieves. But Thomas is working on hacking into Zane's accounts to see if he can find something."

"Good. And Quinn? He must know something."

Gabriel rubbed his neck. "I thought so too, but I can't get anything out of him."

"Has Zane used his credit card anywhere?"

"He's too careful for that. Even if he needed gas for the car, I'm sure he paid cash. Let's face it, if he doesn't want to be found, we won't find him."

"Then we have to figure out a way to draw him out."

"And how are we gonna do that?"

There was a pause of quiet contemplation before Samson replied, "Get me Quinn. He went to see Thomas last night. I want to know what it was about."

"Why not ask Thomas?"

"Because Quinn knows something nobody else does. I just have that gut feeling about it."

"I hope you're right."

"So do I."

A click in the line told Gabriel that Samson had disconnected the call. He sighed.

Behind him, a sound alerted him to the presence of his wife. He turned and smiled at Maya as she floated right into his arms.

"You look worried, baby."

Gabriel sank his face into her long dark hair and inhaled her intoxicating scent. "That's because I am."

"Do you really think Zane will hurt her?"

"If she lied to him, yes." For Portia's sake, he hoped she wasn't hiding anything from Zane.

"But that's not why you're worried. There's something about her father, isn't there?"

There was little he could hide from Maya, and not just because of their blood-bond. Even without it, she would have known when something was wrong.

"He gave me a chill. There was something in his voice that I didn't like."

Maya tilted her head, giving him a questioning look. "More than just a father concerned for his daughter?"

"Oh, he's concerned all right, but the way he said she was his, it wasn't right. He considers her his property."

"Are you sure?"

He nodded. "Which means he thinks he can do with her what he wants." And Gabriel wasn't sure Lewis' intentions were in the best interest of his daughter, whatever they were.

"Then you think that Zane might be right after all, that her father wants her to remain a virgin?"

"And if Zane is right, the only question is: why?"

Maya stroked her hand over the pulsing scar on his face. "What if it doesn't matter anymore?"

He raised a questioning eyebrow. "My sweet wife, I'm not sure I'm following."

"Whatever the reason for it was, it won't matter anymore. After spending over twenty-four hours alone with Zane, do you really think she's still a virgin?"

Not a chance, Gabriel mused.

Exactly, Maya responded, sending her thoughts directly to his mind.

***

"Listen, Samson," Quinn insisted, pacing in his boss' study, "if I knew where he was, I'd tell you."

"Portia's father will be here in less than twelve hours. What do you want me to tell him?"

"Tell him the truth?"

"And what is the truth, Quinn?"

"The truth?" Quinn exhaled, collecting his thoughts. "I baited Zane to come back. I dangled in front of him what he wants most."

"Explain."

"I left him a voicemail and sent an email with information he's been looking for for years."

"You made something up? He might have smelled a rat."

"He probably did smell a rat, but I didn't make it up. I found what he was looking for."

"Does this have anything to do with your visit to Thomas or was that a social call?"

Surprised, Quinn stood still. "It doesn't matter. Don't pry any further. I can't tell you anything without breaking Zane's confidence."

Samson nodded his understanding. "And still he won't come out of hiding? Why do you think that is?"

Quinn let himself fall onto the couch, more weary than tired all of a sudden. He rubbed the bridge of his nose. "Do I really have to spell it out for you?"

"Don't make me guess. You know how I hate that."

"He isn't coming out of hiding because he'd rather be with Portia. Isn't that telling you enough?"

"You can't possible think that Zane … No, he's not capable of …" Samson shook his head in slow motion.

"And why not? He's a man just like any of us. Just because he's never shown any feelings doesn't mean he doesn't have any. Maybe she triggered something in him. Maybe she's exactly what he needs."

Samson jaw dropped. "An innocent? You can't be serious."

"I bet she's not that innocent anymore."

"What do you think he's planning to do with her?"

Fuck her, mate her, Quinn wanted to say, but held his tongue. Samson could figure that out for himself. "How long until her twenty-first birthday?"

Samson dropped his head to the file in front of him, his eyes scanning the paper. "Four and a half weeks."

"You asked me what I think he'll do. Here's my best guess: he'll keep her hidden until she's of age."

"To keep her away from her father?"

Quinn nodded even though he knew it wasn't the complete answer. If Zane had really fallen for Portia, then he would want something more from her. He'd have to wait until her twenty-first birthday before she was old enough to give her consent to mate her. Her father would never give it; that much was clear already. If he didn't want his daughter to lose her virginity, he didn't want her to mate the meanest vampire out there.

Chapter Twenty-Nine

Zane turned his back to the computer and smiled at Portia. He hadn't smiled as much in over sixty years as he'd smiled in the last twenty-four hours.

"Your pizza is on its way. Just explain one thing to me: the fridge is chock-full with human food, and you want take-out food?"

"It's not any different from you wanting one particular type of blood. Don't you ever have cravings?" she teased.

Zane rose and went for her, but she ran toward the door and swung it open. Z instantly came running from his place in front of the fireplace, wagging his tail.

"Oh, I have cravings, baby girl." And right now he had a very particular one. Ever since he'd tasted her blood and confessed his love to her, something had changed. A carefree atmosphere suddenly filled the cabin, and his heart. They both laughed and joked more freely. Yet whenever their gazes met, the heat was instantly there, the fire between them burning brighter than before.

Portia giggled and snatched her jacket off the hook next to the door. "Then you understand." She cast a look over her shoulder and winked mischievously. "And if you want me to satisfy your particular craving later, I'd better get my pizza to get my strength back."

A rumble from deep in his chest left his lips as a suppressed moan. "I ordered you an extra large one."

Portia crouched down and stroked the excited pup's fur. "Come, let's go outside and play in the snow."

"May I join in the fun?" Zane asked and reached for his own jacket, not waiting for a reply.

Her thick dark lashes swept upwards in a graceful move. "Only if you behave."

"Depends on what you call behaving."

She chuckled. "I think I'm going to have my hands full with you. Your dog has much better manners than you." She turned to the pooch and rubbed his neck. "Don't you think so, Z?"

With two steps he was at the door, pulling her up and against him. "I can behave, but I'll need an incentive."

"What kind of incentive?" her voice was breathy, and despite the thick clothes she wore, he smelled her blooming arousal.

"A little treat afterwards." Zane pressed his hips into her, letting her feel what he had in mind. He was used to his constant hard-on by now and had given up trying to hide it or trying to get it down. There was no point. Portia would get used to it, and by the looks of it, she didn't mind his constant hunger for her one bit. She hadn't turned him down once yet.

In fact, it appeared as if she'd bloomed and opened up like a beautiful flower in the summer. Everything about her was more feminine, softer, and more sensual than before. Even her movements had become more graceful. She was all woman now.

"I see you have a present for me." She rubbed herself against him, confidently and seductively.

The dog's impatient barking made him shift his gaze away from his prize. "I'm afraid you've spoiled him already. We'd better take him out, or he's going to interrupt us later ..."

" ... and we don't want that," she finished his sentence.

Minutes later, they were playing in the snow, chasing the dog and each other. There was sufficient light from the cabin to illuminate the flat ground in front of it, and Zane's vampire night vision allowed him to survey the area, making sure they were alone. Despite his carefree attitude, he never forgot his training. He was still her bodyguard. But things had changed. Now he protected her because he loved her and couldn't bear losing her. If anything happened to her, it would destroy him.

But there were still obstacles to overcome until he could make Portia his. She wasn't of age yet, and from all he'd heard about her father, he knew he wouldn't consent to a union between them. It left him no choice but to wait the few weeks until she turned twenty-one. Then she could make her own decisions.

Sure, he could mate with her now, but her father could appeal to the vampire council and nullify their union. And their decision would be clear: Zane would be in the wrong, and Portia would be taken from him. As a blood-bonded mate, it would mean certain death to him. While Portia as a hybrid would be able to continue eating human food, his body would only accept her blood as nourishment after the blood-bond.

Deprived of the only blood his body would recognize, he would starve.

If Portia were a full blooded vampire, things would be different. They would feed off each other but not at the exclusion of other blood. But a hybrid's blood initiated the same changes in a blood-bonded vampire male as a human's blood did. Both Samson and Amaury had experienced this change when they had blood-bonded with humans. Now they were entirely vulnerable and dependent on the women they loved. At their mercy. At the same time, they had bestowed part of their immortality onto their mates: as long as their human wives drank their vampire husbands' blood, they wouldn't age. But they remained human.

And while he wasn't bonded to Portia yet, Zane felt as much at her mercy as if he were. And strangely enough, the thought didn't frighten him.

A snow ball hit him squarely in the chest. He stared in the direction it had come from.

"Penny for your thoughts," Portia offered with a laugh that reached all the way to her eyes.

"Not for sale." She would get into his head soon enough. Once they were bonded, they would have a connection more intense and intimate than any human couple could ever dream of. He could barely wait for that moment when their bodies and mind connected, never to be separated.

Bending down, Zane gathered some snow in his hands and formed a ball. His aim was dead on, and he hit her sweet bottom as she ran away from him. He chased her, knowing it was what she wanted.

Z ran between him and his target, tripping him just as he reached her. As he fell, he snatched her and brought her down with him. She landed next to him, and he didn't waste any time pinning her down in the snow. Portia wouldn't feel the cold at her back, just as he wouldn't have. Not only was she dressed in a warm jacket, her hybrid body tolerated extreme temperatures as well as his vampire body did.

Stretched out above her, his head close to hers, he issued his demand. "Now for my prize."

"What prize?" She gave him a coquettish smile that he hadn't seen her use on him before.

Oh yes, she was getting more confident each minute, and he liked it. She would be a strong partner, somebody to keep him in check. And he knew he needed that if he wanted to keep the darkness at bay.

"You're my prize, didn't you know that?"

She giggled uncontrollably.

"What's so funny about that?"

"Z. He's tugging at my leg. I'm ticklish."

Zane turned his head to find the dog happily pulling on the bottom of Portia's pants, alternately licking the skin underneath and biting the fabric.

"Z! Get lost! Get your own girl. She's mine!"

When he turned his head back to Portia, he collided with her gaze. "If I'm yours, does that mean you're mine?"

Her voice was like a soft trickle that slowly but steadily slid along his skin to pool at the base of his spine.

"I'm yours, baby girl, like it or not."

"Like it," she whispered and lifted her lips to press them against his mouth. They were cold, but within seconds they heated and the now-familiar hunger for her came back in full force. His fangs lengthened instantly, and his cock hardened further, wanting to claim her here and now.

The sound of a car's tires on the snow made him interrupt the kiss. "Company," he murmured, quickly darting a look behind him before he rose, pulling her up effortlessly to stand next to him.

The kid getting out of the beat up Honda wore a hideous red jacket with the emblem of the pizza joint in the village embossed on the cheap fabric. He slowed his step up the porch when he noticed Zane and Portia approach from the yard, the dog barreling toward him.

"Pizza delivery," he announced the obvious.

"I'll get some cash," Zane told Portia by his side and rushed ahead.

"I've got some here," she called after him, making him stop.

Having reached the pizza delivery guy waiting on the steps, Portia dug into her jacket pocket and pulled out a wallet. Zane watched her as she paid for the pizza.

When the guy handed her the flat box, she set her wallet on top.

"Thanks!"

"Bye guys, enjoy," the kid called out and rushed back to his car, limbs shaking from the cold.

Zane reached for the pizza box, wanting to carry it inside for Portia, when Z ran excitedly around Portia's legs, barking, and clearly smelling the food. Portia took a step forward, but stumbled, narrowly avoiding stepping on the dog.

Her hold on the box faltered for a split-second, tilting it and making the wallet on top fall onto the snow-covered porch.

"Z!" Zane admonished.

"He thinks he'll get some of the food!" Portia added as she bent toward the wallet.

"I'll get it, baby girl."

Zane crouched down and pulled the wallet out of the snow while Portia walked back inside, the over-excited pup on her heels. The wallet had fallen open in the middle, revealing one compartment that contained a couple of credit cards, and the other side with a photo.

He wiped the snow off it, revealing the photo fully.

His heart stopped. Suddenly, everything blurred. Nausea overwhelmed him as his knees buckled. He braced his hand against the door frame to prevent himself from falling. The acrid stench of death and misery filled his nostrils and clamped an icy hand around his heart.

"No," he breathed, trying to make his eyes refocus. But no matter how much he tried to wish the picture away, it was there to stay, mocking him.

An older version of Portia smiled at him, the family resemblance evident. She had gotten her looks from her mother. Nothing from her father, not the eyes, the nose, or the chin. That's why he'd never seen it, never could have guessed.

But he had to be her father. There was no other reason why Portia would carry a photo of Franz Müller in her wallet.

"Zane, you're letting the cold in," her angelic voice called out from inside the cabin.

His throat constricted, preventing him from responding.

He'd made love to the spawn of Franz Müller, the man he hated most in this world. He'd thought himself in love with his daughter. Only minutes ago he'd dreamed of a blood-bond with her, a union for eternity.

His hands shook with rage at the injustice of it all. What had he ever done to warrant this? To fall in love with a woman he could never allow in his life? Because all she represented was evil. Nothing good could come from a man like Franz Müller. Whatever he touched was evil. His seed could only create evil.

"Aren't you coming?"

Portia stood at the door, her gaze suddenly dropping to the wallet in his hands.

"Oh thanks …" She paused. "Those are my parents."

Slowly, like the killer he was, he lifted his head and perused her. Even now that he looked at her closer, he could see no resemblance between her and her father.

"What's wrong?" Worry laced her voice.

"Is this your biological father?" he pressed out, pointing at the picture and holding onto the last straw, hoping against all odds that she wasn't his daughter after all.

"Of course, why?"

A wave of pain crashed onto him, turning into rage. And as he'd taught himself in the years of waiting for his revenge, he stilled his body and let all emotion drain from it. All that was left now was eternal coldness. He felt the chill of it physically, and it was all that would protect his heart now, a wall of ice.

Before him stood the chance to hurt Müller in the most cruel way possible, to take his daughter from him, to make her suffer. His claws emerged, and his fangs lengthened as he tried to hold the beast in check.

A flicker of fear crossed Portia's features, and instinctively she took a step back. "What's wrong? Is somebody out there?"

He shook his head slowly and deliberately. "No. We're alone."

He was alone with Müller's daughter. His gaze zeroed in on the rapidly beating pulse at her neck. It wouldn't take much to rip her throat out. She would struggle, but he was stronger. Müller had made him stronger. It was all Müller's fault.

"Your father is Franz Müller."

The gasp that escaped Portia's lips, lips he'd kissed only moments earlier, was barely audible. Her head went from side to side, silently denying his claim.

"No," she whispered. "No."

Her eyes darted back to the photo in her wallet.

"It's him." Zane didn't recognize his own voice. It was that of a stranger.

"You must be wrong," she begged, her eyes filling with moisture, the mouth widening in disbelief. "It can't be him. No, it can't be Müller. My father's name is Robert Lewis."

But her words did nothing to change the facts. He never forgot a face. And Müller's face was imprinted on his mind. It had haunted him for over six decades. Now Portia's face would haunt him equally.

"A name means nothing." They had all changed their names: Brandt and the others. Just as Zane had laid his own name to rest.

"You are Müller's daughter."

Evil by birth.

The killer inside him demanded satisfaction. The evil Müller represented had to be annihilated, destroyed, killed. Zane balled his claws into fists, trying to hold back the rage that threatened to overtake him.

"Zane, please. You scare me."

He flashed his fangs, and this time it had nothing to do with desire and passion. "You should be scared. Nothing good comes from a man like Müller. His seed only produces evil," he spat.

Panic settled in her eyes, eyes that now brimmed with tears. "But we love each other. You love me."

Zane let a bitter laugh escape his throat. "Love? You think I could love the daughter of the man who stole my life? Who killed my sister? You took everything from me?" His voice boomed through the night.

"But—"

"Get out! Get out of my cabin!" How long he could keep the killer in him leashed, he didn't know, but it wouldn't be long now until he lunged for her and took the life that her father owed him.

"Get out of my life!"

Like a frightened doe, Portia stared at him, her lips quivering, tears streaming down her face.

"RUN, don't walk!" His clenched fists came up of their own volition, ready to strike. "Run, before I kill you like I'll kill your father."

Zane squeezed his eyes shut for a moment, holding back the urge to hurt her and in turn to hurt Müller. When he opened his eyes, Portia ran past him out the door and into the night. He forced himself not to listen to the sobs that tore from her throat, not to inhale her scent that wafted past him. Not to run after her and hold her back. Not to recant his words and tell her he would never hurt her. Because he couldn't be sure that he wouldn't. Inside him, the killer lurked, waiting for his prey, angry at being deprived of his revenge.

With the last bit of his humanity, he'd battled his inner demon for supremacy, and allowed her to escape, but if she ever crossed his path again, she would be as good as dead. Just as dead as he was now.

He turned his face toward the dark winter sky. "What have I done to you to deserve this? You're a cruel God!" he cursed. A God who'd shown him what love was and then taken it away in the next instant.

Zane felt the darkness encroach. This time, he didn't fight it. There was no reason to. He'd lost everything that had ever meant anything to him. Now he'd lost Portia and his only chance at love. The darkness might as well take him. Maybe it had always been his destiny, and he'd simply not wanted to see it.

He was a killer who lived only for revenge, and he would take his revenge. He would kill Müller now that he knew where to find him.

Chapter Thirty

Her lungs burning from exhaustion, Portia still didn't slow her run. She had to get away from Zane, from the truth and the pain. Hot tears streamed down her cheeks, but she paid them no attention. She couldn't have stopped them just as she couldn't have stopped a waterfall from breaking over the crest.

Zane had to be wrong. She couldn't be Müller's daughter. A monster's daughter. The monster who'd done unspeakable things to Zane and the other prisoners. Her mind didn't want to acknowledge that somebody close to her was capable of such cruelty. Least of all the man who'd sired her, her own father.

She shook her head, strands of her hair catching on her damp cheeks.

Shivering, she remembered the look on Zane's face, a look she would never forget. Murder had been in his eyes. She'd seen it. Every last bit of the love he'd confessed to her such a short time earlier was gone. All that was left, was hatred, rage, and fury.

And disgust.

She felt bile rise at the recollection. He'd looked at her with disgust at who she was. And his thoughts had been so clearly written on his face. He'd regretted ever having touched her, having made love to her, and having confessed his love.

Her stomach clenched in pain as another wave of sobs made its way north.

He'd loved her. How could he hate her so much now?

Portia fell to her knees, landing in the virgin snow. Zane meant everything to her. He'd promised her so much with his touch and his kisses, his whispered words of love and affection. She'd seen it in his eyes. It was true. He'd laughed with her like she'd never seen him before. He'd been a changed man. She'd done that to him, helped him open his heart.

Now he'd shut her out. Frozen her out.

He'd called her an evil seed. But she'd never thought that he would threaten to kill her because of who she was. Not Zane, not *her* Zane. Didn't he remember that he carried her blood inside him, and that she carried his? Didn't he remember how beautiful their lovemaking had been? How intimate and intense their love was?

How could he throw all this away?

Portia buried her head in her hands, letting the tears flow freely. Nobody would hear her out here in the wilderness. Nobody would ask why she wept as if somebody had died.

He'd cast her out without as much as listening to her, without taking a moment to consider the implications. He hadn't even had time to think about it. As soon as Zane had seen her father's picture, his mind had already been made up. She'd never stood a chance.

Portia felt the cold creeping into her bones and flesh, only intensifying her sense of loss. Zane didn't love her. Had he ever really loved her? If he truly had, how could he have treated her like this? How could he have blasted such iciness at her, such hatred?

And how could she go on now? Her heart ached for the only man who'd ever made her feel anything. Zane was her heart, her love, her life. She'd dreamed of a life with him. Eternal life, a family of her own, a life filled with laughter and love, passion and desire. Just what the last two days had been like.

Her breast ached, the place where his fangs had pierced her skin burning hot like a blacksmith's fire. Longing to feel him there again spread and added to the pain in her chest. His love had felt like a cocoon. Without it she felt vulnerable and lost.

Nothing mattered anymore. Maybe if she stayed here in the snow and let the elements take care of her, she would forget the pain in her heart. If she were human, she would simply fall asleep in the icy surroundings and never wake again, but her hybrid body didn't allow this escape. It forced her to continue, to set one foot before the other and keep moving. Its survival instinct was stronger than her own will.

Numb and without direction, she marched through the snow, not caring where her legs carried her. Maybe if she closed her heart, the pain would vanish.

It didn't.

How did other women deal with this? How did they handle being rejected by the man they love? What did Lauren do?

At the thought of her friend, she closed her eyes and sobbed uncontrollably. She needed a friend so badly right now. She needed to hear from somebody that things would get better, that she would get over this, forget Zane, forget that she loved him. She needed help.

Portia didn't know how long she'd wandered the woods when she finally reached a road. There was little traffic. She kept in the shadows of the trees until she'd figured out what to do, planting herself at the side of the road and lifting her thumb.

The first pickup truck halted. She didn't hesitate and grabbed the door handle to open the door.

The driver was a man in his forties. He gave her an encouraging look, and she let herself fall onto the passenger bench.

"Where to, honey?"

"Just drive."

She could sense his intentions instantly, but it didn't matter. He wouldn't lay a hand on her.

You have the sudden urge to drive to San Francisco. You don't see me. I'm not in your car. Just drive.

She pushed her thoughts into his mind until he turned his face away from her as if he didn't even see her and put the truck back in gear.

As she put more and more distance between Tahoe and Zane's cabin, her heart continued weeping in silence. Nothing in her life had ever hurt as much as losing Zane. Without Zane, she had nothing to look forward to.

She looked out the passenger side window seeing a faint reflection of herself pasted over the darkness outside. She didn't deserve this. Somehow she had to prove that she wasn't the daughter of a monster. Then Zane would love her again.

Chapter Thirty-One

Zane packed the remaining weapons into the back of the Hummer and shut the trunk. He'd loaded up everything he'd stacked in the cabin, knowing he wouldn't return here. Portia knew this place and how to get here, which meant Müller would eventually find out about it. He had no doubt that blood was thicker than water and that once Portia had gotten over the initial shock of what had happened, she would side with her father.

In hindsight it had been stupid not to kill her on the spot, but the thought of shedding her blood had made him recoil. As much as he knew that he had to eliminate her just like her father so that no evil remained, there was a part of him that protested loudly. He tried not to listen, but the voice inside nagged.

"Z! Where the fuck are you?" he yelled for the dog, looking for an outlet for his anger.

There was a soft whine coming from the inside of the cabin. Zane stalked inside, his boots causing the porch to vibrate as he trampled across and barreled inside.

He found the animal curled up in front of the fireplace, his snout buried in a piece of fabric. Zane stepped closer and recognized what Z was suddenly so fond of: one of Portia's bras.

Zane stopped in his tracks. He hadn't even given her a chance to pack or take any of her things. Even her wallet was still here, as was her cell phone and all her clothes. He'd sent her out into the cold without anything, being the heartless bastard he was.

The dog snuggled deeper into one of the cups of the bra, inhaling her lingering scent.

"Stop it, Z!" he admonished. "She's not coming back. Ever!"

Not after the way he'd treated her, the way he'd threatened her. Threatened to kill her. God, what kind of a monster would say that to the woman he loved? What kind of brutal asshole would toss out the love of his life because of where she came from, because of who her sire was? Had he no heart? No compassion? No decency?

The dog looked up at him with big round puppy eyes before digging his snout back into the Portia-scented bra. His dog had no scruples. He followed only his heart, not understanding anything else. If only Zane could do the same, but his mind didn't allow it.

His entire life was based on his one goal of avenging his family, and more specifically his sister, the innocent Rachel, the child who'd never been given a chance at life as a woman. The sister he'd killed because she'd begged him to.

He couldn't suddenly change the direction of his life, throw everything away and betray Rachel because he'd fallen in love with his enemy's daughter. Rachel would never forgive him. And he owed her this. He'd promised her to get justice for her and all the others who had died at Müller's hands. He wouldn't rest until he'd fulfilled that promise.

His own wishes didn't matter. He'd lived without love for the last six decades. So what made things so different now? Why could he not let go of what he felt for her? Didn't his heart understand that the love he'd felt for her couldn't survive, wasn't allowed to survive?

"Stupid dog!" he shouted and yanked the bra from his paws, fully intent on tossing the item into the fire, where a few embers still smoldered. But the strength to do so left him when Portia's scent drifted into his nose and drugged him.

Unable to gather enough strength to keep himself upright, he fell to his knees and caught his head in his palms, feeling as devastated as he had the night he'd ended Rachel's life. How many more losses could he survive before everything was finally too much for him, before he walked into the sun and ended it all?

***

His breakdown had cost him a precious hour, one, it turned out he didn't have to spare. But what was done was done.

When Zane heard the SUV come up the driveway, its lights already illuminating one side of the cabin, he knew his gig was up. They'd found him.

As soon as the car stopped, its engine still running, Samson jumped out of the car, followed by Eddie, Amaury, and Haven. Haven's presence could only mean that Samson had put his crew together in a hurry, taking whoever was available at short notice, because Haven, Yvette's mate, didn't even work for Scanguards. However, that didn't make him a lesser foe.

The four vampires rushed up the stairs. Zane stood there, calmly waiting for them, knowing that a fight would be fruitless. Four vampires against one were odds he didn't like.

"How did you find me?" he asked evenly, meeting Samson's glare.

Eddie replied, Samson clearly too angry to have a civil word. "Thomas traced a utility bill you paid online. It was for this place. You could have invited us for some skiing, but no, you kept this cabin all to yourself."

Zane shrugged, wanting to maintain his outward calm, even if he felt nothing of the sort on the inside. His gut had just been torn out and fed to the wolves. All that was left was an empty shell.

"Where is she? What have you done with her?" Samson yelled only inches from his face.

"She's gone."

Samson jolted back, an expression of utter shock on his face. "You hurt her? You fucking asshole, you hurt her?"

His heart rebelled. "Never!" Even if he'd made her believe that he would, he'd rather catapult himself into a wooden stake than willingly harm a hair on Portia's head. Yeah, that's how screwed up he was.

"Then where are you keeping her?"

Next to Samson, Amaury and Haven stormed into the cabin, calling out her name.

"I told you she's gone."

"What the fuck does that mean?" Samson growled low and dark, his fangs peeking from between his lips, his eyes glaring red in the dark.

"The house is empty," came Amaury's voice from the inside.

Samson grabbed Zane by the elbow and shoved him inside. From his favorite place at the fireplace, Z barked angrily.

Haven came from the bedroom, carrying Portia's backpack. He pulled a pair of panties from it. "Doesn't look like your size, Zane," he snarled.

"She left two hours ago."

Samson narrowed his eyes, scanning the open plan kitchen. His eyes fell onto the spot where Zane had left Portia's wallet. "Without her stuff? How stupid do you think we are?"

Samson motioned to Haven to bring him the bag. He took a whiff of the smell that clung to it, then took a step closer to Zane, inhaling once more.

"You had her, didn't you? You fucking jerk couldn't keep your hands off her, could you?"

Why ask him something Samson already knew? "She begged me to do it."

"And her blood? I can smell her blood on you! You had to take everything, didn't you?"

He shrugged, the motion hurting because he tried to pretend so hard that he didn't care. "She offered. Never turn down a gift horse." God, he hated himself for the way he spoke about her, as if it had meant nothing, when it had meant everything to him.

Samson's fist whipped Zane's head sideways, the pain instantly radiating down his spine. Fuck, his boss was still as fast as ever, and he packed a vicious punch.

"There's blood on the sheets," Eddie's voice suddenly announced.

Everybody turned to where he stood in the door to the bedroom.

Samson rushed past Zane and headed for it. Zane followed, not because he particularly wanted to but because he hated it when others violated his space. He didn't want them touching anything else, and especially not the place where he and Portia had lain together in complete and utter bliss.

As Samson stopped in front of the bed, its sheets tangled from the last time Zane and Portia had made love, the rest of the vampires crowded into the space.

Eddie pointed to a small spot in the center of the bed. "There. That's blood."

When Samson turned slowly, for the first time since he'd arrived at the cabin, his features showed something other than outrage. A small flicker of realization shone through his eyes, together with a sigh of relief. Had Samson really expected to find a bloodbath in the bedroom?

"She was a virgin, just like she told me," Zane admitted. And nobody had believed him. "I did what I had to do."

Samson closed his eyes. "It doesn't change anything about what you did. You kidnapped her."

"She asked me to do it!" Zane snarled.

"It wasn't for her to ask. She's a minor! And she was in your care!"

Samson yelled.

"Oh, I took care of her."

"You were her bodyguard. Nowhere in our rules does that allow you to touch her! You fucking shit!"

That did it. "I don't care about your rules! I quit!"

"You don't get to quit! This is not over! Not by a long shot!" Samson ran his hands through his dark hair and motioned to Haven and Eddie. "Handcuff him and get him to the jet. Amaury and I will take Zane's Hummer."

Then he gave Zane another look. "If you harmed her, I will have you executed."

Haven slipped his gloves on and pulled something from his jacket pocket. Zane glanced at it, recognizing the silver handcuffs instantly.

"Assholes!"

But he didn't protest when they laid the silver restraints on his wrists and clicked them shut, nor did he show any outward signs of the pain the silver caused him. His skin hissed, and the smell of burning flesh spread in the crowded room, but he merely clenched his jaw, not allowing any sound of pain to come over his lips.

"One last time: where is she?" Samson asked.

Zane lifted his head. "She ran away when I told her that I didn't want to see her anymore." It was the truth, in a way. He omitted that he'd also threatened her. It wasn't Samson's business. What was true was that he hadn't harmed her.

"She thinks she loves me," he said more to himself than to the others. She would get over it. She was young, and right now she hated him. It would make things easier. As for how he would survive the pain, he was lost for an answer.

"Amaury," Samson ordered, "you and I, we'll canvass the surroundings, see if we can pick up her scent or any trail in the snow. We have to find her."

Amaury nodded, then tossed Zane a pissed off look. "You've got a lot of explaining to do. And if you think you'll get off easy, think again. Samson is being lenient when he offers you an execution. I have other ideas to make you pay, asshole."

"I haven't done anything to her," Zane hissed.

"You have no clue about women! Maybe you haven't hurt her

physically, but you have no idea what women are capable of doing to themselves when they feel wronged. Ever thought of that?" Amaury turned to follow Samson outside.

No, Portia wouldn't hurt herself. She was strong. She was a survivor. He didn't want to believe it. Trying to push Amaury's last words from his mind, Zane looked at his two jailors. "Great, I got stuck with you two: a civilian and a newbie."

Haven bent closer. "I'm not susceptible to your little digs, so save your breath."

Zane growled and walked into the living room, flanked by Eddie and Haven. Z waddled toward him, a confused look on his face, dragging Portia's bra with him between this teeth.

"We can't leave him here." Zane motioned his bound hands toward the dog.

Haven raised an inquiring eyebrow, and Eddie twisted his lips. "You thought we were gonna leave the pup?" Eddie asked and shook his head. "We're not heartless."

"Unlike other people here," Haven added.

"If I had a heart, I'd be wounded now," Zane snapped, "luckily, I'm all out of heart for today. So get a move on."

But despite his harsh words, relief washed over Zane when Eddie picked up the dog and carried him outside. Zane kept his mouth shut on the drive to the small airport where one of Scanguards' custom-equipped private jets waited. Neither Eddie nor Haven seemed to be in the mood to talk either. Only Z provided some company on the bleak half hour flight, curling up on his lap. But stroking the only creature that still cared for him wasn't possible. Zane's wrists ached from the chafing silver that ate his skin and exposed the flesh beneath.

And he deserved it.

Chapter Thirty-Two

Portia mentally directed the driver of the pickup truck to drop her at the corner of her block. After quickly wiping his memory of her, she sent him on his way back to Tahoe. She felt no guilt for having used him. After all, when he'd picked her up on the side of the street, he'd looked determined to make a pass at her. Luckily her vampire skills had wiped that thought right out of his mind.

She walked toward her house, tired and weary. Coming home to an empty house wasn't going to lift her spirits, but without her cell phone or any money or fresh clothes on her, she had no other place to go, except to Lauren's. However, she could imagine that she had probably landed her best friend in hot water. After all, she'd known about Zane, even though she hadn't had any knowledge about their impromptu trip.

After a hot shower, she would call Lauren and ask her to come over so she could cry on her shoulder. She had little hope, but maybe, just maybe, her friend had some advice that would make her feel better. If not, at least she would not be alone. The loneliness on the four hour drive back to the city had given her a taste of what her life without Zane would be like, and it had frightened her. Sadness had gripped her heart and wouldn't loosen its hold.

Her legs felt heavy when she walked up to her front door. Luckily her habit of keeping her house key in her jacket pocket rather than her handbag assured that she didn't have to break a window to get in. She turned the key and entered the dark interior. It was just like she'd left it.

Portia didn't bother switching on the light and walked toward the stairs. Her hand reached for the railing, her fingers brushing against the smooth wood as she put her foot on the first step. A large hand yanked her back.

The unexpected action robbed her of her breath, and the vice-like grip assured that she couldn't get away. Even before her head snapped toward her attacker, she knew she was in trouble.

Her father was angrier than she'd ever seen him before.

"Where have you been?" The fury in his voice lashed at her like a whip. The red glare in his eyes only underscored the seriousness of the situation she found herself in.

She didn't want a confrontation with him, not now when she was down already. "I'm tired."

Portia turned her face away, trying to avoid his scrutinizing look, but she knew she couldn't hide from him. Zane's smell was still all over her, and his blood coursed through her veins, only intensifying his scent.

When her father's nostrils flared, she shivered instinctively. But she couldn't have been prepared for his next action.

"You whore!"

The back of his hand struck her cheek with such force that she lost her balance and crashed into the wall, leaving a dent in the plaster. The shock of his words and his brutal treatment hurt more than the blow itself. She didn't recognize her father anymore. This was not the man who'd raised her: this was the man Zane had described, the monster of Buchenwald, Franz Müller.

"You're destroying everything!" he accused her, his voice filling the house, making the glass chandelier in the living room vibrate. "You slut! You let yourself be defiled by somebody who's not worthy!"

Portia scrambled to her feet, trembling. She saw the raw brutality in his eyes, and the madness that lurked just behind them. Yes, this was Franz Müller—and he was her father. The mere thought of it made her nauseous.

"Father, please ..."

Another strike of his hand catapulted her against the railing and knocked the wind out of her.

"I have higher plans for you, and what do you do? You behave like a common slut! You are the beginning of a new master race! You'll be its princess, its leader. You and your mate will rule this world." He gave a disgusted look. "If he'll still have you now that you let another man touch you!"

Portia didn't bother getting up the second time. Understanding made her slide to the floor. Still, she couldn't believe her own ears. "Mate?"

"I searched long and hard for the most valiant hybrid for our cause, the strongest, the fiercest. Your children will be stronger than anybody in this world."

"No ..." she whispered breathlessly. This couldn't be. But there was no doubt. Her father wanted to create a master race, a superior race that would rule the world. "No, you can't ..."

He glared down at her. "I own you! You'll do as you're told!"

Self-preservation made her struggle to her feet. He didn't own her. "Nobody owns me!" She would decide who to mate with, and it wouldn't be a man of her father's choosing.

Like a vice, her father's hand clamped around her upper arm, his claws digging into her flesh. An involuntary gasp escaped her. He would stop at nothing. Cold fear gripped her and slithered down her spine.

"Now you listen to me, young lady. From now on, you'll do exactly as I say. In three days, you'll be blood-bonded to your mate, and you'll do it willingly."

"Or what?" she spat. She'd rather die than do as he said. She had nothing more to lose. Zane had cast her out, and now her father turned out to be a monster. She had nobody.

"Or I'll hunt down your lover and kill him, very, very slowly. I promise you, he'll suffer greater pain than this world has ever seen."

Shock stopped her heart, only to make it restart at double the pace. "No!"

"Oh, watch me!"

If she'd ever had any doubts of who her father was, they were all wiped away now. "I didn't want to believe him," she murmured to herself.

Her father jerked her by her arm. "Believe what?" he asked, his eyes narrowing.

Portia lifted her head slowly and calmly. "That you're Franz Müller."

She saw the final confirmation of the truth by the way he jumped back and how his eyes widened and his jaw dropped. It only lasted for a second, before he had himself under control again. He growled and flashed his fangs at her.

"Who told you?" He shook her.

But she didn't open her mouth to speak.

"WHO?" he yelled not inches from her face.

Portia pressed her teeth together, unwilling to give in.

Then his face changed as if something crossed his mind. He gritted his teeth. "There's only one man outside the organization who knows who I am. Only one who'd use this information against me." He snarled.

"Eisenberg."

She recognized Zane's last name, but tried to keep her face emotionless.

But her father knew her too well. As sure as she was his daughter, he could always interpret the little tells her face showed.

He raked his eyes over her body in disgust. "You let Eisenberg fuck you? That dirty, filthy Jew?"

There was no need to deny it now.

Portia lifted her chin in defiance. "And I loved every minute of it." As the revulsion in her father's face spread, she continued, "I drank his blood, and I gave him mine. And I I—"

But she didn't get a chance to finish her sentence. Her father's fists flew into her. She brought her arms up to shield herself, but it was to no avail. Blows to the head were followed by kicks into the stomach, as claws dug into her chest and ripped her clothes to dig into her skin. The scent of her own blood filled the air.

Her strength, already depleted from the events earlier in the night, left her. The next blow hit her temple. Blackness fell over her, and she stopped fighting against it, welcoming the darkness like a cocoon. In the darkness she would be safe.

Chapter Thirty-Three

Zane paced in his cell. After landing in San Francisco, they'd brought him to Scanguards' downtown office and locked him up, waiting for Samson and Amaury to get back from Tahoe. At least, they had taken the silver handcuffs off him, but neither Eddie nor Haven had bothered offering him blood to heal his wrists. Not that he would have taken it anyway. He didn't want any stupid bottled blood.

He kicked his boot against the concrete wall. Then he dropped his forehead against it, feeling the cold smooth surface against his skin.

Fuck, he'd screwed up. What if something had happened after Portia had run off? What if somebody had attacked her, or what if she was injured and couldn't help herself? Logic told him that he shouldn't worry: she was a hybrid and near indestructible, and she could fight off any human with her little finger. But logic didn't rule his mind right now. Emotions did. And they were running high.

He turned and kicked the single chair they'd left for his comfort, then picked it up and slammed it against the wall. The metal bent. Figured that they wouldn't leave a wooden chair in the cell. It would make creating a stake far too easy.

"Does that make you feel any better?" Gabriel's voice droned from the door.

Zane swiveled on his heels and faced his unexpected guest. "No, but it doesn't make me feel any worse either."

Gabriel's hulky form filled the door frame. "Wanna talk before the others get here? They're just crossing the Bay Bridge."

His heartbeat kicked up. "Did they find her?" He held his breath, hoping for the right answer.

"No."

Deflated, he dropped his head. Ah, shit, they might as well kill him now.

"Do you care about her?"

"None of your fucking business!" What did Gabriel want? An outpouring of Zane's heart? Not gonna happen!

"Well, then I guess you don't want to know where she is." Gabriel turned to leave.

Zane stepped forward. "You said they haven't found her."

Without looking back, Gabriel baited him further. "That's right, Amaury and Samson haven't found her. But that doesn't mean I don't know where she is."

Zane jumped toward Gabriel, slammed his hand onto his boss' shoulder and whirled him around. "Then where the fuck is she?"

A half smile played around Gabriel's lips, and Zane had the urge to wipe it off him.

"So you do care."

Zane released his grip and withdrew further back into his cell. "What do you care?"

"I care because I am torn between ripping you a new one and helping you. And right now, with your shitty attitude, I tend toward ripping you a new one. Can you get that into your thick skull?"

To underscore his statement, Gabriel made a fist and rapped his knuckles on Zane's bald head.

Insulted, Zane snarled at him. "Don't pretend you want to help me. You're not any better than the rest of them!"

"And what's that supposed to mean?"

"Just what I said!"

"Goddamn it! Talk if you want me to tell you where she is!"

Zane huffed. "Nobody believed her! Not Samson, none of you. She was telling the truth, damn it! Her father, that sick bastard, was trying to keep her a virgin beyond her twenty-first birthday. Hell, she was asking me to help her. I did. If that makes me a criminal in your eyes, so be it."

"Eddie and Haven already confirmed that she was a virgin."

Impatiently, Zane wiped a trickle of perspiration off his brow. "Then what do you want from me?"

"I want to know what happened in Tahoe."

"We fucked. She left. End of story." The rest was nobody's business, not that he loved her and not that she was Müller's daughter. He'd take on Franz Müller on his own as soon as he got out of this hellhole.

"Stubborn asshole!" Gabriel cursed. "If you don't talk, I can't help you."

Zane crossed his arms over his chest.

"Fine. Be that way. But I'm warning you, Samson won't show you any leniency." He stormed to the door. "And for you, jerk, I stood up to Lewis not two hours ago. A waste of time and energy that was! I should have tossed you at his feet and let him rip you apart!"

He slammed the door shut before Zane could answer.

"He's back? Her father is back?" He hammered his fists against the door, but Gabriel didn't come back.

Müller was in San Francisco? And Gabriel had seen him? And Zane was locked up, unable to get to him. He cursed three ways to heaven. He'd never been so close to him, not in over six decades. All that separated him from this monster now was this damn door.

Then panic struck him. Gabriel knew where Portia was, even though he hadn't said so. This could only mean that she was back. Back at home—with her father.

What would Müller do to her? There was no doubt that he would be able to smell that she'd been with a man. Zane's scent on her, his blood inside her, was still too fresh. In a few days it would have been gone, but Müller had come back too early. He would know instantly, and while he wouldn't know who'd touched his daughter, he would be furious. Knowing his vile temper, anything could happen.

Why hadn't he considered this earlier? He'd been so blinded by the fact that Portia was his greatest enemy's daughter that he'd overlooked the obvious: Müller hadn't wanted her to lose her virginity, and now that he had to assume—and rightly so—that she had, he would be furious. Without a proper outlet, without Müller being able to lash out at the man who'd robbed his daughter of her virginity, he had only one person to direct his anger at: Portia.

"Let me out of here!" he screamed at the closed door and pounded his fists against it. "Gabriel! Get back here! Get me out! NOW!"

He screamed at the top of his lungs. Seconds passed, minutes followed. He was at the border of being hoarse when there was finally a sound at the other side. When the door opened, he burst through it, but both Samson and Amaury pushed him back inside the cell.

"Let me go! I have to get to her!"

"Lock us in, Gabriel," Samson shouted over his shoulder as both he and Amaury used their combined strength to keep him from the door.

When a moment later the door fell shut and the lock clicked, he pulled back. "You have to let me go. She's in danger. I have to help her," Zane breathed.

"That's not how it works, Zane," Samson responded calmly. "Do you really think we'll let you walk out of here after all you've done?"

"You have to! Portia needs me." Desperation clawed at him. He had to convince Samson to let him go.

Amaury tilted his head. "Yeah, like a hole in the head. You have some screwed-up notion of what that means."

"Samson, there's no time to lose. She's in danger. Her father—"

Samson jabbed his finger at Zane's chest. "Her father has every right to be mad at us. You can consider yourself lucky that we're not hanging you out to dry. He hired us for one specific reason, and one reason only, and we didn't do our job. No! What did we do? We screwed him over! We did exactly what he wanted to avoid."

"It was wrong!" Zane yelled.

"You bet it was wrong. What you did was wrong!"

"I had no fucking choice! You wouldn't listen to me. I told you what was at stake. And you ignored it!"

Samson blew out a breath. "I didn't ignore it. I was considering your accusations. I was going to investigate."

"Too late!" Zane planted his hands at his hips and widened his stance.

"Thanks to you!"

"You have to let me go. Her father, he'll hurt her."

Samson shook his head. "He'll ground her, he'll yell at her, that's all. She'll survive."

Zane grabbed Samson's forearm. "You don't understand. I can't let her take his wrath when I'm the one who deserves it."

"First true words out of your mouth," Amaury added.

Zane tossed him a glare. "None of you understands. He'll hurt her. I know him. I know what he's capable of."

"What are you talking about?" Samson asked. "How would you know Lewis? He's been gone the entire time you were Portia's bodyguard."

Zane closed his eyes. "I know him from the war."

"The war?" Amaury echoed.

Zane opened his eyes and looked at the two men who had known him for decades yet knew nothing about his past. This was about to change. "World War II. I was an inmate in Buchwald. The concentration camp."

He noticed the surprise in Samson's and Amaury's eyes, but they remained silent, their bodies rigid in attention.

"Portia's father was a doctor there. His name isn't Lewis, it was Franz Müller. If you think Josef Mengele had a reputation for torturing prisoners with his horrendous experiments, you haven't met Franz Müller. He makes Mengele look like a choirboy. I can't tell you all the things he did, how he tortured us, killed so many of us."

Compassion spread in the eyes of his friends.

"He was obsessed with creating a master race. When they captured a vampire one night, he got what he wanted. I was one of his guinea pigs, so was my sister."

"Are you sure it's he?" Samson interrupted, his voice calmer and quieter than before.

Zane nodded. "It's a face I could never forget. I've hunted him for years. Samson, you have to believe me when I tell you this: he's just as mad and as dangerous as he was then. He's started up an organization to create a new master race."

"What kind of race?"

"A race of hybrids, stronger than any others, stronger than all vampires. He's still obsessed. It was a mistake for me to send Portia away. I know that now."

"You sent her away?" Amaury asked.

He gave his friend a rueful look. "When I saw a picture of her father and realized that she was his flesh, I told her to run or I would kill her. I threatened her."

"Oh God, why?" Samson gasped.

"Don't you see? I'm in love with the daughter of the man who destroyed my family, who tortured and killed my sister. I had to send her away. I couldn't trust myself not to kill her in my rage."

Zane dropped his head. He should have never let her go. Now he knew that even in his rage he wouldn't have harmed her.

"My God, Zane, what now?"

When he met Samson's gaze and realized that his boss believed him and was willing to help him, relief swept over him like a soft breeze. "We have to get her away from her father."

"And then?" Amaury asked, his voice solemn.

"You have to protect her."

"We?" Samson asked softly.

"She won't want me around anymore. She hates me now." And he could live with that as long as he knew she was safe.

Chapter Thirty-Four

There was a cold chill in the air when Zane alighted from his Hummer half a block from Portia's house.

According to Gabriel, Oliver had been assigned to watch the house while Samson and Amaury had searched for Portia in Tahoe. After she had returned home and Oliver had reported that fact to Gabriel, Oliver's assignment had ended, and he'd left his observation point. Considering that Scanguards' assignment had terminated as soon as Portia was back with her father, Gabriel's action was only logical, however, knowing what they all knew now, it would have been more prudent to keep an eye on the house.

Behind Zane, Amaury and Samson got out of the car and quietly eased the doors shut. It was past three in the morning, and the streets were quiet. Any sound they made would carry far, and the last thing Zane wanted was to alert Müller to his presence before he was in position to strike.

The house was shrouded in darkness, not a single lamp illuminating it from the inside. He didn't know what to expect. Had Portia told her father who her lover was? She knew his real name: Zacharias Eisenberg. Had she divulged it to her father? And why wouldn't she? She was angry with him because he'd rejected her and threatened to kill her. What could be more logical than for her to tell her father where he could find his greatest enemy? It would be the easiest way for her to take her ultimate and well-deserved revenge on him.

But what was unclear was how Müller would punish his daughter for going against his wishes. Zane feared the worst. Müller was a fanatic. Would he really tolerate his daughter having slept with a Jew, even if this brought him closer to exterminating said Jew? Would he first lash out at his daughter because she had betrayed him? There was no way of knowing for sure until he actually saw Portia.

For all he knew, Müller could be lying in wait in the dark house, ready to plunge a stake into Zane's heart not only to end the chase that had lasted for over sixty years, but also to punish him for defiling his virgin daughter.

Zane sighed. How ironic that he'd been in Müller's house and never realized it. But there had been no family pictures, nothing that would have given Müller's identity away.

"You okay?" Amaury whispered next to him.

"No."

He would probably never be all right again. Whatever he did now, it would hurt somebody. He had to get Portia out of the house, most likely against her will, because she wouldn't want his help now, and at the same time, he had to take this chance and kill her father. She would hate him even more for that.

They approached the house from the north side, which had no windows. Only the front door was on this side. Their footsteps made no sound on the cold concrete, all three of them were well versed in stealth. Communicating only with hand and eye signals, they positioned themselves around the door.

Zane slid his key into the lock and turned. With a nod to his colleagues, he jerked the door open and lunged inside. Samson and Amaury did likewise. Within a second, they were inside the small house, each positioned against a different wall from which to attack or defend.

Zane inhaled and allowed his senses to reach out. Emptiness greeted him.

"They're gone," Samson said, letting out a breath.

But Zane barely heard his boss' voice, because the scent that drifted into his nostrils had set alarm bells ringing in his head, and catapulted him toward the stairs. He crouched down and wiped his fingers over a spot on the railing.

Blood. It was dried blood.

"Portia ..."

His eyes focused, and he discovered more spots of dried blood.

"Oh God, no!"

Samson's hand clamped down on his shoulder. "We'll find her."

Zane raised his lids. "He hurt her ... She bled. Samson ... it's all my fault. He hurt her because of me."

"She must have told him who you were," Amaury stated.

Zane closed his eyes, pushing back tears he wanted to cry for Portia's pain. "We have to find her ... before he kills her."

"He won't."

Zane turned at the sound of Quinn's voice coming from the door, fury instantly taking over his mind. His erstwhile friend was the reason this situation had gotten to this point in the first place. Had he not sold him out to Samson, Zane would have never had to take Portia away.

As Quinn stepped inside, next to him, another person appeared. Instantly alert at the appearance of the unknown vampire next to Quinn, Zane jumped up and reached for his stake. He'd have to deal with Quinn later.

Quinn quickly raised his hand. "This is Cain. He's the man who identified the pin you found on the assassin."

"Assassin?" Samson interrupted, raising an eyebrow in question.

"Long story. I'll fill you in later," Zane quickly replied.

Samson nodded curtly. "I'll hold you to it."

Zane gave a short nod in agreement and turned his attention back to Quinn and Cain. The vampire was a little over six feet tall, well-built with short dark hair and a permanent shadow where his beard would have grown were he still human.

Cain nodded in greeting. "Quinn flew me in today so I could help."

Quinn shrugged toward Samson. "I borrowed one of the jets."

"We'll talk about that later," Samson replied. "How is Cain gonna help, no offense."

The stranger nodded. "None taken. I might be able to identify some of the members of the breeding program."

"We already know who the head is."

Quinn nudged the vampire. "Tell Zane what you told me."

Cain cleared his throat. "There's going to be a big event in two or three days."

"What kind of event?" Zane asked impatiently.

"A blood-bond. Apparently the leader has found a suitable hybrid to mate with the princess."

"Princess? What the f—?" This wasn't England with royal families and all.

"They say, it's his daughter. She's supposed to start a dynasty of superior hybrids. He's found a hybrid she'll mate with."

Zane's heart stopped. Portia was supposed to blood-bond with some hybrid her father chose for her? "No!"

"That's why he won't kill her," Quinn added. "He needs her. She is his ticket to his master race."

Zane tried to shake off the thought, but couldn't. "He can't do that. She's mine! Portia is mine!"

Voicing it in front of his friends and colleagues, brought reality home. He couldn't kid himself any longer. Without Portia, he was nothing, merely an empty shell without a heart. Only with her, he had a chance at life. Her father might need her to create his master race, but Zane needed her to survive.

"We don't have much time then," Amaury said. "We have to find her before the ceremony or …"

Amaury didn't complete his sentence, and he didn't have to. Zane knew the implications only too well. If Portia was blood-bonded to another man, she was lost to him. Only killing her mate would set her free. And even then, would Portia open her heart to Zane again? Would she be able to forgive him for what he'd done? Because, after all, it was his fault that she found herself in this situation. He'd been the one to cast her out without considering the consequences. He'd driven her back to her father and into hell. Had he thought things through for a moment, he would have seen that it didn't matter who her sire was. She was pure and good despite the seed she came from.

"Do you know where this ceremony will take place?" Samson asked Cain.

"It's somewhere on the West Coast, that much is certain, but I never got to find out where. The location is kept secret. Only a few people know."

Zane glanced at Quinn, remembering something. "You left me a message that you found some phone numbers on Brandt's cell. Was that just bait to get me to come back?"

"Thomas extracted some partial numbers. We have an area code and a prefix."

"Where?"

"Seattle. The prefix identifies a neighborhood called Queen Anne. But—"

"But what?"

"We can't be sure that's the place where Müller went."

"It's all we've got." Just a straw, but Zane clung to it for dear life.

Samson nodded. "It's the best we can do." He turned to Amaury.

"Mobilize the troops. We need everybody we can get."

"I can help," Cain interrupted.

Zane perused the vampire. He'd helped them so far, but could he be trusted? "You wanted to be part of the breeding program. I understand that you're disgruntled about being rejected, but why would you help us now? What's stopping you from running back to them and warning them that we're onto them?"

The tall and well-built vampire ran his hand through his dark hair. Zane silently wondered why Müller had rejected him. He appeared strong and intelligent, and from what Zane could tell, he was fairly decent looking too.

"Listen, I know this must sound odd to you guys, but when I heard of the breeding program I figured it would give me purpose in life. You see, I've been drifting. No family, no friends, no clan."

"Why is that?" Zane shot back, suspicion rising. A loner always meant trouble.

"It's because I don't know who I am. I woke up one night, and I just 'was'. I have no idea when I was turned, by whom, or how. Nor do I remember my human life. Nothing. I've been searching for an answer, and when I heard about the program, I thought it was as good as anything I'd ever be part of."

Zane nodded. He understood the need to find a family, to have friends, to not be alone anymore. "The breeding program, did you believe in it when you applied for it?"

Cain shrugged. "They promised the most enticing women would be at the disposal of any vampire or hybrid who made it into the program. It's not something somebody like me can afford to turn down. I don't understand why they didn't want me. Hey, I'm strong, I'm smart. And I'm told I'm not too bad looking. Beats me what they were looking for that I don't have."

"I think it's your lack of commitment that made you ineligible," Zane mused. "Müller only wants men who believe in his cause. He's a fanatic. He likes to surround himself with other fanatics. You wanted in for the wrong reasons."

"I guess. Well, never mind. Seeing that they're going down anyway, it's just as well that I'm not a part of it." Then he made a motion toward the door. "Well, good luck, guys. Seeing that you have no use for me,

I'll be moving on."

Before Cain could exit through the door, Zane blocked it. "Not so fast. I'm sure you can understand that we can't let you leave and risk you alerting Müller."

Zane glanced at Samson who nodded in agreement.

"That's why," Samson chimed in, "we'd rather have you on our team. Fight on our side, and if you prove yourself, maybe we'll have a place for you in our midst."

Zane noticed Cain's eyes widen in surprise. Then a smile spread on his lips. "You won't regret it."

"Now tell us everything you know, every detail," Samson ordered. Then he turned toward Amaury. "Organize the jet, get everybody up to speed. We'll be leaving before sunrise."

Chapter Thirty-Five

Portia tried to move her arm to relieve the ache in her shoulder but realized she couldn't move. Her eyes flew open. Panicked, she stared into the semidarkness. As her eyes adjusted, she was able to make out her surroundings.

She lay on a large bed in an average sized bedroom with two windows, which were darkened by both heavy curtains and thick blinds. There was an old fireplace with a gas fire burning in it. A dresser sat at the wall near the foot of the bed, and there were three doors. One, she assumed led to a closet, one most likely to the hallway, and the third one, which was ajar, seemed to lead into another room.

Portia craned her neck to get a better look and managed to get a glimpse of the room, which appeared to be a study. But her movements were severely restricted. She jerked her arms, but they were tied around a heavy bar.

Twisting her neck once more, she looked at her restraints. Shit! Her father had handcuffed her with silver handcuffs. However, he had protected her wrists from the effect of the silver by wrapping bandages around them so the silver wouldn't burn her skin. And what she'd thought was a bar, was actually a steel beam that appeared to have been used to retrofit the old house for earthquake safety.

Portia cursed. She couldn't get out of the restraints. Even though the silver didn't hurt her at present, she couldn't break it, not even with her superior hybrid strength.

Frustrated, she let her head fall back onto the pillow and listened for any sound. On the floor beneath her, mumbled voices indicated the presence of others in the house. She was in a house, for sure, an old one, maybe Edwardian or Victorian, evidenced by the crown molding she saw between wall and ceiling. But where she was, she had no idea.

She'd been out cold after her father had beaten her senseless, and she'd welcomed the escape into darkness where she'd felt nothing. Now that she was awake, the memory of her father's beating and Zane's rejection came back full force, even though her physical injuries had healed.

Her stomach growled, reminding her that she hadn't gotten to eat the pizza Zane had ordered for her. A sob escaped her at the thought of him, and she swallowed it down quickly, not wanting to fall apart once more. She needed to be strong now. She had to help herself; nobody else would come to rescue her.

Her father was the evil Dr. Franz Müller, a man so vile and heartless she couldn't believe that he'd ever loved her or her mother. And he wanted to force her to blood-bond with a vampire he'd chosen for her, something she could never accept. If she couldn't have Zane, she didn't want anybody.

A sound from the other room made her snap her head toward it. A door opened, and footsteps entered the study. Two men from what she could tell.

"You should have told me immediately," her father hissed, his voice low and dangerous.

"With all due respect, I was only looking out for Brandt. When he didn't get back like he was supposed to, I followed his trail," a second male voice answered.

"Respect? I'll teach you respect! You should have warned me about Eisenberg!"

Eisenberg—that was Zane's name.

"I didn't see Eisenberg! The man who tinkered with Brandt's locker didn't look like the man you described. He wasn't bald. I didn't know who he was."

"You should have still called me the minute Brandt's locker exploded. We could have made sure to destroy any trail that led to us."

Portia remembered that night only too well.

"Trust me, the locker was blown to bits. Brandt rigged it just like he was taught, so that in case somebody found it, all evidence would be destroyed. He didn't compromise us."

"He was a fool!"

"He simply wanted to prove himself," the stranger contradicted. "When he found out that you were looking for a mate for your daughter, he wanted to—"

"Enough! Brandt wanted to avenge his father, that is all. I wish he had spoken to me before. Eisenberg can't be underestimated. He's grown too strong and too smart. Despite all our efforts, he's found my most trusted supporters. He eradicated them."

"That's unfortunate, but now that we know who and where he is, we'll send a contingent after him," the man suggested.

"I'll give the orders here. Nobody will do anything until after the ceremony," her father barked.

Ceremony? Portia felt bile rise from her stomach.

"Once this is over, we'll get him. And then this chapter will be closed forever. I can't have a filthy Jew interfere with my plans any longer."

Suddenly, heavy steps came toward the door. Portia quickly closed her eyes and pretended to sleep.

"Leave me!"

She heard the other man scurry from the room and close the door behind him.

"Did you hear that, Portia? I'm going to kill your lover and make him regret he ever laid his dirty hands on you."

The door swung open fully, and Portia opened her eyes, glaring at her father who stood in the doorframe. "You're a monster, just like he said."

Her father crossed the distance to the bed with several large strides. "Don't confuse me with him. I'm a creator. I'm creating a new world here, a new race, a dynasty that will rule forever."

Portia shook her head. "No."

"Oh yes, and you'll help me with it." He sat down at the edge of the bed.

"I won't do it."

He slapped her hard with the back of his hand, but she didn't flinch.

"You can't force me to blood-bond with anybody."

"Oh, I can." He flashed is fangs at her, his eyes glaring red with fury.

"What are you gonna do? Hold me down while he fucks me and digs his fangs into me?" she yelled. "You can't force me to take his blood. I'll never do it."

"You'll sink your fangs into anything or anybody I wish once it's time."

"No!"

"You won't have a choice. In two days you'll be so starved for anything, human food or blood, that whatever food source comes within your reach, you'll take it." He let out a sinister laugh.

Shock coursed through her veins. "You can't do that."

"Watch me." He rose.

"I'm your daughter. I thought you loved me." A single tear threatened to dislodge from her eye, but she pushed it back, not wanting to show her weakness. She had looked up to him her entire life. How could he betray her like this?

"That's why I'm giving you this opportunity. If I didn't love you like I do, I would have chosen somebody else to become head of this new race. Don't you see? You'll be a queen."

Portia pressed her lips together, trying to prevent them from trembling. To no avail. She didn't want to be queen or princess or leader of anything. She wanted to be Zane's woman, his mate. Forever.

"No .... no," she whispered and closed her eyes, trying to shut out the world.

"Rest. Two nights from now your mate will be here and you'll see things differently."

He stomped out of the room and shut the door behind him. When she heard his footsteps disappear down the hall, she allowed her tears to flow down her cheeks. She'd awakened to a nightmare, and it was only just beginning.

Chapter Thirty-Six

The well-oiled machine of Scanguards was once again in operation. Within two short hours, everything was organized. Every available vampire in Scanguards' employ had been mobilized and was now sitting on the specially equipped jet. Even Haven, the ex-bounty hunter, was ready to join the fight.

Maya, Gabriel's mate, had been left behind to guard Delilah and the baby, much to her chagrin. She would rather have been by her husband's side, but Samson had learned from experience never again to leave his wife without protection.

Zane understood only too well now. He knew what it felt like to lose the one person that meant everything to him. He promised himself never to leave Portia unguarded after this, no matter whether she took him back or not. If she didn't, he'd simply hire a bodyguard to protect her from afar, to always watch over her so no harm would come to her.

He'd had a long conversation with Samson while they'd waited for the plane to be readied. He'd told his boss about the men he'd chased down, the assassin he'd killed only recently, and his lifelong quest to bring the monsters of Buchenwald to justice. Samson had understood, and Zane was relieved to know he had his boss' full support.

Zane put his seatbelt on when Oliver took the seat next to him.

"You owe me one, bro," he said quietly.

Zane turned his head to face him. "Listen, Oliver, for what it's worth, I'm sorry." He swallowed hard. "But I'd do it again if I had to."

Oliver glared at him. "You could at least have let me in on it. Damn it! I would have covered for you had I known!"

"You what?" Had he heard right? Oliver would have had his back?

His colleague leaned closer. "You know I looked up to you. Why didn't you trust me? Between the two of us we could have made sure nobody knew what was happening. But no, you had to trick me with that stupid phone call."

Oliver jabbed his index finger into Zane's chest, disappointment shining in his eyes.

"I didn't know ..."

Oliver turned and faced forward. "Did you mean any of the things you told me?"

"What things?"

"What you said on the phone about being a vampire. That if I wanted it, you would help me."

Zane ran his hand over his bald head and sighed. "God, I'm such an ass."

"I couldn't agree more."

"Then why would you possibly want to be like me? I lead a miserable life." And it would only get worse.

Oliver spun his face toward him. "Miserable? Do you have any idea what you're saying? You've been given a gift. Do you know how many people are out there who would give anything to get an extra few years of life? A chance at immortality? A life without illness?"

Zane shook his head. "It means nothing when you have to live that life alone."

"What are you talking about? You have Portia. Quinn told me how she looks at you."

Zane suddenly felt his old anger return. "Uh, yeah, Quinn. I still have to settle a score with him. He sold me out to Samson in the first place."

Surprise flitted over Oliver's features. "Quinn didn't sell you out. On the contrary, he kept his mouth shut about you and Portia, even after Samson already knew."

"But then who—?"

"I said nothing, not even that she was at your house that day," Oliver said defensively.

Zane raised his hands. "Hey, I wasn't accusing you. I just want to know."

"I'm not one to rat—"

"Who?" Zane interrupted.

Oliver hesitated. "Samson asked Thomas, and apparently he'd noticed something."

A curse rolled off his lips. Maybe bringing up Thomas' attraction to Eddie hadn't been a good move after all, particularly since everybody knew that Thomas would never act on it. He was Eddie's mentor, and Eddie was straight. No wonder Thomas had felt the need to pay him back for that slap in the face. "I guess I deserved that."

Oliver gave him a confused look.

"Don't ask." He owed Thomas an apology. Shit, he hadn't apologized to anybody in decades, and now he was about to apologize twice in the space of an hour. His life was definitely changing.

"Ready for takeoff," the pilot's voice came through the intercom.

Zane fell silent until they were in the air. But the opportunity to talk to Thomas in private didn't present itself because it was time to work out their action plan.

***

Samson's connections assured that a safe house from which they could operate was available to them upon their arrival in Seattle.

Finding the location where Müller was holed up, wasn't an easy task. Even though the partial phone number narrowed down the search to a specific neighborhood, there was still a large area to cover. While Thomas worked his magic on the computer to pinpoint Müller's headquarters by way of elimination, Amaury used his expertise to dig into title records to search for evidence that Müller had purchased a property, rather than merely rented one. Zane made sure he scanned for all names, Müller or any of his known associates had used in the past.

During the day, the humans who had come onto the mission with him—Oliver, Nina, and two bodyguards—combed the area, but Nina raised a valid point: "We need a picture of Müller."

"There was a picture in Portia's wallet," Zane remembered. "Shit, I didn't think of that." He hadn't had a clear thought since the moment Portia had run off. Some bodyguard he was!

Gabriel's hand came down on his shoulder, making him jerk his head. "Don't worry, I know what Müller looks like. I'll transfer my memories into Samson's mind, and he can draw us a picture."

Gabriel looked over his shoulder at his boss. "Isn't that right?"

Samson nodded. "Not a problem."

"I envy you for your gifts sometimes," Zane admitted. Gabriel's gift of being able to access anybody's memories and transfer them to someone else was probably the coolest skill he'd ever seen in action. And the fact that Samson had a photographic memory and was an expert at painting and drawing, wasn't too shabby either.

"You shouldn't," Amaury said from behind him. "Certain gifts can be a curse too."

Zane nodded. Amaury's gift of sensing everybody else's emotions had been a literal headache until Nina had come along and healed him.

When nighttime traded with daylight once more, the humans ventured out and continued their search, checking out targets Thomas had picked for them. In the meantime, Zane was relegated to pacing. His feet carried him to the room where Thomas had set up his computers and was hacking into every system imaginable.

After a brief knock, Zane opened the door and entered.

"Hey," Thomas greeted him.

"Hey." Zane shifted his weight from one foot to the other while he shut the door behind him.

"What's up?" Thomas asked without taking his eyes off the monitor.

"Can we talk?"

His colleague swiveled in his chair. "What about?"

"About what I said."

"What did you say?" There was an uncharacteristic tightness in Thomas' voice.

"About you and Eddie."

Thomas stiffened and crossed his arms over his chest. "There's nothing to talk about."

"There is. I want to apologize."

Thomas' mouth dropped open.

"You heard right. It's none of my business, and it was inappropriate."

Thomas nodded slowly. "I guess none of us can choose who we are drawn to."

"No. That's why I shouldn't have said it. It must be hard enough for you as is."

Thomas gave a bitter laugh. "I curse the day I met him … Yet, if I could go back in time, I would still offer to be his mentor. Screwed up, huh?"

Zane shook his head. "You're a good man, Thomas. I wish for you to get what you want, because I know how much it hurts not to." He took an awkward step forward, not sure whether to hug Thomas or simply turn to leave.

His friend gave him a tired smile. "You know that I was the one who told Samson, don't you?"

"It doesn't matter. You did what you had to do. If the shoe were on the other foot, I would have done the same. No hard feelings."

"No hard feelings."

Thomas swiveled back to face the screen and Zane turned to the door. When he twisted the door knob, Thomas cleared his throat.

"I hope you get her back, Zane. I think she's good for you."

Chapter Thirty-Seven

Portia felt the hunger pangs getting worse. Her stomach clenched as she writhed on the bed she was still chained to, and her throat felt as dry as sandpaper. Her father had made good on his threat and was starving her to force her compliance. She'd long stopped crying. Disappointment about her father's disregard for her feelings had made way for despair many hours earlier.

With every hour that passed, she became weaker, drifting in and out of sleep, feeling near delirious from the thirst and hunger for anything, be it blood or human food. The state she was in, she would bite into anything that came close enough to her mouth.

Portia clenched her jaw shut, desperately trying to ward off the need to sink her fangs into something. Before her eyes, the room began to swim, the furniture in it seemingly moving on its own, tilting to one side and then the other. The gas fire in the old fireplace flared as if mocking her, its heat intensifying. She knew then that her mind was playing tricks on her and that she was beginning to hallucinate from starvation. If she were human, starvation wouldn't set in for a long time, but her hybrid body demanded more fuel to burn than a human body.

Her father would win after all. Desperate to survive, she would bite any man her father presented to her. It would seal her fate. She would become part of a group of fanatics, imprisoned by their lunatic ideology and their crazy notion of ruling this world.

Portia pulled hard on her restraints, her shoulders and arms feeling virtually numb from the long hours they'd been in this position, stretched out over her head. The silver clanged against the heavy steel beam it was attached to, and now that she was getting weaker, she felt the effects of the silver even through the bandages on her wrists that were meant to protect her skin.

Heat started pouring through the protective cloth, and she felt the start of a burning sensation. She shifted her position, trying to minimize the contact with the silver.

A loud thud from downstairs jolted her. Then a shout. More shouts.

Were her hallucinations getting worse?

Portia lifted her head, trying to focus her eyes, but everything was fuzzy. The door toward the hallway seemed crooked, the dresser opposite the bed seemed to move on its own. Dizziness overwhelmed her, forcing her to drop her head back onto the pillow. More noise pounded in her head, mocking her like drums beating down the time until the midnight ceremony that would seal her fate.

Glass shattered nearby. Vibrations rippled through the house.

Then she felt it, the presence that was comforting and soothing. She sighed contently, allowing herself to drift deeper into her dream. There in her world of fantasy, Zane was by her side, the man who loved her, who looked at her like she meant the world to him.

"Portia!"

His voice was so close, so strong. He would save her from this madness and wipe away the memories of the last two days and nights. In her dream, they were back at his cabin in Tahoe, making love in front of the fireplace.

"Oh, baby girl, what has he done to you?"

Zane's question didn't fit into her dream. No, she didn't want to be reminded of her situation; she wanted to relive happy times.

Her head thrashed from side to side as she tried to shake off the intrusion into her dream. "No!"

A strong hand captured her face.

Her eyes flew open. Her vision was blurry. Somebody was there. A face she recognized but knew couldn't be real.

"No," she breathed.

"Baby girl, look at me."

Portia watched his lips move, his breath ghosting over her skin as he did so, and inhaled his words and his scent. Blinking her eyes, she pushed through the fog that surrounded her.

Shock made her catapult from her prone position, but the restraints jerked her back. "Zane!" Was she still dreaming?

"I came for you."

As the words sank in, her mind sobered. He was real, all right. But it was no reason to rejoice. He'd come for her. What was it he'd said the last time she'd seen him? That he'd kill her like he'd kill her father.

Panicked, she scrambled backwards, and for the first time she truly saw him. Zane was dressed entirely in black. He wore a long sleeved figure hugging t-shirt and black jeans. Over it, his leather jacket was open. She glimpsed an array of weapons in its inside pockets. Weapons to kill a vampire—or a hybrid.

Portia opened her mouth, wanting to scream, not for help, but out of desperation, but Zane clamped his hand over her mouth.

"I'm sorry, baby girl."

Tears brimmed at her eyes. Why was he still calling her this? How could he be so cruel when she already knew he'd come to kill her?

***

Portia looked frightened. Frightened of him. She'd been about to scream, but Zane couldn't allow that.

His colleagues were attacking from outside on the ground floor on the other side of the large Victorian mansion to draw Müller and his cohorts to that side of the house, so he'd been able to slip in through a window on the second floor and search for Portia. He couldn't risk her alerting her father.

Zane glanced at the silver handcuffs around her wrists. He cursed. He had brought weapons to kill vampires, but he hadn't expected that her father would be keeping Portia captive with silver, the only metal he couldn't break. Frustration howled through him, and his free hand clenched into a fist.

Portia's frightened eyes pinned him.

"I would never hurt you," he hastened to assure her.

Her expression went from fear to doubt.

"Please trust me."

When a tear rolled down her cheek, he swept it up with his thumb. "Please don't cry, baby girl."

He slowly removed his hand from her mouth, ready to clamp it back on should she decide to scream. But her lips remained silent, and her eyes drilled into him.

Then he saw the cords in her throat move. "Tell me you don't love me," she murmured so quietly he almost didn't hear it.

"I can't do that." His heart expanded as he noticed a sparkle in her eyes. Hope blossomed. She hadn't given up on him yet. She hadn't stopped loving him despite the cruel things he'd said to her.

"Zane."

Gently, Zane caressed her cheek with his palm, even as he listened to the sounds of fighting from below. "Forgive me for the things I said. I didn't know what I was doing."

She raised her head to come closer, and he took the invitation and lowered his lips to hers. As he took her mouth in a desperate kiss, he pressed her to him. The silver handcuffs clanged against the steel beam as she tried to move her arms. The sound brought reality home. He had to free her. He pulled back, releasing her.

She tried to reach for him, her fangs suddenly protruding farther from her lips.

"What's wrong?"

"I'm thirsty ..." Portia averted her eyes.

"He's been starving you?" He wanted to howl in frustration. Had he known, he would have brought bottled human blood for her.

She nodded. "He wants me to blood-bond tonight. I told him I wouldn't ... mate with the man he's chosen." Her voice broke off, evidence that she was weak.

They had no time to lose. "We have to get you out of here. Now."

Zane pressed his finger against the little wireless device in his ear to connect to the command center. "Thomas, I've found her. He chained her with silver. We need wire clippers, and human blood. Quickly."

"Location," Thomas requested.

"Second floor, south-west corner bedroom."

"Understood."

From downstairs the noise intensified. He hoped his colleagues could keep Müller and his thugs at bay until he had freed Portia and brought her to safety. Only then would he return to finish off Müller.

Portia's eyes darted toward the door. "Who's with you?"

"Half of Scanguards. They're fighting Müller and his people." He refrained from referring to Müller as her father, hoping to keep reality away from them. Because reality was a cruel mistress. The fact was he hated the father of the woman he loved, and he was here to finish him off once and for all.

Their gazes clashed. "You're going to kill him, aren't you?"

Zane withstood her scrutiny for a few seconds before he broke the contact. "I'll kill anybody who hurts you."

When he got no answer, he looked back at her and noticed that she'd closed her eyes again.

Panic seared through him. "Baby girl!"

"So tired," Portia mumbled. "So thirsty."

He had to do something before she slipped too far. He needed her coherent to get her out of here, and the way she looked right now, he wasn't sure she'd be able to walk. Even though he knew that vampire blood would provide her only with temporary nourishment, it would boost her strength for a short while, long enough until he could get her human blood. It had worked for him when he'd fed off the Czech vampire at the camp. It would work now.

"You have to feed." He propped her head up.

Portia opened her eyes halfway, and he placed his wrist at her lips.

"Do it, baby girl, it'll ease the thirst." Even if it would weaken him by a fraction, it needed to be done. He couldn't bear seeing her suffer.

When her mouth opened wider and her fangs grazed his skin, Zane shivered involuntarily. God, he'd missed her. It seemed impossible, but in the short time that he'd known her, she'd become a part of not just his life, but of him.

The sharp tips of her fangs drove into his skin and lodged in his flesh. Heat suffused his body as she began feeding from him.

"Oh, God," he murmured, trying to hold back the clawing need to slide over her and take her. This wasn't the time or the place.

The sound of the door hinges creaking behind him, made him spin his head around.

"You!" Müller's furious glare lashed at him as he charged into the room.

In a split-second, Zane took in his opponent. He looked just like he had then: dark blond hair and high cheekbones. But he was also different. His mouth was twisted into a snarl, and fangs protruded from it. His eyes might have still been brown, but now they shone red. He was in full fighting mode.

With Portia's fangs still lodged in his wrist, Zane lost a valuable second trying to pry his arm from her. Her eyes flew open, and despite her weakened state, she seemed to sense her father in the room. She instantly released his wrist, returning his full range of motion to him.

But Müller was already on him, one claw slicing into Zane's shoulder. The jacket he wore protected him. "Don't touch her, you filthy Jew!"

Zane jumped up and barreled into Müller, both of them crashing against the dresser. "You hurt her, you bastard!" He landed a right hook against his enemy's cheek.

Müller's head whipped to the side but snapped back just as fast. "You sullied her!" He underscored his point by kicking his knee upwards.

But Zane had anticipated the move and blocked it, swiveling sideways to avoid a hit into his groin. Figured that the bastard was going for his nuts.

"She's mine!" Zane bit out between clenched teeth.

A blow against his solar plexus silenced him, the wind rushing from his lungs faster than from a popping balloon. Recovering quickly, Zane counterattacked, serving up his fists by aiming for Müller's head again.

Blood splattered as Müller's skin split open near his eye.

Glaring furiously, Müller used his entire bodyweight to throw himself against Zane, robbing him of his balance. He stumbled backwards, hearing Portia's distressed scream as he crashed into the door to the next room. The impact swung it wide open, putting Zane on his ass in the other room.

Leveraging himself against the desk he'd hit, Zane pulled himself up just as Müller launched himself at him again. Zane kicked his leg out, slamming it sideways into Müller's knees.

Müller's face distorted in pain. "Fucking asshole! I should have killed you back then."

"Too late."

Zane catapulted forward and landed a barrage of blows against his opponent while receiving several vicious ones in return. Both felt good. This fight had been a long time coming. He couldn't simply cut it short by drawing one of the weapons inside his jacket. He needed this, needed to beat the man who'd robbed him of so much, stolen the life of so many, and tortured the most innocent of them all.

Breathing hard, his eyes scanned the room, a study. A desk with computer equipment, a book case, a chair and a chest of drawers was all it contained. Plenty Müller could use against him. And Müller would have to since they were equally strong. Their body mass was similar, and neither had any advantage in strength or agility. At any other time, Zane would have enjoyed fighting an opponent who was his equal, challenging him in every way. Not tonight. Tonight, there were only two things he wanted, making Müller pay and getting Portia out of this hellhole.

From the ground floor, he could now hear a cacophony of sounds— bodies and furniture slamming into walls and floors, shouting, as well as gun shots. Scanguards had managed to storm the house and was battling the enemy from within. Grunts and angry shouts mingled with orders and the confusion of the house's inhabitants. His colleagues would handle them, but Müller he had to take care of himself.

Knowing how Brandt's son had acted irrationally when his emotions had gotten the better of him, he decided to provoke Müller into making the same mistake.

After a blow against his shoulder, Zane whirled around his axis, never losing his sure footing.

"Your daughter wants me. She can't get enough of me, a dirty Jew!" he provoked Müller.

Müller snarled, baring his fangs in aggression.

Zane laughed into his face. "Yes, I've had her. And I'll keep her."

His words seemed to have the right effect.

"Never!" promised Müller. "She's better than you!"

His claw swung so fast, Zane barely saw it coming. Trying to avoid it was futile. It slashed one side of his neck open, blood instantly dripping from the wound. It wasn't deep enough to cause him any immediate harm, but the longer the blood loss continued, the weaker it would render him.

Knowing he had to act fast, Zane delivered his own deluge of blows, kicks, and slashes. Müller successfully blocked some of them, but others hit their target. Zane panted heavily, pumping his body full with much needed oxygen. His brain told him to end it, to pull his silver blade and slice him open as Müller had done with his victims, but his heart protested. It wasn't satisfied yet. He needed to pound into Müller longer, to hurt him, to connect his claws with his flesh, to injure him with his bare hands.

Only like this, Zane felt his need for revenge slowly but steadily trickling away. Only as he felt his claws connect with Müller's skin and the blood from his wounds run over his hands, was the beast in him happy. He was finally paying him back. Zane soaked up that knowledge, just as he inhaled the stench of Müller's blood and the smell of his sweat. The more he pounded into him, the more adrenaline he felt shooting through him.

A high spread in his body despite the injuries Müller inflicted on him. And he wanted to make it last until he was truly ready to send his enemy to hell where he belonged.

Zane cornered his opponent, trapping him against the wall, the bookcase to his left preventing him from sliding past him.

From his right, Müller grabbed a wall lamp with its frilly lampshade and yanked it from its connection, ripping the electrical cord from the wall. He raised his arm to hit Zane with it, but Zane sidestepped him, and the lamp crashed through the open door, landing in the bedroom next door instead.

From the corner of his eye, he saw it crashing against the grill in front of the fireplace.

A startled scream from Portia made him take his eyes off his opponent. It was his mistake.

Müller's hand had reached for a heavy iron bookend and now slammed it in the direction of Zane's head. By snapping to the side, he avoided a direct blow to the head, but the bookend hit his collarbone instead. He heard the sound of bones breaking, and felt the corresponding pain radiate through his body.

Shit! It was time to stop fooling around and end this.

Zane reached his hand into the inside pocket of his jacket and jerked out the first thing his fingers gripped. The wooden stake felt smooth in his palm. It would have to do. He would have rather used his silver knife to provide a more painful death for Müller, but there was no time to change his weapon now with Müller attacking him even more ferociously than before.

He wasn't the only one who wanted to take the fight to the next level. Müller had obviously also decided to kick things up a notch.

As Müller jumped toward the desk, he snatched the chair in the next instant, smashing it against the wall with such force that it splintered.

Zane went after him but couldn't prevent Müller from taking one of the chair's broken feet and gripping it like a stake. As he clashed with his opponent, Zane's free hand snapped around Müller's neck and squeezed. Müller's hand holding the stake shot forward, but Zane blocked it with his elbow and continued squeezing.

"This is for all those you tortured," Zane hissed and raised his arm holding the stake. He swung.

"Help me! Zane! Fire!"

Chapter Thirty-Eight

Portia's scream rocketed through Zane's bones. In the same instant he smelled it, the smoke his brain had blocked out to deal with Müller. He blinked.

Without completing his swing, Zane dropped his arm and released Müller in the same breath. His eyes snapped to the door of the bedroom were Portia was captured. Flames engulfed the area in front of the fireplace. The armchair in front of it was already in flames that now shot up to the ceiling, the smoke they created billowing below.

Thinking only one thought, Zane charged into the room, the flames licking at him as he rushed passed the fireplace.

Portia jerked on her restraints, her eyes filled with panic. Her face was bathed in sweat, her feet scrambling to move closer to the head of the bed and farther away from the fire.

"Portia!" he screamed. "Oh, God!"

He reached her and jerked on the silver handcuffs, ignoring the searing pain on his flesh. But the steel beam behind the bed to which the cuffs were fastened didn't budge.

Touching the button on his earpiece he tried to connect with his colleague. "Thomas, where are those wire cutters?"

Only static came through the line. Shit!

"Help me," Portia pleaded.

They both knew she would die if the fire engulfed her. It wasn't the smoke inhalation that would kill her, not like it would kill a human, but the fire itself that would burn her flesh from her bones while she was still alive.

Pushing the ugly thoughts from his mind, he tried to calm her. "I'll get you free. I promise."

"Oh, God, Portia!" came Müller's voice from the door.

Zane glanced back at him for a second and saw him standing there, hesitating. Pulling his silver blade from his jacket, Zane took one of Portia's wrists.

"Keep still."

She pressed her lips together and watched him with fear-filled eyes that now brimmed with unshed tears.

He stuck his knife into the lock of the cuff and twisted. Back and forth he tried, first pushing in the tip of the knife only a fraction, then pressing deeper and trying again. But he found no traction. No clicking sound indicated that the cuffs would spring open. Pain seared through his injured shoulder, making his hand shake and the knife slip from the lock. He tried again.

The heat at his back made pearls of sweat drip from his forehead. He had to try harder. Without taking his eyes off the handcuffs, he wedged the knife's blade in between a ridge and twisted it. The blade bent.

"I love you, Zane," Portia whispered, a tear rolling down her cheek. He realized she was saying goodbye.

Her eyes strayed past him, where he knew the fire was encroaching on the bed.

But he couldn't turn to see how close it was already. And he couldn't let her believe that he would let her die.

"No, Portia, I won't leave you here."

He turned his face back to the door, where Müller still stood in horror, but the flames were about to cut off that route. "The keys!" Zane pleaded. "You must have the keys!"

Casting a cautious look at the flames, Müller answered, "Your life in exchange for hers."

Zane stared at him in disbelief. There was no time to lose, and her father was bargaining when any second the room would be entirely engulfed in flames?

"What's your answer?" Müller taunted and pulled the keys from his pants pockets, dangling them in the air.

Zane stood. "Free her first, then kill me."

"No!" Portia screamed with more force than her weakened state should allow her. "Never! I'd rather die!"

Her gaze collided with Zane's. "If you're dead, he'll use me just like he planned." Her eyes pleaded with him.

For a moment, time froze, and the wheels in his mind worked. She was right of course, but he couldn't let her die. Nor could he allow her father to use her for his nefarious plans.

There was one other way of freeing her though, but it was the most desperate one. And the most barbaric. He shuddered at what he had to do.

"Do you trust me?"

Portia nodded.

"If I cut one of your hands with the silver knife, you're free from the cuffs." The other handcuff would remain on her other wrist, but he could slip the silver chain connecting them from around the steel beam, freeing her.

A gasp issued from her lips, and her eyes squeezed shut.

"Your body will heal itself and grow you a new hand."

Her throat worked hard as she parted her lips. "It's the only way, isn't it?"

He nodded solemnly. He wished there were another.

"Do it."

"No!" Müller screamed from the door, suddenly advancing on the flames as if he wanted to burst through them. "You can't do that!"

Zane paid him no heed. Instead, he pulled another stake from his pocket. "Bite on this."

He put the wooden piece between her teeth. His brave Portia held onto it and nodded.

"I will make it quick," he promised, his heart clenching in pain. He couldn't wait for Thomas and the wire cutters. In a minute, it would be too late.

He set the knife's blade at her wrist.

"Noooooo!" Müller's scream broke through his thoughts.

He instinctively jerked his head and saw how Müller rushed through the flames that had now taken over two thirds of the room. Despite his speed, his clothes caught on fire.

"The key! Take it!" he yelled and raised his hand. Flames reflected on the metal as he threw the key.

Purely reacting on instinct, Zane caught the tiny key in his hands. As he rushed to stick it into the lock, Portia's eyes reflected back at him what was happening behind his back.

The bottom of the bed had caught fire and was now rapidly licking its path toward Portia. Müller, himself engulfed in flames, frantically pulled on the bedclothes to drag them away from his daughter.

As the lock clicked open, Zane ripped the open handcuff from her and released the chain from the steel beam. He lifted her into his arms and glanced over his shoulder.

Müller was a fireball, still moving, but no more sounds came from him. His hands still moved in all directions as if trying to put out the fire, but Zane knew it was too late for him.

He pushed the curtain aside and kicked the window with his boot, shattering the glass. The fresh air that rushed in fuelled the flames, creating a back draft that hit him instantly. Not losing a second, he jumped out of the window, Portia pressed tightly to him.

Zane landed amidst a few bushes that cushioned his fall. However, his injured shoulder gave out on impact, making him release his hold on Portia. Thankfully, she had her arms slung around him so firmly, she remained glued to him despite his slip.

"Are you all right?" he asked, his breath deserting him.

He felt her nod.

An explosion rocked through the night. Instinct made him scramble to his feet, reassert his hold on Portia, and jump several yards away from the house before he turned.

Flames shot from several windows on the second floor, and the roof was catching fire too. Zane could only assume that a gas line or something else highly flammable had exploded as a result of the fire in the bedroom.

The old Victorian, built entirely from wood, burned like kindling.

Portia buried her head in the crook of his neck, and he suddenly felt tears trickle onto his skin.

"I'm sorry, baby girl." Then he swallowed, because the next words he said were the hardest of his long life. "Your father loved you after all." In his own way, even if it had come almost too late.

A floodgate opened, and Portia sobbed against his chest.

"I love you, baby girl. Always."

***

By the time Portia's tears stopped flowing minutes later, she sensed the approach of other vampires. Her spine stiffened.

"We have to run," she urged Zane, looking up at him.

He gave her a faint smile, and only now as she pulled away from him did she notice blood gushing from one side of his neck. There were slashes on his shoulder, which he held in an awkward way.

Panicked, she grabbed his arm, but he stood firm. "Friends."

With a sigh of relief, she turned toward the approaching vampires and instantly recognized one of them: Quinn. More came running from the burning house behind them. She focused her eyes. Eddie dragged an injured Thomas from the house, trying to keep him upright but when Thomas' knees suddenly buckled and his head fell forward, Eddie swiftly picked him up and carried him.

One authoritative vampire with raven-black hair bellowed orders into the night that the others followed without question. He could only be the leader of Scanguards, Samson.

"Get the injured into the vans! Amaury! Gabriel! Damage control."

She watched as two vampires approached Samson, both with long dark hair.

"Keep any humans away. Wipe their memories. We can't risk exposure."

"All because of me," she whispered to herself.

Portia felt Zane's hand on her chin, tilting it up and making her look at him.

"It's not your fault." He motioned to the burning house. "They needed to be taken down, either way. We couldn't allow what they were planning."

Before she could answer, Samson ran to them.

"You're injured," he stated matter of factly, running his eyes over Zane.

"I'm fine. But Portia needs blood. Her father was starving her."

"I'm all right," she protested. "Zane needs blood."

She sensed Zane wanting to protest again, but Samson cut him off. "You both need blood. Bottled blood will be sufficient for Portia, but Zane needs fresh blood." He looked over his shoulder and scanned the garden, before he waved. "Oliver! Over here."

Portia suddenly remembered the conversation she'd had with Oliver only a few days earlier, how he'd told her that he let the vampires feed off him in emergencies.

Oliver ran toward them, giving her a smile as he approached. Immediately, Zane pulled her closer. She felt his possessiveness physically, and it sent a wave of heat through her body.

"Zane needs you," Samson explained. Then he reached into the bag that hung from Oliver's shoulder and pulled out a bottle with red liquid. He handed it to Portia. "Here, drink."

The moment she put the bottle to her lips and let the blood run down her throat, she realized how starved she'd truly been. Zane had been right. His blood had given her a short boost, but it hadn't lasted long. When she removed the empty bottle from her lips and looked in Zane's direction, she saw that he'd dug his fangs into Oliver's arm.

But his eyes were open, watching her, telling her with that longing gaze that what he truly wanted was to lodge his fangs in her. Not wanting to dissolve into a puddle of need, she turned toward Samson.

"Is anybody dead?" she asked quietly, worried that she was responsible for someone's death.

"None of our guys. A few are injured. But there were casualties on the other side, and we took some prisoners." He cleared his throat. "We didn't see your father ..."

Portia squeezed her eyes shut for a moment, pushing back the threatening tears. "He burned to death."

"I'm sorry."

Her throat constricted. Was she sorry? Truly, she didn't know. She felt numb. He had saved her after all. Maybe one day she would find it in her heart to forgive him. But right now, the pain was too fresh.

An approaching siren pulled her from her trance.

"Fire engines. We've got to leave." Samson raised his voice. "Into the vans, everybody, now!"

Vampires rushed to the waiting blackout vans that were parked at the curb. With a last look at the burning house that contained her father's ashes, Portia turned and ran out to the sidewalk, flanked by Samson and Zane.

Chapter Thirty-Nine

They spent the entire day at the safe house in Seattle, tending to their wounds, guarding the prisoners, and making arrangements for transferring them to the council, the high court of vampires that punished infractions within their society.

The house Müller had used as his headquarters had burned to the ground, despite the swift arrival of the fire engines. Any knowledge of the vampires' existence had been successfully contained, and according to Samson's local sources, the fire department suspected arson but had no leads. No bodies had been found in the debris, confirming that only vampires had perished, their bodies dissolving into ash without leaving any DNA.

Zane hadn't had any private time with Portia, the house being too crowded and people like Samson making sure that both he and Portia recovered from the ordeal, at least physically.

Thomas' injuries were healing under Eddie's and Oliver's care.

When Samson finally gave the all-okay for everybody to return to San Francisco, Zane was relieved. He needed to be alone with Portia to talk about their future and didn't want an audience for that conversation.

He squeezed Portia's hand as they walked down the gangway from the plane.

"Zane," Samson called after him.

He turned, not at all eager for a drawn-out goodbye when all he wanted was to get Portia home, into his arms and his bed.

"Yes?"

"Forgot to mention Isabella's naming ceremony is next Saturday. As her godfather, we expect you there after sunset."

He nodded. During that event, he would officially be recognized as her godfather, her mentor for life, and he would choose a middle name for her. "It'll be an honor."

"Oh, and another thing: I arranged for your dog to stay at Yvette's tonight. I figured you wanted to be alone."

Zane was stunned by his boss' foresight and almost choked up. Shit, he was turning into such an emotional freak!

He glanced at Portia by his side and saw that she too was eager to be alone with him. There were still things they hadn't talked about. "Yes, we have much to discuss."

Quickening his step, he headed home, never letting go of Portia's hand.

When the entrance door fell shut behind him, his eyes searched hers. For the first time in his life, he didn't know where to start. They had barely had a chance to talk since the fire had killed her father, and except for the few words he'd said after they'd jumped from the window, he'd not mentioned her father's death. But it was an issue they had to resolve.

"I know," she whispered.

Could Portia really read him so well? "Know what?"

"That this is hard for you. I am his daughter. Nothing will ever change that. When you look at me, you must think of him, of the things he did to you and your family. I don't know how I can ever make that go away."

He silenced her by pressing a finger to her lips. "You have nothing to prove to me. I know who you are." He pressed his hand to his chest. "I feel it in here. You're nothing like him. When I look at you, I only see you. But I hurt you. The things I said to you, the way I threatened you ..."

Zane closed his eyes, wishing he could undo it all.

"How can you even trust me after how I treated you?"

"You were willing to give your life in exchange for mine." She sucked in a quick breath. "I would have never accepted it, of course, but to know that you were willing to do that ... it showed me what's in your heart."

"I would offer it again."

"I hope you'll never have to again."

Zane dropped his lids and studied his boots for a moment. "There's something else you need to know." When he looked up, she gave him a curious look. "Without a living parent, and considering your age, you'll automatically be considered mature and legally of age. It means you can make your own decisions."

A smile pasted itself onto her lips. "What kind of decisions?"

"Any." He shifted his weight to the other foot, suddenly nervous.

Portia took a step closer, then another one, bringing her flush to his body. "Is there anything you want to ask me?"

Her eyelashes fluttered slightly, and he suddenly heard a tremble in her voice.

"I have no right to ask you."

Her eyebrows twisted. "I don't understand."

"You're young, and I'm your first. It would be wrong of me to offer you a ... a union."

Startled, Portia jerked back. "You don't love me?"

He swallowed past the lump in his throat. "I didn't say that. But I can't ask you to make a decision that will affect your entire life. You need time to figure out for yourself what you want. I can wait."

He'd thought about it long and hard on the flight back. If he asked her to blood-bond with him now, he would be exploiting her vulnerability. She was still grieving for her father, even if she didn't want to admit it. And she was on her own. He didn't want her to choose him simply because she had nobody else to turn to.

"Wait?"

"Yes, baby girl. I'll wait until you're ready, until you know for sure that you want me. Because once you say yes, I'll never let you go."

Her eyes softened. "And in the meantime?"

"You could live with me ..." Zane searched her eyes for approval.

"In sin?" Portia teased, her lashes swinging upwards gracefully.

"Lots of sin, I can promise you that."

Her hand came up and stroked over his bottom lip, the touch electrifying, her gaze hungry. "Can I have a taste of that now? I wouldn't wanna buy a pig in a poke, if you know what I mean."

His lips nipped at her finger. "I thought you'd never ask."

Without giving Portia time to think, he swept her into his arms and carried her into his bedroom where he set her onto her feet. Seconds later, their clothes littered the floor, torn off their bodies in haste and with impatience. It had been too long.

Only when he felt her naked skin beneath his hands and her warm lips pressed to his, did the tension of the last few days desert his body and fade into the distance.

There was no finesse in the way he brought her down on the sheets, his body simply demanding its due. He'd promised not to bond with her tonight, to give her time to adjust to her new situation, but now with a pliable Portia in his arms, he knew he had to fight every cell in his body to keep his promise.

Zane kissed a path down her neck and filled his hands with her breasts, kneading the firm flesh and thrumming her nipples with his thumbs. He had one leg wedged between hers, with his hard-on pressed against her thigh, impatient to find its home. He forced back the need to drive into her without any sort of foreplay, but his leg urged hers to part wider, not caring that he was behaving like a savage.

Portia's body arched as she pressed into his touch. Her voice was hoarse when she spoke. "Don't be cruel; don't make me wait. You know what I want."

He raised his head to gaze at her flushed face. "Tell me then."

She slid her hand to the back of his neck and pulled him to her. "I want your cock inside me. And your fangs in my neck."

Her blunt demand was all it took to free the barely leashed beast inside him. His fangs descended and extended to their full length, their tips peeking from between his lips. And his cock had never been harder.

Complying with her wishes, Zane covered her with his body. The scent of her arousal filled the room and drugged him, making him unable to hold back. With a triumphant grunt, he thrust into her in one continuous slide. Her muscles gripped him like a tight fist, robbing him of his sanity once more. Whether he would ever get used to the way she took him into her beautiful body, he had no idea.

A light sheen of sweat built on his body, and with every thrust he delivered, with every impact of flesh against flesh, more sweat accumulated. He tried to delay biting her, not wanting to lose his head and drown in her essence too quickly. But it was only a matter of time. He couldn't ignore Portia's soft moans, her panting breaths, and her scent that only intensified as sweat covered her own skin.

The graceful curve of her neck called to him, and the vein beneath it pulsed in a frantic rhythm, beckoning him to approach.

Her hips undulated beneath him, urging him to drive harder into her. Beneath her half-closed lids, her eyes shone with passion and love, silently repeating her request.

"Zane!" she begged.

The sound of her voice undid him. With a groan, he slid his lips onto the spot where her neck met her shoulder. Shivering, he grazed her skin with the tips of his fangs, the contact shooting a flame of liquid heat through his body. Portia moaned in response. Then he pierced her skin and drove inside.

Her sweet blood touched his tongue, her essence so potent and so rich, the effect hitting him instantly. A high spread through his body, which was humming with pleasurable electricity. He drew more of her blood into his body, and the feeling only intensified.

"I love you, Zane," he heard her whisper.

He wanted to respond and tell her how he felt, but was unable to let go of her neck. He needed this; he needed her.

His cock worked her frantically, driving them both higher and higher, and the sounds of their lovemaking echoed in his house.

"I've made my decision, Zane."

Her words pushed through the bliss he was cocooned in. His brain didn't work fast enough to understand what she meant, when he suddenly felt her lips on his shoulder, her teeth scraping against his skin.

"I don't want to wait."

All of a sudden Zane understood. His heart stopped only to restart the instant he felt her fangs drive into his flesh.

By drinking from him as he took her blood into his body while they were joined in love, she was accepting him as her blood-bonded mate.

Forever together.

Forever one.

As their blood comingled and their bodies exploded in carnal bliss, Zane's heart opened wide. There would never again be a wall around it or chains locking it down.

He was free. Free to love.

His mind reached out to her. *Baby girl, I love you.*

And then, for the first him, he felt her presence inside him, warmth and love spreading in his heart and mind. When her voice sounded inside his body while her fangs were still lodged in his flesh, he knew that he'd never heard a sweeter sound.

You're mine, Zane, forever mine.

Epilogue

One week later

Zane paced the full length of his living room, little Z running around under foot. Where was she? He'd awakened alone when it was still daylight, and that fact prevented him from chasing after her.

"You could have woken me," he chastised the dog. "Ever thought of barking when she left the house?"

Z turned his face up to him, turning on his puppy charm.

"Yeah, you're a great help."

Even a week after bonding with Portia, he still felt nervous about losing her. His nightmares of seeing her in the burning house were only just beginning to wane. Feeling her in his arms was the only thing that chased them away completely.

Where are you, baby girl?

A warm tingle reached his mind.

I'm almost home, her response came.

Hearing her voice in his head settled his unease somewhat. Thank God for the telepathic bond that came with their blood bond. It allowed them to communicate when they were apart.

When he heard the key in the front door a few minutes later, his heart beat excitedly into his throat and as soon as the door closed, he rushed into the hallway and pulled Portia into an embrace.

Hungrily devouring her lips, he didn't even give her a chance for a greeting. Only when the dog started barking did Zane release her lips.

"Now he barks. What a watchdog we've got ourselves there."

"Going by that kiss," Portia hedged, "you must have missed me."

Her coquettish smile made his heart flip as if it were jumping up and down a trampoline. "What do you think?"

Her eyes locked with his. "Tell me you don't love me."

Zane smiled. "I can't do that, baby girl."

She brushed her lips against his. "Why not?"

"Because it would be a lie," he whispered back and took her lips once more.

Breathless, he released her a few minutes later. "Now tell me what was so important that you had to leave our bed."

Portia pulled away from him and reached into the inside of her leather jacket, pulling out a small plastic bag.

"You have no idea how hard it was to find this in the Mission."

Curious, Zane watched her as she pulled a silken item from the bag. His eyes recognized the round piece of fabric. He raised his eyes to stare at her.

His mouth dropped open. "You bought a yarmulke?"

She nodded with a smile. "I want you to wear it at Isabelle's ceremony tonight."

His lips trembled as he pushed back the emotions that threatened to unman him. "I haven't … it's been such a long time …"

Portia put her hand on his forearm where his skin was now bare. Thanks to her, he wasn't hiding his tattoo anymore and had started wearing short sleeved shirts instead of the long sleeved ones that had served him so well over the last decades.

"You should be proud of who you are." She gave him a warm smile. "I am."

Then she reached up and placed the yarmulke on his head. The unfamiliar piece of fabric slid into place right where it belonged, where it had always belonged. Suddenly he felt whole, the one last piece that made him complete finally clicking into place.

Slowly, he stroked his hand over the head cover, but he was too choked up to say a single word. He was free now, free to love and to believe. His faith in the good was restored, because even from evil, something good could emerge. Or some*one* good.

"Let's get ready. We don't want to keep Samson and the others waiting." Portia caressed his cheek.

"They can't start without me," Zane murmured and pulled her against him. "And I have something important to do first."

"What's that?" she asked, but the excited flicker in her eyes told him she already knew.

"I have to thank my wife for saving me."

"But you were the one who saved me," she protested.

He moved his head from side to side. "No, baby girl, without you, I'd still be lost."

THE END

About Buchenwald

Buchenwald was one of the largest Nazi concentration camps in Germany. It was established in July 1937 and liberated by Patton's army in April 1945. During most of this time, only male prisoners occupied the camp. Few female prisoners were at the camp in the early years, and those brought in were forced to work in the camp's brothel. The majority of female prisoners arrived at the camp during 1944 and 1945.

Dr. Franz Müller is a figment of my imagination, however, doctors like him existed, and many of the experiments I described in Zane's Redemption took place, in one form or another, if not at Buchenwald, then at camps like Auschwitz and Mauthausen. The most famous concentration camp doctor is Josef Mengele. After the war, he escaped to Brazil where he died in 1979, never having paid for his crimes.

Adolf Hitler and some of his followers did indeed believe in the occult and the supernatural. They searched, rather unsuccessfully, for the Holy Grail, hoping that once the artifact was in their possession, they would win the war.

The Holocaust is the darkest spot in modern German history. May it never be repeated.

Tina Folsom

ABOUT THE AUTHOR

Tina Folsom is a member of the Romance Writers of America and writes predominantly paranormal romance. She lives in Northern California with her husband where she enjoys great food, changeable weather, and tolerates the occasional earthquake.

Her ideas for her books come from her many different careers— CPA/Accountant, Real Estate Broker, Chef, Secretary, Au-pair amongst others—as well as the many different countries she's lived in, and the people she's met over the years. And the vampires? Well, chalk them up to her active imagination.

For more about Tina Folsom:

www.tinawritesromance.com
http://authortinafolsom.blogspot.com
http://www.facebook.com/AuthorTinaFolsom
Twitter: @Tina_Folsom
Email: tina@tinawritesromance.com

Made in the USA
Lexington, KY
24 June 2012